出题与做题

（大学英语四级阅读与综合）

主　编　乔爱玲

副主编　魏　蕾　黄建平　谭　丽
　　　　高　扬　符文慧

上海交通大学出版社

图书在版编目(CIP)数据

大学英语四级阅读与综合/乔爱玲主编. －上海：上海交通大学出版社，2006
（出题与做题）
ISBN 7-313-04523-9

Ⅰ.大… Ⅱ.乔… Ⅲ.英语-阅读教学-高等学校-水平考试-习题 Ⅳ.H319.9-44

中国版本图书馆 CIP 数据核字(2006)第 082885 号

出 题 与 做 题

（大学英语四级阅读与综合）

乔爱玲 主编

上海交通大学出版社出版发行

（上海市番禺路 877 号　邮政编码 200030）

电话：64071208　出版人：张天蔚

立信会计出版社常熟市印刷联营厂印刷　全国新华书店经销

开本：880mm×1230mm 1/32　印张：12.875　字数：456 千字

2006 年 7 月第 1 版　　2006 年 7 月第 1 次印刷

印数：1～5 050

ISBN 7-313-04523-9/H・891　　定价：19.50 元

前　言

　　《出题与做题大学英语四级阅读与综合》一书主要是针对大学英语四级考试新题型阅读理解和综合部分的要求编写而成,其读者对象为欲参加全国大学英语四级考试的高等院校学生和参加含有此类题型的其他种类考试的社会考生。

　　目前,尽管教学界对全国大学英语四、六级考试本身存在着多种看法,考试中心自 2005 年 6 月起也取消了大学英语四、六级考试证书,但是社会上对于把四、六级考试结果当作就业等的参照指标的热情始终不减当年。因而使得许多大专院校不敢轻言放弃该考试。加之考试成绩公开化而非以一张合格证书面世,致使 60 分与 90 分有了本质的区别。此外,目前许多院校仍然把该考试结果与毕业证书挂钩,这又使得学生不敢轻视该考试。

　　本书的编写目的是通过归纳总结该考试阅读理解与综合部分的测试技巧,分析做题规律和提供相关实践素材,帮助考生在提高阅读理解与综合应试的能力的同时,提高考试成绩。本书既适合考前强化训练之用,也可用于含有相应内容的教学辅导或培训。

　　本书共由四个部分组成。第一部分与第二部分分别为阅读理解与综合测试技巧解析与技能训练。两个部分根据各类阅读理解与综合测试题的自身特点,分门别类地加以归纳总结试题的类型与解析试题的出题特点,提供做题技巧或方法,并辅以一定量的相关练习,以期通过一定量的练习实践,使考生熟练掌握做题技巧,提高得分胜算。

　　第三部分为综合应试训练,共由 10 套阅读与综合试题组成。该部分把各类试题题型按照考试的要求组合在一起,旨在供考生实践操练之用。

第四部分为前三部分练习的参考答案与解析。

由于水平所限,书中纰漏在所难免。望广大专家或读者不吝赐教,予以指正。

编　者

2006 年 7 月

目　　录

第一部分　阅读理解技巧解析与技能训练…………………… 1

　第一节　篇章阅读理解与解题方法 ……………………… 1

　第二节　阅读技能解说与实践操练 ……………………… 5

　　一、主旨类题 ………………………………………… 5

　　二、细节类题 ………………………………………… 49

　　三、判断/推理类题 ………………………………… 74

　　四、词义辨析类题 …………………………………… 111

　第三节　篇章词汇理解 ………………………………… 135

　第四节　快速阅读理解 ………………………………… 140

第二部分　综合测试解题技巧与技能训练……………… 161

　第一节　完型填空 ……………………………………… 161

　第二节　改错 …………………………………………… 172

　第三节　篇章问答(简短回答) ………………………… 179

第三部分　综合训练…………………………………… 189

　Test One ………………………………………………… 189

　Test Two ………………………………………………… 201

　Test Three ……………………………………………… 213

　Test Four ………………………………………………… 226

　Test Five ………………………………………………… 238

　Test Six …………………………………………………… 250

　Test Seven ……………………………………………… 262

　Test Eight ……………………………………………… 274

　Test Nine ………………………………………………… 286

Test Ten ·· 299

第四部分　参考答案与解析············· 311
第一部分·· 311
第二部分·· 343
第三部分·· 354

第一部分　阅读理解技巧解析与技能训练

　　为进一步推进大学英语教学改革,国家教育部自 2004 年新颁布了《大学英语教学要求》,其目的是培养学生的英语综合应用能力。新的大学英语四级考试模式也随之发生了变化,由原来相对单一的语言能力测试改为综合性的语言能力测试。就阅读理解部分而言,虽说总比例有所下降,由原来占总题量的 40％减少到 35％。但其中新增加的新题型种类及所占的比例则大大地增加了。其中快速阅读理解部分占总题量的 10％,旨在测试考生的快速阅读技能,考察考生在阅读文章的过程中寻找信息、解决问题的能力;仔细阅读部分占总题量的 25％。该部分除了测试传统的篇章阅读理解外,还将原来的词汇测试纳入阅读中来,以此考查学生在篇章语境中对词义的推测与理解能力。

　　新题型从不同的角度和不同的层面对大学英语考生进行阅读能力的考查。同时也对考生的综合语言应用能力提出了更高的要求:要求考生在规定的时间内完成各类阅读材料四篇,并对提供的多项选择、选词填空、短句问答、句子填空、是非判断等多种题型做出快速准确的判断,找出正确答案。因此,学生通过阅读学习与训练,仅仅掌握大量的词汇、熟悉语法结构、积累文化知识背景等、是远远不够的,还需要掌握一些科学合理的阅读方法与阅读技巧,经过专项技能训练来提高阅读理解速度,保证阅读质量,做到"快速＋准确"最终产生"效率"。本部分的主要内容将服务于考生在这一方面的实际需求。

第一节　篇章阅读理解与解题方法

　　大学英语四级阅读理解试题要求考生必须在指定的时间内读完一定量的英语短文。要做到快速读完并正确理解所读的英语文章,达到预期的阅读目的,就必须养成一种良好的阅读习惯,要根据不同的习惯,不同的需要和不同的阅读目的使用不同的阅读方法。

　　通常,阅读方法大致可分为两种类型:先阅读相关文章,后做试题,或先阅读文章后的问题再阅读文章,然后再做试题。考生可以根据自己的做题习惯,既可以采取先阅读后做题的做题程序,也可以采取先读相关文章后的问题后阅读再做题的方法。前者为传统的做题程序,按部就班,先了解文章的大致内容,再根据问题的内容通过复读或略读或查读等阅读方法,寻找答案的参考依据,以便从四个选项中确定一个正确的答案;后者则是通过先读文章,预先了解阅读的重点所在,再根据问题的具体内容去有目的地阅读文章寻找所需的信息。两种阅读程序各有利弊。前者的"利"在于通过阅读整篇文章,即可以大致了解文章的内容,同时又不会漏掉什么细节。其弊端在于费时费力,部分时间浪费在与问题不相关的信息上;后者的"利"在于阅读前"胸有成竹",知道自己在为解决什么问题而读,而不会在与问题不相关的信息上多费时间,有益于提高单位时间里的阅读效率。其弊端在于不容易全部记住所看过的问题。至于采用何种阅读程序,考生应视自己的具体情况而定。对于记忆力较强的考生,较适合第一种阅读方法,否则最好采用第二种阅读方法。因此,在阅读训练过程中,考生有必要先试用不同的程序阅读几篇文章,选定适合自己的那一种,并据其反复操练,直到熟练掌握。

就具体阅读方法而言,英语的篇章阅读方法有多种,常用的,也是最有效的阅读方法有三种:略读(skimming)、查读(scanning)和细读(reading for full understanding/reading in depth/careful reading)。

1. 略读

略读又称作快读、浏览或跳读是一种"全景式"的阅读方法,也是一种浏览全文的快速阅读方法,要求考生在阅读过程中以高度集中的精力,达到迅速准确地获取整篇文章的主题思想或者是段落的大意,并使考生对文章的总体结构有一个整体概念的目的。

由于略读技巧的自身特点,通常略读一篇文章时,要求考生只读文章的主标题、副标题、段落标题、文章的开头与结尾、每段的主题句、关键句以及由 first second 等引导的表示归类总结性的语句,或者是由 because, as a result 等引导的表示因果关系的语句,或者是由 but, however 等引导的表示转折的语句等,而不是阅读全文的每一个词句或者是由 for example 引出的佐证。遇到个别非频繁性重复生词、难句或举例时应略过。此外,为了更好地抓住全文的中心思想,除上述阅读重点外,还要特别注意文章中某些反复出现的词语和与之相关的信息,因为这些词语常常与文章的主题密切相关。

略读方法主要适于解决以下主旨题所涉及的几个方面问题:

(1) 文章的中心思想(the main idea)。

(2) 作者的观点(the author's point of view)。

(3) 文章的体裁(the method of treatment)。

(4) 文章的风格(the style)。

(5) 作者的口吻(the tone of the passage)。

(6) 文章的题目(the title)。

考生若遇到判断主旨性的问题时,应采取略读法。有些考生由于受到自己固有的一些阅读习惯,尤其是精读习惯的影响,略读文章时总是担心漏掉某些信息。其实,这些担心是多余的。因为文章中的某些细节、数字、举例、事实、描写,都是用来支持、说明或发展文章的中心思想的,而这些细节常常不是主旨性问题的考查重点。

略读法常采用的步骤如下:

(1) 阅读文章的标题和副标题。文章若有标题和副标题时,应该先阅读该部分。但大学英语四级考题(后称四级题)中的阅读文章通常是没有标题或副标题的。

(2) 阅读每一段的第一句话,扫视其他文字。四级题阅读短文常用的文体是议论文。作为议论文,其标准段落通常由三个部分组成:主题句(topic sentence)、推展句(developing sentences)和结论据(concluding sentence)。主题句作为段落论述的主题,即段落的中心思想,在大多数情况下位于句首。阅读段落的第一句话,实际上就等于了解段落的中心思想。

(3) 阅读文章的第一段和最后一段。文章的第一段又称开首段,主要引入文章将要讨论的问题;文章的最后一段通常是文章的结论段,总结归纳了文章的主要观点和看法。因此,读完这两个段落,就可大致上了解了文章的大意。当然,不同体裁的文章开头不尽相同。在记叙文中,开首段主要交待故事的背景和人物;在议论文中,开首段的作用是引入和揭示全文的主题或概述文章的内容。最后一段通常为结尾段——全文的总结,故事的结局或文章的落点。因此,阅读文章的第一段和最后一段时,应特别仔细。

(4) 充分利用文中一些有助于对文章进行预测的印刷细节,如各种标题、斜体词、黑体词和标点符号等,通过这些印刷细节来了解作者的基本思路、行文方式,从而把握文章的大意、某些有关细节及相互关系。

(5) 关注文中某些标志词。如转折词 however, in spite of, yet 等,递进词 furthermore, moreover, in addition 等,叙述词 firstly, secondly, next 等。这些标志词有助于理解该句与上下文的逻辑关系,并使考生能够更准确地把握作者的思路,提高阅读理解效率。

2. 查读

查读又称寻读、检索或搜索,是一种搜寻式的快速阅读方法,旨在帮助考生查寻所需要的各种特定具体信息,如数字、时间、人名、地名、原因等。该阅读方法主要用于回答事实细节性的问题。与略读相比,查读是在对材料比较熟悉的前提下进行的,也是在有针对性地选择问题的答案时才采用的,因此带有明确的目的性,而略读则是在对所读材料的内容一无所知的情况下进行的。

查读时,目光要自上而下、一目数行地巡视与答题内容相关的词句。当回答有关 who,when,where,what,which 等文章细节问题的时候,采用此种阅读方法可以很快就找到答案。不过有些与文章细节有关的问题如:why,how 等问题则不宜采用这种阅读方法,这时就要求考生先通过"查读"的阅读方法找到文中与答题内容相关的信息范围,然后再用下面将要讨论的"细读"方法去寻找准确的答案,以确保答案的参考依据准确无误。

阅读试题中针对事实细节性的主要提问方式如下:

(1) When is the deadline for...?

(2) When did the scientist discover that...?

(3) Where did Alice spend most of her childhood?

(4) Which of the following is most probably an example of...?

(5) Which of the following is NOT true?

(6) Why does the author think...is very important?

(7) How did she manage to...?

(8) In the passage, the author advocates all of the following EXCEPT

_____.

3. 细读

细读即详细阅读。阅读文章时,除了需要了解文章大意或段落的主旨以及所需的特定信息外,有时还需要仔细阅读、揣摩阅读文章的某一特定语句或部分,以期达到对文章的准确深刻理解和领会的目的。对于某些词语和句子,特别是关键词句,不仅要理解其字面意思,还要通过分析、判断、推理等阅读方法,弄清文章字里行间的内涵。

细读法有助于回答较为复杂或更深层面的问题。在阅读理解试题中,这种阅读方法更适用于做词汇题、语义题及逻辑判断推理题。

细读注意事项如下:

(1) 细读时如遇到不熟悉的词语,可通过联系上下文,同时根据有关常识、背景知识,或利用构词法来猜测词义。

(2) 细读时如遇到难以理解或结构复杂的长句,可借助所学的语法知识,通过分析句子结构,弄清主谓关系、修饰与被修饰关系等来理解句子大意。

以上提到的三种阅读方法,虽然分而论之,但是在阅读过程中却需要根据阅读问题的实际情况灵活交替使用。如果使用恰当,这些阅读方法将会从不同的方面帮助考生在阅读文章的过程中快速获取问题答案的参考依据,提高阅读理解效率和考分。

第二节　阅读技能解说与实践操练

据分析归纳历届真题的出题特点得知,大学英语四级阅读理解试题的设计思路存在着一定的出题规律。基于这些规律,该项试题可大致分为四种类型:主旨题、细节题、判断推理题、词义辨析题。本部分将针对这四种类型试题分别进行阐述、解析,以帮助考生突破英语阅读难关,收到事半功倍的效果。

一、主旨类题

主旨又称作中心思想(main idea),是阅读理解考试的一个重要内容,旨在考察学生的概括、归纳和总结阅读文章的能力,位于四类常考题型之首。根据具体的考点设置,主旨题可分为篇章主旨和段落主旨两种。从考查的角度上来看,主旨题又可细分为主题类主旨题即篇章类和段落类主旨题(全文或段落的主旨大意)、目的类主旨题(全文或某段的写作目的)及标题类主旨题(即要求考生为文章选出最佳标题)和语气类主旨题等五种形式,其常用的提问关键词有 main idea, main point, key point, mainly explain, mainly about, purpose, best title, mainly discuss, the general tone, attitude 等。常用的提问形式如下:

(1) What's the main idea of this passage?

(2) What is the best title for this article?

(3) What is the main subject of the passage?

(4) What is the writing style of this article?

(5) What's the key point of the passage?

(6) The general tone of the passage is _____(critical, positive, negative, indifferent, sensitive, doubtful, impartial, suspicious, sympathetic, indignant, admiring, confidential, optimistic, pessimistic, etc.)

(7) The passage is written to explain _____.

(8) What conclusion can be drawn from the passage?

(9) Which of the following sentences can best summarize the article?

(10) This is a letter of _____ (request, application, complaint, advice...).

(11) The main purpose of this passage is to _____.

注意,做主旨题时,要尽量使用快速阅读法,从头到尾将全文浏览一遍关键信息,不要因为个别生词或难句而停滞不前。要从上下文的连贯、整体意思上来理解文章,确定全文是在围绕一个什么主题(subject),又是从哪几个方面对其进行阐述的,从而做到有把握地概括主旨。

在做主旨题时,应避免以下几个错误:

(1) 以局部信息或将某一段的大意当成全文的主旨文章致使以偏概全或归纳不充分。

(2) 给文章扣大帽子致使概括范围过广,归纳过头。

1. 篇章主旨题

篇章主旨题是针对全篇文章的主题进行提问的,要求考生学会识别文章中那些最主要的信息,准确地概括文中所阐述的内容,其涵盖面不能太宽,也不能过窄。如果概括面太宽,会包含文中没有阐述的内容;过窄则不足以概括文章的全部内容。例如:

Sugar history in the Hawaiian Island is filled with pioneering. In sailing ship days, Hawaiian sugar growers were many months from sources of suppliers and from markets. This isolation built up among the Hawaiian growers an enduring spirit of cooperation. Growers shared with one another improvements in production. Without government aid of any sort, they build great irrigation projects. Without government help, they set up their own research and experiment organization. Pioneering together cover the years, they have provided Hawaii with its largest industry.

Question

What does the passage mainly talk about?

A. In sailing days, Hawaiian sugar growers were many months away from supplies and markets.

B. Hawaiian sugar growers built their great industry without government help.

C. Hawaiian sugar growers had set up their own research organization and had shared improvements.

D. By pioneering together, sugar growers had provided Hawaii with its largest industry.

【例题解析】选项 A,B 和 C 只是文中提到的各项具体内容,作为主题思想,所涉及的面均窄,不足以涵盖全文的中心思想。而只有选项 D 才能概括全文要说明的问题。因此,应为正确答案。

Exercise 1

Directions: *In this section, there are ten passages. For each passage there is a question or unfinished statement followed by four choices marked A, B, C and D. You should decide on the best choice for the question and then mark the corresponding letter on it.*

Passage 1

More and more, the operations of our businesses, governments, and financial institutions are controlled by information that exists only inside computer memories. Anyone clever enough to modify this information for his own purposes can reap big reward. Even worse, a number of people who have done this and been caught at it have managed to get away(逃脱) without punishment.

It's easy for computer crimes to go undetected if no one checks up on what the computer is doing. But even if the crime is detected, the criminal may walk away not only unpunished but with a glowing recommendation from his former employers.

Of course, we have no statistics on crimes that go undetected. But it's disturbing to note how many of the crimes we do know about were detected by accident, not by systematic inspections or other security procedures. The computer criminals who have been caught may have been the victims of uncommonly bad luck.

Unlike other lawbreakers, who must leave the country, commit suicide, or go to jail, computer criminals sometimes escape punishment, demanding not only that they not be charged but that they be given good recommendations and perhaps other benefits. All too often, their demands have been met.

Why? Because company executives are afraid of the bad publicity that would result if the public found out that their computer had been misused. They hesitate at the thought of a criminal boasting in open court of how he juggled(诈骗) the most confidential(保密) records right under the noses of the company's executives, accountants, and security staff. And so another computer criminal departs with just the recommendations he needs to continue his crimes elsewhere.

Question

1. The passage is mainly about _____.
   A. why computer criminals are often able to escape punishment
   B. why computer crimes are difficult to detect by systematic inspections
   C. how computer criminals manage to get good recommendations from their former employers
   D. why computer crimes can't be eliminated

Passage 2

Any talk of the energy needs of the United States should include a discussion of the Tennessee Valley Authority, a successful but sometimes quiet federal agency. The Tennessee Valley Authority began life in 1933 as one of the public works agencies designed to help fight the Great Depression. The TVA was first meant to employ thousands of men to build a chain of dams down the Tennessee River. These dams were to include electric plants for generating electricity to provide cheap power for the rural land in the valley area.

Within ten years, most of the homes in the TVA area had electricity. In twenty years, there were four times as many homes in the area with power. At first, TVA electricity cost a penny per kilowatt. Many homes in the area relied on electricity for heating. This results in criticism now that electricity is more than three pennies per kilowatt. Other criticism has been aimed at the TVA's other methods of generating power in 1975. The Authority was sued(控告，提出诉讼) for polluting the air with its coal-generating plants. Anti-nuclear groups point out that the TVA would soon have a total of seventeen atomic reactor plants supplying power for its service area. But the Tennessee Valley Authority has adjusted to the new times. It quickly became a model for pollution control at its coal plants. Just as quickly the TVA found itself an energy conserver as well as a producer. The TVA conducts free home energy consultations and offers cheap loans to consumers who want to install insulation storm windows, solar energy equipment or wood burning stoves. The resulting decrease in demand has allowed the TVA to postpone or delay construction of two nuclear reactors. Instead, the Authority is building a plant to extract coal gas from low-grade(品质低劣的) coal. Their first step will be to use the coal gas to make an ammonia (氨) fertilizer for farmers in the TVA service area. Their ultimate goal is to produce a synthetic fuel from the coal gas. The TVA will then be once again producing a cheaper source of energy and helping solve the nation's problems, several at a time.

Question

2. The main idea of this passage is that _____.

A. electricity purchased by TVA's customers has tripled in price.

B. the TVA has not served its function well.

C. the TVA is dangerous to the environment.

D. the TVA has always been a pioneer in the energy field.

Passage 3

Basic to any understanding of Canada in 20 years after the Second World War is the country's impressive population growth. For every three Canadians in 1945, there were over five in 1996. In September 1966 Canada's population passed the 20 million mark. Most of this surging(迅猛的) growth came from natural increase. The depression of the 1930's and the war had held back marriages and the catching-up process began after 1945. The baby boom continued through the decade of the 1950's, producing a population increase of nearly fifteen percent in the five years from 1951 to 1956. This rate of increase had been exceeded only once before in Canada's history, in the decade before 1911, when the prairies were being settled. Undoubtedly, the good economic conditions of the 1950's supported a growth in the population, but the expansion also derived from a trend toward earlier marriages and an increase in the average size of families. In 1957 the Canadian birth rate stood at 28 per thousand, one of the highest in the world.

After the peak year of 1957, the birth rate in Canada began to decline. It continued falling until in 1966 it stood at the lowest level in 25 years. Partly this decline reflected the low level of births during the depression and the war, but it was also caused by changes in Canadian society. Young people were staying at school longer, more women were working, young married couples were buying automobiles or houses before starting families; rising living standards were cutting down the size of families.

It appeared that Canada was once more falling in step with the trend toward smaller families that had occurred all through the Western world since the time of the Industrial Revolution.

Although the growth in Canada's population has slowed down by 1966 (the increase in the first half of the 1960's was only nine percent), another large population wave was coming over the horizon. It would be composed of the children of the children who were born during the period of the high birth rate prior to 1957.

Question

3. What does the passage mainly discuss?

    A. Educational changes in Canadian society.

    B. Canada during the Second World War.

    C. Population trends in postwar Canada.

    D. Standards of living in Canada.

Passage 4

Orchids are unique in having the most highly developed of all blossoms, in which the usual male and female reproductive organs are fused in a single structure called the column. The column is designed so that a single pollination (授粉) will fertilize hundreds of thousands, and in some cases millions, of seeds, so microscopic and light they are easily carried by the breeze. Surrounding the column are three sepals(萼片) and three petals(花瓣), sometimes easily recognizable as such, often distorted into gorgeous, weird(怪异的), but always functional shapes. The most noticeable of the petals is called the flabellum, or lip. It is often dramatically marked as an unmistakable landing strip to attract the specific insect the orchid has chosen as its pollinator.

To lure their pollinators from afar, orchids use appropriately intriguing shapes, colors, and scents. At least 50 different aromatic compounds have been analyzed in the orchid(兰花) family, each blended(混合) to attract one, or at most a few, species of insects or birds. Some orchids even change their scents to interest different insects at different times.

Once the right insect has been attracted, some orchids present all sorts of one-way obstacle courses to make sure it does not leave until pollen has been accurately placed or removed. By such ingenious adaptations to specific pollinators, orchids have avoided the hazards of rampant(繁茂的) crossbreeding in the wild, assuring the survival of species as discrete(分离的) identities. At the same time they have made themselves irresistible to collectors.

Question

4. What does the passage mainly discuss?

   A. Birds.   B. Insects.

   C. Flowers.   D. Perfume.

Passage 5

American women experience a great variety of lifestyles. A "typical" American woman may be single. She may also be divorced or married. She may be a homemaker, a doctor, or a factory worker. It is very difficult to generalize about American women. However, one thing that many American women have in common is their attitude about themselves and their role in American life.

Historically, American women have always been very independent. The first colonists to come to New England were of ten young couples who had left behind their extended family (i. e. their parents, sisters, cousins, etc.). The women were alone in a new, undeveloped country with their husbands. This had two important effects. First of all, this as yet uncivilized environment demanded that every person share in developing it and in survival. Women worked along side their husbands and children to establish themselves in this new land. Second, because they were in a new land without the established influence of older members of society, women felt free to step into nontraditional roles.

This role of women was reinforced in later years as Americans moved west, again leaving family behind and encountering a hostile environment. Even later, in the East, as new immigrants arrived, the women often found jobs more easily than men. Women became the supporters of the family.

Within the established lifestyle of industrialized twentieth century America, the strong role of women was not as dramatic as in the early days of the country. Some women were active outside the home; others were not. However, when American men went to war in the 1940s, women stepped into the men's jobs as factory and business workers. After the war, some women stayed in these positions, and others left their jobs with a new sense of their own capabilities.

Question

5. What is the main idea of this passage?

   A. Different life styles led by the American women.

   B. American women were free to step into nontraditional roles.

C. American women worked hard to establish their roles in American history.

D. American women were independent because they did not have to follow the regulations at all.

Passage 6

Cooperation is the only safeguard we have against the development of neurotic tendencies. It is therefore very important that children should be trained and encouraged in cooperation, and should be allowed to find their own way amongst children of their own age, in common tasks and shared games. Any barrier to cooperation will have serious consequences. The spoilt child, for example, who has learned to be interested only in himself, will take this lack of interest in others to school with him. His lessons will interest him only in so far as he thinks he can gain his teachers' favor. He will listen only to what he considers advantageous to himself. As he approaches adulthood, the result of his lack of social feeling will become more and more evident. When he first misconstrued the meaning of life, he ceased training himself for responsibility and independence. By now he is painfully ill equipped for any of life's tests and difficulties.

We cannot blame the adult for the child's early mistakes. We can only help him to remedy them when he begins to suffer the consequences. We do not expect a child who has never been taught geography to score high marks in an examination paper on the subject. Similarly, we cannot expect a child who has never been trained in cooperation to respond appropriately when tasks that demand cooperation are set before him. But all of life's problems demand an ability to cooperate if they are to be resolved; every task must be mastered within the framework of human society and in a way that furthers human welfare. Only the individual who understands that life means contribution will be able to meet his difficulties with courage and with a good chance of success.

If teachers, parents and psychologists understand the mistakes that can be made in ascribing(把······归于) a meaning to life, and provided they do not make the same mistakes themselves, we can be confident that children who lack social feeling will eventually develop a better sense of their own capacities and of the opportunities in life. When they meet problems, they will not stop trying;

they will not look for an easy way out, try to escape or throw the burden onto the shoulders of others; they will not demand extra consideration or special sympathy; they will not feel humiliated and seek revenge, or ask, "What is the use of life? What do I get from it?" They will say, "We must make our own lives. It is our own task and we are capable of performing it. We are masters of our own actions. If something new must be done or something old replaced, no one can do it but us. If life is approached in this way, as a cooperation of independent human beings, there are no limits to the progress of our human civilization. "

Question

6. What is the main idea of the passage?
   A. The importance of learning to cooperate.
   B. The early education of children.
   C. The progress of human civilization.
   D. Facing difficulties with courage.

Passage 7

Being less than perfectly well-dressed in a business setting can result in a feeling of profound discomfort that may well require therapy to dispel. And the sad truth is that "clothing mismatches" on the job can ruin the day of the person who is wearing the inappropriate attire(着装)—and the people with whom he or she comes in contact.

Offices vary when it comes to dress codes. Some businesses have very high standards for their employees and set strict guidelines for office attire, while others maintain a more relaxed attitude. However, it is always important to remember that no matter what your company's attitude is regarding what you wear, you are working in a business environment and you should dress accordingly. Certain items may be more appropriate for evening wear than for a business meeting, just as shorts and a T-shirt are better suited for the beach than for an office environment. Your attire should reflect both your environment and your position. A senior vice president has a different image to maintain than that of a secretary or sales assistant. Like it or not, you will be judged by your personal appearance.

This is never mere apparent than on "dress-down days", when what you wear can say mere about you than any business suit ever could. In fact, people will pay more attention to what you wear on dress-down days than on "business professional" days. Thus, when dressing in "business casual" clothes, try to put some flair into your wardrobe choices, recognize that the "real" definition of business casual is to dress just one notch（等级）down from what you would normally wear on business-professional attire days.

Remember, there are boundaries between your career and our social life. You should dress one way for play and another way when you mean business. Always ask yourself where you are going and how other people will be dressed when you get there. Is the final destination the opera, the beach, or the office? Dress accordingly and you will discover the truth in the axiom（公理）that clothes make the man and the woman. When in doubt, always err on the side of dressing slightly more conservatively than the situation demands.

Question

7. What is the passage mainly about?
   A. The difference between professional and casual dress.
   B. A president of a company should dress differently from a secretary or sales assistant.
   C. How to dress properly in a business setting.
   D. Improper dress will make a person feel uncomfortable.

Passage 8

Standing on the rim of the Grand Canyon gazing across this giant wound in the Earth's surface, a visitor might assume that the canyon had been caused by some ancient convulsion（突变）. In fact, the events that produced the canyon, far from being sudden and cataclysmic（巨变的）simply add up to the slow and orderly process of erosion.

Many millions of years ago the Colorado Plateau in the Grand Canyon area contained 10,000 more teat（凸出部分）of rock than it does today and was relatively level. The additional material consisted of some 14 layered formations of rock. In the Grand Canyon region these layers were largely worn away over the course of millions of years.

Approximately 65 million years ago the Plateau's flat surface in the Grand Canyon area bulged upward from internal pressure: geologists refer to this bulging action as awarding; it was followed by a general elevation of the whole Colorado Plateau, a process that is still going on. As the plateau gradually rose shallow rivers that meandered（蜿蜒）across it began to run more swiftly and cut more definite courses. One of these rivers, located east of the upward, was the ancestor of the Colorado. Another river system called the Hualapai, flowing west of the upward, extended itself eastward by cutting back into the upward: It eventually connected with the ancient Colorado and captured its waters. The new river then began to carve out the 277-mile long trench that eventually became the Grand Canyon. Geologists estimate that this initial cutting action began no earlier than 10 million years ago.

Since then, the Canyon forming has been cumulative. To the corrosive force of the river itself have been added other factors. Heat and cold, rain and snow, along with the varying resistance of the rocks, increase the opportunities for erosion. The canyon walls crumble the river acquires a cutting rottens of debris（废墟）; rainfall running off the high plateau creates feeder streams that carve side canyons. Pushing slowly backward into the plateau, the side canyons expose new rocks, and the pattern of erosion continues.

Question

8. The passage mainly discusses _____.

   A. patterns of erosion in different mountain ranges
   B. forces that made the Grand Canyon
   C. the increasing pollution of the Colorado River
   D. the sudden appearance of Grand Canyon

Passage 9

Most people would probably agree that many individual consumer adverts function on the level of the day dream. By picturing quite unusually happy and glamorous people whose success in either career or sexual terms, or both, is obvious, adverts construct an imaginary world in which the reader is able to make come true those desires which remain unsatisfied in his or her everyday life.

An advert for a science fiction magazine is unusually explicit about this. In addition to the primary use value of the magazine, the reader is promised access to a wonderful universe through the product—access to other mysterious and tantalizing（逗惹）worlds and epochs, the realms of the imagination. When studying advertising, it is therefore unreasonable to expect readers to decipher （辨认）adverts as factual statements about reality. Most adverts are just too meager in informative content and too rich in emotional suggestive detail to be read literally. If people read them literally, they would soon be forced to realize their error when the glamorous promises held out by the adverts didn't materialize.

The average consumer is not surprised that his purchase of the commodity does not redeem（买回，挽回）the promise of the advertisement, for this is what he is used to in life: the individual's pursuit of happiness and success is usually in vain. But the fantasy of his is to keep; in his dream world he enjoys a "future endlessly deferred".

The Estivalia advert is quite explicit about the fact that advertising shows us not reality, but a fantasy; it does so by openly admitting the day-dream but in Estivalia, which is "for daydream believers", those who refuse to give up trying to make the hazy ideal of natural beauty and harmony come true.

If adverts function on the day dream level—it clearly becomes inadequate to merely condemn advertising for channeling readers' attention and desires towards an unrealistic, paradisiacal（天堂似的）nowhere land. Advertising certainly does that, but in order for people to find it relevant, the Utopia（乌托邦）visualized in adverts must be linked to our surrounding reality by a causal connection.

Question

9. What is this passage mainly concerned with?

A. Many adverts can be read literally.

B. Everyone has a day dream.

C. Many adverts function on the level of the day dream.

D. Many adverts are deceitful because they can not make their promises.

Passage 10

The term "Hudson River school" was applied to the foremost representatives of nineteenth-century North American landscape painting. Apparently unknown during the golden days of the American landscape movement, which began around 1850 and lasted until the late 1860s, the Hudson River school seems to have emerged in the 1870s as a direct result of the struggle between the old and the new generations of artists, each to assert its own style as the representative American art. The older painters, most of whom were born before 1835, practiced in a mode often self-taught and monopolized by landscape subject matter and were securely established in and fostered by the reigning American art organization, the National Academy of Design. The younger painters returning home from training in Europe worked more with figural subject matter and in a bold and impressionistic technique; their prospects for patronage(赞助,支持) in their own country were uncertain, and they sought to attract it by attaining academic recognition in New York. One of the results of the conflict between the two factions was that what in previous years had been referred to as the "American Native" or occasionally "New York school"—the most representative school of American art in any genre—had by 1890 become firmly established in the minds of critics and public alike as the Hudson River school.

The sobriquet(假名,绰号) was first applied around 1879. While it was not intended as flattering, it was hardly inappropriate, the Academicians at whom it was aimed had worded and socialized in New York, the Hudson's port city, and had painted the river and its shores with varying frequency. Most important, perhaps, was that they had all maintained with a certain fidelity(忠诚), a manner of technique and composition consistent with those of America's first popular landscape artist. Thomas Cole, who built a career painting the term applied to the group of landscapists, was that many of them had, like Cole lived on or near the banks of the Hudson. Further the river had long served as the principal route to other sketching grounds favored by the Academicians, particularly the Adirondacks and the mountains of Vermont and New Hampshire.

Question

10. What is the main idea of the passage?

   A. The early history of North American landscape paintings.

   B. The emergence of Hudson River school and the origin of its name.

   C. The development of American art.

   D. The conflict between old and young artists.

2. 段落主旨题

段落主旨题是对文章的某一段或几个段落的主题进行设问，要求考生从文章的段落结构来判断段落的中心思想。虽说标准段落通常会有一个主题句来概括段落的主题思想，但是选项句意所概括的信息面就像篇章主旨题一样有偏有全。因此，考生同样要根据段落所涵盖的信息情况来选择段落主旨。例如：

Washington Irving was American's first man of letters to be known as internationally. His works were received enthusiastically both in England and the United States. He was, in fact, one of the most successful writers of his time in either country, delighting a large general public and at the same time winning the admiration of fellow writers like Scott in Britain and Poe and Hawthorne in the United States. The respect in which he was held was partly owing to the man himself, with his warm friendliness, his good sense, his urbanity（雅致）, his gay spirits, his artistic integrity（完美）, his love of both the Old World and the new. Thackeray described Irving as "a gentleman, who, though himself born in no very high sphere, was most finished, polished, witty; socially the equal of the most refined Europeans." In England he was granted an honorary degree from Oxford—as unusual honor for a citizen of a young, uncultured nation—and he received the medal of the Royal Society of Literature; America made him ambassador to Spain.

Irving's background provides little to explain his literary achievements. A gifted but delicate child, he had little schooling. He studied law, but without zeal, and never did practice seriously. He was immune to his strict Presbyterian （长老会） home environment, frequenting both social gatherings and the theater.

Question

The main point of the first paragraph is that Washington Irving was _____.

A. America's first man of letters

B. a writer who had great success both in his own country and outside it

C. a man who was able to move from literature to politics

D. a man whose personal charm enabled him to get by with basically inferior or work

【例题解析】该题的正确选项是 B。原文的第一句，也是本段落的主题句

Washington Irving was American's first man of letters to be known as internationally. 的句意是：Washington Irving 是享誉国际的美国第一才子；而选项 A 的意思则是：Washington Irving 是美国的第一才子，这显然是两种概念，因此，不合题意。选项 C 的意思显然离题太远。因为 Washington Irving 实际上学的是法律，后来才改行搞文学了。选项 D 内容文中没有提到，不足为答案。

Exercise 2

Directions：*In this section, there are five passages or paragraphs. After each passage or paragraph there are some questions or unfinished statements followed by four choices marked A, B, C and D. You should decide on the best choice and mark the corresponding letter on it.*

Passage 1

In a time of low academic achievement by children in the United States, many Americans are turning to Japan, a country of high academic achievement and economic success, for possible answers. However, the answers provided by Japanese preschools are not the ones Americans expected to find. In most Japanese preschools, surprisingly little emphasis are put on academic instructions. In one investigation, 300 Japanese and 210 American preschool teachers, child development specialists, and parents were asked about various aspects of early childhood education. Only 2 percent of the Japanese respondents (答问卷者) listed "to give children a good start academically" as one of their top three reasons for a society to have preschools. In contrast, over half the American respondents chose this as one of their top three choices. To prepare children for successful careers in first grade and beyond, Japanese schools do not teach reading, writing, and math, but rather skills such as persistence, concentration, and the ability to function as a member of a group. The vast majority of young Japanese children are taught to read at home by their parents.

In the recent comparison of Japanese and American preschool education, 91 percent of Japanese respondents chose providing children with a group experience as one of their top three reasons for a society to have preschools. Sixty-two percent of the more individually oriented (强调个性发展的) Americans listed group experience as one of their top three choices. An emphasis on the importance of the group seen in Japanese early childhood education continues into elementary school education.

Like in America, there is diversity in Japanese early childhood education. Some Japanese kindergartens have specific aims, such as early musical training or potential development. In large cities, some kindergartens are attached to universities that have elementary and secondary schools.

Some Japanese parents believe that if their young children attend a university-based program, it will increase the children's chances of eventually being admitted to top-rated schools and universities. Several more progressive programs have introduced free play as a way out for the heavy intellectualizing in some Japanese kindergartens.

Questions

1. We learn from the first paragraph that many Americans believe _____.

    A. Japanese parents are more involved in preschool education than American parents

    B. Japan's economic success is a result of its scientific achievements

    C. Japanese preschool education emphasizes academic instruction

    D. Japan's higher education is superior to theirs

2. What is the second paragraph mainly about?

    A. Japanese attach more importance to education of group experience than Americans do.

    B. Japanese attach more importance to academic education.

    C. Americans are not satisfied with the current education in US.

    D. Americans think high of individually-oriented education than Japanese.

Passage 2

Galaxies are the major building blocks of the universe. A galaxy is giant family of many millions of stars, and it is held together by its own gravitational field(引力场). Most of the material universe is organized into galaxies of stars together with gas and dust.

There are three main types of galaxy: spiral, elliptical(椭圆形), and irregular. The Milky Way is a spiral galaxy, a flattish(稍平的) disc of stars with two spiral arms emerging from its central nucleus. About one-quarter of all galaxies have this shape. Spiral galaxies are well supplied with the interstellar gas in which new stars form: as the rotating spiral pattern sweeps around the galaxy it compresses gas and dust, triggering the formation of bright young stars and in its arms. The elliptical galaxies have a symmetrical elliptical(对称的椭圆形) or spherical shape with no obvious structure. Most of their member stars are very old and since elliptical are devoid of(缺少……的)interstellar gas, no new stars are forming in them. The biggest and brightest galaxies in the universe are elliptical with masses of about 1013 times that of the Sun; these giants may frequently be sources of strong radio emission, in which case they are called radio galaxies. About two-thirds of all galaxies are elliptical. Irregular galaxies comprise about one-tenth of all galaxies and they come in many subclasses.

Measurement in space is quite different from measurement on Earth. Some terrestrial distances can be expressed as intervals of time, the time to fly from one continent to another or the time it takes to drive to work, for example. By comparison with these familiar yardsticks, the distances to the galaxies are incomprehensibly large, but they too are made more manageable by using a time calibration(刻度), in this case the distance that light travels in one year. On such a scale the nearest giant spiral galaxy, the Andromeda galaxy, is two million light years away. The most distant luminous objects seen by telescopes are probably ten thousand million light years away. Their light was already halfway here before the Earth even formed. The light from the nearby Virgo galaxy set out when reptiles still dominated the animal world.

Question

3. What does the second paragraph mainly discuss?

   A. The Milky Way.

   B. Major categories of galaxies.

   C. How elliptical galaxies are formed.

   D. Differences between irregular and spiral galaxies.

Passage 3

In bringing up children, every parent watches eagerly the child's acquisition (学会) of each new skill—the first spoken words, the first independent steps, or the beginning of wading(费力地前进) and writing. It is often tempting to hurry the child beyond his natural learning rate, but this can set up dangerous feelings of failure and states of worry in the child. This might happen at any stage. A baby might be forced to use a toilet early. A young child might be encouraged to learn to read before he knows the meaning of the words he reads. On the other hand, though, if a child is left alone too much, or without any learning opportunities, he loses his natural enthusiasm for life and his desire to hold out new things for himself.

Parents vary greatly in their degree of strictness towards their children. Some may be especially strict in money matters. Others are severe over times of coming home at night or punctuality for meals. In general, the controls imposed represent the needs of the parents and the values of the community as much as the child's own happiness.

As regents the development of moral standards in the growing child, consistency is very important in parental teaching. To forbid a thing one day and encase it the next is no foundation for morality(道德). Also, parents should realize that "example is better than precept". If they are not sincere and do not practice what they preach(说教), their children may grow confused and emotionally insecure when they grow old enough to think for themselves, and realize they have been in some extent fooled.

A sudden awareness of a marked difference between their parents' principles and their morals can be a dangerous disappointment.

Question

4. The second paragraph mainly tells us that _____.
   A. parents should be strict with their children
   B. parental controls reflect only the needs of the parents and the values of the community
   C. parental restrictions vary, and are not always enforced for the benefit of the children alone
   D. parents vary in their strikes towards their children according to the situation

Passage 4

The importance and focus of the interview in the work of the print and broadcast journalist is reflected in several books that have been written on the topic. Most of these books, as well as several chapters, mainly in, but not limited to, journalism and broadcasting handbooks and reporting texts, stress the "how to" aspects of journalistic interviewing rather than the conceptual aspects of the interview, its context, and implications. Much of the "how to" material is based on personal experiences and general impressions. As we know, in journalism as in other fields, much can be learned from the systematic study of professional practice. Such study brings together evidence from which broad generalized principles can be developed.

There is, as has been suggested, a growing body of research literature in journalism and broadcasting, but very little significant attention has been devoted to the study of the interview itself. On the other hand, many general texts as well as numerous research articles on interviewing in fields other than journalism have been written. Many of these books and articles present the theoretical and empirical aspects of the interview as well as the training of the interviewers. Unhappily, this plentiful general literature about interviewing pays little attention to the journalistic interview. The fact that the general literature on interviewing does not deal with the journalistic interview seems to be surprising for two reasons. First, it seems likely that most people in modern Western societies are more familiar, at least in positive manner, with journalistic interviewing than any other form of interviewing. Most of us are probably somewhat familiar with the clinical interview, such as that conducted by physicians and psychologists. In these situations the professional person or interviewer is interested in getting information necessary for the diagnosis and treatment of the person. Another familiar situation is the job interview. However, very few of us have actually been interviewed personally by the mass media, particularly by television. And yet we have a vivid acquaintance with the journalistic interview by virtue of our roles as readers, listeners, and viewers. Even so the understanding of the journalistic interview, especially television interviews, requires thoughtful analyses and even study, as this book indicates.

Questions

5. The main idea of the first paragraph is that _____.

   A. generalized principles for journalistic interviews are the chief concern for writers on journalism

   B. importance should be attached to the systematic study of journalistic interviewing

   C. concepts and contextual implications are of secondary importance to journalistic interviewing

D. personal experiences and general impressions should be excluded from journalistic interviews

6. What does the second paragraph mainly talk about?

A. More attention should be given to research literature in journalism and broadcast.

B. More attention should be given to the research in journalistic interview only.

C. Dissatisfaction with the current research on interview.

D. Dissatisfaction with the television interview.

Passage 5

Teaching is unquestionably one of the most important commitments one can make for the future economic prosperity of a society. Sadly, it is a profession that has largely underpaid its workers while increasing the complexity of the responsibilities its workers face. The recent budget revision proposal by Governor Gray Davis of California seeks to recognize the important contribution of teachers to the California economy by permanently excluding teachers from paying state personal income taxes. On the surface it is indeed a good gesture, but it is bad public policy.

In order to attract teachers it makes sense to raise their salaries. Public school teachers in the United States make an average of $39,300 according to the American Federation of Teachers, with a starting salary of $25,700. Comparing the starting salary of a teacher with that of a service occupation in the private sector (单位) such as a computer programmer, at present in much demand in California, where the starting salary is $40,800, the wage differential(差额) is stark(不折不扣的). As a result, for many young adults looking for jobs after graduation with a Bachelor's degree going into the private sector is a more economically rewarding option.

Removing state income taxes in California, however, is not the way to create incentives for graduates to become teachers. The first consideration is that financially the gain from non-payment of income taxes is not very large. In the governor's budget plan, a teacher making $30,000 will gain $502 more by not paying the state income tax. It is simply ridiculous to think a few hundred dollars a year is going to make anyone reevaluate their career plans.

Also，in offering state exemption（免税）to teachers，the governor is opening up a Pandora's Box. Exempting teachers is a nice fed-good policy，but it singles out teachers as being somehow more valuable than other public services workers such as police officers or social workers. Pretty soon，various types of public servants will be asking the governor for tax exemptions for their important contributions to the public. Where would the limit be set?

Questions

7. The first paragraph is intended to tell the readers that _____ .

   A. the state exemption to teachers from income taxes is ill-advised

   B. teachers are indispensable to the development of economy

   C. the recent budget revision was proposed by the state Governor

   D. the exclusion of teachers from paying income taxes is sensible

8. What does the last paragraph tell us?

   A. Teachers are more valuable than other public services workers.

   B. Public service workers make more contribution to the public.

   C. Offering exception to teachers is a start of other various troubles.

   D. The state governor will give exception to the public service workers in the future.

3. 目的类主旨题

目的类主旨题是针对全文或某段文章的写作目的进行提问。该类型试题与主题类主旨句试题的不同之处在于前者要求考生就短文内容进行综合判断,而后者则是要求考生就短文的蕴含目的进行推导判断。例如:

Men usually want to have their own way. They want to think and act as they like. No one，however，can have his own way all the time. A man cannot live in society without considering the interests of others as well as his own interests. "Job Society" means a group of people with the same laws and the same way of life. People in society may make their own decisions，but these decisions ought not to be unjust or harmful to others. One man's decisions may so easily harm another person. For example，a motorist may be in a hurry to get to a friend's house. He sets out，driving at full speed like a competitor in a motor race. There are other vehicles and also pedestrians on the road. Suddenly there is a crash. There are screams and confusion. One careless motorist has struck another car. The collision has injured two of the passengers and killed the third.

Too many road accidents happen through the thoughtlessness of selfish drivers.

We have governments, the police and the law courts to prevent or to punish such criminal acts. But in addition, all men ought to observe certain rules of conduct. Every man ought to behave with consideration for other men. He ought not to steal, cheat, or destroy the property of others. There is no place of this sort of behavior in a civilized society.

Question

The purpose of this passage is to _____.

A. tell people how to behave in society

B. illustrate the importance of laws

C. teach people how to prevent criminal acts

D. persuade people not to make their own decisions

【例题解析】选项 A 为正确答案。本文以实例为依据,说明人作为社会的一份子不能生活在社会里却不考虑自己或他人的利益。藉其暗示人们应当如何行为处事。文章在第二段第一句中确实出现过法律一词,但该词只是一句起定语作用的名词而已,不是段落中的关键词。此外,第二段第四句中作者说人们不该偷窃、欺骗或破坏他人财物,实际上也是在告诉人们该做什么,不该做什么,以支持文章的主要观点,而不是选项 B,C 和 D 中所说的目的。

Exercise 3

Directions: *In this section, there are ten passages. After each passage there is a question or unfinished statement followed by four choices marked A, B, C and D. You should decide on the best choice and mark the corresponding letter on it.*

Passage 1

In the late 1960's, many people in North America turned their attention to environmental problems, and new steel-and-glass skyscrapers were widely criticized. Ecologists pointed out that a cluster of tall buildings in a city often overburdens public transportation and parking lot capacities.

Skyscrapers are also lavish consumers, and wasters, of electric power. In one recent year, the addition of 17 million square feet of skyscraper office space in New York City raised the peak daily demand for electricity by 120,000 kilowatts—enough to supply the entire city of Albany, New York, for a day.

Glass-walled skyscrapers can be especially wasteful. The heat loss (or gain) through a wall of half-inch plate glass is more than ten times that through a typical masonry（砖石建筑）wall filled with insulation board. To lessen the strain on heating and air-conditioning equipment, builders of skyscrapers have begun to use double-glazed panels of glass, and reflective glasses coated with silver or gold mirror films that reduce glare as well as heat gain. However, mirror-walled skyscrapers raise the temperature of the surrounding air and affect neighboring buildings.

Skyscrapers put a severe strain on a city's sanitation（卫生,卫生设施）facilities, too. If fully occupied, the two World Trade Center towers in New York City would alone generate 2.25 million gallons of raw sewage（污水）each year—as much as a city the size of Stamford, Connecticut, which has a population of more than 109,000.

Skyscrapers also interfere with television reception, block bird flyways（飞行线路）, and obstruct air traffic. In Boston in the late 1960's, some people even feared that shadows from skyscrapers would kill the grass on Boston Common.

Still, people continue to build skyscrapers for all the reasons that they have always built them—personal ambition, civic pride, and the desire of owners to have the largest possible amount of rentable space.

Question

1. The main purpose of the passage is to _____.
   A. discuss the advantages and disadvantages of skyscrapers
   B. compare skyscrapers with other modern structures
   C. describe skyscrapers and their effect on the environment
   D. illustrate various architectural designs of skyscrapers

Passage 2

Exercise is one of the few factors with a positive role in long-term maintenance of body weight. Unfortunately, that message has not gotten through to the average American, who would rather try switching to "light" beer and low-calorie bread than increase physical exertion. The Centers for Disease Control, for example, found that less than one-fourth of overweight adults who were trying to shed pounds said they were combining exercise with their diet.

In rejecting exercise, some people may be discouraged too much by caloric-expenditure charts; for example, one would have to briskly walk three miles just to work off the 275 calories in one delicious Danish pastry (小甜饼). Even exercise professionals concede half a point here. "Exercise by itself is a very tough way to lose weight," says York Onnen, program director of the President's Council on Physical Fitness and Sports.

Still, exercise's supporting role in weight reduction is vital. A study at the Boston University Medical Center of overweight police officers and other public employees confirmed that those who dieted without exercise regained almost all their old weight, while those who worked exercise into their daily routine maintained their new weight.

If you have been sedentary (极少活动的) and decide to start walking one mile a day, the added exercise could burn an extra 100 calories daily. In a year's time, assuming no increase in food intake, you could lose ten pounds. By increasing the distance of your walks gradually and making other dietary adjustments, you may lose even more weight.

Question

2. What is the author's purpose in writing this article?

    A. To justify the study of the Boston University Medical Center.

    B. To stress the importance of maintaining proper weight.

    C. To support the statement made by York Onnen.

    D. To show the most effective way to lose weight.

Passage 3

Joyce Carol Oates published her first collection of short stories. *By The North Gate*, in 1963, two years after she had received her master's degree from the University of Wisconsin and become an instructor of English at the University of Detroit. Her productivity since then has been prodigious (巨大的, 庞大的), accumulating in less than two decades to nearly thirty titles, including novels, collections of short stories and verse, plays, and literary criticism. In the meantime, she has continued to teach, moving in 1967 from the University of Detroit to the University of Windsor, in Ontario, and, in 1978, to Princeton University. Reviewers have admired her enormous energy, but find a productivity of such magnitude difficult to assess.

In a period characterized by the abandonment of so much of the realistic tradition by authors such as John Barth, Donald Barthelme, and Thomas Pynchon, Joyce Carol Oates has seemed at times determinedly old-fashioned in her insistence on the essentially mimetic(模仿的，类似的) quality of her fiction. Hers is a world of violence, insanity, fractured love, and hopeless loneliness. Although some of it appears to come from her direct observations, her dreams, and her fears, much more is clearly from the experiences of others. Her first novel, *With Shuddering Fall* (1964), dealt with stock car racing, though she had never seen a race. In *Them* (1969) she focused on Detroit from the Depression through the notes of 1967, drawing much of her material from the deep impression made on her by the problems of one of her students. Whatever the source and however shocking the events or the motivations, however, her fictive world remains strikingly akin(类似的) to that real one reflected in the daily newspapers, the television news and talk shows, and the popular magazines of our day.

Question

3. What is the main purpose of the passage?

   A. To review Oates's By the North Gate.

   B. To compare some modern writers.

   C. To describe Oates's childhood.

   D. To outline Oates's career.

Passage 4

The term "culture shock" has already begun to creep into the popular vocabulary. Culture shock is the effect that immersion in a strange culture has on the unprepared visitor. Culture shock is what happens when a traveler suddenly finds himself in a place where "yes" may mean "no", where a "fixed price" is negotiable, where to be kept waiting in an outer office is no cause for insult, where laughter may signify anger. It is what happens when the familiar psychological cues that help an individual to function in society are suddenly withdrawn and replaced by new ones that are strange or incomprehensible.

The culture shock phenomenon accounts for much of the bewilderment, frustration, and disorientation(使不辨方向，使精神混乱) that plague Americans in their dealings with other societies. It causes a breakdown in communication, a misreading of reality, an inability to cope. Yet culture shock is relatively mild in comparison with the much more serious malady, future shock. Future shock is the dizzying disorientation brought on by the premature arrival of the future. It may well be the most important disease of tomorrow.

Take an individual out of his own culture and set him down suddenly in an environment sharply different from his own, with a different set of cues to react to—different conceptions of time, space, work, love, religion, sex, and everything else that cut him off from any hope of retreat to a more familiar social landscape, and the dislocation he suffers is doubly severe. Moreover, if this new culture is itself in constant turmoil(骚乱), and if worse yet its values are incessantly changing, the sense of disorientation will be still further intensified. Given few clues as to what kind of behavior is rational under the radically new circumstances, the victim may well become a hazard to himself and others.

Now imagine not merely an individual but an entire society, an entire generation including its weakest, least intelligent, and most irrational members—suddenly transported into this new world. The result is mass disorientation, future shock on a grand scale.

This is the prospect that man now faces. Change is avalanching(纷至杳来) upon our heads and most people are absurdly unprepared to cope with it.

Question

4. This passage was probably written to _____.

   A. warn the readers of today against possible dangers of tomorrow

   B. prepare travelers for the unfamiliar environments

   C. help psychologists understand certain irrational behavior better

   D. enable sociologists to predict more accurately what will happen to mankind

Passage 5

My objective is to analyze certain forms of knowledge, not in terms of repression or law, but in terms of power. But the word power is apt to lead to misunderstandings about the nature, form, and unity of power. By power, I do not mean a group of institutions and mechanisms that ensure the subservience(贡献) of the citizenry. I do not mean, either, a mode of subjugation(顺从,统治) that, in contrast to violence, has the form of the rule. Finally, I do not have in mind a general system of domination exerted by one group over another, a system whose effects, through successive derivations(诱导), pervade the entire social body. The sovereignty of the state, the form of law or the overall unity of domination are only the terminal forms power takes.

It seems to me that power must be understood as the multiplicity of force relations that are immanent(内在的) in the social sphere; as the process that, through ceaseless struggle and confrontation, transforms, strengthens, or reverses them; as the support that these force relations find in one another, or on the contrary, the disjuncture(相悖,反意) and contradictions that isolate them from one another and lastly, as the strategies in which they take effect, whose general design or institutional crystallization is embodied in the state apparatus, in the formulation of the law, in the various social hegemonies(霸权, 领导权).

Thus, the viewpoint that permits one to understand the exercise of power, even in its mere "peripheral(边缘的)" effects, and that also makes it possible to use its mechanisms as a structural framework for analyzing the social order, must not be sought in a unique source of sovereignty from which secondary and descendent forms of power emanate(放射) but in the moving substrata(隐藏的特点) of force relations that, by virtue of their inequality, constantly engender local and trustable states of power, if power seems omnipresent(无所不在的), it is not because it has the privilege of consolidating everything under its invincible(无法征服的) unity, but because it is produced from one moment to the next, at every point, or rather in every relation from one point to another. Power is everywhere, not because it embraces everything, but because it comes from everywhere. And if power at times seems to be permanent, repetitious, invert, and self-reproducing, it is simply because the overall effect that emerges from all these nobilities is a concatenation(连结,连续) that rests on each of them and seeks in turn to arrest their movement. One needs to be nominalistic, no doubt: power is not an institution, and not a structure; neither is it certain strength we are endowed with; it is the name that one attributes to a complex strategic situation in a particular society.

Question

5. The author's primary propose in defining power is to _____.
   A. counteract self-serving and confusing uses of the term
   B. establish a compromise among those who have defined the term in different ways

C. increase comprehension of the term by providing concrete examples

D. avoid possible misinterpretations resulting from the more common uses of the term

Passage 6

One-room schools are part of the heritage of the United States, and the mention of them makes people feel a vague longing for "the way things were". One-room schools are an endangered species, however. For more than a hundred years, one-room schools have been systematically shut down and their students sent away to centralized schools. As recently as 1930 there were 149,000 one-room schools in the United States. By 1970 there were 1,800. Today, of the nearly 800 remaining one-room schools, more than 350 are in Nebraska. The rest are scattered through a few other states that have on their road maps wide-open spaces between towns.

Now that there are hardly any left, educators are beginning to think that maybe there is something yet to be learned from one-room schools, something that served the pioneers that might serve as well today. Progressive educators have come up with progressive sounding names like "peer-group teaching" and "multi-age grouping" for educational procedures that occur naturally in the one-room schools. In a one-room school the children teach each other because the teacher is busy part of the time teaching someone else. A fourth grader can work at a fifth-grade level in math and a third-grade level in English without the stigma (污名) associated with being left back or the pressures of being skipped ahead. A youngster with a learning disability can find his or her own feel without being separated from the other pupils. In larger urban and suburban schools today, this is called "mainstreaming". A few hours in a small school that has only one classroom and it becomes clear why so many parents feel that one of the advantages of living in Nebraska is that their children have to go to a one-room school.

Question

6. What is the author's main purpose in the passage?

   A. To discuss present-day education in the United States.

   B. To mention some advantages of one-room schools.

   C. To persuade states to close down one-room schools.

D. To summarize the history of education in the United States.

Passage 7

There are various ways in which individual economic units can interact with one another. Three basic ways may be described as the market system, the administered system and the traditional system.

In a market system individual economic units are free to interact among each other in the marketplace. It is possible to buy commodities(商品) from other economic units or sell commodities to them. In a market, transactions may take place via barter or money exchange. In a barter economy, real goods such as automobiles, shoes, and pizzas are traded against each other. Obviously, finding somebody who wants to trade my old car in exchange for a sailboat may not always be an easy task. Hence, the introduction of money as a medium of exchange eases transactions considerably. In the modern market economy, goods and services are bought or sold for money.

An alternative to the market system is administrative control by some agency over all transactions. This agency will issue edicts(法令) or commands as to how much of each commodity and service should be produced, exchanged and consumed by each economic unit. Central planning may be one way of administering such an economy. The central plan, drawn up by the government, shows the amounts of each commodity produced by the various firms and allocated to different households for consumption. This is an example of complete planning of production, consumption, and exchange for the whole economy.

In a traditional society, production and consumption patterns are governed by tradition; every person's place within the economic system is fixed by parentage, religion, and custom. Transactions take place on the basis of tradition, too. People belonging to a certain group or caste(阶级，等级) may have an obligation to care for other persons, provide them with food and shelter, care for their health, and provide for their education. Clearly, in a system where every decision is made on the basis of tradition alone, progress may be difficult to achieve. A stagnant(停滞，不发展的) society may result.

Question

7. What is the main purpose of the passage?

A. To outline contrasting types of economic systems.
B. To explain the science of economics.
C. To argue for the superiority of one economic system.
D. To compare barter and money-exchange markets.

Passage 8

Without regular supplies of some hormones(荷尔蒙) our capacity to behave would be seriously impaired; without others we would soon die. Tiny amounts of some hormones can modify moods and actions, our inclination to eat or drink, our aggressiveness or submissiveness, and our reproductive and parental behavior. And hormones do more than influence adult behavior; early in life they help to determine the development of bodily form and may even determine an individual's behavioral capacities. Later in life the changing outputs of some endocrine glands(内分泌腺) and the body's changing sensitivity to some hormones are essential aspects of the phenomena of aging.

Communication within the body and the consequent integration of behavior were considered the exclusive province of the nervous system up to the beginning of the present century. The emergence of endocrinology(内分泌学) as a separate discipline can probably be traced to the experiments of Baytiss and Starling on the hormone secretion. This substance is secreted from cells in the intestinal(肠道的) walls when food enters the stomach; it travels through the bloodstream and stimulates the pancreas(胰) to liberate pancreatic juice, which aids in digestion. By showing that special cells secrete chemical agents that are conveyed by the bloodstream and regulate distant target organs or tissues. Bayliss and Starling demonstrated that chemical integration can occur without participation of the nervous system

The term "hormone" was first used with reference to secretion Starling derived the term from the Greek hormone, meaning "to excite or set in motion. " The term "endocrine" was introduced shortly thereafter "exocrine"(外分泌的) is used to refer to glands that secrete products into the bloodstream. The term "endocrine" contrasts with "exocrine", which is applied to glands that secrete their products through ducts(导管) to the site of action. Examples of exocrine glands are the tear glands, the sweat glands and the pancreas, which secretes pancreatic juice through a duct into the intestine. Exocrine glands are also called duct glands, while endocrine glands are called ductless.

Question

8. What is the author's main purpose in the passage?

    A. To explain the specific functions of various hormones.

    B. To provide general information about hormones.

    C. To explain how the term "hormone" evolved.

    D. To report on experiments in endocrinology.

Passage 9

Jogging has become the most popular individual sport in America. Many theories, even some mystical ones, have been advanced to explain the popularity of jogging. The plain truth is that jogging is a cheap, quick and efficient way to maintain (or achieve) physical fitness.

The most useful sort of exercise is exercise that develops the heart, lungs, and circulatory systems. If these systems are fit, the body is ready for almost any sport and for almost any sudden demand made by work or emergencies. One can train more specifically, as by developing strength for weight lifting or the ability to run straight ahead for short distances with great power as in football, but running trains your heart and lungs to deliver oxygen more efficiently to all parts of your body. It is worth doing that, this sort of exercise is the only kind that can reduce heart disease, the number one cause of death in America.

Only one sort of equipment is needed a pair of good shoes. Physicians advise beginning joggers not to try to run in a tennis or gym shoe. Many design advances have been made in only the last several years that make an excellent running shoe indispensable if a runner wishes to develop as quickly as possible, with as little chance of injury as possible. A good running shoe will have a soft pad for absorbing shock, as well as a slightly built-up heel and a full heel cup that will give the knee and ankle more stability. A wise investment in good shoes will prevent blisters（水泡）and the foot ankle and knee injuries and will also enable the wearer to run on paved or soft surfaces.

No other special equipment is needed: you can jog in any clothing you desire, even your street clothes. Many joggers wear expensive, flashy warm-up suite, but just as any wear a simple pair of gym shoes and T-shirt, in fact, many people just jog in last year's clothes. In cold weather, several layers of clothing are better than one heavy sweater or coat. If joggers are wearing several layers of clothing, they can add or subtract layers as conditions change.

It takes surprisingly little time to develop the ability to run. The American Jogging Association has a twelve-week program designed to move from a fifteen-minute walk (which almost anyone can manage who is in reasonable health) to a thirty-minute run. A measure of common sense, a physical examination, and a planned schedule are all it takes.

Question

9. The main purpose of this passage is to _____.
   A. discuss jogging as a physical fitness program
   B. describe the type of clothing needed for jogging
   C. provide scientific evidence of the benefits of jogging
   D. distinguish between jogging as a "common sense" fitness program and a cult(崇拜) movement.

Passage 10

A study of art history might be a good way to learn more about a culture than is possible to learn in general history classes. Most typical history courses concentrate on politics, economics, and war. But art history focuses on much more than this because art reflects not only the political values of a people, but also religious beliefs, emotions, and psychology. In addition, information about the daily activities of our ancestors or of people very different from our own can be provided by art. In short, art expresses the essential qualities of a time and a place, and a study of it clearly offers us a deeper understanding than can be found in most history books.

In history books, objective information about the political life of a country is presented; that is, facts about politics are given, but opinions are not expressed. Art, on the other hand, is subjective: it reflects emotions and opinions. The great Spanish painter Francisco Goya was perhaps the first truly "political" artist. In his well-known painting *The Third of May*, 1808, he criticized the Spanish government for its misuse of power over people. Over a hundred years later, symbolic images were used in Pablo Picasso's Guernica to express the horror of war. Meanwhile, on another continent, the powerful paintings of Diego Rivera, Jose Clemente Orozco, and David Alfaro Siqueiros as well as the works of Alfredo Ramos Martinez depicted these Mexican artists' deep anger and sadness about social problems.

In the same way, art can reflect a culture's religious beliefs. For hundreds of years in Europe, religious art was almost the only type of art that existed. Churches and other religious buildings were filled with paintings that depicted people and stories from the Bible. Although most people couldn't read, they could still understand biblical stories in the pictures on church walls.

By contrast, one of the main characteristics of art in the Middle East was (and still is) its absence of human and animal images. This reflects the Islamic belief that statues are unholy.

Question

10. The purpose of this passage is to mainly discuss _____.

    A. the difference between general history and art history

    B. the making of art history

    C. what we can learn from art

    D. the influence of artists on art history

4. 标题类主旨题

标题类主旨题要求考生从四个选项中为文章选出一个恰当的标题。这类考题实际上还是在考查考生的归纳和概括能力,因为短文的标题就是短文中心思想的高度凝练,其不同之处在于前者只是就短文的标题进行提问。做这类试题时,除了要关注短文的信息内容外,还要特别注意短文的写作文体,因为文体往往与文章的标题密切相关。例如:

Artificial flowers are used for scientific as well as for decorative purposes. They are made from a variety of materials, such as wax and glass, so skillfully that they can scarcely be distinguished from natural flowers. In making such models, painstaking skill and artistry are called for, as well as thorough knowledge of plant structure. The collection of glass flowers in the Botanical Museum of Harvard University is the most famous in North America and is widely known throughout the scientific world. In all, there are several thousand models in colored glass, the work of two artist-naturalists, Leopold Blaschka and his son Rudolph.

The intention was to have the collection represent at least one member of each flower family native to the United States. Although it was never completed, it contains more than seven hundred species representing 164 families of flowering plants, a group of fruits showing the effect of fungus（由真菌引起的）diseases, and thousands of flower parts and magnified details. Every detail of these is accurately reproduced in color and structure. The models are kept in locked cases as they are too valuable and fragile for classroom use.

Question

Which of the following is the best title for the passage?

A. An Extensive Collection of Glass Flowers

B. The Lives of Leopold and Rudolph Blaschka

C. Flowers Native to the United States

D. Materials Used for Artificial Flowers

【例题解析】选项 A 为正确答案。虽然在文章的段首曾提到过其他假花的制作材料,但那只是一个过渡和铺垫,随后文章的主题很快就切入了正题,并且自此之后始终围绕着这个主题拓展行文,说明广泛收集玻璃花的目的、意图和状况。选项 B 的中心词是 lives,限定范围是 Leopold and Rudolph Blaschka。基于该标题的文章首先应以 lives 为主题,在 Leopold and Rudolph Blaschka 的范围内进行拓展论述。然而,文章的内容并非如此。因此,选项 B 不是正确答案。选项 C 所界定的范围太广,涵盖了所有以不同形式呈现的生长在美国本地的花,而文章谈的只是外形神似真花的假花;选项 D 所涵盖的内容又太偏,用于制作假花的材料。因此,这两个选项均不可为正确答案。

Exercise 4

Directions: *In this section, there are five passages. For each passage there is a question or unfinished statement followed by four choices marked A, B, C and D. You should decide on the best choice and mark the corresponding letter on it.*

Passage 1

Scientists estimate that about 35,000 other objects, too small to detect with radar but detectable with powerful Earth-based telescope, are also circling the Earth at an altitude of 200 to 700 miles. This debris（碎片）poses little danger to us on the Earth, but since it is traveling at average relative speeds of six miles per second, it can severely damage expensive equipment in a collision. This threat was dramatized by a hole one-eighth of an inch in diameter created in a window of a United States space shuttle in 1983. The pit was determined to have been caused by a collision with a speck（微片）of paint traveling at a speed of about two to four miles per second. The window has been replaced.

As more and more nations put satellites into space, the risk of collision can only increase. Measures are already being taken to control the growth of orbital debris. The United State has always required its astronauts to bag their wastes and return them to Earth. The United States Air Force has agrees to conduct low-altitude rather than high-altitude tests of objects it puts into space so debris from tests will reenter the Earth's atmosphere and burn up. Extra shielding will also reduce the risk of damage. For example, 2000 pounds of additional shielding (防护物) is being considered for each of six space-station crew modules(乘务舱). Further, the European Space Agency is also looking into preventive measures.

Question

1. Which of the following would be the best title for the passage?

   A. The Problem of Space Debris

   B. The Space Shuttle of 1983

   C. The Work of the European Space Agency

   D. A Collision in Space

Passage 2

The preschool movement can be traced back as far as the 4th century B. C. when Plato stressed the importance of early childhood, and the necessity of family cooperation. A study of ancient history reveals that some of the early philosophers, preachers(布道师) and educational reformers considered the significance of parent-child relationships, and made plans for improved education for infants and young children. However, it is in the 17th century that early childhood education as we know received its impetus(推进).

In the history of education, several educational leaders have made valuable early contributions to the preschool movement. The pioneer work of Comenius, Rousseau, Basedow, Pestalozzi and Froebel in this field is particularly noteworthy. More recently, important additions were made by Montessori, Dewey, and others. Early in the 20th century, organized planning for preschool training led to the introduction of institutions designed specially for this purpose. In England, for example, the Consultation Committee of the Board of Education recommended good nursery schools to take care of children too young to attend regular schools.

The first preschools in America were adaptations of the English idea, differing however in aims, motives, and organization. The American preschool was promoted in the interest of psychological and educational research and was concerned with what could be learned from children rather than taught them. Social forces that prevailed in the country after 1890 further influenced their development. The number of schools increased rapidly following the close of World War.

Question

2. Which of the following would be the best title for the passage?

    A. The Early Contributions to the Preschool.

    B. Education in Parent Child Relationships.

    C. The Development of the Preschool Movement.

    D. The First Preschools in America.

Passage 3

Money spent on advertising is money spent as well as any I know of. It serves directly to assist a rapid distribution of goods at reasonable prices, thereby establishing a firm home market and so making it possible to provide for export at competitive prices. By drawing attention to new ideas it helps enormously to raise standards of living. By helping to increase demand it ensures an increased need for labor, and is therefore an effective way to fight unemployment. It lowers the costs of many services: without advertisements your daily newspaper would cost four times as much. The price of your television license would need to be doubled and travel by bus or tube would cost 20 per cent more.

And perhaps most important of all advertising provides a guarantee of reasonable value in the products and services you buy. Apart from the fact that twenty-seven Acts of Parliament govern the terms of advertising, no regular advertiser dare promote a product that fails to live up to the promise of his advertisements. He might fool some people for a little while through misleading advertising. He will not do so for long for mercifully the public has the good sense not to buy the inferior article more than once. If you see an article consistently advertised, it is the surest proof I know that the article does what is claimed for it, and that it represents good value.

Advertising does more for the material benefit of the community than any other force I can think of. There is one more point I feel I ought to touch on. Recently I heard a well known television personality declare that he was against advertising because it persuades rather than informs. He was drawing excessively fine distinctions. Of course advertising seeks to persuade.

If its message were confined(限制) merely to information and that in itself would be difficult if not impossible to achieve, for even a detail such as the choice of the color of a shirt is subtly persuasive—advertising would be so boring that no one would pay any attention. But perhaps that is what the well known television personality wants.

Question

3. The best title for the passage would probably be _____.
   A. Positive and Negative Aspects of Advertising
   B. Benefits Brought by Advertising and Its Persuasive Function
   C. Advertising the Best Persuasive and Informative Medium
   D. Advertising the Most Effective Way to Promote Products

Passage 4

If you intend using humor in your talk to make people smile, you must know how to identify shared experiences and problems. Your humor must be relevant to the audience and should help to show them that you are one of them or that you understand their situation and are in sympathy with their point of view. Depending on whom you are addressing, the problems will be different. If you are talking to a group of managers, you may refer to the disorganized methods of their secretaries; alternatively if you are addressing secretaries, you may want to comment on their disorganized bosses.

Here is an example, which I heard at a nurses' convention, of story which works well because all of the audience shared the same view of doctors. A man arrives in heaven and is being shown around by St. Peter. He sees wonderful accommodations, beautiful gardens, sunny weather, and so on. Everyone is very peaceful, polite and friendly until, waiting in a line for lunch, the new arrival is suddenly pushed aside by a man in a white coat that rushes to the head of the line, grabs his food and stomps over to a table by himself. "Who is that?" the new arrival asked St. Peter. "Oh, that's God," came the reply, "but sometimes he thinks he's a doctor. "

If you are part of the group which you are addressing, you will be in a position to know the experiences and problems which are common to all of you and it'll be appropriate for you to make a passing remark about the inedible canteen food or the chairman's notorious bad taste in ties. With other audiences you mustn't attempt to cut in with humor as they will resent an outsider making disparaging（诋毁，贬低）remarks about their canteen or their chairman. You will be on . safer ground if you stick to, scapegoats（替罪羊）like the Post Office or the telephone system.

If you feel awkward being humorous, you must practice so that it becomes more natural. Include a few casual and apparently humorous remarks which you can deliver in a relaxed and unforced manner. Often it's the delivery which causes the audience to smile, so speak slowly and remember that a raised eyebrow or an unbelieving look may help to show that you are making a light-hearted remark.

Look for the humor. It often comes from the unexpected. A twist on a familiar quote "If at first you don't succeed, give up" or a play on words or on a situation. Search for exaggeration and understatements. Look at your talk and pick out a few words or sentences which you can turn about and inject with humor.

Question

4. The best title for the text may be _____.

    A. Use Humor Effectively   B. Various Kinds of Humor

    C. Add Humor to Speech   D. Different Humor Strategies

Passage 5

The study of ecology is important for everyone who cares about our world. Air, water, and land—we would not live without any of these. But what do we mean by land? It is the earth beneath our feet, wherever we are. It is mountains and plains. It is wide field for growing corn and wheat. Or it may be an airfield or a parking lot or a highway or a whole city—land covered with cement, asphalt （沥青）, and buildings. Land is the solid part of the earth.

Land is the soil plants grow in. That is the most important thing about the land—it is the place where green plants grow. Without green plants there would be no life on Earth. Green leaves make oxygen. All of us—ants, elephants, people, and every living creature—must have oxygen to stay alive. We breathe in oxygen and our bodies use it. Carbon dioxide is formed in the process and we breathe it out. Leaves use carbon dioxide along with water to make food for plants. Then they give off oxygen.

This process has been going on for millions of years. It is part of the pattern of our natural life on Earth. This pattern had changed very little for millions of years before people arrived on Earth. People found ways to improve their lives by changing nature, by trying to make nature fit in with their way of life. Warm houses in winter, electric lights at night, factories to produce our food, our clothes, our gadgets(小装置)—all this people have accomplished. And we learned to grow more food on the land than nature could grow without our help.

All this is good—up to a point. But it has gone too far. We have produced too much and we have failed to see what this was doing to our world. We have not understood the ways in which all living things on Earth depend on one another. We ourselves have increased until the sheer numbers of people on Earth have upset the balance of nature.

Question

5. The best title for this passage is _____.

    A. The Products of Nature   B. The Life Pattern on Earth

    C. The Exhausted Balance of Nature D. The Broken Balance of Nature

5. 语气类试题

作者在写文章时会通过语用及其他各自的独特表述方式为文章奠定某种基调,直接或间接地透露出自己对所谈论的主题的语气或者是主观倾向。前者易于确定,因为作者在文章中对某个问题所表达的语气或者看法相对明确,可谓立场坚定,旗帜鲜明。但间接或表述含蓄的语气则需要透过文章的字里行间来领悟归纳和推导。语气类试题的测试目的就是要检查考生在这方面的推断能力。对于此类阅读理解试题,应特别关注作者在文章中所使用的语气。例如:

Turn on the world news broadcast any evening, and the predominant mood is one of semi-darkness and hopelessness. Maybe Brazil and Peru haven't gone to war, but the news is that some other countries have. Thousands of people have been left homeless by earthquakes, floods, and fires, but nobody reports on the millions of people unharmed by natural disasters. In the cities, men and women go about the daily affairs of earning a living, quietly and calmly, without making the news, but crime, greed, and corruption seem to be on every street corner according to the latest news report.

Question

The tone of the passage would be _____.

A. pessimistic

B. critical

C. angry

D. one of gloom

【例题解析】本题的正确答案为选项 B。根据问题中 tone 一词可知该试题显然是一道语气判断题。短文主要讲的是新闻广播的内容太过阴暗绝望。其中作者采用了正反对比手法，指出广播新闻只看到了灾难性的邪恶一面，却忽视了生活中无处不在的另一面：祥和与光明。在论述过程中，作者的语气客观平和，就事论事，既没有愤怒沮丧，又没有消极失望，只是实事求是地评论着现实中存在于新闻广播中的一种现象。

Exercise 5

Directions: *In this section, there are five passages. For each passage there is a question or unfinished statement followed by four choices marked A, B, C and D. You should decide on the best choice and mark the corresponding letter on it.*

Passage 1

In only two decades Asian Americans have become the fastest-growing US minority. As their children began moving up through the nation's schools, it became clear that a new class of academic was emerging. Their achievements are reflected in the nation's best universities, where mathematics, science and engineering departments have taken on a decidedly Asian character. This special liking for mathematics and science is partly explained by the fact that Asian-American students who began their educations abroad arrived in the US with a solid grounding(基础) in mathematics but little or no knowledge of English . They are also influenced by the promise of a good job after college. Asians feel there will be less unfair treatment in areas like mathematics and science because they will be judged more objectively. And the return on the investment in education is more immediate in something like engineering than with an arts degree.

Most Asian-American students owe their success to the influence of parents who are determined that their children take full advantage of what the American educational system has to offer. An effective measure of parental attention is homework. Asian parents spend more time with their children than American parents do, and it helps. Many researchers also believe there is something in Asian Culture that breeds success, such ideals that stress family values and emphasize education.

Both explanations for academic success worry Asian Americans because of fears that they feed a typical racial image. Many can remember when Chinese, Japanese and Filipino immigrants were the victims of social isolation. Indeed, it was not until 1952 that laws were laid down giving all Asian immigrants the right to citizenship.

Question

1. What is the author's tone in this passage?

   A. Sympathetic.   B. Doubtful.

   C. Critical.   D. Objective.

Passage 2

If I sounded all out of breath, it's because I had three repairmen here this afternoon.

You've probably noticed that the first thing every repairman does, right after he spreads his tools all over the floor, is to ask if he can use your telephone. It became a problem today only because all three of them wanted to use the phone at the same time. And as it happened, each of them had to make several calls, so the phone was busy for half an hour.

Since I mentioned three repairmen, you will suppose I had the misfortune of having three appliances break down on a single day. Not at all. Years of experience may have taught that no repairman ever comes on the day he says he will. Nevertheless, you do have to stay right there waiting faithfully. Once I went into the garden for three minutes and missed the plumber.

Perhaps I exaggerate the incompetence of these gentlemen. Perhaps they are just unfortunate. Maybe they each have only one bad day a year and I get that day. Every one of them dismantled(拆除) whatever he was repairing, then put it back together while muttering, "definitely you've got an order a new switch," and left.

As for the man who came to replace the broken stove leg, I really liked him. He had honesty. When I brought up the always sensitive subject of the oven 1 switch, he said, "lady, I'm a maintenance man, those things are a mystery to me. " This honesty was not only refreshing; it did a lot to restore my faith in human nature. It did nothing, however, to restore the oven.

Question

2. What's the author's tone in telling the story?

    A. Angry.   B. Satire.

    C. Indifferent.   D. Humorous.

Passage 3

After watching my mother deal with our family of five, I can't understand why her answer to the question, "What do you do?" is always, "Oh, I'm just a housewife. " JUST a housewife? Anyone who spends most of her time in meal preparation and cleanup, washing and drying clothes, keeping the house clean, leading a scout troop, playing taxi driver to us kids when it's time for school, music lessons or the dentist, doing volunteer work for her favorite charity, and making sure that all our family needs are met is not JUST a housewife. She's the real Wonder Woman.

Why is it that so many mothers like mine think of themselves as second-class or something similar? Where has this notion come from? Have we males made them feel this way? Has our society made "going to work" outside the home seem more important than what a housewife must face each day?

I would be very curious to see what would happen if a housewife went on strike. Dishes would pile up. Food in the house would run out. No meals would appear on the table. There would be no clean clothes when needed. High boots would be required just to make it through the house scattered with garbage. Walking and bus riding would increase. Those scout troops would have to break up. Charities would suffer.

I doubt if the man of the house would be able to take over. Oh, he might start out with the attitude that he can do just as good a job, but how long would that last? Not long, once he had to come home each night after work to more household duties.

There would be no more coming home to a prepared meal; he'd have to fix it himself. The kids would all be screaming for something to eat, clean clothes and more bus fare money. Once he quieted the kids, he'd have to clean the house, go shopping, make sure that kids got a bath, and fix lunches for the next day. Once the kids were down for the night, he might be able to crawl into an unmade bed and try to read the morning newspaper.

No, I don't think many males are going to volunteer for the job. I know I don't want it. So, thanks, mom! I'll do what I can to create a national holiday for housewives. It could be appropriately called Wonder Woman Day.

Question

3. What is the tone does the writer use in the passage?
   A. Critical.   B. Indifferent.
   C. Ironical.   D. Appreciative.

Passage 4

So far there have been discovered no limits to man's capacity to learn. From earliest times, however, men in positions of power or influence have suggested that the learning capacity of certain individuals or groups is severely limited and that they should not be expected to profit greatly, if at all from education. These "inequitable" individuals have usually been members of minority or disadvantaged groups. But, repeatedly, when their cultural disadvantages have been removed, these groups have shown that their previous failure to learn has been due not to incapacity but to lack of fully realized opportunity.

These findings have led educators to be much more modest and less hasty in their labeling and classifying procedures. It has been realized that labels affixed (附加上,贴上) to children tend to become self-fulfilling prophecies, that those who are expected to learn usually do so, and those who are expected to fail to learn also usually do so. Hence, when educators try to classify children at all, they increasingly tend to use their labels as temporary rather than permanent, as saying something only about a quality of the child rather than about his person, and, as something to be abandoned as soon as the child's performance proves the label wrong.

Similarly, no one has been able to confirm any certain limits to the speed with which man can learn. Schools and universities have usually been organized as if to suggest that all students learn at about the same rather tedious and regular speed. But, whenever the actual rates at which different people learn have been tested, nothing has been found to justify such an organization. Not only do individuals learn at vastly different speeds and in different ways, but man seems capable of astonishing feats of rapid learning when the attendant circumstances are favorable. It seems that, in customary educational settings, one habitually uses only a tiny fraction of one's learning capacities.

Question

4. The author's tone towards man's capacity to learn is _____.

    A. objective   B. optimistic

    C. amazed   D. reserved

Passage 5

Cyberspace, data superhighways, multi mediator(解读者) those who have seen the future, the linking of computers, television and telephones will change our lives for ever. Yet for all the talk of a forthcoming technological utopia little attention has been given to the implications of these developments for the poor. As with all new high technology, while the West concerns itself with the "how", the question of "for whom" is put aside once again.

Economists are only now realizing the full extent to which the communications revolution has affected the world economy. Information technology allows the extension of trade across geographical and industrial boundaries, and transnational corporations take full advantage of it. Terms of trade, exchange and interest rates and money movements are more important than the production of goods. The electronic economy made possible by information technology allows the "haves" to increase their control on global markets—with destructive impact on the "have-nots".

For them the result is instability. Developing countries which rely on the production of a small range of goods for export are made to feel like small parts in the international economic machine. As "futures" are traded on computer screens, developing countries simply have less and less control of their destinies. So what are the options for regaining control? One alternative is for developing countries to buy in the latest computers and telecommunications themselves—so-called "devil omens communications" modernization. Yet this leads to long-term dependency and perhaps permanent constraints on developing countries' economies.

Communications technology is generally provided by the very countries whose companies stand to gain.

Furthermore, when new technology is introduced there is often too low a level of expertise to exploit for native development. This means that while local elites, foreign communities and subsidiaries of transnational corporations may benefit, those whose lives depend on access to the information are denied it.

Question

5. The author's tone toward the communications revolution is _____.

A. positive   B. critical

C. indifferent   D. tolerant

二、细节类题

细节类试题的考查内容主要有时间、地点、原因、结果、方式等几种类型。这类题型的特点是针对原文的细节内容设计考题。通常这些考题比较直观,只要读懂了原文意思,基本上就能选对答案。当然,前提是应先掌握全文大意,因为文章的大意是与文章的具体细节内容密切地联系在一起的,或者说文章的大意是建立在事实或细节的基础上。注意,做题时细节问题的表述常常不采用文章中的原话,而是使用不同表达形式的同义词语进行提问。因此,在回答此类问题时,首先要认真审题,弄明白问题问的究竟是什么。然后再根据所涉及的问题,快速扫视文章中与之相关的信息部分,锁定与答题内容相关的关键词或关键语句细读一两遍。在确信理解了原文的基础上,来选定正确答案。切忌脱离文中内容而根据自己的想象或其他来源的知识选择答案。此外,考生在浏览文章时还要留意一些表示主要事实细节的标志性词语,以帮助考生快速、准确地找到相关问题的答案。

根据出题特点,细节题又可分作直接细节题、间接细节题和排除式等类型试题。

该类试题常用的提问方式如下:

(1) According to the passage, when (where, why, how, who, what, which)...?

(2) According to the passage, which of the following is true/not true?

(3) Which of the following is not mentioned in the passage?

(4) All of the following are true except...

(5) The author (or the passage) states that...

1. 直接细节题

直接细节题指的是考生可在原文中直接找出答案的试题。做这类试题时，考生可利用词性的变换、同义、近义词等的替换手段来选择正确回答。例如：

When the current American President Bill Clinton was re-elected to the White House for a second four-year term on November 5, 1996, his victory over Senator Bob Dole was seen as the triumph of youth over maturity, the mastery of a president who offered promises of a bridge to the 21st century against the solid guarantee of a Kansas senator who pledged the service of his determined and homely character.

Clinton was 46 years old and one of the youngest American Presidents ever when he was elected in 1992 (President John F. Kennedy was the youngest at 42 years old when he was sworn in 1960). Bob Dole turned 73 during the tough and exhausting 1996 campaign. The contrast in ages was not overplayed by either candidate, but it was evident in their style of campaign—Clinton, jazzy (活泼的, 华而不实的) and comfortable with Hollywood style presentations, not above playing (不齿于) his saxophone (萨克斯管) to entertain the crowds. Dole, on the other hand, was serious and forthright about the lessons to be learnt from hardship, like the war hero he was. But the American crowd was in the mood for the entertainer rather than the teacher. Clinton loved the crowds and television appearances, and liked to emphasize his look-alike Kennedy style, said one American political scientist: "Watching Clinton with an audience is like watching a virtuoso (演奏家) play a fine musical instrument. Being able to sense at what level you have to pitch your appeal to an audience is the mark of a gifted politician."

Questions

1. Bill Clinton's re-election was considered as _____.
   A. something out of the question
   B. the triumph of youth over maturity
   C. promises of a bridge to the 21st century against the solid guarantee
   D. both B and C

2. When he took office in 1992, Clinton became _____.
   A. the youngest president ever since Kennedy
   B. the second youngest president in American history

C. one of the youngest presidents

D. all of the above

3. One of the differences which is not overstated between the two candidates is
_____.

    A. their styles   B. the contrast in their ages

    C. their promises   D. their characters

【例题解析】

1. D。该答案主要根据第一自然段所提供的细节而得出的。此题干 was considered as 与原文中的 was seen as 是一个意思,所以正确答案是"年青战胜了成熟"又是"展望 21 世纪的承诺战胜了生硬的保证",即选项 B 和选项 C 都是正确的。而选项 A 的意思是"根本不可能的事",则原文不符。

2. D。根据第二段第一句话(Clinton was 46 years old and one of the youngest American Presidents ever when he was elected in 1992)可知选项 A 和选项 C 是正确答案;再根据历史知识的常识进行推断,可知选项 B 也是正确的。所以,选项 A,B 和 C 的内容都正确。

3. B。根据第二段第三句"双方候选人都没有过分强调年龄上的差距"可知选项 B 是正确答案。此句中 over-played 和题干中的 overstated 是一个意思。而选项 A 的意思是"他们的风格",选项 C"他们的承诺"和选项 D"他们的性格"在文章中都分别有不同的描述。

2. 间接细节题

间接细节题是指一种隐含的事实细节题,该类试题往往要求考生依据文中某几个细节进行归纳、概括、比较,然后才能得出正确结论。例如:

Time was—and not so many years ago, either—when the average citizen took a pretty dim view of banks and banking. That this was so, it should be said, was to no small extent the fault of banks and bankers themselves. Banks used to be—and a few still are—forbidding structures. Behind the little barred windows were, more often than not, elderly gentlemen whose expression of friendliness reflected the size of the customer's account, and nothing less than a few hundred thousand in the bank could have inspired the suggestion of a smile.

And yet the average bank for many years was, to the average citizen, a fearful, if necessary, instrument for dealing business—usually big business. But somewhere in the past quarter century, banks began to grow human, even pleasant, and started to attract the little man. It is possible that this movement began in medium-sized towns, or in small towns where people know each other by their first names, and spread to big towns. At any rate, the results have been remarkable.

The movement to "humanize" banks, of course, received a big push during the war, when more and more women were employed to do work previously performed by men. Also more and more "little" people found themselves in need of personal loans, as taxes became heavier and as the practice of installment(分期付款) buying broke down the previously long held concept that there was something almost morally wrong about being in debt. All sorts of people began to discover that the intelligent use of credit(信贷) could be extremely helpful.

Questions 1 to 3 are based on the following passage you have just read.

1. The author believes that the unfriendly atmosphere in banks many years ago was chiefly due to _____.
   A. the outer appearance of bank buildings
   B. unfriendliness of customers toward banks
   C. economic pressure of the time
   D. the attitude to bankers

2. The banks of many years ago showed interest only in _____.
   A. regular visitor's   B. rich customers
   C. friendly businessmen   D. elderly gentlemen

3. When did banks begin to grow human?
   A. Sometime before the war.   B. A few years ago.
   C. During the war.   D. In the last century.

【例题解析】

1. A。由第一段"That this was so, it should be said, was to no small extent the fault of banks and bankers themselves"和"little barred windows"可知这种不友好的气氛是由银行的结构和外观造成的。

2. B。该答案由第一段最后一句"and nothing less than a few hundred thousand in the bank could have inspired the suggestion of a smile"推知。

3. A。从第二段第二句话提到的从二十五年前，一些银行就开始 grow human，又可从第三段第一句话"received a big push during the war"两方面推知。

Exercise 6

Directions: *In this section, there are ten passages. For each passage there are some questions or unfinished statements followed by four choices marked A, B, C and D. You should decide on the best choice and mark the corresponding letter on it.*

Passage 1

It is not often realized that woman held a high place in southern European societies in the 10th and 11th centuries. As a wife, the woman was protected by the setting up of a dowry(嫁妆) or decorum. Admittedly, the purpose of this was to protect her against the risk of desertion(遗弃), but in reality its function in the social and family life of the time was much more important. The decorum was the wife's right to receive a tenth of all her husband's property. The wife had the right to withhold(不给) consent, in all transactions the husband would make. And more than just a right: the documents show that she enjoyed a real power of decision, equal to that of her husband. In no case do the documents indicate any degree of difference in the legal status of husband and wife.

The wife shared in the management of her husband's personal property, but the opposite was not always true. Women seemed perfectly prepared to defend their own inheritance against husbands who tried to exceed their rights, and on occasion they showed a fine fighting spirit. A case in point is that of Maria Visas, a Catalan woman of Barcelona. Having agreed with husband Miro to sell a field she had inherited, for the needs of the household, she insisted on compensation. None being offered, she succeeded in dragging her husband to the scribe(法学家) to have a contract duly(及时的) drawn up assigning her a piece of land from Miro's personal inheritance. The unfortunate husband was obliged to agree, as the contract says, "for the sake of peace." Either through the dowry or through being hot-tempered, the Catalan wife knew how to win herself, within the context of the family, a powerful economic position.

Questions

1. A decorum (in Para. 1) was _____.

   A. the wife's inheritance from her father

   B. a gift of money to the new husband

   C. a written contract

D. the wife's right to receive one-tenth of her husband's property

2. In the society described in the Passage the legal standing of the wife in marriage was _____.
   A. higher than that of her husband
   B. lower than that of her husband
   C. the same as that of her husband
   D. higher than that of a single woman

3. What compensation did Maria Visas get for the field?
   A. Some of the land Miro had inherited.
   B. A tenth of Miro's land.
   C. Money for household expenses.
   D. Money from Miro's inheritance.

Passage 2

During the seventeenth and eighteenth centuries, almost nothing was written about the contributions of women during the colonial period and the early history of the newly formed United States. Lacking the right to vote and absent from the seats of power, women were not considered as important force in history. Anne Bradstreet wrote some significant poetry in the seventeenth century, Mercy Otis Warren produced the best contemporary history of the American Revolution, and Abigail Adams penned important letters showing she exercised great political influence over her husband, John, the second President of the United States. But little or no notice was taken of these contributions. During these centuries, women remained invisible in history books.

Throughout the nineteenth century, this lack of visibility continued, despite the efforts of female authors writing about women. These writers, like most of their male counterparts, were amateur historians. Their writings were celebratory(著名的) in nature, and they were uncritical in their selection and use of sources.

During the nineteenth century, however, certain feminists showed a keen sense of history by keeping records of activities in which women were engaged. National, regional, and local women's organizations compiled accounts of their doings. Personal correspondence, newspaper clippings, and souvenirs were saved and stored. These sources from the core of the two greatest collections of women's history in the United States one at the Elizabeth and Arthur Schlesinger Library at Radcliffe College, and the other the Sophia Smith Collection at Smith College. Such sources have provided valuable materials for later generations of historians.

Despite the gathering of more information about ordinary women during the nineteenth century, most of the writing about women conformed(遵照) to the "great women" theory of history, just as much of mainstream American history concentrated on "great men". To demonstrate that women were making significant contributions to American life, female authors singled out women leaders and wrote biographies, or else important women produced their autobiographies. Most of these leaders were involved in public life as reformers, activists working for women's right to vote, or authors, and were not representative at all of the great of ordinary woman. The lives of ordinary people continued, generally, to be untold in the American histories being published.

Questions

4. In the first paragraph, Bradstreet, Warren, and Adams are mentioned to show that _____.
   A. a woman's status was changed by marriage
   B. even the contributions of outstanding women were ignored
   C. only three women were able to get their writing published
   D. poetry produced by women was more readily accepted than other writing by women

5. In the second paragraph, what weakness in nineteenth-century histories does the author point out?
   A. They put too much emphasis on daily activities.
   B. They left out discussion of the influence of money on politics.
   C. The sources of the information they were based on were not necessarily accurate.
   D. They were printed on poor-quality paper.

6. On the basis of information in the third paragraph, which of the following would most likely have been collected by nineteenth-century feminist organizations?
   A. Newspaper accounts of presidential election results.
   B. Biographies of John Adams.

C. Letters from a mother to a daughter advising her how to handle a family problem.

D. Books about famous graduates of the country's first college.

7. What use was made of the nineteenth-century women's history materials in the Schlesinger Library and the Sophia Smith Collection?

A. They were combined and published in a multivolume encyclopedia.

B. They formed the basis of college courses in the nineteenth century.

C. They provided valuable information for twentieth-century historical researchers.

D. They were shared among women's colleges throughout the United States.

Passage 3

Young people in the United States have a wide variety of interests apart from their school work. As children, both boys and girls play many of the same games. They swim, play baseball and basketball, go boating and camping, and have fun in many kinds of sports and outdoor activities.

Numerous youth organizations give young people a chance to develop and broaden their interests, and to gain experience in working with others. Among these groups are the Boy Scouts which serves more than four million boys, the Girl Scouts, with nearly three million girls, and the Boys' Club of America, with over one million participants. These and other groups are guided by adults who volunteer their services. Civic, cultural and religious groups also sponsor special programs for young people.

In farm areas, boys and girls learn to work together in agriculture, homemaking and citizenship activities through more than 158,360 clubs which have about 4,420,932 members. In these clubs youths compete for prizes in raising farm animals and growing crops.

Secondary schools offer students a wide variety of activities to develop talents and skills. There are clubs for photography, music, theater, art, stamp collecting, natural science and debating. Often schools have orchestras, bands and singing groups as well as a variety of competitive sports for boys and girls.

Most schools and colleges have some form of student government with election to choose class representatives. These elected officers speak for their fellow students at student council meetings with teachers and school officials.

They also organize social activities and take part in such community projects as raising money for public welfare.

Many young people hold part-time jobs after school hours. Thousands earn money delivering newspapers or helping care for infants and young children in private homes. Later, when they go to college, many youths continue to work part-time at a variety of jobs to help pay their expenses.

For several weeks during the summer vacation, about five million school-age children go to camps where they get plenty of recreational activity and learn various skills. There are more than 10,000 camps operated by private citizens and organizations. College students often work as counselors at these camps.

Questions

8. Youth organizations in the US try to _____.
   A. develop the students' interests and social abilities
   B. help improve the students' academic performance
   C. develop students' ability to participate in the school management
   D. help students obtain part-time jobs

9. American students _____.
   A. work on farms to compete only for handsome prizes
   B. learn how to cooperate with each other through farm work
   C. usually do not do any farm work
   D. treat farm work as a necessary experience in their life

10. Student governments in American schools _____.
    A. often do not cooperate with teachers or school authorities
    B. only work for the benefits of the students
    C. also deals with activities and programs out of school
    D. also raise money to support their activities

Passage 4

Today, the majority of Americans belong to the Protestant church. Over 60% of Americans are said to be Protestant believers, among whom the Baptists are the largest group. From the beginning in 17th century England, the Baptists have continued on a small scale in England where they are about 1% of the population. But in the United States, they have their main strength, with over 25 million members, divided among more than 20 branches and concentrated

job because their normal growth, employee retirements, and turnover create thousands of jobs nationwide each year.）。由于大公司人员的自然增加和减少，每年在全国范围内创造了数以千计的工作机会，因此，大公司已成为寻找工作的最好去处，这符合选项 B 所陈述的内容。选项 A "大公司只雇佣大学毕业生"与事实不符；选项 C "大公司在全国各地有许多分公司"在文中并未提及；选项 D "大公司的要求非常高"在文中也没有明确说明。不能视作正确答案。

2. A。由第二段第三句可知，小公司不会委派雇员去大学寻求毕业生是因为时间、财力不足或工作上不需要，而不是没有必要（Such firms may not have the time, money, or need to send people around to your college; you'll probably have to contact them yourself either directly or through an employment agency.）。因此，选项 A 内容与原文不符，为正确答案。选项 B "小公司难以支付其人员去大学"，选项 C "小公司雇员被提升得更快"以及选项 D "小公司可能提供你需要的职位"在文中都提及过。因此，不是本题的正确答案。

Exercise 7

Directions: *In this section, there are five passages. For each passage there are some questions or unfinished statements followed by four choices marked A, B, C and D. You should decide on the best choice and mark the corresponding letter on it.*

Passage 1

International airlines have rediscovered the business travelers, the man or woman who regularly jets from country to country as part of the job. This does not necessarily mean that airlines ever abandoned their business travelers. Indeed, companies like Lufthansa and Swissair would rightly argue that they have always catered best for the executive class passengers. But many lines could be accused of concentrating too heavily in the recent past on attracting passengers by volume, often at the expense of regular travelers. Too often, they have seemed geared for quantity rather than quality. Operating a major airline in the 1980s is essentially a matter of finding the right mix of passengers. The airlines need to fill up the back end of their wide-bodied jets with low fare passengers, without forgetting that the front end should be filled with people who pay substantially more for their tickets.

It is no coincidence(巧合) that the two major airline bankruptcies in 1982 were among the companies specializing in cheap flights. But low fares require consistently full aircraft to make flights economically available, and in the recent recession the volume of traffic has not grown. Equally the large number of airlines jostling(竞争) for the available passengers has created a huge excess of capacity. The net result of excess capacity and cut-throat competition driving down fares has been to push some airlines into collapse and leave many others hovering on the brink.

Against this grim background, it is no surprise that airlines are turning increasingly towards the business travelers to improve their rates of return. They have invested much time and effort to establish exactly what the executive demands for sitting apart from the tourists.

High on the list of priorities is punctuality; an executive's time is money. In-flight service is another area where the airlines are jostling for the executive's attention. The free drinks and headsets and better food are all part of the lure.

Question

1. The following are all used to attract passengers except _____.

    A. punctuality   B. sound system

    C. free drinks   D. charge-free food

Passage 2

Halloween, this is a holiday widely celebrated with different names in many countries. Although it originated as a religious holiday, it has lost its religious connections in the United States. It is now celebrated largely as a children's day, and many American children look forward to it for days and weeks beforehand.

The orange pumpkin is harvested at this time of year and is hollowed out, a funny face cut into it, and a candle placed inside as a decoration in the window. City folks, nowadays, sometimes use paper pumpkins for decorations.

Some years ago, the holiday was celebrated by dressing up in strange and frightening costumes and playing tricks on one's neighbors and friends, such as ringing door bells, throwing bits of corn on the window panes, and in other ways making minor disturbances.

More recently, children come to the door to have friends and neighbors admire their costumes and guess who are behind the false faces and receive treats of candy, fruit or cookies. They say, "Trick or Treat", meaning, "I will play a trick on you if you will not give me a treat." This practice has even more recently developed into a significant international activity. Instead of asking for money along with candy, the children collect money for UNICEF (United Nations International Children's Emergency Fund). This special collection of money by children for needy children throughout the world is known as "UNICEF Trick of Treat". Begun only recently, it results in several million dollars each year contributed to UNICEF. The collection box is orange, reminiscent(怀旧的,忆往事的) of the pumpkin.

Question

2. Which of the following is not mentioned some years ago how the children celebrate the Halloween?

   A. Dressing up in strange and frightening costumes and playing tricks on one's neighbors friends.

   B. Ringing door bells.

   C. Throwing bits of corn on the window panes.

   D. Dressing up in the best holiday clothes.

Passage 3

The most thoroughly studied cases of deception strategies employed by ground-nesting birds involve plovers(海鸟), small birds that typically nest on beaches or in open fields, their nests merely scrapes in the sand or earth. Plovers also have an effective repertoire(爬行动物) of tricks for distracting potential nest predators from their exposed and defenseless eggs or chicks. The ever-watchful plover can detect a possible threat at a considerable distance. When she does, the nesting bird moves inconspicuously(悄悄地) off the nest to a spot well away from eggs or chicks. At this point she may use one of several ploys. One technique involves first moving quietly toward an approaching animal and then setting off noisily through the grass or brush in a low, crouching run away from the nest.

The effect mimics a sly mouse or vole(仓鼠), and the behavior attracts the attention of the type of predators that would also be interested in eggs and chicks. Another deception begins with quiet movement to an exposed and visible location well away from the nest. Once there, the bird pretends to incubate(孵

卵）a brood. When the predator approaches, the parent flees, leaving the false nest to be searched. The direction in which the plover "escapes" is such that if the predator chooses to follow, it will be led still further away from the true nest.

The plover's most famous trick is the broken-wing display, actually a continuum of injury-mimicking behaviors spanning the range from slight disability to near-complete helplessness. One or both wings are held in an abnormal position, suggesting injury. The bird appears to be attempting escape along an irregular route that indicates panic. In the most extreme version of the display, the bird flaps one wing in an apparent attempt to take to the air, flops over helplessly, struggles back to its feet, runs away a short distance, seemingly attempts once more to take off, flops over again as the "useless" wing fails to provide any lift, and so on. Few predators fail to pursue such obviously vulnerable prey. Needless to say, each short run between "flight attempts" is directed away from the nest.

Questions

4. Which of the following is mentioned in the passage about plovers?

   A. Their eggs and chicks are difficult to find.

   B. They are generally defenseless when away from their nests.

   C. They are slow to react in dangerous situations.

   D. Their nests are on the surface of the ground.

5. According to the passage, a female plover utilizes all of the following deception techniques EXCEPT _____.

   A. appearing to be injured   B. sounding like another animal

   C. pretending to search for prey   D. pretending to sit on her eggs

Passage 4

Hunting is at best a precarious way of get food, even when the diet is supplemented with seeds and fruits. Not long after the last Ice Age, around 7, 000 B. C. (during the Neolithic period), some hunters and gatherers began to rely chiefly on agriculture for their sustenance. Others continued the old natural and nomadic(游牧的) ways. Indeed, agriculture itself evolved over the course of time, and Neolithic peoples had long known how to grow crops. The real transformation of human life occurred when huge numbers of people began to rely primarily and permanently on the grain they grew and the animals they domesticated.

Agriculture made possible a more stable and secure life. With it Neolithic (新石器时代) peoples flourished, fashioning an energetic, creative era. They were responsible for many fundamental inventions and innovations that the modern world takes for granted. First, obviously, is systematic agriculture—that is, the reliance of Neolithic peoples on agriculture as their primary, not merely subsidiary(辅助的), source of food.

Thus they developed the primary economic activity of the entire ancient world and the basis of all modern life. With the settled routine of Neolithic farmers came the evolution of towns and eventually cities. Neolithic farmers usually raised more food than they could consume, and their surpluses permitted larger, healthier populations. Population growth in turn created an even greater reliance on settled farming, as only systematic agriculture could sustain the increased numbers of people. Since surpluses of food could also be bartered(易货交易) for other commodities, the Neolithic era witnessed the beginnings of large-scale exchange of goods.

In time the increasing complexity of Neolithic societies led to the development of writing, prompted by the need to keep records and later by the urge to chronicle(将……载于编年史中) experiences, learning, and beliefs.

The transition to settled life also had a profound impact on the family. The shared needs and pressures that encourage extended-family ties are less prominent in settled than in nomadic societies. Bonds to the extended family weakened. In towns and cities, the nuclear family was more dependent on its immediate neighbors than on kinfolk(亲戚).

Questions

6. According to the passage, all of the following led to the development of writing EXCEPT the _____.

   A. need to keep records   B. desire to write down beliefs

   C. extraction of ink from plants   D. growth of social complexity

7. The author mentions all of the following as results of the shift to agricultural societies EXCEPT _____.

   A. an increase in invention and innovation

   B. emergence of towns and cities

C. development of a system of trade

D. a decrease in warfare

8. Which of the following is true about the human diet prior to the Neolithic period?

A. It consisted mainly of agricultural products.

B. It varied according to family size.

C. It was based on hunting and gathering.

D. It was transformed when large numbers of people no longer depended on the grain they grew themselves.

Passage 5

World Trade Organization (WTO) is an open, nondiscriminatory trading system, inaugurated on 1, January 1995 as the successor to the General Agreement on Tariffs and Trade (GATT). Initially composed of 81 members, the WTO will eventually be open to all 125 members of GATT upon their ratification(批准，认可) of the Uruguay Round Final Act. WTO has a wider role than GATT, covering commercial activities beyond the operational scope of the latter body, such as intellectual property, trade in services, and arbitration of disputes.

Members of WTO follow three most important principles:

— the most favored nation concept, i. e. , every contracting party grants all other parties, any tariff advantages that it grants to any other country.

— although customs duties are recognized as a legitimated instrument of protection, they should be reduced as far as possible.

— the abolition of quantitative restrictions on imports; there are permissible, however, if necessitated by reasons relating to the balance of payments, and these exceptions are carefully supervised.

WTO was born out of GATT which conducted such multilateral(多边的) negotiations on customs tariffs as the Uruguay Round. Now WTO is also pledged to reduce tariffs and other barriers and to eliminate discriminatory treatment in international trade.

Thanks to GATT and other international organizations, the protective measures taken by numerous countries during world-wide recessions(萧条) are restricted to the minimum. There is no general relapse(退步) into strict protectionism such as that which followed the world economic crisis of 1929-1932, because the basic principles of GATT are upheld.

Questions

9. According to the passage, which of the following is NOT mentioned as the common goal of the WTO members in regard to international trade?
   A. To strike balance of payment.
   B. To get rid of discriminatory treatments.
   C. To reduce tariffs.
   D. To cut down non-tariff barriers.

10. Which of the following is NOT TRUE according to the passage?
    A. Initially made up of 81 members, the WTO will be open to all 125 members of GATT sooner or later.
    B. WTO was originated from GATT which conducted such negotiations among many countries on customs tariffs as the Uruguay Round.
    C. The protective measures taken by numerous countries during world-wide recessions are restricted to the minimum.
    D. WTO has a narrower role than GATT, covering only commercial activities beyond the operational scope.

11. Which of the following is NOT mentioned in the passage?
    A. The abolition of quantitative restrictions on imports.
    B. The General Agreement on Tariffs and Trade.
    C. Country-wide recessions.
    D. A legitimated instrument of protection

三、判断/推理类题

在阅读理解考题中,判断/推理题是一种比较难解的题型。该类试题要求考生根据短文所提供的事实或细节,按照逻辑发展的规律进行分析和概括,并以此为依据得出一个合乎逻辑的结论,或者是以已知的事实为依据,挖掘作者的隐含意思,来获取未知的信息。(注意,凡是要求通过推理判断的方法来获得答案的试题,在文中均不能直接找到答案。)

该类试题要求考生根据问题的具体内容细读文章,不但掌握文章的表层含义,而且还要理解文章的深层内涵,准确地掌握作者的观点和态度。答题时,要认真审题,特别要注意原文中的意思在题目中的表达形式,准确地理解题意和试题要求。

该类考题中常用的关键词有：infer，imply，suggest，draw a conclusion，assume，learn，show 等；常用的提问形式如下：

(1) The passage/writer implies/suggests that...

(2) The passage is intended to...

(3) It can be concluded from the passage that...

(4) It can be inferred from the passage that...

(5) We can infer/see/conclude from the passage that...

(6) Which of the following can be readily inferred from the passage?

(7) The paragraph proceeding/following this one would most likely state/discuss/deal with...

(8) Where would the paragraph most probably appear/be found?

(9) What does the author conclude about...?

(10) What is the author's attitude towards...?

(11) The writer is trying to present a point of view in...

(12) The author wants to advocate...

(13) The author's tone would be best described as...

(14) The author seems to think that...

做判断/推理题时，考生应尽量避免以下几种错误：

(1) 根据自己的观点、看法进行推理或判断。

(2) 概括过度，推理过头，即主次不分，本末倒置。

(3) 将文中明确表达的信息当成推理得出的结论。

(4) 把文中的原因与选项中的结果关系倒置。

根据问题的性质，该类试题可分为以下几种类型：

1. 含义类试题

推断语句含义实际上就是找出作者蕴含于语句中的言外之意。该类试题主要考查考生通过已获取的直接信息来推导判断字里行间中所蕴含的意思的能力。通常这类试题在阅读理解考试中所占的比例最大。例如：

Under the Earth's topsoil, at various levels, sometimes under a layer of rock, there are deposits of clay. Look at cuts where highways have been built to see exposed clay beds; or look at a construction site, where pockets of clay may be exposed. Rivers also reveal clay along their banks, and erosion on a hillside may make clay easily accessible.

What is clay made of? The Earth's surface is basically rocky, and it is this rock that gradually decomposes into clay. Rain, streams, alternating freezing and thawing(解冻), roots of trees and plants forcing their way into cracks, earthquakes, volcanic action, and glaciers—all of these forces slowly break down the Earth's exposed rocky crust into smaller and smaller pieces that eventually become clay.

Rocks are composed of elements and compounds of elements. Feldspar, which is the most abundant mineral on the Earth's surface, is basically made up of the oxides silica(硅) and alumina combined with alkalis(碱) like potassium (钾) and some so-called impurities such as iron. Feldspar is an essential component of granite rocks, and as such it is the basis of clay.

When it is wet, clay can be easily shaped to make a variety of useful objects, which can then be fired to varying degrees of hardness and covered with impermeable(不透水或空气的) decorative coatings of glasslike material called glaze. Just as volcanic action, with its intense heat, fuses the elements in certain rocks into a glasslike rock, so can we apply heat to earthen materials and change them into a hard, dense material. Different clays need different heat levels to fuse, and some, the low-fire clays, never become watertight like highly fired stoneware. Each clay can stand only a certain amount of heat without losing its shape through sagging(凹陷) or melting. Variations of clay composition and the temperatures at which they are fired account for the differences in texture and appearance between a china teacup and an earthenware flower pot.

Questions

1. It can be inferred from the passage that _____.
   A. climate has a hand in the formation of clay.
   B. clay is resulted completely from the contents of minerals in it.
   C. there is no clay at all in the forests.
   D. all kinds of clay can stand the same heat.

2. Based on the information in the passage, it can be inferred that low-fire clays are MOST appropriate for making objects that _____.
   A. must be strong   B. can be porous(透空气的)
   C. have a smooth texture   D. are highly decorated

【例题解析】

1. A。第二段第三句"Rain, streams, alternating freezing and thawing, roots of trees and plants forcing their way into cracks, earthquakes,..."中所罗

列的现象均为气候现象，由此可以推知由于不同的气候现象而使岩石风化瓦解而最终使之变成粘土。此意与选项 A 相吻合；选项 B 的意思过于绝对，参照第三自然段；选项 C 的内容文中没有提到；选项 D 错在句意过于绝对化。文章的最后一段倒数第二句说的是每一种粘土只能承受一定程度的热度，而不是同样的温度。

2. B。根据最后一段倒数第二句"Different clays need different heat levels to fuse, and some, the low-fire clays, never become watertight like highly fired stoneware."可知有些"low-fire"粘土是决不会像高温烧制石器一样具有防水的性能。这就意味着低火粘土至少说具有透水性。

Exercise 8

Directions: *In this section, there are five passages. For each passage there are several questions or unfinished statements followed by four choices marked A, B, C and D. You should decide on the best choice and mark the corresponding letter on it.*

Passage 1

Two important gaps are growing in and between nations of the world. One is between rich and poor nations as well as people, the other, between old and young within nations. Both will have profound consequences.

The rich-poor gap goes to the heart of the popular opposition to globalization. This is the tendency of multilateral corporations to seek the most favorable manufacturing conditions anywhere in the world: the fewest possible environmental regulations and the lowest possible labor costs. Poor countries see this as bringing them jobs; rich countries see it as taking jobs away.

Concern over labor and the environment was dismissed as modern version for the old arguments of protectionism. Now, it is seen as more complicated. Consider the issue in a multilateral relationship such as a Western Hemisphere wide Free Trade Area of the Americas, if one is negotiated. When there are many poor countries involved, such as all of Central America, they compete against each other to attract foreign business through tax, if any, environmental and labor regulation. The same situation prevailed among poor states in the United States before the federal government imposed nationwide uniform standards for the environment and labor. It would make sense to agree on worldwide standards, if agreement can be reached.

The second gap—between young and old has to do with the surplus(剩余) of labor in the poor world, where the young are more numerous, and the shortage of labor in the rich world, where the old are more numerous. The American computer industry has already imported, on a temporary basis, hundreds of thousands of workers from India to make up for a shortage of qualified American workers. In fact, the pressure of population growth in developing nations since World War II has generated a growing and irresistible flood of immigrants that is changing the American people from basically European to a heterogeneous(异质的) mix of Europeans, Hispanics(西班牙人), Asians and Africans with Europeans slipping into the minority.

Besides, the rest of the rich world—namely Europe and Japan—needs immigrants. By 2050, only half of all Europeans and 58 percent of all Japanese will be under the age of 60. This will not sustain present economies. It is only immigration that is driving American population growth.

This combination of rich-poor, old-young trends is woven together in a complex relationship that has too many conflicting interests for neat solutions. Industrial economies will continue to seek export markets and advantageous investment opportunities.

There will continue to be enough people hurt by this growth in world trade to make themselves heard—at the polls in democracies and in the streets of other countries. Enough people will continue to benefit to make themselves similarly heard. In most instances, the balance is probably on the side of the beneficiaries. But there are enough legitimate complaints that governments should curb(抑制) the more greedy instincts of their corporations.

Questions

1. It is implied in the first two paragraphs that globalization will _____.
   A. bring no country any good
   B. benefit poor countries
   C. harm poor countries
   D. benefit poor and rich countries alike

2. Opposition to globalization used to be thought of as _____.
   A. an attempt to narrow down the rich-poor gap
   B. another argument for protectionism
   C. an attempt to bring more jobs to the poor countries

    D. being central to bridging over the rich-poor gap

3. In face of the increasing globalization, the author believes that _____.

    A. worldwide environmental and labor regulation is necessary

    B. competition for capital between poor countries should be discouraged

    C. fairer agreement should be reached between poor and rich countries

    D. rich countries should restrict overseas investment made by their corporations

4. Which opinion assumes a dominant role in the present argument about globalization?

    A. The voice against the increasing globalization.

    B. The support for the increasing globalization.

    C. The appeal that governments should curb the greed of their corporations.

    D. The call for stopping the rich-poor and old-young trends.

Passage 2

Scientific explanations require objective thinking. Both theoretical research and experimental exploration have shown that no child below school age is truly able to grasp these two concepts, without which abstract understanding is impossible. In his early years, until age eight or ten, the child can develop only highly personalized concepts about what he experiences. Therefore it seems natural to him, since the plants which grow on this earth nourish him as his mother did from her breast, to see the earth as a mother or a female god, or at least as her abode(住所).

Even a young child somehow knows that he was created by his parents; so it makes good sense to him that, like himself, all men and where they live were created by a super-human figure not very different from his parents—some male or female god. Since his parents watch over the child and provide him with his needs in his home, then naturally he also believes that something like them, only much more powerful, intelligent, and reliable—a guardian angel will do so out in the world.

A child thus experiences the world order in the image of his parents and of what goes on within the family. The ancient Egyptians, as a child does, saw heaven and the sky as a motherly figure who protectively bent over the earth, enveloping it and them serenely(安详地). Far from preventing man from later developing a more rational explanation of the world, such a view offers security where and when it is most needed—a security which, when the time is ripe, allows for a truly rational world view. Life on a small planet surrounded by limitless space seems awfully lonely and cold to a child—just the opposite of what he knows life ought to be. This is why the ancients needed to feel sheltered and warmed by an enveloping mother figure. To depreciate protective imagery like this as mere childish projections of an immature mind is to rob the young child of one aspect of the prolonged safety and comfort he needs.

Questions

5. The ancient people are similar to children in their _____.
   A. ignorance and passivity
   B. search for protection
   C. resistance to godlike authority
   D. desire to be superhuman
6. It can be inferred from the passage that children in their early years are capable of _____.
   A. objective thinking
   B. rational thinking
   C. religious thinking
   D. subjective thinking
7. In the author's opinion, the way young children get to know the world _____.
   A. leads them to some mistaken ideas about the world
   B. provides them with a sense of security necessary to later development
   C. is too personalized to be useful for the development of rational thinking
   D. leads them easily to irrational religious beliefs

Passage 3

The energy crunch(危机), which is being felt around the world, has dramatized how the reckless despoiling of the earth's resources has brought the whole world to brink(边缘) of disaster. The overdevelopment of motor transport, with its spiral of more cars, more highways, more pollution, more suburbs, more commuting, has contributed to the near-destruction of our cities, the disintegration of the family, and the pollution not only of local air, but also of the earth's atmosphere. The catastrophe(灾难) has arrived in the form of the energy crunch.

Our present situation is unlike war, revolution, or depression. It is also unlike the great natural catastrophes of the past. Worldwide resources exploitation and energy use have brought us to a state where long-range planning is crucial. What we need is not a continuation of our present perilous state, which endangers the future of our country, our children, and our earth, but a movement forward to a new norm in order to work rapidly and effectively on planetary problems.

This country has been reeling under the continuing exposures of loss of moral integrity and the revelation(暴露) that lawbreaking has reached into the highest places in the land. There is a strong demand for moral reinvigoration(重新振作) and for some commitment that is vast enough and yet personal enough to enlist the loyalty of all. In the past it has been only in a war in defense of their own country and their own ideals that any people have been able to invoke a total commitment.

This is the first time that we have been asked to defend ourselves and what we hold dear in cooperation with all the other inhabitants of this planet, who share with us the same endangered air and the same endangered oceans. There is a common need to reassess our present course, to change that course, and to devise new methods through which the world can survive. This is a priceless opportunity.

To grasp it, we need a widespread understanding of the nature of the crisis confronting us—and the world—a crisis that is no passing inconvenience, no by-product of the ambitions of the oil-producing countries, no figment(虚构) of environmentalists' fears, no by-product of any present system of government. What we face is the outcome of the invention of the last four hundred years. What we need is a transformed life-style. This new life style can flow directly from science and technology, but its acceptance depends on an overriding commitment to a higher quality of life for the world's children and future generation.

Questions

8. Which condition does the writer feel has nearly destroyed our cities?

    A. Lack of financial planning.

    B. The breakup of the family.

    C. Natural disasters in many regions.

    D. The excessive growth of motor transportation.

9. According to the passage which example listed below can be inferred as our

loss of moral integrity?

    A. Disregard for law.   B. Lack of dedication.

    C. Lack of cooperation.   D. Exploitation of resources.

10. What commitment does the speaker feel people must now make?

    A. Search for new energy sources.

    B. Outlaw(取缔,摒弃) motor transportation.

    C. Accept a new lifestyle.

    D. Adopt a new form of government.

Passage 4

The relationship between a man and fatherland is always disturbed by conflict if either man or fatherland is highly developed. A man's demands for liberty at some point challenge the limitations the state imposes on the individual for the sake of the mass. If he is to carry on the national tradition, he must wrestle with those who, speaking in its name, desire to crystallize it at the point reached by the previous generation. In any cases national life itself must frequently irritate him because it is the medium in which he is expressing himself, and every craftsman or artist is repelled by the resistance of his medium to his will. All men should have a drop or two of resistance spirit in them, if the nations are not to go soft like so many sleepy pears. Yet to be a traitor is most miserable. All the men described in this book were sad as they stood their trials, not only because they were going to be punished. They would have been sad even if they had never been brought to justice. They had forsaken the familiar medium; they had trust themselves to the mercies of those who had no reason to care for them; knowing their protector's indifference, they had lived for long in fear; and they were aware that they had thrown away their claim on those who might naturally have felt affection for them. Strangers, as King Solomon put it, were filled with their wealth, and their labors were in the house of a stranger, and they mourned at the last when their flesh and body were consumed. As a divorce sharply recalls what a happy marriage should be, so the treachery of these men recall what a nation should be; a shelter where all talents are generously recognized, all forgivable oddities(奇特) forgiven, all evils quietly frustrated, and those who lack talent honored for equivalent contributions of graciousness(和蔼). Each of those men was as dependent on the good opinion of others as one is of one self; they needed a nation which was also a heart. It was sad to see them, chilled to the bone of their souls, because the intellectual leaders of their time had professed a philosophy which was scarcely more than a lapse(过失) of memory, and had forgotten, among much else, that a hearth gives out warmth.

Questions

11. This passage is probably _____.
    A. a preface of a book   B. a review of an historical event
    C. a literary review   D. an editorial

12. What can be inferred from the word "a man who wants to develop the national tradition come into a conflict with his country"?
    A. He must be more highly developed than his fatherland.
    B. The man and his country must be highly developed.
    C. What he does must do no good to his country-men.
    D. He must want to change the tradition and the government.

13. Which of the following words could best describe the writer's attribute to "resistance to a crystallized tradition" is _____.
    A. necessary   B. destructive
    C. punishable   D. pitiable

14. How did the people who came into conflict with their fatherland in the book mentioned feel?
    A. They felt uncomfortable as they lived in poverty.
    B. They felt the pains of being denied and deserted.
    C. They were usually emotionally indifferent.
    D. They were all put to death by the country.

Passage 5

For the generation that grew up during the feminist revolution and the rapid social change of the 1960s and 1970s, it at first seemed achievement enough just to "make it" in a man's world. But coupled with their ambition, today's women have developed a fierce determination to find new options for being both parent and professional without sacrificing too much to either role or burning themselves out beyond redemption(偿还,弥补).

Women have done all of the accommodating in terms of time, energy, and personal sacrifice that is humanly possible, and still they have not reached true integration in the workplace. For a complicated set of reasons—many beyond their control—they feel conflict between their careers and their children. All but a rare few quickly dispel（驱散，消除）the myth that superwoman ever existed.

For many women, profession and family are pitied against one another on a high-stakes collision course. Women's values are stacked against the traditions of their professions. In the home, men and women struggle to figure out how dual-career marriages should work. Role conflict for women reaches far beyond the fundamental work/family dilemma to encompass（包含）a whole constellation（星座）of fiercely competing priorities. Women today find themselves in an intense battle with a society that cannot let go of a narrowly defined work ethic that is supported by a family structure that has not existed for decades. The unspoken assumption persists that there is still a woman at home to raise the children and manage the household. But the economic reality is that most people, whether in two, parent or single-parent families, need to work throughout their adult lives. As a consequence, the majority of today's mothers are in the labor market.

The first full-fledged（羽毛丰满的）generation of women in the professions did not talk about their overbooked agenda or the toll it took on them and their families. They knew that their position in the office was shaky at best. With virtually no choice in the matter, they brought into the traditional notion of success in the workplace—usually attained at the high cost of giving up an involved family life. If they suffered self-doubt or frustration about how hollow professional success felt without complementary（补偿性的）rewards from the home, they blamed themselves—either for expecting too much or for doing too little. And they asked themselves questions that held no easy answers: Am I expecting too much? Is it me? Am I alone in this dilemma? Do other women truly have it all?

Until now, this has been a private dilemma, unshared, as each woman wishes to forge her own unique solution to merging her dual loyalties to work and family. Too often she felt that she alone had failed to achieve a comfortable balance between the two.

Questions

15. According to the passage today's women _____.

A. want to achieve a balance between her loyalties to work and family

B. are stronger advocates of gender equality than the older generation

C. do not want to sacrifice anything at all for the desired liberation

D. are getting no nearer to achieving their ambition

16. What is the possible myth held by some "superwomen" according to the passage?

A. That they can reconcile their careers with parental responsibilities.

B. That they can devote themselves to their career without regard for their children.

C. That they can resist the temptation of their ambition to make great achievements.

D. That they can resolve the conflicts between their careers and children without any sacrifice.

17. In what way do women today find themselves in an intense battle with the society?

A. The society regards women as less able to perform social tasks.

B. Women do too much about their career and too little about their families.

C. The society still holds the traditional image about a family.

D. Women no longer regard the family as a basic unit of the society.

2. 结论类试题

结论类试题要求考生根据从文章中获取的信息,通过归纳总结的方法,去得出某个合乎逻辑的结论。该类试题设计的主要目的是考查考生的阅读归纳总结能力。例如:

Although social changes in the United States were being brought throughout most of the nineteenth century, public awareness of the changes increased to new levels in the 1890's. The acute, growing public awareness of the social changes that had been taking place for some time was tied to tremendous growth in popular journalism in the late nineteenth century, including growth in quantity and circulation of both magazines and newspapers. These developments, in addition to the continued growth of cities, were significant factors in the transformation of the society from one characterized by relatively isolated self-contained communities into an urban, industrial nation. The decade of the 1870's, for example, was a period in which the sheer number of newspapers doubled, and by 1880 the New York Graphic had published the first photographic reproduction in a newspaper, portending(成为……先兆) a dramatic rise in newspaper readership. Between 1882 and 1886 alone, the price of daily newspapers dropped from four cents a copy to one cent, made possible in part by a great increase in demand. Furthermore, the introduction in 1890 of the first successful linotype(胶版印刷) machine promised even further growth. In 1872 only two daily newspapers could claim a circulation of over 100,000, but by 1890 seven more newspapers exceeded that figure. A world beyond the immediate community was rapidly becoming visible.

But it was not newspapers alone that were bringing the new awareness to people in the United States in the late nineteenth century. Magazines as they are known today began publication around 1882 and in fact, the circulation of weekly magazines exceeded that of newspapers in the period which followed. By 1892 for example, the circulation of the *Ladies' Home Journal* had reached an astounding 700,000. An increase in book readership also played a significant part in this general trend. For example, Edward Bellamy's Utopian(空想主义) novel, *Looking Backward*, sold over a million copies in 1888, giving rise to the growth of organizations dedicated to the realization of Bollamy's vision of the future. The printed word, unquestionably, was intruding on the insulation that had characterized United States society in an earlier period.

Question

It can be concluded from the passage that _____.

A. it was newspapers that were developing people's awareness of social changes

B. the society has experienced the transformation because of development of journalism

C. growth of popular journalism including newspapers and magazines has contributed to growing public awareness of social change

D. an increase in readership helped to drop the price of journalism

【例题解析】本选项的正确答案是 C。原文第二句说社会变革意识与 19 世纪末剧增的杂志和报纸的数量和发行量的增长密切相关。接下来又按照历史时间的顺序分别叙述了后者对前者的推动作用。选项 C 全面表述了文章的目的：杂志和报纸的流行提高了人们的社会变革意识。因此，应为正确答案。选项 A 仅说到报纸，不全面；选项 B 只说社会变更是因为新闻业的发展，也不全面。第一段第三句话中"in addition to the continued growth of cities"表明不仅新闻业，城市发展也是社会变革的一个原因；选项 D 只符合一个细节，含义太窄，不能概括文章的全貌,所以不足为答案。

Exercise 9

Directions: *In this section, there are five passages. For each passage there is a question or unfinished statement followed by four choices marked A, B, C and D. You should decide on the best choice and mark the corresponding letter on it.*

Passage 1

I'm usually fairly skeptical about any research that concludes that people are either happier or unhappier or more or less certain of themselves than they were 50 years ago. While any of these statements might be true, they are practically impossible to prove scientifically. Still, I was struck by a report, which concluded that today's children are significantly more anxious than children in the 1950s. In fact, the analysis showed, normal children ages 9 to 17 exhibit a higher level of anxiety today than children who were treated for mental illness 50 years ago.

Why are America's kids so stressed? The report cites two main causes: increasing physical isolation—brought on by high divorce rates and less involvement in community, among other things—and a growing perception that the world is a more dangerous place. Given that we can't turn the clock back, adults can still do plenty to help the next generation.

At the top of the list is nurturing(培育) a better appreciation of the limits of individualism. No child is an island. Strengthening social ties helps build communities and protect individuals against stress.

To help kids build stronger connections with others, you can pull out the plug on TVs and computers. Your family will thank you later. They will have more time for face-to-face relationships, and they will get more sleep.

Limit the amount of virtual(虚拟的) violence your children are exposed to. It's not just video games and movies; children see a lot of murder and crime on the local news. Keep your expectations for your children reasonable. Many highly successful people never attended Harvard or Yale.

Make exercise part of your daily routine. It will help you cope with your own anxieties and provide a good model for your kids. Sometimes anxiety is unavoidable. But it doesn't have to ruin your life.

Question

1. What conclusion can be drawn from the passage?

    A. Anxiety, though unavoidable, can be coped with.

    B. Children's anxiety has been enormously exaggerated.

    C. Children's anxiety can be eliminated with more parental care.

    D. Anxiety, if properly controlled, may help children become mature.

Passage 2

There are people in Italy who can't stand soccer. Not all Canadians love hockey. A similar situation exists in America, where there are those individuals you may be one of them who yawn or even frown when somebody mentions baseball. Baseball to them means boring hours watching grown men in funny tight outfits standing around in a field staring away while very little of anything happens. They tell you it's a game better suited to the 19th century, slow, quiet and gentlemanly. There are the same people you may be one of them who love football because there's the sport that glorifies "the hit".

By contrast, baseball seems abstract, cool, silent, still. On TV the game is fractured into a dozen perspectives, replays, close ups. The geometry(几何学) of the game, however, is essential to understanding it. You will contemplate the game from one point as a painter does his subject; you may, of course, project yourself into the game. It is in this projection that the game affords so much space and time for involvement. The TV won't do it for you.

Take, for example, the third baseman. You sit behind the third base dugout and you watch him watching home plate. His legs are apart, knees flexed (弯曲). His arms hang loose. He does a lot of this. The skeptic still cannot think of any other sports so still, so passive. But watch what happens every time the pitcher(投手) throws: the third baseman goes up on his toes, flexes his arms or brings the glove to a point in front of him, takes a step right or left, backward or forward, perhaps he glances across the field to check his first baseman's position. Suppose the pitch is a ball. "Nothing happened," you say. "I could have had my eyes closed."

The skeptic and the innocent must play the game. And this involvement in the stands is no more intellectual than listening to music is. Watch the third baseman. Smooth the dirt in front of you with one foot; smooth the pocket in your glove; watch the eyes of the batter, the speed of the bat, the sound of horsehide on wood. If football is a symphony of movement and theatre, baseball is chamber music, a spacious interlocking of notes, chorus and responses.

Question

2. We can safely conclude that the author _____.

   A. likes football   B. hates football

   C. hates baseball   D. likes baseball.

Passage 3

Unless we spend money to spot and prevent asteroids(小行星) now, one might crash into Earth and destroy life as we know it, say some scientists.

Asteroids are bigger versions of the meteoroids(流星) that race across the night sky. Most orbit the sun far from Earth and don't threaten us. But there are also thousands of asteroids whose orbits put them on a collision course with Earth.

Buy $50 million worth of new telescopes right now. Then spend $10 million a year for the next 25 years to locate most of the space rocks. By the time we spot a fatal one, the scientists say, we'll have a way to change its course.

Some scientists favor pushing asteroids off course with nuclear weapons. But the cost wouldn't be cheap.

Is it worth it? Two things experts consider when judging any risk are:

1) How likely the event is; and 2) How bad the consequences if the event occurs. Experts think an asteroid big enough to destroy lots of life might strike Earth once every 500,000 years. Sounds pretty rare—but if one did fall, it would be the end of the world. "If we don't take care of these big asteroids, they'll take care of us," says one scientist. "It's that simple."

The cure, though, might be worse than the disease. Do we really want fleets of nuclear weapons sitting around on Earth? "The world has less to fear from doomsday(毁灭性的) rocks than from a great nuclear fleet set against them," said a *New York Times* article.

Question

3. We can conclude from the passage that _____.

   A. while pushing asteroids off course nuclear weapons would destroy the world

   B. asteroids racing the night sky are likely to hit Earth in the near future

C. the worry about asteroids can be left to future generations since it is unlikely to happen in our lifetime

D. workable solutions still have to be found to prevent a collision of asteroids with Earth

Passage 4

Like many of my generation, I have a weakness for hero worship. At some point, however, we all begin to question our heroes and our need for them. This leads us to ask: What is a hero?

Despite immense differences in cultures, heroes around the world generally share a number of characteristics that instruct and inspire people.

A hero does something worth talking about. A hero has a story of adventure to tell and a community who will listen. But a hero goes beyond mere fame.

Heroes serve powers or principles larger than themselves. Like high-voltage transformers, heroes take the energy of higher powers and step it down so that it can be used by ordinary people.

The hero lives a life worthy of imitation. Those who imitate a genuine hero experience life with new depth, enthusiasm, and meaning. A sure test for would-be heroes is what or whom do they serve? What are they willing to live and die for? If the answer or evidence suggests they serve only their own fame, they may be famous persons but not heroes. Madonna and Michael Jackson are famous, but who would claim that their fans find life more abundant?

Heroes are catalysts (催化剂) for change. They have a vision from the mountaintop. They have the skill and the charm to move the masses. They create new possibilities. Without Gandhi, India might still be part of the British Empire. Without Rosa Parks and Martin Luther King, Jr., we might still have segregated(隔离的) buses, restaurants, and parks. It may be possible for large-scale change to occur without leaders with magnetic personalities, but the pace of change would be slow, the vision uncertain, and the committee meetings endless.

Question

4. The author concludes that historical changes would _____.

    A. be delayed without leaders with inspiring personal qualities

B. not happen without heroes making the necessary sacrifices
C. take place if there were heroes to lead the people
D. produce leaders with attractive personalities

Passage 5

Nike is one of the world's best-known sports shoe and apparel(服装) companies with annual revenues exceeding $1 billion. It markets running shoes, walking shoes, basketball shoes, jogging suits, and many other related products. Yet, despite its success, Nike (like many of its competitors) relies heavily on celebrity endorsement(支持,认可) to stimulate consumer sale.

And over the past few years, Nike has capitalized on one of the best celebrity endorsements in sports history: Michael Jordan for Air Jordan basketball shoes and clothing. In the first two years on the market, Nike sold 2 million pairs of Air Jordans; and sales from the shoes and clothing reached $100 million. What about Michael Jordan's fee? $2.5 million over five years, a royalty on all items sold, and a number of fringe benefits.

Nike's promotion efforts for Air Jordan have been impressive. It decided to hire Michael Jordan after he starred for and co-captained the gold-medal winning 1984 U. S. Olympic basketball team. He has since become an exciting all-pro player in the National Basketball Association. The name Air Jordan was derived from the shoe's air-sole and Michael Jordan's name. The original shoe was a high-top black and red model, designed to be functional, and fashionable. Magazine and television commercials, for which Nike has invested $5 million, have shown Jordan leaping, blocking shots, and "slam dunking." Enormous billboards of him in action also have appeared in major cities. McDonald's and coke commercials featuring Jordan have enhanced his public stature. Nike received early publicity when the Chicago Bulls (his basketball team) refused to let Jordan wear the red and black shoes, since they did not match the team's colors. After getting hardness everywhere, Nike supplied Jordan with shoes in the Bulls' colors, and took out ads teasing the National Basketball Association.

Question

5. It can be concluded from this passage that _____.
   A. both Jordan and Nike benefited from advertising
   B. Nike could not have survived without Jordan, the basketball star

C. the American National Basketball Association also depends heavily on Jordan

D. The Chicago Bulls hated Jordan because he did not wear shoes in the Bulls' colors

3. 态度或观点类试题

态度或观点类试题设置的目的是考查考生通过分析作者的行文语气、表述方式、选词以及观点等来推导作者的态度或观点,判断文章的主观倾向。由于这类试题常常没有明显的解题线索,所以考生必须通过个别带有主观色彩的词语来推断作者对某个问题所持有的态度或观点,或通过作者所叙述的客观事实的行文语气等来推断隐藏在词句背后或字里行间的真正意图,因为作者在叙述客观事实时总是会有所取舍,有主观倾向的,而这种取舍和主观倾向恰恰表明了作者对同一事实的不同态度。因此,考生要充分利用作者的这这些特点来确定作者的真实态度。切忌以自己的观点或对问题的态度或凭常识枉自判断。例如:

It is hard to predict how science is going to turn out, and if it is really good science it is impossible to predict. If the things to be found are actually new, they are by definition unknown in advance. You cannot make choices in this matter. You either have science or you don't, and if you have it you are obliged to accept the surprising and disturbing pieces of information, along with the neat and promptly useful bits.

The only solid piece of scientific truth about which I feel totally confident is that we are profoundly ignorant about nature. Indeed, I regard this as the major discovery of the past hundred years of biology. It is, in its way, an illuminating piece of news: It would have amazed the brightest minds of the 18th century Enlightenment to be told by any of us how little we know and how bewildering seems the way ahead. It is this sudden confrontation with the depth and scope of ignorance that represents the most significant contribution of the 20th century science to the human intellect. In earlier times, we either pretended to understand how things worked or ignored the problem, or simply made up stories to fill the gaps. Now that we have begun exploring in earnest, we are getting glimpses of how huge the questions are, and how far from being answered. Because of this, we are depressed. It is not so bad being ignorant if you are totally ignorant; the hard thing is knowing in some detail the reality of ignorance, the worst spots and here and there the not-so-bad spots, but no true light at the end of the tunnel nor even any tunnels that can yet be trusted.

But we are making a beginning, and there ought to be some satisfaction. There are probably no questions we can think up that can't be answered, sooner or later, including even the matter of consciousness. To be sure, there may well be questions we can't think up, ever, and therefore limits to the reach of human intellect, but that is another matter. Within our limits, we should be able to work our way through to all our answers, if we keep at it long enough, and pay attention.

Question

What is the author's attitude towards science?

A. He is depressed because of the ignorance of scientists.

B. He is doubtful because of the enormous difficulties confronting it.

C. He is confident though he is aware of the enormous difficulties confronting it.

D. He is delighted because of the illuminating scientific findings.

【例题解析】选项 C 为正确答案。作者在前两段中花了大量的笔墨谈论科学的不可预测性和对科学的无知,特别是对最近一个世纪的科学的不了解,进而产生沮丧和迷茫等情绪。但是,作者在最后一段笔锋一转,充分地表示面对种种困难的自信心和乐观的态度,"There are probably no questions we can think up that can't be answered, sooner or later","Within our limits, we should be able to work our way through to all our answers, if we keep at it long enough, and pay attention."本文所采用的写作手法是反衬法,即先抛出问题的消极一面,以便与最后所表现的积极的一面形成反衬,从而产生了画龙点睛的作用。

Exercise 10

Directions: *In this section, there are ten passages. For each passage there is a question or unfinished statement followed by four choices marked A, B, C and D. You should decide on the best choice and mark the corresponding letter on it.*

Passage 1

Are organically grown foods the best food choices? The advantages claimed for such foods over conventionally grown and marketed food products are now being debated. Advocates of organic foods—a term whose meaning varies greatly—frequently proclaim that such products are safer and more nutritious than others.

The growing interest of consumers in the safety and more nutritional quality of the typical North American diet is a welcome development. However, much of this interest has been sparked by sweeping claims that the food supply is unsafe or inadequate in meeting nutritional needs. Although most of these claims are not supported by scientific evidence, the preponderance（优势）of written material advancing such claims makes it difficult for the general public to separate fact from fiction. As a result, claims that eating a diet consisting entirely of organically grown foods prevents or cures disease or provides other benefits to health have become widely publicized and form the basis for folklore（民俗）.

Almost daily the public is besieged by claims for "no-aging" diets, new vitamins, and other wonder foods. There are numerous unsubstantiated reports that natural vitamins are superior to synthetic ones, that fertilized eggs are nutritionally superior to unfertilized eggs, that untreated grains are better than fumigated（熏蒸消毒）grains and the like.

One thing that most organically grown food products seem to have in common is that they cost more than conventionally grown foods. But in many cases consumers are misled if they believe organic foods can maintain health and provide better nutritional quality than conventionally grown foods. So there is real cause for concern if consumers, particularly those with limited incomes, distrust the regular food and buy only expensive organic foods instead.

Question

1. What is the author's attitude toward the claims made by advocates of health foods?

A. Very enthusiastic
B. Somewhat favorable
C. Neutral
D. Skeptical

Passage 2

Here's my simple test for a product of today's technology. I go to the bookstore and check the shelves for remedial books. The more books, the more my suspicions are raised. If computers and computer programs supposedly are getting easier to use, why are so many companies still making a nice living publishing books on how to use them?

Computers manipulate information, but information is invisible. There's nothing to see or touch. The programmer decides what you see on the screen.

Computers don't have knobs like old radios. They don't have buttons, not real buttons. Instead, more and more programs display pictures of buttons, moving even further into abstraction and arbitrariness(任意). I like computers, but I hope they will disappear, that they will seem as strange to our descendants as the technologies of our grandparents appear to us. Today's computers are indeed getting easier to us, but look where they started so difficult that almost any improvement was welcome.

Computers have the power to allow people within a company, across a nation or even around the world to work together. But this power will be wasted if tomorrow's computers aren't designed around the needs and capabilities of the human beings who must use them—a people centered philosophy. In other words, that means retooling computers to mesh(使缠住) with human strengths—observing, communicating and innovation—instead of asking people to conform to the unnatural behavior computers demand. That just leads to error.

Many of today's machines try to do too much. When a complicated word processor attempts to double as a desktop pulsing program or a kitchen appliance comes with half a dozen attachments, the product is bound to be unwieldy(不便利的) and burdensome. My favorite example of a technological product is on just the right scale in an electronic dictionary. It can be made smaller, lighter and far easier to use than a print version, not only giving meanings but even pronouncing the words. Today's electronic dictionaries, with their tiny keys and barely legible displays, are primitive but they are on the right track.

Question

2. Concerning the author's attitude towards computers, which of the following is most suitable?

   A. He doubts the convenience of computers.

   B. He loves them, but proposes to change them.

   C. He doesn't like them at all, but has to rely on it for his job.

   D. He is dissatisfied with nowadays-technological development.

Passage 3

A child who has been pleased with a tale likes, as a rule, to have it retold in identically the same words, but this should not lead parents to treat printed fairy stories as sacred texts. It is always much better to tell story than read it out of a book and, if a parent can produce what, in the actual circumstances of the time and the individual child, is an improvement on the printed text, so much the better.

A charge made against fairy tales is that they harm the child by frightening him or arousing evil desire. To prove the latter, one would have to show in a controlled experiment that children who have read fairy stories were more often guilty of cruelty than those who had not. As to fears, there are, I think, many cases of children being dangerously terrified by some fairy story. Often, however, this arises from the child having heard the story once. Familiarity with the story by repetition turns the pain into the pleasure of fear faced and mastered.

There are also people who object to fairy stories on the grounds that they are not objectively true, that giants, two-headed dragons, magic carpets, etc, do not exist; and that, instead of indulging his fantasies in a fairy tale, the child should be taught how to adapt to reality by studying history and mechanics. I find such people, I must confess, so unsympathetic and peculiar that I do not know how to argue with them. If their case were sound, the world should be full of mad men attempting to fly from New York to Philadelphia on a broomstick or covering a telephone with kisses in the belief that it was their lovely girl-friend.

No fairy story ever claimed to be a description of the external world and no normal child has ever believed that it was.

Question
3. Which of the following is the author's attitude toward fairy tales?
   A. They do no harm to children.
   B. They are harmful because they may make children cruel.
   C. They harm the child by frightening him.
   D. They are not sacred texts because they are not objectively true.

Passage 4
We find that bright children are rarely held back by mixed-ability teaching. On the contrary, both their knowledge and experience are enriched. We feel that there are many disadvantages in streaming pupils. It does not take into account . the fact that children develop at different rates. It can have a bad effect on both

the bright and the not-so-bright child. After all, it can be quite discouraging to be at the bottom of the top grade!

Besides, it is rather unreal to grade people just according to their intellectual abilities. This is only one aspect of their total personality. We are concerned to develop the abilities of all our pupils to the full, not just their academic ability. We also value personal qualities and social skills, and we find that mixed-ability teaching contributes to all these aspects of learning.

In our classrooms, we work in various ways. The pupils often work in groups: this gives them the opportunity to learn to cooperate, to share, and to develop leadership skills. They also learn how to cope with personal problems as well as how to think, to make decisions, to analyze and evaluate, and to communicate effectively. The pupils learn from each other as well as from the teacher.

Sometimes the pupils work in pairs; sometimes they work on individual tasks and assignments, and they can do this at their own speed. They also have some library, and we teach them the skills they need in order to do this effectively. And expect our pupils to do their best, not their least, and we give them every encouragement to attain this goal.

Question

4. In the passage the author's attitude towards "mixed-ability teaching" is

_____.

    A. questioning   B. approving

    C. objective   D. critical

Passage 5

The subject of my study is a woman who is initiating social change in a small region in Texas. The women are Mexican Americans who are, or were, migrant agricultural workers. There is more than one kind of innovation at work in the region, of course, but I have chosen to focus on three related patterns of family behavior.

The pattern I life style represents how migrant farm workers of all nationalities lived in the past and how many continue to live. I treat this pattern as a baseline with which to compare the changes represented by pattern II and III. Families in pattern I work and travel in extended kin units, with the eldest male occupying the position of authority. Families are large? Eight or nine children are not unusual? And all members are economic contributor in this strategy of family migration. Families in pattern II manifest some differences in behavior while still maintaining aspects of pattern I. They continue to migrate but on a reduced scale, often modifying their schedules of migration to allow children to finish the school year. Parents in this pattern often find temporary local jobs as checkers to make up for lost farming income. Pattern II families usually have fewer children than do pattern I families.

The greatest amount of change from pattern I, however, is in pattern III families, who no longer migrate at all. Both Parents work full time in the area and have an average of three children. Children attend school for the entire year. In pattern III, the women in particular create new roles for themselves for which no local models exist. They not only work full time but may, in addition, return to school. They also assume a greater responsibility in family decisions than do women in the other patterns. Although these women are in the minority among residents of the region, they serve as role models for others, causing moderate changes to spread in their communities.

Now opportunities have continued to be determined by pre-existing values. When federal jobs became available in the region, most involved working under the direction of female professionals such as teachers or nurses. Such positions were unaccepted to many men in the area because they were not accustomed to being subordinate to women. Women therefore took the jobs, at first, because the income was desporately needed. But some of the women decided to stay at their jobs, at first, after the family's distress was over. These women enjoyed their work, its responsibility, and the companionship of fellow women workers. The steady, relatively high income allowed their families to stop migrating. And, as the benefits to these women became increasingly apparent, they and their families became even more willing to consider changes in their lives that they would not have considered before.

Question

5. The author's attitude towards the three patterns of behavior mentioned in the passage is best described as one of _____.

A. great admiration   B. unbiased objectivity

C. dissatisfaction   D. indifference

Passage 6

Sport is not only physically challenging, but it can also be mentally challenging. Criticism from coaches, parents, and other teammates, as well as pressure to win can create an excessive amount of anxiety or stress for young athletes. Stress can be physical, emotional, or psychological and research has indicated that it can lead to burnout. Burnout has been described as dropping or quitting of an activity that was at one time enjoyable.

The early years of development are critical years for learning about oneself. The sport setting is one where valuable experiences can take place. Young athletes can, for example, learn how to cooperate with others, make friends, and gain other social skills that will be used throughout their lives. Coaches and parents should be aware, at all times, that their feedback(反馈) to youngsters can greatly affect their children. Youngsters may take their parents' and coaches' criticisms to heart and find a flaw in themselves.

Coaches and parents should also be cautious that youth sport participation does not become work for children. The outcome of the game should not be more important than the process of learning the sport and other life lessons. In today's youth sport setting, young athletes may be worrying more about who will win instead of enjoying themselves and the sport. Following a game many parents and coaches focus on the outcome and find fault with youngsters' performances. Positive reinforcement should be provided regardless of the outcome. Research indicates that positive reinforcement motivates and has a greater effect on learning than criticism. Again, criticism can create high levels of stress, which can lead to burnout.

Question

6. The author's purpose in writing the passage is _____.
    A. to persuade young children not to worry about criticism
    B. to stress the importance of positive reinforcement to children
    C. to discuss the skill of combining criticism with encouragement
    D. to teach young athletes how to avoid burnout

Passage 7

The standardized educational or psychological tests, which are widely used to aid in selecting, assigning or promoting students, employees and military personnel, have been the target of recent attacks in books, magazines, the daily press, and even in the Congress. The target is wrong, for in attacking the tests, critics divert attention from the fault that lies with ill-informed or incompetent users. The tests themselves are merely tools, with characteristics that can be measured with reasonable precision under specified condition. Whether the results will be valuable, meaningless, or even misleading depends partly upon the tool itself but largely upon the user.

All informed predictions of future performance are based upon some knowledge of relevant past performance. How well the predictions will be validated by later performance depends upon the amount, reliability and appropriateness of the information used and on the skill and wisdom with which it is interpreted. Anyone who keeps careful score knows that the information available is always incomplete and that the predictions are always subject to error.

Standardized tests should be considered in this context: they provide a quick, objective method of getting some kind of information about what a person has learned, the skills he has developed, or the kind of person he is. The information so obtained has, qualitatively, the same advantages and shortcomings as other kinds of information. Whether to use tests, other kinds of information, or both in a particular situation depends, therefore, upon the empirical evidence concerning comparative validity, and upon such factors as cost and availability.

In general, the tests work most effectively when the traits or qualities to be measured can be most precisely defined (for example, ability to do well in a particular course of training program) and least effectively when what is to be measured or predicted cannot be well defined, for example, personality or creativity. Properly used, they provide a rapid means of getting comparable information about many people. Sometimes they identify students whose high potential has not been previously recognized.

Question

7. The author's attitude toward standardized tests is _____.

    A. critical   B. vague

    C. optimistic   D. positive

Passage 8

Icebergs are among nature's most spectacular creations, and yet most people have never seen one. A vague air of mystery envelops them. They come into being somewhere—in faraway, frigid waters, and with thunderous noise and splashing turbulence, which in most cases no one hears or sees. They exist only a short time and then slowly waste away just as unnoticed.

Objects of sheerest beauty, they have been called. Appearing in an endless variety of shapes, they may be dazzlingly white, or they may be glassy blue, green, or purple, tinted faintly of darker hues. They are graceful, stately, inspiring in calm, sunlit seas.

But they are also called frightening and dangerous, and that they are in the night, in the fog and in storms. Even in clear weather one is wise to stay a safe distance away from them. Most of their bulk is hidden below the water, so their underwater parts may extend out far beyond the visible top. Also, they may roll over unexpectedly, churning the waters around them.

Icebergs are parts of glaciers that break off, drift into the water, float about a while, and finally melt. Icebergs afloat today are made of snowflakes that have fallen over long ages of time. They embody snows that drifted down hundreds, or many thousands, or in some cases, maybe a million years ago. The snows fell in Polar Regions and on cold mountains, where they melted only a little or not at all, and so collected to great depths over the years and centuries.

As each year's snow accumulation lay on the surface, evaporation and melting caused the snowflakes slowly to lose their feathery points and become tiny grains of ice. When new snow fell on top of the old, it too turned to icy grains. So blankets of snow and ice grains mounted layer upon layer and were of such great thickness that the weight of the upper layers compressed the lower ones. With time and pressure from above, the many small ice grains joined and changed to larger crystals, and eventually the deeper crystals merged into a solid mass of ice.

Question

8. The attitude of the author's tone toward icebergs is one of _____.

    A. disappointment   B. humor

    C. disinterest   D. wonder

Passage 9

In general, our society is becoming one of giant enterprises directed by a bureaucratic(官僚主义的) management in which man becomes a small, well-oiled cog(齿轮) in the machinery. The oiling is done with higher wages, well-ventilated factories and piped music, and by psychologists and "human-relations" experts; yet all this oiling does not alter the fact that man has become powerless, that he is bored with it. In fact, the blue and the white-collar workers have become economic puppets(木偶) who dance to the tune of automated machines and bureaucratic management.

The worker and employee are anxious, not only because they might find themselves out of a job; they are anxious also because they are unable to acquire any real satisfaction of interest in life. They live and die without ever having confronted the fundamental realities of human existence as emotionally and intellectually independent and productive human being.

Those higher up on the social ladder are no less anxious. Their lives are no less empty than those of their subordinates. They are even more insecure in some respects. They are in a highly competitive race. To be promoted or to fall behind is not a matter of salary but even more a matter of self-respect. When they apply for their first job, they are tested for intelligence as well as for the right mixture of submissiveness and independence. From that moment on they are tested again and again by the psychologists, for whom testing is a big business, and by their superiors, who judge their behavior, sociability, capacity to get along, etc. This constant need to prove that one is as good as or better than one's fellow-competitor creates constant anxiety and stress, the very causes of unhappiness and illness.

Am I suggesting that we should return to the pre-industrial mode of production or to nineteenth-century "free enterprise" capitalism? Certainly not. Problems are never solved by returning to a stage which one has already outgrown. I suggest transforming our social system from a bureaucratically managed industrialism in which maximal production and consumption are ends in themselves into a humanist(人文主义者) industrialism in which man and full development of his potentialities—those of all love and of reason—are the aims of social arrangements. Production and consumption should serve only as means to this end, and should be prevented from ruling man.

Question

9. The author's attitude towards industrialism might best be summarized as one of _____.

A. approval   B. dissatisfaction

C. suspicion   D. susceptibility

Passage 10

How often do you sit still and do absolutely nothing? The usual answer these days is "never" or "hardly ever". As the pace of life continues to increase, we are fast losing the art of relaxation. Once you are in the habit of rushing through life, being on the go from morning till night, it is hard to slow down and unwind(放松). But relaxation is essential for a healthy mind and body.

Stress is a natural part of everyday life. There is no way to avoid it, since it takes many and varied forms—driving in traffic, problems with personal relationships are all different forms of stress. Stress, in fact, is not the "baddy" which is often reputed to be. A certain amount of stress is vital to provide motivation and give purpose to life. It is only when the stress gets out of control that it can lead to low-level performance and ill health.

The amount of stress a person can withstand depends very much on the individual. Some people thrive on stress, and such characters are obviously prime material for managerial responsibilities. Others crumple at the sight of unusual difficulties.

When exposed to stress, in whatever form, we react both chemically and physically. In fact, we invoke the "fight" mechanism which in more primitive days made the difference between life and death. The crises we meet today are unlikely to be so extreme, but however minimal the stress, it involves the same response. All the energy is diverted to cope with the stress, with the result that other functions, such as digestion(消化力) are neglected。

It is when such a reaction is prolonged, through continued exposure to stress, that health becomes endangered. Such serious conditions as high blood pressure, coronary heart disease(冠心病) all have established links with stress. The way stress affects a person also varies with the individual. Stress in some people produces stomach disorders, while others succumb(屈服) to tension headaches. Since we cannot remove stress from our lives, we need to find ways to cope with it.

Question

10. What is the writer's attitude to stress according to the passage?

    A. Stress as well as relaxation is essential for a healthy mind and body.

    B. Stress produces both positive and negative effects on people.

    C. Stress should not be eliminated completely from the life.

    D. People usually work better under stress if they are healthy.

4. 逻辑推理类试题

逻辑推理是指由一个或几个已知的信息作为判断前提,推导出新的结论。逻辑推理类试题就是通过这个推理的过程来获取一个合乎情理的结论。例如:

In a family where the roles of men and women are not sharply separated and where many household tasks are shared to a greater or lesser extent, notions of male superiority are hard to maintain. The pattern of sharing in tasks and in decision makes for equality and this in turn leads to further sharing. In such a home, the growing boy and girl learn to accept equality more easily than did their parents and to prepare more fully for participation in a world characterized by cooperation rather than by the "battle of the sexes".

If the process goes too far and man's role is regarded as less important—and that has happened in some cases—we are as badly off as before, only in reverse.

It is time to reassess the role of the man in the American family. We are getting a little tired of "Momism"—but we don't want to exchange it for a "neo-Popism". What we need, rather, is the recognition that bringing up children involves a partnership of equals. There are signs that psychiatrists, psychologists, social workers, and specialists on the family are becoming more aware of the part men play and that they have decided that women should not receive all the credit, or the blame. We have almost given up saying that a woman's place is in the home. We are beginning, however, to analyze man's place in the home and to insist that he does have a place in it. Nor is that place irrelevant to the healthy development of the child.

The family is a co-operative enterprise for which it is difficult to lay down rules, because each family needs to work out its own ways for solving its own problems.

Excessive authoritarianism(命令主义) has unhappy consequences, whether it wears skirts or trousers, and the ideal of equal rights and equal responsibilities is pertinent(相关的,切题的) not only to a healthy democracy, but also to a healthy family.

Question

With which of the following statements would the author be most likely to agree?

A. A healthy, co-operative family is a basic ingredient of a healthy society.

B. Men are basically opposed to sharing household chores.

C. Division of household responsibilities is workable only in theory.

D. A woman's place in the home—now as always.

【例题解析】该选项的正确答案是 A。作者在第一段最后一句中所表达的观点是 In such a home, the growing boy and girl learn to accept equality more easily than did their parents and to prepare more fully for participation in a world characterized by cooperation rather than by the "battle of the sexes".(在这种家庭里,成长中的男女孩子们就会比他们的父母更能轻松地学会接受平等的观点,为加入以合作为特色的世界而不是为性别而战斗的世界做好准备)。试想一个"为性别而战斗的世界"而不是"以合作为特色的世界"会是什么样子,必定是一个充满了硝烟弥漫的世界。这样的世界必定不是一个健康的世界。作为社会的细胞,家庭对社会的安定团结必定是一个很重要的因素。因此,选项 A 应为正确答案。选项 B、C 和 D 中所提到的内容文中没有提到,况且根据文中的观点也不可得出那些种结论。因此,不可视作正确答案。

Exercise 11

Directions: *In this section, there are five passages. Each passage is followed by a question or unfinished statement followed by four choices marked A, B, C and D. You should decide on the best choice and mark the corresponding letter on it.*

Passage 1

British universities, groaning under the burden of a huge increase in student numbers, are warning that the tradition of a free education is at risk. The universities have threatened to impose an admission fee on students to plug a gap in revenue if the government does not act to improve their finances and scrap some public spending cutbacks.

The government responded to the universities' threat by setting up the most fundamental review of higher education for a generation, under a non-party troubleshooter, Sir Ron Dearing.

One in three school leavers enters higher education, five times the number when the last review took place thirty years ago.

Everyone agrees a system that is feeling the strain after rapid expansion needs a lot more money—but there is little hope of getting it from the taxpayer and not much scope for attracting more finance from business.

Most colleges believe students should contribute to tuition costs, something that is common elsewhere in the world but would mark a revolutionary change in Britain. Universities want the government to introduce a loan scheme for tuition fees and have suspended their own threatened action for now. They await Dearing's advice, hoping it will not be too late—some are already reported to be in financial difficulty.

As the century nears its end, the whole concept of what a university should be is under the microscope. Experts ponder how much they can use computers instead of classrooms, talk of the need for lifelong learning and refer to students as "consumers".

The Confederation of British Industry, the key employers' organization, wants even more expansion in higher education to help fight competition on world markets from booming Asian economies. But the government has doubts about more expansion. The *Times* newspaper agrees, complaining that quality has suffered as student numbers soared, with close tutorial supervision giving way to "mass production methods more typical of European universities. "

Question

1. It can be inferred from the passage that _____.
    A. British employers demand an expansion in enrollment at the expense of quality
    B. the best way out for British universities is to follow their European counterparts
    C. the British government will be forced to increase its spending on higher education
    D. British students will probably have to pay for their higher education in the near future

Passage 2

Design of all the new tools and implements is based on careful experiments with electronic instruments. First, a human "guinea pig" is tested using a regular tool. Measurements are taken of the amount of work done, and the buildup of heat in the body. Twisted joints and stretched muscles cannot perform as well, it has been found, as joints and muscles in their normal positions. The same person is then tested again, using a tool designed according to the suggestions made by Dr. Tichauer. All these tests have shown the great improvement of the new designs over the old.

One of the electronic instruments used by Dr. Tichauer, the myograph（肌动描记器）, makes visible through electrical signals the work done by human muscle.

Another machine measures any dangerous features of tools, thus proving information upon which to base a new design. One conclusion of tests made with this machine is that a tripod stepladder is more stable and safer to use than one with four legs.

This work has attracted the attention of efficiency experts and time-and-motion-study engineer, but its value goes far beyond that. Dr. Tichauer's first thought is for the health of the tool user. With the repeated use of the same tool all day long on production lines and in other jobs, even light manual work can put a heavy stress on one small area of the body. In time, such stress can cause a disabling disease. Furthermore, muscle fatigue is a serious safety hazard.

Efficiency is the by-product of comfort, Dr. Tichauer believes, and his new designs for traditional tools have proved his point.

Question

2. It can be inferred from the passage that _____.
   A. a stepladder used to have four legs
   B. it is dangerous to use tools
   C. a tripod is safer in a tool design
   D. workers are safer on production lines

Passage 3

The name Chunlan might mean little or nothing to the average man or woman in the street at the present time but things change and the Chinese-owned multinational manufacturing giant is already well established across the

Far East, North America and Europe. Amongst a multitude of other things, from refrigerators to DVD players, Chunlan produces a range of high quality scooters(小型摩托车) and motorcycles at their hi-tech, state-of-the-art factory.

These vehicles combine Chunlan's significant innovation and manufacturing expertise with a design flair(天资)and build quality that is a match for anything else on the UK market. Ranging from 50cc scooters to 125cc motorcycles, there's plenty to choose from and the prices are amongst the most competitive you'll find.

The tempting pricing levels of the Chunlan range in the UK can be attributed, in part to the sales and distribution network for the vehicles. The entire process is handled by the local company, Starway Motorcycles who are the sole importers and suppliers of Chunlan bikes and scooters in this country.

Initially starting out as a mail order service, supplying catalogues like Littlewoods Kays, Gus and Empire Stores. Starway have sold in excess of 3000 Chunlan vehicles onto the UK market. The increasing demand and the profitability of the business has been such that, two weeks ago, Starway Motorcycles opened their own showroom in Armley from which they can now offer the Chunlan product range for sale direct to the public.

Essentially the new facility is a factory outlet with exclusivity of the supply and the absence of a "middle-man" enabling Starway to provide unbeatable value for money on all the Chunlan designs. The range opens with the 50cc CL50QT-A and this is a first-class modern, stylish design. The single cylinder, two-stroke, air-cooled engine is quiet economical while providing a decent amount of poke of negotiating steep inclines. Next up is the CL125T which provides the same elegant lines and an injection of fun courtesy of the sporty 125cc engine. Here customers get top-line shock absorbers, a front disc brake and alloy wheels.

The Chunlan motorcycles come in three versions, a sports model, a tauter (拉紧的) and a fully chromed-up retro design. All three are powered by the same 125cc double cylinder, air-cooled, four-stroke engine and come with generous specifications including disc brakes and alloy wheels.

Question

3. The passage implies that the prices of Chunlan motorcycles are made competitive by _____.

A. Chunlan's hi-tech and state-of-the-art technology

B. the absence of any "middle-man" sales agency

C. the promotional efforts made on the part of Starway

D. the opening of showrooms in nationwide locations

Passage 4

Some people believe that international sport creates goodwill between the nations and that if countries play games together they will learn to live together. Others say that the opposite is true that international contests encourage false national pride and lead to misunderstanding and hatred. There is probably some truth in both arguments, but in recent years the Olympic Games have done little to support the view that sports encourage international brotherhood. Not only was there the tragic incident involving the murder of athletes, but the Games were also ruined by lesser incidents caused principally by minor national contests.

One country received its second place medals with visible indignation after the hockey(曲棍球) final. There had been noisy scenes at the end of the hockey match, the losers objecting to the final decisions. They were convinced that one of their goals should not have been disallowed and that their opponents' victory was unfair. Their manager was in a rage when he said: This wasn't hockey. Hockey and the International Hockey Federation are finished. The president of the Federation said later that such behavior could result in the suspension of the team for at least three years.

The American basketball team announced that they would not yield first place to Russian, after a disputable end to their contest. The game had ended in disturbance. It was thought at first that the United States had won by a single point, but it was announced that there were three seconds still to play. A Russian player then threw the ball from one end of the court to the other, and another player popped it into the basket. It was the first time the USA had ever lost an Olympic basketball match. An appeal jury debated the matter for four and a half hours before announcing that the result would stand. The American players then voted not to receive the silver medals.

Incidents of this kind will continue as long as sport is played competitively rather than for the love of the game. The suggestion that athletes should compete as individuals, or in non national teams, might be too much to hope for. But in the present organization of the Olympies there is far too much that encourages aggressive patriotism.

Question

4. The author gives the two examples in paragraphs 2 and 3 to show _____.
   A. how false national pride led to undesirable incidents in international games
   B. that sportsmen have been more obedient than they used to be
   C. that competitiveness in the games sometimes discourages international friendship
   D. that unfair decisions are common in Olympic Games

Passage 5

Mass transportation revised the social and economic fabric of the American city in three fundamental ways. It catalyzed physical expansion, it sorted out people and land uses, and it accelerated the inherent instability of urban life. By opening vast areas of unoccupied land for residential expansion, the omnibuses, horse railways, commuter trains, and electric trolleys pulled settled regions outward two to four times more distant from city centers than they were in the pre-modern era. In 1850, for example, the borders of Boston lay scarcely two miles from the old business district: by the turn of the 20th century the radius (半径) extended ten miles. Now those who could afford it could live far removed from the old city center and still commute there for work, shopping and entertainment. The new accessibility of land around the periphery(周边，力缘) of almost every major city sparked an explosion of real estate development and fueled what we now know as urban sprawl. Between 1890 and 1920, for example, some 250 000 new residential lots were recorded within the borders of Chicago, most of them located in outlying areas. Over the same period, another 550 000 were plotted outside the city limits but within the metropolitan area. Anxious to take advantage of the possibilities of commuting, real estate developers added 800 000 potential building sites to the Chicago region in just thirty years—lots that could have housed five to six million people.

Of course, many were never occupied; there was always a huge surplus of subdivided, but vacant land around Chicago and other cities. These excesses underscore a feature of residential expansion related to the growth of mass transportation; urban sprawl was essentially unplanned. It was carried out by thousands of small investors who paid little heed to coordinated land use or to future land users. Those who purchased and prepared land for residential purposes, particularly land near or outside city borders where transit lines and middle-class inhabitants were anticipated, did so to create demand as much as to respond to it. Chicago is a prime example of this process. Real estate subdivision there proceeded much faster than population growth.

Question

5. The author mentions both Boston and Chicago in order to _____.

   A. contrast their rates of growth with each other

   B. show that mass transit changed many cities

   C. demonstrate positive and negative effects of growth

   D. exemplify cities with and without mass transportation

四、词义辨析类题

在阅读过程中不可避免地会遇到一些生词。如果这些生词不影响对整个句子或意群大意的理解,最好跳过去,不必细究;如果影响了对整个句子或意群大意的理解,可以利用文中的定义、解释、对比与比较关系、上下文逻辑关系、同位替代关系,结合常识以及举例等进行推断。

此类试题常为考生标明需要辨析词意的词或者是词组在文中的具体所在位置,如该词在第几段、第几行或者是哪句话、哪个词等,并要求考生说明该词在句中的具体含义是什么。

此类试题常考查的重点如下:

(1) 某个多义词在具体语境中的特定含义

(2) 超纲的生词或词组在文中的意义

(3) 替代词所指代的内容

(4) 引用的句子在上下文中的含义

常用的提问形式如下:

(1) Which of the following can best describe the word…?

(2) Which of the following is nearest (closest) in meaning to "…"?

(3) What does the word in line…of paragraph…probably mean?

(4) The word in Line…of Paragraph…means…

(5) According to the author, the word "…" means…

(6) By "…" the author means…

(7) The word "…" in the paragraph means…

(8) The word "..." most likely means...

1. 多义词在具体语境中的特定含义

Stewardess Tallinn Barsan said she escaped from the burning wreckage by driving a hole in the cockpit window with the aid of the pilot, Capt. Turban Goker. "It was a fearful moment, with flames all around and the possibility of being grilled to death," she said.

Question

Line 4, the word "grilled" means _____.

A. shocked   B. thrilled

C. feared   D. burned

【例题解析】选项 D 为正确答案。根据段落中 escaped from the burning wreckage 和 with flames all around 两个语句的含义以推知 grilled 的意思是 burned。

Exercise 12

Directions: *In this section, there are seven passages. For each passage there are some questions or unfinished statements followed by four choices marked A, B, C and D. You should decide on the best choice and mark the corresponding letter on it.*

Passage 1

The interrelationship of science, technology, and industry is taken for granted today—summed up, not altogether accurately, as "research and development." Yet historically this widespread faith in the economic virtues of science is a relatively recent phenomenon, dating back in the United States about 150 years, and in the Western world as a whole not over 300 years at most. Even in this current era of large scale, intensive research and development, the interrelationships involved in this process are frequently misunderstood. Until the coming of the Industrial Revolution, science and technology evolved for the most part independently of each other. Then as industrialization became increasingly complicated, the craft techniques of pre-industrial society gradually gave way to a technology based on the systematic application of scientific knowledge and scientific methods. This changeover started slowly and progressed unevenly. Until late in the nineteenth century, only a few industries could use scientific techniques or cared about using them. The list expanded noticeably after 1870, but even then much of what passed for the application of science was "engineering science" rather than basic science. Nevertheless, by the middle of the nineteenth century, the rapid expansion of scientific knowledge and of public awareness—if not understanding—of it had created a belief that the advance of science would in some unspecified manner automatically generate economic benefits. The widespread and usually uncritical acceptance of this thesis led in turn to the assumption that the application of science to industrial purposes was a linear process, starting with fundamental science, then proceeding to applied science or technology, and through them to industrial use. This is probably the most common pattern, but it is not invariable. New areas of science have been opened up and fundamental discoveries made as a result of attempts to solve a specific technical or economic problem. Conversely, scientists who mainly do basic research also serve as consultants on projects that apply research in practical ways. In sum, the science-technology-industry relationship may flow in several different ways, and the particular channel it will follow depends on the individual situation. It may at times even be multidirectional.

Questions

1. The underlined word "altogether" is closest in meaning to _____.

   A. completely   B. realistically

   C. individually   D. understandably

2. The underlined word "intensive" is closest in meaning to _____.

   A. decreased   B. concentrated

   C. creative   D. advanced

3. The underlined word "list" mentioned refers to _____.

   A. types of scientific knowledge

   B. changes brought by technology

   C. industries that used scientific techniques

   D. applications of engineering science

4. The underlined word "assumption" is closest in meaning to _____.

   A. regulation   B. belief

   C. contract   D. confusion

Passage 2

Glass fibers have a long history. The Egyptians made coarse fibers by 1600 B. C. , and fibers survive as decorations on Egyptian pottery dating back to 1375 B. C.. During the Renaissance (15th and 16th centuries A. D.), glassmakers from Venice used glass fibers to decorate the surfaces of plain glass vessels. However, glassmakers guarded their secrets so carefully that no one wrote about glass fiber production until the early seventeenth century.

The eighteenth century brought the invention of "spun glass" fibers. Rene-Antoine de Reaumur, a French scientist, tried to make artificial feathers from glass. He made fibers by rotating a wheel through a pool of molten glass, pulling threads of glass where the hot thick liquid stuck to the wheel. His fibers were short and fragile, but he predicted that spun glass fibers as thin as spider silk would be flexible and could be woven into fabric. By the start of the nineteenth century, glassmakers learned how to make longer, stronger fibers by pulling them from molten glass with a hot glass tube. Inventors wound the cooling end of the thread around a yarn reel(纱线绕线筒), and then turned the reel rapidly to pull more fiber from the molten glass. Wandering trades-people began to spin glass fibers at fairs, making decorations and ornaments as novelties for collectors, but this material was of little practical use; the fibers were brittle, ragged, and no longer than ten feet, the circumference of the largest reels. By the mid-1870's, however, the best glass fibers were finer than silk and could be woven into fabrics or assembled into imitation ostrich(鸵鸟) feathers to decorate hats. Cloth of white spun glass resembled silver; fibers drawn from yellow-orange glass looked golden.

Glass fibers were little more than a novelty until the 1930's, when their thermal(热的) and electrical insulating properties were appreciated and methods for producing continuous filaments were developed. In the modern manufacturing process, liquid glass is fed directly from a glass-melting furnace into a bushing, a receptacle pierced with hundreds of fine nozzles, from which the liquid issues in fine streams. As they solidify, the streams of glass are gathered into a single strand and wound onto a reel.

Questions

5. The underlined word "coarse" is closest in meaning to _____ .

    A. decorative   B. natural

    C. crude   D. weak

6. The underlined phrase "this material" refers to _____.
   A. glass fibers
   B. decorations
   C. ornaments
   D. novelties for collectors
7. The underlined word "brittle" is closest in meaning to _____.
   A. easily broken
   B. roughly made
   C. hairy
   D. shiny

Passage 3

Scientists have discovered that for the last 160,000 years, at least, there has been a consistent relationship between the amount of carbon dioxide in the air and the average temperature of the planet. The importance of carbon dioxide in regulating the Earth's temperature was confirmed by scientists working in eastern Antarctica. Drilling down into a glacier(冰川), they extracted a mile-long cylinder of ice from the hole. The glacier had formed as layer upon layer of snow accumulated year after year. Thus drilling into the ice was tantamount to drilling back through time.

The deepest sections of the core are composed of water that fell as snow 160,000 years ago. Scientists in Grenoble, France, fractured portions of the core and measured the composition of ancient air released from bubbles in the ice.

Instruments were used to measure the ratio of certain isotopes(同位素) in the frozen water to get an idea of the prevailing atmospheric temperature at the time when that particular bit of water became locked in the glacier.

The result is a remarkable unbroken record of temperature and of atmospheric levels of carbon dioxide. Almost every time the chill of an ice age descended on the planet, carbon dioxide levels dropped. When the global temperature dropped 9 ℉ (5 ℃), carbon dioxide levels dropped to 190 parts per million or so. Generally, as each ice age ended and the Earth basked in a warm interglacial period, carbon dioxide levels were around 280 parts per million. Through the 160,000 years of that ice record, the level of carbon dioxide in the atmosphere fluctuated between 190 and 280 parts per million, but never rose much higher—until the Industrial Revolution beginning in the eighteenth century and continuing today.

Questions

8. The underlined word "accumulated" is closest in meaning to _____.
   A. spread out   B. changed
   C. became denser   D. built up
9. The underlined phrase "tantamount to" is closest in meaning to _____.
   A. complementary to   B. practically the same as
   C. especially well suited to   D. unlikely to be confused with
10. The underlined word "remarkable" is closest in meaning to _____.
    A. genuine   B. permanent
    C. extraordinary   D. continuous

Passage 4

Newspaper publishers in the United States have long been enthusiastic users and distributors of weather maps. Although some newspapers that had carried the United States Weather Bureau's national weather map in 1912 dropped it once the novelty had passed, many continued to print the daily weather chart provided by their local forecasting office. In the 1930's, when interest in aviation and progress in air-mass analysis made weather patterns more newsworthy, additional newspapers started or resumed the daily weather map. In 1935, The Associated Press (AP) news service inaugurated(为……举行仪式) its Wire-photo network and offered subscribing newspapers morning and afternoon weather maps redrafted by the AP's Washington, D. C. office from charts provided by the government agency. Another news service, United Press International (UPI), developed a competing photo wire network and also provided timely weather maps for both morning and afternoon newspapers. After the United States government launched a series of weather satellites in 1966, both the AP and UPI offered cloud-cover photos obtained from the Weather Bureau.

In the late 1970's and early 1980's, the weather map became an essential ingredient in the redesign of the American newspaper. News publishers, threatened by increased competition from television for readers' attention, sought to package the news more conveniently and attractively. In 1982, many publishers felt threatened by the new *USA Today*, a national daily newspaper that used a page-wide, full-color weather map as its key design element.

Today's not including information about weather fronts and pressures

<u>attests</u> to the largely symbolic role it played. Nonetheless, competing local and metropolitan newspapers responded in a variety of ways. Most substituted full-color temperature maps for the standard weather maps, while others dropped the comparatively <u>drab</u> satellite photos or added regional forecast maps with pictorial (用图片表示的) symbols to indicate rainy, snowy, cloudy, or clear conditions. A few newspapers, notably *The New York Times*, adopted a highly informative yet less visually prominent weather map that was specially designed to explain an important recent or imminent weather event. <u>Ironically</u>, a newspaper's richest, most instructive weather maps often are comparatively small and inconspicuous.

Questions

11. The underlined word "resumed" is closest in meaning to _____.

  A. began again   B. held back

  C. thought over   D. referred to

12. The underlined phrase "attests to" is closest in meaning to _____.

  A. makes up for   B. combines with

  C. interferes with   D. gives evidence of

13. The underlined word "drab" is closest in meaning to _____.

  A. precise   B. poor

  C. simple   D. dull

14. The author uses the term "Ironically" in the last sentence of the last paragraph to indicate that a weather map's appearance _____.

  A. is not important to newspaper publishers

  B. does not always indicate how much information it provides

  C. reflects how informative a newspaper can be

  D. often can improve newspaper sales

Passage 5

No two comets ever look <u>identical</u>, but they have basic features in common, one of the most obvious of which is a coma. A coma looks like a misty patch of light with one or more tails often streaming from it in the direction away from the Sun.

At the <u>heart</u> of a comet's coma lies a nucleus of solid material, typically no more than 10 kilometers across. The visible coma is a huge cloud of gas and dust that has escaped from the nucleus, which it then surrounds like an extended atmosphere. The coma can extend as far as a million kilometers outward from the nucleus. Around the coma there is often an even larger invisible envelope of hydrogen gas.

The most graphic proof that the grand spectacle of a comet develops from a relatively small and inconspicuous chunk of ice and dust was the close-up image obtained in 1986 by the European Giotto probe of the nucleus of Halley's Comet. It turned out to be a bit like a very dark asteroid, measuring 16 by 8 kilometers. Ices have evaporated from its outer layers to leave a crust of nearly black dust all over the surface. Bright jets of gas from evaporating ice burst out on the side facing the Sun, where the surface gets heated up, carrying dust with them. This is how the coma and the tails are created.

Comets grow tails only when they get warm enough for ice and dust to boil off. As a comet's orbit brings it closer to the Sun, first the coma grows, then two distinct tails usually form. One, the less common kind, contains electrically charged (i. e. , ionized) atoms of gas, which are blown off directly in the direction away from the Sun by the magnetic field of the solar wind. The other tail is made of neutral dust particles, which get gently pushed back by the pressure of the sunlight itself. Unlike the ion tail, which is straight, the dust tail becomes curved as the particles follow their own orbits around the Sun.

Questions

15. The underlined word "identical" is closest in meaning to _____.
    A. equally fast   B. exactly alike
    C. near each other   D. invisible

16. The underlined word "heart" is closest in meaning to _____.
    A. center   B. edge
    C. tail   D. beginning

17. The underlined word "graphic" is closest in meaning to _____.
    A. mathematical   B. popular
    C. unusual   D. vivid

18. The underlined word "distinct" is closest in meaning to _____.
    A. visible   B. gaseous
    C. separate   D. new

Passage 6

Science has long had an uneasy relationship with other aspects of culture. Think of Galileo's 17th century trial for his rebeling belief before the Catholic Church or poet William Blake's harsh remarks against the mechanistic worldview of Issac Newton. The <u>schism</u> between sciences and the humanities has, if anything, deepened in this century.

Until recently, the scientific community was so powerful that it could affort to ignore its critics—but no longer. As funding for science has declined, scientists have attacked "antiscience" in several books, notably Higher Superstition, by Paul Regress, biologist at the University of Virginia, and Norman Leavitt, a mathematician at Rutgers University; and The Demon Haunted World, by Car Satan of Cornell University.

Defenders of science have also voiced their concerns at meetings such as "The Flight from Science and Reason" held in New York City in 1995, and "Science in the Age of (Miss) information", which assembled last June near Buffalo.

Antiscience clearly means different things to different people. Gross and Leavitt find fault primarily with sociologists, philosopher and other academics, that have questioned science's objectivity. Saga is more concerned with those who believe in ghost, creationism and other phenomena that contradict the scientific worldview.

A survey of news stories in 1996 reveals that the antiscience tag has been attached to many other groups as well, from authorities who advocated the elimination of the last remaining stocks of smallpox virus to Republicans who advocated decreased funding for basic research.

Few would dispute that the term applies to the Unabonlber, those manifesto, published in 1995, scorns science and longs for return to a pre-technological utopia. But surely that does not mean environmentalists concerned about uncontrolled industrial growth are antiscience, as an essay in US News &. World Report last May seemed to suggest.

The environmentalists, inevitably, respond to such critics. The true enemies of science, argues Paul Ehrlich of Stanford University, a pioneer of environmental studies, are those who question the evidence supporting global warming, the <u>depletion</u> of the ozone layer and other consequence of industrial growth.

Indeed, some observers fear that the antiscience epithet(表示特性的修饰词) is in danger of becoming meaningless. "The terra 'cantiscience' can lump together too many, quite different things," notes Harvard University philosopher Gerald Holton in his 1993 work Science and Antiscience, "They have in common only one thing that they tend to annoy or threaten those who regard themselves as more enlightened."

Questions

19. The underlined word "schism" in the context probably means _____.
    A. confrontation   B. dissatisfaction
    C. separation   D. contempt
20. What does the underlined word "depletion" may mean?
    A. repletion   B. completion
    C. reception   D. reduction

Passage 7

One of the most interesting paradoxes in America today is that Harvard University, the oldest institution of higher learning in the United States, is now engaged in a serious debate about what a university should be, and whether it is measuring up.

Like the Roman Catholic Church and other ancient institutions, it is asking—still in private rather than in public—whether its past assumptions about faculty, authority, admissions, courses of study, are really relevant to the problems of the 1990's.

Should Harvard or any other university be an intellectual sanctuary, apart from the political and social revolution of the age, or should it be a laboratory for experimentation with these political and social revolutions; or even an engine of the revolution? This is what is being discussed privately in the big clapboard houses of faculty members around the Harvard Yard.

The issue was defined by Walter Lippmann, a distinguished Harvard graduate, several years ago. "If the universities are to do their work," he said, "they must be independent and they must be disinterested... They are places to which men can turn for judgments which are unbiased by partisanship and special interest. Obviously, the moment the universities fall under political control, or under the control of private interests, or the moment they themselves take a

· 120 ·

hand in politics and the leadership of government, their value as independent and disinterested sources of judgment is impaired. "

This is part of the argument that is going on at Harvard today. Another part is the argument of the militant and even many moderate students: that a university is the keeper of our ideals and morals, and should not be "disinterested" but activist in bringing the nation's ideals and actions together.

Harvard's men of today seem more troubled and less sure about personal, political and academic purpose than they did at the beginning. They are not even clear about how they should debate and resolve their problems, but they are struggling with them privately, and how they come out is bound to influence American university and political life in the 1990's.

Questions

21. What does the underlined phrase "an intellectual sanctuary" implies?

    A. a holy place dedicated to a certain god

    B. a temple or nunnery of middle age

    C. a certain place you can hide in and avoid mishaps

    D. a higher learning institution where learners and teachers are free from outside social and political influences

22. What did Walter Lippmann mean by saying "If the universities are to do their work, they must be independent and they must be disinterested..."?

    A. Universities must finance itself if they want to get rid of political influence

    B. Universities must be immune to social and political influences and make independent judgments to function properly

    C. Universities should not be interested in sociology and politics

    D. Universities must be independent from any governmental organs and only serve the interests of other social groups

2. 超纲词或词组在文中的意义

How should we live? Shall we aim at happiness or at knowledge, virtue, or the creation of beautiful objects? If we choose happiness, will it be our own or the happiness of all? And what of the more particular questions that face us: Is it fight to be dishonest in a good cause? Can we justify living in opulence while elsewhere in the world people are starving? If conscripted to fight in a war we do not support, should we disobey the law? What are our obligations to the other creatures with whom we share this planet and to the generations of humans who will come after as?

Ethics deals with such questions at all levels. Its subject consists of the fundamental issues of practical decision making, and its major concerns include the nature of ultimate value and the standards by which human actions can be judged right or wrong.

The terms ethics and morality are closely related. We now often refer to ethical judgments or ethical principles where it once would have been more common to speak of moral judgments or moral principles. These applications are an extension of the meaning of ethics. Strictly speaking, however, the term refers not to morality itself but to the field of study, or branch of inquiry, that has morality as its subject matter. In this sense, ethics is equivalent to moral philosophy.

Although ethics has always been viewed as a branch of philosophy, its all-embracing practical nature links it with many other areas of study, including anthropology, biology, economics, history, politics, sociology, and theology. Yet, ethics remains distinct from such disciplines because it is not a matter of factual knowledge in the way that the sciences and other branches of inquiry are. Rather, it has to do with determining the nature of normative theories and applying these sets of principles to practical moral problems.

Question

The underlined word "opulence" in the first paragraph most probably means
_____.

A. elegance   B. indigence
C. plenty   D. scarcity

【例题解析】本题的答案为选项 C。句中 while 为 conj,意思是"而,然而",表示对比。"while elsewhere in the world people are starving"的意思是:然而世界其他地方的人却在忍饥挨饿。根据词句进行逆向推导可知这里的"we"显然是过着一种衣食无忧的生活。因此,选项 C 的意思与之相吻合,应为正确答案。elegance 意为"雅致,优雅";indigence 意为"贫困,贫寒";scarcity 意为"缺乏"。

Exercise 13

Directions: *In this section, there are five passages. For each passage there are* *some questions or unfinished statements followed by four choices marked A, B, C and D. You should decide on the best choice and mark the corresponding letter on it.*

Passage 1

It is estimated that over 99 percent of all species that ever existed have become extinct. What causes extinction? When a species is no longer adapted to a changed environment, it may perish. The exact causes of a species' death vary from situation to situation. Rapid ecological change may render an environment hostile to a species. Food resources may be affected by environmental changes, which will then cause problems for a species requiring these resources. Other species may become better adapted to an environment, resulting in competition and, ultimately, in the death of a species.

The fossil record reveals that extinction has occurred throughout the history of Earth. Recent analyses have also revealed that on some occasions many species became extinct at the same time—a mass extinction. One of the best-known examples of mass extinction occurred 65 million years ago with the demise of dinosaurs and many other forms of life.

Perhaps the largest mass extinction was the one that occurred 225 million years ago. When approximately 95 percent of all species died, mass extinctions can be caused by a relatively rapid change in the environment and can be worsened by the close interrelationship of many species. If, for example, something were to happen to destroy much of the plankton in the oceans, then the oxygen content of Earth would drop, affecting even organisms not living in the oceans. Such a change would probably lead to a mass extinction.

One interesting, and controversial finding is that extinctions during the past 250 million years have tended to be more intense every 26 million years. This periodic extinction might be due to intersection of the Earth's orbit with a cloud of comets, but this theory is purely speculative. Some researchers have also speculated that extinction may often be random. That is, certain species may be eliminated and others may survive for no particular reason. A species' survival may have nothing to do with its ability or inability to adapt. If so, some of evolutionary history may reflect a sequence of essentially random events.

Questions

1. The underlined word "demise" is closest in meaning to _____ .

A. change   B. recovery

C. help   D. death

2. The underlined word "plankton" may mean _____.

  A. the very small forms of plant and animal life that live in water, especially the sea

  B. the food resources in preventing mass extinction

  C. the organisms that live on the land and those that live in the ocean

  D. certain species could never become extinct

Passage 2

Divorce rates have markedly increased in many countries since World War II and in some countries have been on the increase since the early 20th century. Attitudes toward divorce have changed dramatically in this period, with the general trend toward tolerance of the practice. Although the statistics are highly variable for overall rates, a number of correlations can be drawn between divorce and other factors.

First, divorce rates are affected by national conditions. Historical studies have shown that, in general, fewer divorces occur in times of economic depression and more in times of prosperity or war. The frequency of divorce in the United States, for example, nearly doubled during World War II.

Second, divorce rates are affected by factors related to social circumstances, including ethnic group, religion, class, and economic background. Divorce rates can be expected to be higher in groups that attach fewer stigmas to divorce than in those that attach more. The backgrounds of partners have a more complicated effect on divorce. Studies of racially mixed marriages, for example, show that these may yield specific patterns within specific cultures. One study in the United States suggested far greater stability in marriages of black husbands and white wives than of white husbands and black wives. Such differences no doubt depend on factors derived from sex roles in American society generally, or they may be related to the kinds of people who are most likely to marry outside their group.

Third, divorce rates vary according to the family cycle itself. Many studies have pointed to the fact that the longer a couple has been married, the more likely it is to remain so. Divorce rates are highest among the young, and, if a marriage survives its first few years, there is an increased likelihood that it will continue. Another factor often cited is the presence of children as a determinant to divorce. Empirical studies have shown, however, that this factor is much less significant than commonly believed.

Questions

3. The underlined word "stigma" most probably means _____.
   A. apprehension   B. dishonor
   C. sign   D. token

4. What does the underlined word "empirical" probably mean _____?
   A. something based on impression   B. something learned from others
   C. something based on experience   D. something based on science only

Passage 3

Information systems are a major tool for improving the cost-effectiveness of societal investments. In the realm of the economy, they may be expected to lead to higher productivity, particularly in the industrial and service sectors in the former through automation of manufacturing and related proceeds, in the latter through computer-aided decision making, problem solving, administration, and support of clerical functions. Awareness that possession of information is tantamount to a competitive edge is stimulating the gathering of technical and economic intelligence at the corporate and national levels. Similarly, concern is mounting over the safeguarding and husbanding of proprietary and strategic information within the confines of organizations as well as within national border. Computer crime, a phrase denoting illegal attempts to invade data banks in order to steal or modify records or to release over computer networks software (called a virus) that corrupts data and programs, has grown at an alarming rate since the development of computer communications. In worst case, computer crime is capable of causing large-scale chaos in financial, military, transportation, municipal, and other systems and service, with attendant economic consequences.

The growing number of information-processing applications is altering the distribution of labor in national economies. The deployment of information systems has resulted in the dislocation of labour and has already had an appreciable effect on unemployment in the United States. That country's economic recession during the early 1990s saw thousands of middle-management jobs relinquished, most permanently. The growth of computer-based information systems encourages a change in the traditional hierarchical(等级制度的) structure of management. As heavy automation is reverting production facilities from the labor-intensive nations to industrialized countries, the competitive potential of some of these nations is also likely to suffer an economic setback, at least in the short run. Singapore, a city-state of some three million people, has become very prosperous as giant foreign electronic firms located their manufacturing facilities there. It is bracing against such an economic setback by seeking to become the world's most intensive user and provider of electronic information systems for public services, international commerce and banking, and communications.

Questions

5. What does the underlined word "tantamount" possibly mean _____?

    A. equal   B. same

    C. different   D. likely

6. The underlined word "relinquished" most probably means _____.

    A. given away   B. given in

    3. given out   D. given up

Passage 4

Ours has become a society of employees. A hundred years or so ago only one out of every five Americans at work was employed, i. e., worked for somebody else. Today only one out of five is not employed but working for himself. And when fifty years ago "being employed" meant working as a factory laborer or as a farmhand, the employee of today is increasingly a middle-class person with a substantial formal education, holding a professional or management job requiring intellectual and technical skills. Indeed, two things have characterized American society during these last fifty years: middle-class employees have been the fastest-growing groups in our working population— growing so fast that the industrial worker, that oldest child of the Industrial Revolution, has been losing in numerical importance despite the expansion of industrial production.

Yet you will find little if anything written on what it is to be an employee.

You can find a great deal of very dubious advice on how to get a job or how to get a promotion. You can also find a good deal of work in a chosen field, whether it be the mechanist's trade or bookkeeping. Every one of these trades requires different skills, sets different standards, and requires a different preparation. Yet they all have employeeship in common. And increasingly, especially in the large business or in the government, employeeship is more important to success than the special professional knowledge or skill. Certainly more people fail because they do not know the requirements of being an employee than because they do not adequately possess the skills of their trade; the higher you climb the ladder, the more you get into administrative or executive work, the greater the emphasis on ability to work within the organization rather than on technical abilities or professional knowledge.

Question

7. The underlined word "dubious" most probably means _____.

    A. valuable   B. useful

    C. doubtful   D. helpful

Passage 5

    Acculturation(文化交流，文化移入), which begins at birth, is the process of teaching new generations of children the customs and values of the parents' culture. How people treat newborns, for example, can be indicative of cultural values?In the United States it is not uncommon for parents to put a newborn in a separate room that belongs only to the child. This helps to preserve parents' privacy and allows the child to get used to having his or her own room, which is seen as a first step toward personal independence. Americans traditionally have held independence and a closely related value, individualism, in high esteem. Parents try to instill these prevailing values in their children. American English expresses these value preferences: children should "cut the (umbilical) cord" and are encouraged not to be "tied to their mothers' apron strings." In the process of their socialization children learn to "look out for number one" and to "stand on their own two feet".

    Many children are taught at a very early age to make decisions and be responsible for their actions. Often children work for money outside the home as a first step to establishing autonomy. Nine-or-ten-year-old children may deliver newspapers in their neighborhoods and save or spend their earnings. Teenagers (13 to 18 years) may baby-sit neighbors' homes in order to earn a few dollars a week. Receiving a weekly allowance at an early age teaches children to budget their money, preparing them for future financial independence. Many parents believe that managing money helps children learn responsibility as well as appreciate the value of money.

Questions

8. What does the underlined phrase "cut the cord" and "not to be tied to the apron strings" imply?
   A. Children shouldn't be caught in their mothers' aprons
   B. Children must always wear an apron when they eat
   C. Children should be very dependent on their mothers
   D. Children should be independent from their parents

3. 替代词所指代的内容

The economic depression in the late-nineteenth-century United States contributed significantly to a growing movement in literature toward realism and naturalism. After the 1870's, a number of important authors began to reject the romanticism(浪漫主义) that had prevailed immediately following the Civil War of 1861-1865 and turned instead to realism.

Determined to portray life as it was, with loyalty to real life and accurate representation without idealization, they studied local dialects, wrote stories which focused on life in specific regions of the country, and emphasized the "true" relationships between people. In doing so, they reflected broader trends in the society, such as industrialization, evolutionary theory which emphasized the effect of the environment on humans, and the influence of science.

Realists such as Joel Chandler Harris and Ellen Glasgow depicted life in the South; Hamlin Garland described life on the Great Plains; and Sarah Orne Jewett wrote about everyday life in rural New England. Another realist, Bret Harte, achieved fame with stories that portrayed local life in the California mining camps.

Samuel Clemens, who adopted the pen name Mark Twain, became the country's most outstanding realist author, observing life around him with a humorous and skeptical eye. In his stories and novels, Twain drew on his own experiences and used dialect and common speech instead of literary language, touching off a major change in American prose style.

Other writers became impatient even with realism. Pushing evolutionary theory to its limits, they wrote of a world in which a cruel and merciless environment determined human fate. These writers, called naturalists, often focused on economic hardship, studying people struggling with poverty, and other aspects of urban and industrial life.

Naturalists brought to their writing a passion for direct and honest experience. Theodore Dreiser, the foremost naturalist writer, in novels such as *Sister Carrie*, grimly portrayed a dark world in which human beings were tossed about by forces beyond their understanding or control. Dreiser thought that writers should tell the truth about human affairs, not fabricate romance, and *Sister Carrie*, he said, was "not intended as a piece of literary craftsmanship, but was a picture of conditions."

Question

The underlined word "they" refers to _____.

A. authors   B. dialects

C. stories   D. relationships

【例题解析】本题的正确答案应为选项 A。本段主要谈论的是如何在文学作品中忠实地反映现实生活,其作者显然指代的是文学作品的作者了。

Exercise 14

Directions: *In this section, there are five passages. For each passage there is one or more questions or unfinished statement followed by four choices marked A, B, C and D. You should decide on the best choice and mark the corresponding letter on it.*

Passage 1

For surgery to be curative, it must be performed before the cancer has spread into organs and tissues that cannot be safely removed. Since the late 19th century increasingly radical operations for cancer have become standard. Despite the increasing extent of these procedures, risk has been reduced by improvements in surgical techniques, anesthesiology, and preoperative and postoperative care, especially in the control of infection. Heart-lung pumps, artificial kidneys, and methods of maintaining electrolyte balance and metabolic equilibrium have permitted patients with impaired cardiovascular（心血管）and kidney functions or poor general metabolism to survive cancer surgery.

Major advances have been made in the restoration of structures altered by cancer surgery and in the rehabilitation of people who have undergone radical surgery. Patients undergoing certain surgical procedures for cancer of the colon or rectum（直肠）, for instance, can be equipped with simple devices for the elimination of solid waste. For patients with cancer of the head and neck, the use of grafting methods and of tissue flaps make it possible to apply reconstructive techniques at the time the cancer is removed.

Rehabilitation of the patient also plays an important role. Women who have extensive surgery for breast cancer are given treatment for restoration of muscle tone needed for movement of the arms. Progress has also been made in teaching new mechanisms（机制）of speech to people who have undergone surgical removal of the larynx（喉）.

In addition to saving lives by cut off cancer, surgery also may improve the remaining months or years of life for persons whose cancers cannot be eradicated（切除）, restoring comfort and a sense of usefulness. When severe pain accompanies cancer, surgery may bring relief by severing the nerve pathways that carry the painful sensations. In addition, surgery is sometimes necessary to treat abscesses（脓肿）resulting from either the tumor or infection and to relieve intestinal obstructions（肠道阻塞）.

Surgery is also valuable as a preventive measure in controlling cancer. It may be used to eliminate precancerous conditions in the mouth, chronic ulcers（溃疡）(ulcerative colitis) that may lead to cancer of the colon, and certain precancerous polyps in the colon and rectum. It may be used to remove burn scars that may lead to cancer, precancerous nodules in the thyroid gland, and certain precancerous pigmented moles.

Question

1. The underlined word "It" in the last paragraph refers to _____.

    A. surgery   B. a preventive measure

    C. to remove burn scars   D. that may lead to cancer

Passage 2

    Native Americans from the southern part of what is now United States believed that the universe in which they lived was made up of these separated but related world: the Upper World, the Lower World and This World. In <u>the last</u> there lived humans, most animals, and plants.

This World, a round island resting on the surface of waters, was suspended from the sky by four cords attached to the island at the four cardinal points of the compass. Lines drawn to connect the opposite points of the compass, from north to south and from the east to west, intersected This World to divide it into four wedge-shaped segments. Thus a symbolic representation of the human world was a cross within a circle the shape of This World.

Each segment of This World was identified by its own color. According to Cherokee doctrine, east was associated with the color red because it was the direction of the Sun, the greatest deity(崇拜) of all. Red was also the color of fire, believed to be directly connected with the Sun, with blood, and therefore with life. Finally, red was the color of success. The west was the Moon segment; it provided no warmth and was not life-giving as the Sun was. So its color was black. North was the direction of cold, and so its color was blue (sometimes purple), and it represented trouble and defeat. South was the direction of warmth; its color, white, was associated with peace and happiness.

The southeastern native Americans' universe was one in which opposites were constantly at war with each other, red against black, blue against white. This World hovered somewhere between the perfect order and predictability of the Upper World and the total disorder and instability of the Lower World. The goal was to find some kind of halfway path, or balance, between those other worlds.

Question

2. "The last" in the last sentence of first paragraph refers to _____.

    A. all planets   B. this World

    C. the universe   D. the Upper World

Passage 3

    The environment contains three major natural sources of radiation: radioactive elements in mineral deposits, ultraviolet(紫外线) light from the Sun, and cosmic rays. The carcinogenic(致癌的) potential of radioactive elements and ultraviolet light has been established, while <u>that</u> of highly energetic cosmic radiation remains to be documented. Clearly, chronic exposure to intense sunlight is a major cause of skin cancer in humans; incidence is high in farmers, sailors, and habitual sunbathers. Since the most effective natural screen for ultraviolet light is the natural skin pigment(色素), melanin(人的皮肤、毛发黑色素), and individuals with large amounts of melanin—blacks, for example—are resistant to the carcinogenic effects of ultraviolet light. Fair-complexioned(皮肤白皙) people, on the other hand, are quite susceptible. It is important to point out that the term skin cancer, as it is generally used, includes not only malignant tumors of the nonpigmented cells of the skin but also tumors of the pigmented cells (melanoma). Under the proper conditions ultraviolet light can cause cancer to develop in the very cells that produce the pigment that affords protection from solar radiation.

The environment also contains dangerous ionizing(离子化的) radiation from artificial sources. These include X-rays used for medical diagnosis and therapy, radioactive chemicals, radioactive elements used in atomic reactors, and radioactive fallout arising from the testing of nuclear devices. Home appliances have been known to emit potentially harmful X-rays under certain circumstances, as was the case with some color television sets made during the 1950s. Radiation leaks from improperly constructed or operated microwave ovens can also occur, but the health hazards from such exposures have yet to be established.

Question

3. The underlined word "that" in the first paragraph refers to _____.

    A. ultraviolet light   B. radioactive element

    C. carcinogenic potential   D. cosmic ray

Passage 4

For any given task in Britain there are more men than are needed. Strong unions keep them there in Fleet Street, home of some London's biggest dailies, it is understood that when two unions quarrel over three jobs, the argument is settled by giving each union two. That means 33 per cent over manning, 33 per cent less productivity than could be obtained.

A reporter who has visited plants throughout Europe has an impression that the pace of work is much slower here. Nobody tries too hard. Tea breaks do matter and are frequent. It is hard to measure intensity of work, but Britons give a distinct impression of going at their tasks in a more leisurely way.

But is all this so terrible? It certainly does not improve the gross national product or output per worker. Those observant visitors, however, have noticed something else about Britain. It is a pleasant place.

Street crowds in Stockholm. Paris and New York move quickly and silently heads down, all in a hurry. London crowds tend to walk at an easy pace (except in the profitable, efficient City, the financial district).

Every stranger is struck by the patient and orderly way in which Britons queue for a bus—if the saleswoman is slow and out of stock she will likely say, "Oh dear, what a pity"; the rubbish collectors stop to chat and call the housewives "Luv". Crime rises here as in every city but there still remains a gentle tone and temper that is unmatched in Berlin, Milan or Detroit.

In short, what is wrong with Britain may also be what is right. Having reached a tolerable standard, Britons appear to be choosing leisure over goods.

Question

4. The word "this"(Para 3, Line 1) refers to the fact that _____.

   A. there are more men on any given job than are needed

   B. 33 per cent over-manning leads to 33 per cent less productivity

   C. it is difficult to measure the intensity of work

   D. Britons generally do not want to work too hard

Passage 5

The *Reader's Digest* investigation asked Americans which was the biggest threat to the nation's future—big business, big labor or big government. A whopping 67 percent replied "big government".

Opinion researchers rarely see such a vast change in public attitude. When put in historical perspective, from the time of Franklin Roosevelt's New Deal to the present, the fallen status of government as a protector and benefactor is extraordinary. We've returned to the instinctive American wariness of Washington so common before the Great Depression.

In our poll, taken before the November elections, the overwhelming majority of our respondents wanted to stop or roll back the impact of government. In answer to another question posed by the *Digest*, 79 percent said they wanted either no more than the current level of government services and taxes, or less government and lower taxes.

"It seems to me that we in the middle class bear most of the burden," says Jene Nell Norman 61, a nurse in Dyersburg Tenn, who often wonders about the government's judgment in spending her money.

Of Americans in our sample, 62 percent believe that politician's ethics and honesty have fallen. And what about Congress? Is it doing a good job? Or do members "spend more time thinking about their political futures than passing good legislation?" Across generations, a thumping 89 percent thought the latter. "Congress always seems to be screwing up." says one young Xer.

However, Americans are satisfied with their own lives and jobs. Four of five respondents were "completely" or "somewhat" satisfied. The fibers held up across all ages—including Xers, whom many pundits(学者) have claimed are pessimistic about their belief.

Looking deeper at jobs, we found 70 percent of Americans believe they are about where they should be, given their talents and efforts. This is an issue where age always makes a difference, since older people, who are more established in their ions, tend to be more satisfied, while younger workers are still trying to find the right niche(谋求适当的职务). Sure enough, Xers scored 65 percent, about five points below average.

Questions

5. "Xers" is repeated several times to refer to _____.

    A. accusers   B. younger respondents

    C. college students   D. blue-collar workers

6. "Screwing up"(Last sentence, Para. 5) may be referred to _____.

    A. indecisive in making decisions

    B. benefiting the nation in earnest

    C. making a mess of everything

    D. debating hotly

7. "Political future"(Sentence 3, Para. 5) may be replaced as _____.

    A. the future of the whole nation

    B. people's well-being in the future

    C. a position of higher rank

    D. awareness of consistency in politics

第三节 篇章词汇理解

篇章词汇理解(Banked Cloze)是阅读理解部分中仔细阅读理解的一个必考项目之一,类属于篇章语境中的词汇理解测试。该类试题的出题特点是在Word Bank 里给出多于填空实际所需要的词汇(填空实际需要10个词,Word Bank 提供15个英语单词),供考生根据填空的需要来选用,旨在考查考生在篇章层次的词汇理解能力。该类试题的具体做题方法和做题技巧与第二部分中的完型填空说明大致相同,此处不再赘述。例如:

Inflation and its opposite ___1___ are situations which basically arise from the operations of the law of supply and ___2___. Briefly, this law states that the price of a commodity is determined by the supply of it and the demand for it: if it is in ___3___ supply and many people wish to buy it, the price ___4___ to rise; ___5___, if the supply is bountiful and the demand small, the price tends to fall. When personal incomes rise and credit is easily and cheaply available, the demand for goods is high. In a country like Britain, ___6___ has a large volume of imports, any increase in production to meet increased demand at home causes imports to rise, and unless this is accompanied by an expansion of exports, it has an adverse effect on the country's balance of ___7___. There are also psychological factors. When there is inflation, people fear for the value of their money; there is a ___8___ to withdraw savings in the form of investments in stocks and interest-bearing bonds; and ___9___ to buy houses, land, pictures, antique silver and furniture, and so on, which the buyers hope will at least ___10___ their value and may even appreciate.

A. inflation	E. payments	I. instead	M. adverse
B. which	F. conversely	J. tends	N. retain
C. deflation	G. short	K. demand	O. exports
D. effect	H. tendency	L. volume	

【例题解析】

1. C。因为 inflation 的反义词就是 deflation。这一点文中通过 opposite 一词明确地予以示明。

2. K。英语"供与需"是一个词组,即 supply and demand。

3. G。根据上下文逻辑可知,只有在物资供应不足,且人人都想购买时,物价才有可能上涨。

4. J。道理同上。这里 tend 意为"趋势,倾向"。

5. F。实际上,这句话是与前一句意思相反的一种假设,即"相反的话,否则",物价就会下降。

6. B。这里 which 显然引导的是一个非限制性定语从句。

7. E。payment 意为"支付情况"。根据上文,物价的上涨或下降都与支付问题有着密切的联系。balance of payments 意为"支付平衡"。

8. H。通货膨胀时,人们因担心货币的价值而去提现以股票等形式呈现的投资是一种惯性的做法。因此,在此处填入 tendency 符合题意。

9. I。根据上文,人们把提现的钱用于购买房产等东西,以期保值,即做一件与上述情况相反的事。

10. N。参见8,9解析。

Exercise 15

Directions: *In this section, there are five passages which are followed separately by ten blanks. You are required to select one word for each blank from a list of choices given in a word bank following the passage. Read the passage through carefully before making your choices. Each choice in the bank is identified by a letter. Please mark the corresponding letter for each item with a single line through the center. You may not use any of the words in the bank more than once.*

Passage 1

I strongly believe that it is rather important to be a good listener. And although I have become a better listener than I was ten years ago, I have to ___1___ I'm still only an adequate listener.

Effective listening is more than simply avoiding the bad habit of ___2___ others while they are speaking or finishing their sentences. It's being content to listen to the entire ___3___ of someone ___4___ than waiting impatiently for your chance to ___5___. In some ways, the way we fail to listen is symbolic of the ___6___ we live. We often treat communication as if it were a race. It's almost like our goal to have no gaps between the conclusion of the sentence of the person we are ___7___ with and the beginning of our own. My wife and I were recently at a cafe having lunch, overhearing the conversations ___8___ us. It seemed that no one was really listening to another; ___9___ they were taking turns not listening to one another. I asked my wife if I still did the same thing. With a smile on her face she said, "Only sometimes".

Slowing down your __10__ and becoming a better listener aids you in becoming a more peaceful person. It takes pressure from you. If you think about it, you'll notice that it takes an enormous amount of energy and is very stressful to be sitting at the edge of your seat trying to guess what the person in front of you is going to say so that you can fire back your response.

A. other	E. rather	I. energy	M. thought
B. admit	F. respond	J. responses	N. instead
C. between	G. notice	K. way	O. symbolic
D. interrupting	H. around	L. speaking	

Passage 2

Nowadays in many companies there is a relatively new office __1__ of dress-down Fridays. Yet people still seem to be unsure how to __2__ it. Plus, even dress-down days have their unwritten rules.

Many people want to know if they actually have to dress down. Some people are __3__ doing so or don't think they look their best in casual clothes. Actually, a formal suit does stand out when everyone else is __4__ T-shirts and jeans, so you won't want to ignore the custom entirely. On the other hand, if you like how you look __5__, then do a little of both. Wear jeans or casual pants and a nice shirt and a jacket. This way you won't stand out, and you will still feel __6__.

Don't err too far in the other direction, __7__. Nowhere do dress-down days mean that you can come to work __8__ your dirty clothes. Some clothes are never __9__ to be seen by your fellow workers. Office casual typically means carefully tailored, well-made casual clothes. Leisure suits, sweaters, or exercise clothes are best __10__ at home—or in your locker at the gym.

Dressing up for work can be just as hard as dressing down. Dressy(衣着考究的) office occasions include dinner with a client, dinner at the boss's house, a banquet, a client's party, or an office holiday. For women especially, dressy clothes for business occasions are not the same as dressy clothes for purely social occasions.

A. dressed down	E. either	I. left	M. meant
B. custom	F. wearing	J. comfortable	N. too
C. interpret	G. dressed up	K. making up	O. entirely
D. uncomfortable	H. putting on	L. in	

Passage 3

Old people are always saying that the young are not what they were. The same comment is made from generation to ___1___ and it is always true. It has never been truer ___2___ it is today. The young are better educated. They have a lot of money to ___3___ and enjoy more freedom. They grow up more quickly and are not so ___4___ on their parents. They think more for themselves and do not ___5___ accept the ideas of their elders. Events which the older generation remember vividly are nothing ___6___ than past history. This is as it should be. Every ___7___ generation is different from the one that preceded it. Today the difference is very marked indeed.

The old always ___8___ that they know best for the simple reason that they have been around a bit longer. They don't like to feel that their values are being questioned or threatened. And this is precisely ___9___ the young are doing. They are questioning the assumptions of their elders and disturbing their complacency （满足）. They take leave to doubt that the ___10___ generation had created the best of all possible worlds. What they reject more than anything is conformity.

A. think	E. precisely	I. what	M. blindly
B. spend	F. than	J. assume	N. educated
C. dependent	G. more	K. generation	O. enjoy
D. reason	H. new	L. older	

Passage 4

When your parents advise you to "get an education" in order to ___1___ your income, they tell you only half the truth. What they really ___2___ is to get just enough education to provide manpower for your society, but not so much that you prove an embarrassment to your ___3___.

Get a high school diploma, at least. Without that, you will be occupationally dead unless your name ___4___ to be George Bernard Shaw or Thomas Alva Edison, and you can successfully drop out in grade school. Get a

college degree, if possible. With a B. A. , you are on the launching pad(发射台,
起点). But now you have to start to put on the brakes. If you go for a master's
degree, __5__ it is an M. B. A. , and the famous law of diminishing returns
begins to take __6__ .

A Ph. D. is the highest degree you can get. __7__ for a few specialized
fields such as physics or chemistry __8__ the degree can quickly be turned to
industrial or commercial purposes, if you pursue such a degree in any other field,
you will face a dim future. There are more Ph. D. s __9__ or underemployed(学
非所用的) in this country than any other __10__ of the world.

A. mean	E. part	I. make sure	M. Except
B. happens	F. where	J. education	N. effect
C. degree	G. unemployed	K. raise	O. truth
D. famous	H. diploma	L. society	

Passage 5

A plan is needed for the World Trade Center site but not a big plan. There
are times for building Central Park, and there are times for remedial(补救的)
gardening. Lower Manhattan should not be remade __1__ to some new grand
vision. A framework needs to be put in place and some principles agreed on, and
city life will take its __2__ . "There's no rush" is a phrase often heard in
discussion of the site. Actually, there is a __3__ , because there's a reason why
most cities struck by disaster— __4__ or man-made—generally end up rebuilding
 __5__ or less what was there before. The reason is not a lack of imagination or
will. Rather, while the planners and architects are thoughtfully discussing the
options, decisions are being made on the ground(当场). There is infrastructure
(基础设施) to be __6__ , fire hydrants(消防栓) to be reconnected, materials to
be transported, neighborhood to be knitted back together. And in the absence of
a new plan, the old street pattern emerges by default. And soon it's too __7__ :
the blank slate is no longer blank. Yes, the World Trade Center __8__ offer a
rare opportunity, as many have been __9__ out, but the window of opportunity
will not stay open long. There is no __10__ pressure to build a lot of office
space, since it's as yet unclear how strong the demand will be and how the
current upswing will affect New York...

A. course	E. absence	I. immediate	M. pointed
B. imagination	F. repaired	J. demand	N. demand
C. rush	G. late	K. according	O. transported
D. more	H. site	L. natural	

第四节　快速阅读理解

1. "是非"判断与句子填空

"是非"判断与句子填空类试题属于阅读理解部分中的快速阅读理解范畴。该类试题共分两个部分：句意判断(Statement Judgment)(7句)和完成句子(Sentence Completion)(3句)。该试题要求考生根据文章的内容对所给出的句意做出正误判断和完成所给出的不完整的句子，旨在测试考生的浏览阅读和查读的能力。

2. "是非"判断与句子填空题的出题特点

"是非"判断与句子填空题的出题特点是，前者以综述性或概括性很强的语句归纳文中来自各个不同层面、视角或信息段等的信息大意，要求考生根据已获取的信息进行综合归纳判断，注意，所使用的词语通常不同于原文的语句，后者是把考点落在文中所提到的某些具体的信息上。要求考生在规定的时间内找到相关信息，并对所给出的句子进行正误判断。此外，该试题的篇幅较长，大学英语四级样题的篇幅约为1100余字，大约是阅读理解试题篇幅的3倍。

3. "是非"判断与句子填空题的做题技巧

"是非"判断与句子填空题的做题技巧同仔细阅读理解技巧。例如：

The American Association for the Advancement of Science (AAAS) has just held its annual meeting. One highlight was a session on new techniques for tracking marine animals. Making a living as a fisherman has never been easy. With the continual decline in fish stocks currently under way, it is becoming an even harder way to grind out a living. And it is not only fish that are disappearing, but marine fauna(动物群) generally. In the past 20 years, for example, 90% of leatherback turtles and large predatory fish, such as sharks, have disappeared.

Where and how this is happening has been difficult to say, since the ocean is something of a black box. Things go in, and things come out, but what happens in between is hard to unravel(阐明). According to researchers presenting their work at the AAAS meeting in Seattle, Washington, this is now changing. Today, when many marine biologists swig(大口喝,痛饮) their morning coffee and download their messages, they receive special e-mails from their research subjects. These messages, relayed by a satellite, tell them exactly where their animals have been. This has been made possible thanks to advances in underwater electronic tagging, and it is causing a revolution in marine biology.

One of the leading researchers in oceanic tagging is Barbara Block of Hopkins Marine Station in Pacific Grove, California. She tags blue fin tuna, which are commercially valuable animals that can reach 680kg (1,500lb) in weight, and swim at speeds of up to 80kph (50mph). So far, her group has tagged around 700 blue fins. Many of the tags are surgically implanted, a tricky thing to do while on board a moving boat. These tags archive(存档) their data in memory chips, and are eventually recovered when a fish is caught and butchered. (The tags carry a healthy reward.)

Other tags, though, are fastened to the outside of a fish, and pop off(突然伸出) at a pre-programmed time and date. They then broadcast their results to a satellite. Dr Block's work has shown that blue fin can migrate thousands of kilometers across the Atlantic, ignoring boundaries that have been set to protect stocks in the western Atlantic.

Tagging is also helping David Welch, head of the Canadian government's salmon program, to find out where and why large numbers of the fish are vanishing. He uses small acoustic(传音的) tags (the size of a large multivitamin capsule) that are sewn into the body cavities of salmon. These tags broadcast their signals to microphones on the sea-bed.

Dr Welch can now track where an individual salmon spends its life and watch trends in an entire population. He was surprised to find that most salmon do not die as they leave the river and enter the sea, as previously believed. And he is finding that climatic fluctuations play an important role in determining population.

Dr Welch and his colleagues are planning to install a system of microphones stretching from the coast of Washington state to southeastern Alaska. This could follow the movements of some 250,000 fish—collecting data on their direction of travel, speed, depth and position. If that works, the plan is to extend the system from Baja California in Mexico to the Bering Sea—a project that would involve about 1,000 underwater tracking stations.

Meanwhile, Andrew Read, a marine biologist at Duke University in North Carolina, is following 45 tagged loggerhead turtles. These animals must come to the surface to breathe. When they do so, the tags (which are glued to their shells) talk to the nearest convenient satellite. Dr Read told the meeting that the tracking data he collects are now available online, to allow fishermen to follow the movements of turtles and, if they wish, to modify the deployment of their nets accordingly. Bill Foster, a fisherman from Hatteras, North Carolina, and Dr Read, proposed the project because the Pamlico Sound near Hatteras was closed to large-mesh gill nets (which are dragged behind a boat like a curtain) for four months a year because too many turtles were being caught by accident. Now, the fishermen are helping the researchers, and attaching tags to healthy turtles that are accidentally caught in their nets.

Together, all this work is beginning to fill in the map of marine "highways" used by particular species, and their preferred habitats. It is also showing where particular animals prefer to stay close to the surface, and where they prefer deeper waters. As in the ease of Dr Read's turtles, this is helping scientists to devise ways of protecting rare species in an efficient manner, without interfering too much with the exploitation of common ones.

Larry Crowder, also at Duke University, has overlaid maps of marine highways for loggerhead and leatherback turtles in the Pacific onto those of "longline" fisheries, in which people catch prey on fishing lines that are several kilometers long. Turtles often take the bait on the hooks that these lines carry. Dr Crowder wants to identify the places of greatest danger to these turtles, in the hope that such places will be considered for protection. This need not, he says, mean a ban on fishing, but rather the use of different hooks, and other sorts of gear that are less damaging to turtles. It also turns out that turtles spend 90% of their time within 40 meters of the surface, so setting hooks deeper than this would reduce the chance of catching them accidentally.

Conservationists are now pushing the notion of "ocean zoning". Like the land, parts of the sea—such as turtle highways—would be defined as sensitive, and subject to restrictions on how extractive industries operate. If this idea is ever to work，tagging data will be crucial. And because tagging data come in continually，this could mean that sensitive areas in the ocean could be flexible，changing in both time and space. Enforcing such zones might be difficult. But it would help fish，and other marine fauna，breathe a bit easier. And careful management might leave the fishermen on top as well.

1. The passage mainly talks about marine exploration.

2. Blue fin tuna will possible be caught to make profit.

3. All of rare animals have disappeared in the past 20 years.

4. The purpose of David Welch to tag salmon is to investigate the case of its disappearance.

5. Andrew Read's research concentrates both on loggerhead turtle and shark.

6. Tagging marine animals is the most effective way scientists have ever used to trace the animals for sake of knowing their living habits.

7. Fishermen can get the information on Dr. Read's tracking data now if they like.

8. The salmon population change is affected by _____.

9. All marine scientific researchers' work will be useful in mapping out _____.

10. The tagging data would be critical only when the _____.

【例题解析】

1. Y。参见全文。

2. Y。参见第三段第二句。

3. N。参见第一段第五、六句。

4. Y。参见第五段。

5. N。参见第八段。

6. NG。参见全文。

7. Y。参见第八段第三句。

8. climatic fluctuations。

参见第六段第二句。

9. the marine "highway" used by particular species and preferred habitat。

参见第九段第一句。

10. notion of "ocean zoning" is pushed。

参见第十一段第一句。

Exercise 16

Directions: *In this part, you will have 15 minutes to go over the passage quickly and answer the questions.*

For questions 1-7, mark

Y (*for YES*)   *if the statement agrees with the information given in the passage;*

N (*for NO*)   *if the statement contradicts the information given in the passage;*

NG (*for NOT GIVEN*)   *if the information is not given in the passage.*

For questions 8-10, complete the sentences with the information given in the passage.

Passage 1

We are filled with the attitudes that we acquire from our family, friends, and the environment. They are also in the very fiber of our being, inherited through our genes. Many of our attitudes are fine, while others are less than stellar(优秀的,出色的). However, if we can identify a bad attitude, and make an effort to change it, we will find that life will suddenly respond to our efforts, and bring us good fortune.

A salesperson was intimidated about meeting a very large customer. He felt that the effort was a waste of time since the company was too large and could never be penetrated. As it turned out he didn't get the sale. However, a number of months later he changed his attitude about approaching such larger-type customers. The very day that he changed his attitude, the very same customer, who turned him down, gave him a huge order!

As we can see, the power of a positive or a changed attitude has an amazing way of attracting positive responses from life. We call this phenomenon "life response." Whenever we change our inner attitudes and consciousness, life has a most astounding(令人震惊的) and miraculous way of responding positively and instantaneously(即刻的,瞬间的) in kind. Life brings success, fortune, and joy to those who make this psychological adjustment.

Attitudes About Ourselves, Others, Life

There are three basic types of attitudes: attitudes about ourselves, attitudes towards others and things around us, and attitudes towards life itself. Examples of attitudes about ourselves are having high or low self-esteem, or having a high or low degree of self-confidence. Examples of attitudes about others are our good or bad feelings towards others, trust or mistrust of others, concern or indifference toward others, and so on. Attitudes about life include the feeling that good things will always come our way, or that we are doomed to difficulty and failure. Let's then first consider an example of the benefit of having a positive attitude toward others:

A woman was working as a temporary employee for a large medical organization. For months she complained about others around her. Then she developed a 30-day plan to change her attitude toward those around her. She made the decision to carry out her plan. Almost every day she stayed true to her decision. Just after the 30 day period ended, she was suddenly asked to work full time for the organization; her first full time job in nearly a decade.

As we can see, a positive attitude can overcome a negative situation, and enable positive circumstances to suddenly emerge. We also see how people respond better to our shifts in attitude, as in this case, where another individual is suddenly elevated to a new position in life. As a result of shifting one's attitude, life suddenly, abundantly, miraculously responds in kind; defying all of the normally accepted perceptions of logic of cause and effect, and even space and time.

Negative Expressions Attracts Negative Responses

Whereas we see that positive improvements in attitudes attract positive responses from life, sudden negative attitudes attract the reverse. For example, if one speaks negatively about another person or about a situation or circumstance, it tends to suddenly attract negative circumstances from life. Consider this example:

A man "A" met a fellow instructor "B" before a class he was to perform that day. They discussed problems they had in previous classes with certain students in certain situations. In particular, A kept talking about how the students were difficult at a certain client(客户) he worked at. For a long time the instructor A had not had such problems, though that morning he complained negatively about such incidents in the past. That day, and in his next two classes, A had continuous difficulties with students in his class.

The best approach is to avoid all negative expressions towards others, things, and situations. Negative expressions are reflections of a wanting attitude, habit, or opinion, which has the tendency to suddenly attract negative responses from life. It can even destroy work.

People You Think Negative Of May Be Your Allies

One interesting related point about negative feelings toward others is that you might find that the very person you have these negative feelings towards are often the very keys to your success in an activity you are involved in! Consider this example:

An instructor stopped having negative feelings toward certain individuals who attended his classes. He then suddenly found that instead of avoiding them and feeling negative toward them, these individuals were helping him in ways he never thought possible in the class. For example, a few of the students helped him understand how to better interact with certain students in the class; or were telling him what training resources were available to him at the company, something very useful to other students; or were informing him what were some underlying issues of the participants, also helpful to conducting a good class, etc. This information was very useful to him in conducting the classes. Thus, these formerly "bothersome" students became the very keys to the success of his classes!

Attitudes about Things, Objects

Now here's an example that show how one person changed a negative attitude about some physical thing and, as a result, saw a positive outcome.

"In a department store while I was paying to the cashier I noticed that the currency I was giving was a torn one but fixed by a transparent adhesive tape. I had other good currency. But my attitude was that if the cashier accepts the currency let me part with it. The cashier accepted it.

After returning home when I reexamined my attitude, I felt ashamed of myself and felt very guilty for my conduct. I at once rushed back to the department store and explained to the cashier that I had deliberately passed a torn currency to him and that I wanted to replace it with a good currency and profusely(大方地) apologized for my petty mentality. Back home I received a long over-due payment from a client of mine who was avoiding the payment."

That is the power of a changed attitude to attract positive responses from life! There are dozens of major attitudes that each of us have. Examples of attitudes are whether one is—considerate, cooperative, expansive, open-minded, mature, persistent, responsive, respectful, caring, sincere, serious, truthful, and dozens of others. To truly understand where our attitudes are lacking, we would need to measure each of them, discover which ones we are lacking in, and make the concerted, determined effort to improve ourselves in those areas.

1. We can have good fortune if we make an effort to change our bad attitude into good one.

2. The purpose of the passage is to tell us that everybody should hold a positive attitude no matter what has happened otherwise bad fortune would catch up with us.

3. Attitude, either positive or negative, may be nothing important to one person but extremely crucial to others.

4. The woman mentioned in Paragraph 5 never had a full time job in about past 10 years.

5. Negative expressions, or rather attitude, can always attract negative responses.

6. Positive expressions may tend to sudden attraction of positive response from life.

7. The reason why the writer receives a long over-due payment from his client is a coincidence.

8. The salesperson failed the first time when he has business with a large company because of _____.

9. Instructor's or A's mood was affected by _____.

10. That the "bothersome" students became the keys to the success of his class is just because _____.

Passage 2

Decoding and comprehension are the two main tasks for reading: In English learning, the elements, which influence the reading are linguistic knowledge, cultural background knowledge, language skills, and intelligent elements (the abilities of thought such as motivation, purpose, emotion and control). Mastering linguistic knowledge of phonetics, vocabulary and grammar is helpful to decode the word symbols. However, in the process of reading, many Chinese students already possess the above knowledge, but they still cannot comprehend the texts completely, so understanding the cultural content of what one reads is a crucial factor in reading comprehension. Because language is the carrier of culture, people's words and deeds reflect certain cultural connotation（内涵）consciously or unconsciously. Every social communication possesses its own certain thought pattern, value, custom, and way of life, for "The influence of background to comprehension is larger than language knowledge." Many studies indicate that without sufficient background knowledge of social culture, the readers cannot comprehend the deep meaning of texts.

The Role of Cultural Knowledge in Reading Comprehension

Along with the development of Applied Linguistics and Psycholinguistics, the American scholar, Goodman negated（否定）the traditional reading theory and posed a "psycholinguistic reading model", which considers that reading is not the process of passive decoding and reading literally any more. Rather it is the process of active "guessing—confirming" and interaction between the readers and the reading contents.

Reading comprehension is a complex process of the interaction between the writer's language and the readers' prior background knowledge or memory schemata. It is also true that in the reading process, sometimes we cannot read behind the lines except by the help of background knowledge of culture, because the meanings of words are acquired in a certain circumstance of culture. Therefore, if a student does not know about the English culture, such as histories, values, mode of thinking, customs, religion and life style, he may fail to understand the exact meaning of the texts.

The Cultural Background Knowledge of and the Reading Comprehension of English

For a long time, in China, English teaching has just focused on the language forms and ignored the effect of background knowledge of culture. As the carrier of culture, the cultural background of language is rather extensive. Lacking of the necessary cultural background may hinder people from comprehending language. For instance, when the President Reagan took up his post, an American told a Chinese teacher: "the United States has gone from peanuts to popcorn." The syntax of this sentence is very simple. However, the Chinese teacher did not understand the sentence at that time until her friend explained to her that former president Jimmy Carter owned a big peanut farm while the present president Reagan is an actor and people eat popcorn while they watch TV. She suddenly realized the real humorous meaning of this sentence.

I. Historical Culture

Historical culture refers to the culture that is formed by the developing process of certain history and social heritage which varies between nations at often times. In the process of cross-cultural reading, we often meet the comprehension barriers that are caused by such differences of historical cultures. For example: At a science museum you can feel your hair stand on end as harmless electricity passes through your body. The phrase one's hair stands on end is an idiom, from a criminal's expression. In 1825, an Englishman named Robert was sentenced to death by hanging for stealing horses. While waiting for his execution at the gallows(绞刑台), Robert was extremely scared, the result of which made his hair stand straight up. Therefore, in English, one's hair stands on end means fear. The writer uses this idiom to emphasize that the museum is very weird and strange. However, if Chinese students do not know this idiom, they may fail to understand its idiomatic meaning over and above the direct meaning.

II. Regional Culture

Regional culture, here, refers to the culture that can be shaped by natural conditions and geographical environment of an area. These effects on culture may lend themselves to creating comprehension barriers to Chinese students of English reading. For example, British poet Shelley's poem "Ode to the West Wind" compares the west wind to the warm and delightful wind that brings forth spring. However, to Chinese people, the west wind not only means cold but also means declining and depressed.

III. Social Culture

Language is an important component of culture, the existence and development of language are influenced by society, and the social phenomenon and vocabulary of a certain historical periods reflect the objective history of society. Such vocabulary may confuse foreign readers. For instance, when American President Nixon was in his second term of office, Watergate became a well-established and common term. It stands for a political scandal in the Nixon era associated with burglarizing an office of the Democrat Party located at the

Watergate Hotel in Washington. Elements within the Nixon administration created a large number of euphemisms（委婉说法）to hide the scandal. For example, intelligence gathering replaces eavesdropping（偷听）, plumber for eavesdropper. Chinese students may have difficulty in understanding these words.

IV. Religious Culture

Religious culture is an important component in the lives of many human beings. It refers to the culture that is formed by religious belief of nation and can be embodied in the cultural differences of taboo of different nations. Confucianism, Taoism and Buddhism are three main religions of China, which deeply influence Chinese people. On the contrary, many people living in European based and/or founded cultures believe in Christianity—or have been seriously influenced by Christian values. They believe that a single God created and organized the world. Because of differences of religious culture, Chinese students can misunderstand English reading, at times. For example, a sentence in the article "Why Measure Life in Heartbeats" is that I believe, because of my religious faith, that I shall "return to father" in an after life that is beyond description. Many Chinese readers comprehend an after life in the sentences as the next life. The reason of this misunderstanding is the differences of the two religious cultures. The next life is the term of oriental Buddhism, which refers to the samaras（翼果）. On the contrary, Christianity does not have this concept, considering that after the death of human being, his soul will stay in Heaven or Hell and will not disappear. Therefore, they do not have the saying of the next life. So according to its religious background, an after life refers to the time after people's death.

Again, there is a need to emphasize cultural differences as being potentially extensive and complex. In the process of English reading, at times, we should focus on the understanding of cultural background to get a deeper understanding of the whole text.

1. The passage holds the opinion that effective reading comprehension based on enough knowledge in culture, background, history as well as religions.
2. The background influence on understanding efficiency is more important than language knowledge.
3. English culture, like histories, values, mode of thinking is critical to reading

comprehensive efficiency.

4. Historical culture here mainly denotes certain history and social heritage that are different from nation to nation.

5. Besides the influential elements on effective reading comprehension, the writer also tell the readers that the knowledge of the various cultures is "musts" for language learners too.

6. Social culture is more important than other cultures.

7. In order to have a good command of a foreign language, it is equally important to know some knowledge about the culture concerned.

8. English teaching now in China realizes the importance of _____.

9. Regional culture is different from other cultures in that it shaped by _____.

10. Watergate, a well-established term for a political scandal in the Nixon area, is a good case in point _____.

Passage 3

Moves by the central banks of the United States and Japan have been the object of attention all over the world during the past week. First came the Bank of Japan's announcement on the 19th, in the face of currency deflation and an ongoing drop in commodity prices, that funds would be injected into the banking system with the aim of pushing interest rates down to zero and of maintaining a zero-interest policy until consumer prices start to rise again. Then came the U. S. Federal Reserve's decision to cut interest rates by 0.5 percentage points; this was the Fed's third interest-rate reduction in three months, but the size of the cut was less than the financial markets had expected and Wall Street reacted with disappointment and selling. Stock prices fell, with the Dow Jones index dropping below 9,300 points at one time before a resurgence(复苏) of buying sentiment turned prices upward again, bringing stability to European markets as well. After experiencing this kind of instability in the financial markets, along with the moves by the central banks of the two economic powers, there appeared a certain psychology of apprehension(见解,理解) about the prospects of global economics and finance. What the people of the world are worried about is to do the bear markets in the U. S. , Japan, and Europe presage(预感) a turn toward economic recession? More importantly, are the world's two leading economies, the U. S. and Japan, moving simultaneously toward recessions that will drag the entire global economy down with them?

That the U. S. economy is showing its first signs of weakness in 10 years cannot be doubted. In its statement about the interest-rate reduction last weak, the Fed emphasized that the U. S. economy would remain weak for the foreseeable future and that a further interest-rate cut was not excluded from the realm of possibility. The "anti-wealth effect" of a possible reduction in consumer spending brought on by the recent stock market weakness has been the object of especially intense attention. Judging from economic indexes released by the U. S. government, industrial production has fallen for five months in a row and the equipment utilization ratio has dropped to its lowest level in nine years...

In its cover story this week, *The Economist*, one of the world's best news weeklies, addressed the question of whether the world can avoid economic recession, giving voice to some extent the widespread concerns in the international community about the world's economic prospects at a time of instability in financial markets and of the cutting of interest rates by the American and Japanese central banks. In truth, at this time of increasingly deep economic and trade globalization and global financial market linkage, the stock market instability and economic weakness in the U. S. and Japan, which together account for 46% of total world output, could easily and quickly infect other countries. This is especially true because these two economic powers have not encountered simultaneous economic recessions since the time of the energy crisis in the early 1970s; and in the past 10 years, as the Japanese economy sank into a slump(沼地), the U. S. economy experienced its longest period of prosperity ever. Now, judging from current indexes, the Japanese economy remains stuck in its morass(困境) while the American economy may be headed for a "hard landing." However, housing starts, consumer confidence, and other indexes are still moving in a direction that gives cause for optimism; and so long as there is no misstep in macroeconomic policy, the American economy will not necessarily encounter an appreciable(可觉察的) recession. On Mar. 22 Horst Kohler, managing director of the International Monetary Fund, emphasized that the probability of the U. S. sinking into economic recession this year is under 25%, and this should be considered a fair assessment.

However that may be, it can be said with certainty that the international economy is not as strong this year as it was in 2000. The global economic growth rate reached 4.8% last year, the highest level in 16 years. The IMF, which originally predicted that the world economy would expand at a rate of 4.2% this year, has decided to reduce its forecast by almost a full percentage point, to 3.4%. Last week, Merill Lynch pushed its own forecast down to 2.4%. Asia is being influenced by this situation; and except the Philippines, where the economy is benefiting from political stability; the company has also adjusted its forecast for most of the other countries of the region downward as well. According to its forecast, Taiwan will maintain a growth of 4.3%, lower only to Singapore's 4.45% among the "Four Little Dragons of Asia." At the same time, the Council of Economic Planning and Development points out that the speed of the domestic and external downturn will be faster than originally expected; the domestic economic growth for the first quarter is projected at only about 3%, and in the second half of the year the economic recovery is expected to slow down further; with this factor, plus a sharp increase in the unemployment rate, it is obvious that the deterioration(恶化) in the internal and external environments will have some effect.

At the present time, with the Central Bank's monetary policy generally maintaining a loose-money situation via continued reductions in the interest rate and with the interest rate of the New Taiwan dollar depreciating along with the Japanese yen, the main question that merits our attention is whether or not other Asian currencies will evidence a competitive depreciatory situation. Asian stock markets turned in the worst performance in the world last year. This year they have become relatively stable. At the same time, Taiwan's economic and financial authorities are obviously attempting to work on the major sectors that constitute the national income account in the hope of revitalizing(使恢复元气) economic growth. Aside from this, it may not be possible to boost private consumption at a time when the unemployment rate is rising; but if the implementation of the two-day weekend this year can have an active effect in developing domestic tourist and leisure activities, it may be able to create new opportunities. Finally, viewed from the economic level, the current weakness of the economy also presents opportunities for readjustment and reform, an example of which is provided by the mergers(合并)of private enterprises which have occurred recently. Financial reform, especially, will admit of no delay.

1. The passage mainly talks about the far-reaching financial problems of the world.

2. The interest-rate reduction was expected much more than what had been done in fact.

3. People of the world are very disappointed about the world economic situation and held pessimistic attitude to it.

4. The world economic situation fluctuation is mainly under the impact of economic tendency of America and Japan.

5. If there were no other problems with American macro-economic policy, its economic situation would be improved soon.

6. All countries in the world are suffering from economic recessions and no one is an exception.

7. The implementation of two-day-weekend is an effective way to encourage economic revival.

8. The America and Japan are moving simultaneously toward recessions that will drag the entire global economy down with them, but American economy is _____.

9. The highest level of the global economic growth rate in 16 years is _____.

10. Viewing from the economic level, the current weakness of economy also present _____.

Passage 4

Hypnosis(催眠术) is an intriguing and fascinating process. A trance-like (恍惚状的) mental state is induced in one person by another, who appears to have the power to command that person to obey instructions without question. Hypnotic experiences were described by the ancient Egyptians and Greeks, while references to deep sleep and anesthesia(麻醉) have been found in *the Bible* and in the Jewish *Talmud*. In the mid-1700s Franz Mesmer, an Austrian physician, developed his theory of "animal magnetism", which was the belief that the cause of disease was the "improper distribution of the invisible magnetic fluid". Mesmer used water tubs and magnetic wands to direct these supposed fluids to his patients. In 1784, a French commission studied Mesmer's claims, and concluded that these cues were only imagined by patients. However, people continued to believe in this process of "mesmerism（催眠术）" and it was soon realized that successful results could be achieved, but without the need for magnets and water.

The term hypnotism was first used by James Braid, a British physician who studied suggestion and hypnosis in the mid-1800s. He demonstrated that hypnosis differed from sleep, that it was a physiological response and not a result of secret powers. During the same period, James Esdaile, a Scottish doctor working in India, used hypnotism instead of anesthetic in over 200 major surgical operations, including leg amputations（截肢）. Later that century a French neurologist（神经学家）, Jean Charcot, successfully experimented with hypnosis in his clinic for nervous disorders.

Since then, scientists have shown that the state of hypnosis is a natural human behavior, which can affect psychological, social and/or physical experiences. The effects of hypnotism depend on the ability, willingness and motivation of the person being hypnotized. Although hypnosis has been compared to dreaming and sleepwalking, it is not actually related to sleep. It involves a more active and intensive mental concentration of the person being hypnotized. Hypnotized people can talk, write and walk about and they are usually fully aware of what is being said and done.

There are various techniques used to induce hypnosis. The best known is a series of simple suggestions repeated continuously in the same tone of voice. The subject is instructed to focus their attention on an object of fixed point, while being told to relax, breathe deeply, and allow the eyelids to grow heavy and close. As the person responds, their state of attention changes, and this altered state often leads to other changes. For example, the person may experience different levels of awareness, consciousness, imagination, memory and reasoning or becoming more responsive to suggestions. Additional phenomena may be produced or eliminated such as blushing, sweating, paralysis, muscle tension or anesthesia. Although these changes can occur with hypnosis, none of these experiences is unique to it. People who are very responsive to hypnosis are also more responsive to suggestions when they are hypnotized. This responsiveness increases during hypnotism. This explains why hypnosis takes only a few seconds for some, whilst other people cannot be easily hypnotized.

It is a common misunderstanding that hypnotists are able to force people to perform criminal or any other acts against their will. In fact, subjects can resist suggestions, and they retain their ability to distinguish right from wrong. This misunderstanding is often the result of public performances where subjects perform ridiculous or highly embarrassing actions at the command of the hypnotist. These people are usually instructed not to recall their behavior after re-emerging from the hypnotic state, so it appears that they were powerless while hypnotized. The point to remember, however, is that these individuals chose to participate, and the success of hypnotism depends on the willingness of a person to be hypnotized.

Interestingly there are different levels of hypnosis achievable. Thus deep hypnosis can be induced to allow anesthesia or surgery, childbirth or dentistry. This contrasts to a lighter state of hypnosis, which deeply relaxes the patient who will then follow simple directions. This latter state may be used to treat mental health problems, as it allows patients to feel calm while simultaneously (同时地) thinking about distressing feelings or painful memories. Thus patients can learn new responses to situations or come up with solutions to problems. This can help recovery from psychological conditions such as anxiety, depression or phobias. Sometime after traumatic incidents memory of the incidents may be blocked. For example some soldiers develop amnesia (loss of memory) as a result of their experiences during wartime. Through hypnosis these repressed (抑制) memories can be retrieved and treated. A variation of this treatment involves age regression (退化), when the hypnotist takes the patient back to a specific age. In this way patients may remember events and feelings from that time, which may be affecting their current well-being.

Physicians also have made use of the ability of a hypnotized person to remain in a given position for long periods of time. In one case, doctors had to graft skin onto a patient's badly damaged foot. First, skin from the person's abdomen was grafted onto his arm; then the graft was transferred to his foot. With hypnosis, the patient held his arm tightly in position over his abdomen for three weeks, then over his foot for four weeks. Even though these positions were unusual, the patient at no time felt uncomfortable!

Hypnosis occasionally has been used with witnesses and victims of crime to enable people to remember important clues, such as a criminal's physical appearance or other significant details that might help to solve a crime.

However, as people can both lie and make mistakes while hypnotized, the use of hypnotism in legal situations can cause serious problems. Also hypnosis cannot make a person divulge(泄露) secret information if they don't want to. This was confirmed by the Council on Scientific Affairs of American Medical Association, which in 1985 reported that memories refreshed through hypnosis may include inaccurate information, false memories, and confabulation (facts and fantasy combined).

1. Hypnosis was once used successfully in medical world.
2. According to the writer, hypnosis is a result of secret power.
3. Hypnosis can be fully effective on any people who receive it.
4. During the process of hypnosis, the subjects would fall in a sound sleep.
5. Hypnotists are able to force people to commit crimes or any other acts against their will.
6. Both deep and lighter hypnosis can be used in medical treatment.
7. After surgery, hypnosis may be used to make drugs unnecessary.
8. As a natural human behavior, the state of hypnosis can affect _____.
9. The best known technique to induce hypnosis is _____.
10. What people worried about hypnosis is _____.

Passage 5

It is usually a bad sign when a firm looks outside its own ranks for its next boss. The revolt by shareholders of Walt Disney demonstrates if nothing else, how difficult it is for a public company's owners to remove a boss who does not want to go. Despite 43% of shareholders withholding their votes from Michael Eisner in the board election at the firm's annual meeting on March 3rd, the long-serving boss retained his position as chief executive, although he relinquished (让出) his position as chairman in what will sorely be an unsuccessful attempt to placate(得到谅解) his opponents.

Yet almost as hard as getting rid of a chief executive is the task of finding a suitable replacement, such has been the dominance of Mr. Eisner at Disney that, when he finally goes, the company may struggle to find a successor within the cowed ranks of its top management. But Disney is by no means alone in failing to groom(推荐) a new leader from its in-house talent pool. ABB is a multinational engineering business with some 115,000 employees in around 100 countries. Yet not one of these employees is deemed capable of running the company. ABB announced last week that its next chief executive will be an outsider. Fred Kindle, currently the boss of Sulzer, a much smaller Swiss engineering business, will join Zurich-based ABB on September 1st and take over as chief executive from Jurgen Dormann in January.

ABB used a firm of head-hunters, Egon Zehnder, to carry out "a thorough and careful search and evaluation". It took a year to come up with half a dozen candidates, some of them internal, some external. The winner has an MBA and four years' experience with McKinsey, a consulting firm with a decidedly mixed record among Switzerland's leading firms.

Choosing an outsider as chief executive is more common in America than it is in Europe. Coca-Cola recently announced that its boss, Douglas Daft, will be retiring at the end of this year and, more controversially, that it will employ a firm of head-hunters to carefully consider external candidates along with the internal candidate in Steve Heyer. Given that Mr. Heyer only joined the company in 2001—from AOL Time Warner—all the candidates are, in effect, outsiders.

Yet even in America, this is still the exception, not the rule. Recent regime changes at the top of other big companies have followed the more traditional pattern. This week, Lockheed Martin said that its boss, Vance Coffman, will step down on August 6th to be replaced by Robert Stevens, currently the defense company's chief operating officer, while ExxonMobil, by promoting Rex Tillerson, its head of production, to president last week, suggested that he is being groomed to take over from Lee Raymond, the current chief executive. Both Mr. Stevens and Mr. Tillerson are long-time employees of the firms that they are in line to lead.

Every one of the top ten (nine of them American) on the list of the world's most admired companies—admittedly, not an infallible(确实可靠的) yardstick of corporate merit—in the latest issue of *FORTUNE* magazine has a boss who was appointed from inside. None of them has spent less than 20 years with their current employer. The bosses of the top three British firms on the list (Tosco, BP and Shell) had notched(搭) up between them almost a century of employment with their respective firms. The first company on the world-wide list about to break that mould is 11th-placed Coca-Cola. HUNTING FOR

CHARISMA Boards have traditionally turned to outsiders when their companies have been in trouble. Scandal-hit firms such as Tyco and WorldCom probably had no choice—any internal appointment would have been viewed with too much suspicion, not least by investors and regulators. But in several less dramatic cases the injection of fresh blood has worked. Lou Gemtner, brought into IBM from RJR Nabisco, famously converted a failing manufacturer of mainframe computers into a thriving IT-services business. Chuck Lueier, of consultants Booz Allen Hamilton, has examined the performance of insiders and outsiders over time and found that, in general, outside chief executives do very well in the early part of their tenure(在职期间) and very badly in the latter part. Insiders have a "remarkably even" performance over time. Outsiders are good at doing the rapid cost-cutting and divestment often needed by firms in trouble, but they are less good at building and sustaining long-term growth, says Mr. Lucier.

Michael Eisner's track record at Disney is a bit like this, argues Mr. Lucier. Hired from outside in 1984 to be chief executive, Mr. Eisner had some good years followed by a lot of bad ones, exacerbated(使烦恼) by the death in 1994 of Frank Wells, his trusted operational chief, in a helicopter crash.

In recent years, it has become almost a matter of course for boards at least to look outside for their next leader, even if most still decide, in the end, to pick an insider. One of the reasons for this, says Dayton Ogden, a head-hunter with Spencer Stuart and co-author of *CEO SUCCESSION* (OUP, 2000), is "to benchmark their insiders". High-tech firms (not all of them struggling), such as Motorola, Hewlett-Packard and Yahoo, have led the way in appointing outside chief executives.

In *SEARCHING FOR A CORPORATE SAVIOUR* (Princeton University Press, 2002), Rakesh Khurana, a Harvard Business School professor, suggests that this is part of a growing "irrational quest for charismatic(有感召力的) chief executives". Mr. Khurana argues that the process for finding a chief executive from outside (which invariably involves head-hunters) is so flawed that it "frequently fails to hire the best people available" and "tends to produce leaders with almost identical social, cultural, and demographic characteristics." Spencer Stuart's Mr. Ogden says that this is "ballocks(胡说八道)".

Roselinde Torres, US president of Mercer Delta Consulting, a firm that advises companies on chief-executive succession, suggests that boards are being tempted to look outside because they can more easily fantasies about the charisma of unknowns with great resumes than they can about the all too-familiar insiders they meet in the lifts. But she finds that chief executives fail most often when they "cannot provide the contextual stuff", the right networks and culture within the company—a particularly difficult task for an outsider.

One way to resolve the outsider-insider dilemma is to look for an outsider with inside knowledge of the business. Disney may yet find just such a person to succeed Mr. Eisner. If Comcast, the 148 cable-TV firm which has launched a hostile bid for Disney, succeeds in taking over the firm, it is likely to put Stephen Burke in charge of the acquired Disney operations. Mr. Burke joined Comcast in 1998, after spending 12 years working for Disney. He is a classic "insider-outsider", a man with experience of the company, but with a long enough absence from it to shake off much of the baggage that insiders bring to the top job. Perhaps if Disney shareholders want a solution to the unresolved issue of Mr. Eisner's succession, they could do worse than vote in favor of the Comcast bid.

1. Disney is just one of many U.S. companies to try to find an outsider to chair the company board.
2. Head-hunting firms find it profitable to get right replacement for the big company bosses.
3. Mr. Heyer is capable as he used to work for such a big company as AOL.
4. Companies in trouble would tend to find an outsider to rearrange the business.
5. There are many showcases that outsiders would do better than the previous leadership.
6. Outsiders and insiders have their strengths and weaknesses in running the company at different stages.
7. High-tech companies arc more open to the choice of leaders from outside.
8. The way suggested in the passage to resolve the outsider-insider dilemma is

_____.

9. ABB's new chief executive will be an outsider who has _____.
10. According to Rakesh Khurana, it is unwise to get an outsider as the chief executive with almost _____.

第二部分　综合测试解题技巧与技能训练

第一节　完型填空

　　完型填空为大学英语综合测试形式之一,主要目的是测试考生综合运用语言的能力。该部分试题共有20道选项填空题,占试题分值的10%,涉及到语言应用的各个方面。该类试题的选材通常是考生们熟悉、难度适中的短文,要求考生在全面理解短文内容的基础上选择最佳答案,使短文的意思和结构恢复完整。

1. 完形填空题的出题特点与考试重点

　　完形填空题的出题特点是选项的设计建立在特定语言环境的基础上,即考生必须在充分理解短文的基础上才能准确地做出恰当的选择。该类试题出题的侧重点通常落在逻辑推理、句子结构、惯用法、语法和语用等方面。

2. 完形填空题解题方法及技巧

　　完形填空题的解题方法及技巧如下:
　　(1)了解大意,先易后难。即做题时应先跳过空白,通读全文,了解短文的大意,尽可能多地获取信息,特别是文章的开首和结尾部分。因为文章的开头第一句和最后一句常分别提示全文的基本内容和总结文章的大意,而且大多不设置填空题,这对理解全文起着关键的作用。做题要先易后难,如遇有考查语法或惯用法填空题,不必通过上下文推敲,只看本句,利用已掌握的知识,来推敲并确定正确答案,然后以其为突破口,弄通与此句有关的上下文意思,完成其余试题部分。
　　(2)依据语意,推理判断。即做题时,要参照文章的整体和选项所处的语言环境,根据上下文的语境、逻辑关系、情节发展、因果关系等确定正确选项。切忌撇开语境选答案。
　　(3)顺水推舟,前呼后应。短文中的每个语句都不是孤立存在的,而是上下关联,相互依存的。如果第一题选对了,第二题就不难解了。此外,有些选题必须参照上下文的暗示才能做出正确的选择。如果只把理解思路限制在短文的局部句子的水平上,很容易造成判断失误。

(4) 仔细推敲,认真检查。做完试题目后,必须对各题进行认真的检查:把选定的答案纳入原文中,从头至尾检查一遍,仔细推敲选择的答案,看看是否正确,有没有把握不定或似是而非的地方,是否符合上下文的逻辑,是否符合科学道理或故事情节的发展规律等。例如:

Inflation is an economic condition in ___1___ prices for consumer goods ___2___, and the ___3___ of money or purchasing power decreases. There are three important causes of inflation. The first and most important cause may be excessive government spending. For example, in order to ___4___ a war or carry ___5___ social programs, the government may spend more money than it has received through taxes and other revenue(税收), thus creating deficit. In order to ___6___ this deficit, the Treasury Department can simply, ___7___ the money supply by issuing more paper money to ___8___ the debts of government. This increase in the money supply will cause the value of the dollar to ___9___ decrease. The second cause of inflation occurs when the money supply increases faster than the supply of goods ___10___ people have more money, they will run out to buy popular goods ___11___ televisions and computers, for example, and a shortage will result. Industry will then produce more at higher prices, to ___12___ demand. ___13___, if people think that the prices of popular goods are going up, they will buy and even borrow money at high ___14___ rates to pay for them. Finally, if labor unions demand that workers' wages ___15___ to ___16___ the high cost of living, industry will meet this demand and add other costs of production on to the ___17___. ___18___ summary, all of these causes can ___19___ inflationary problems that can affect the welfare of a nation. However, of these three causes, ___20___ government spending may be the most important.

1. A. that   B. which   C. this   D. what
2. A. raise   B. lower   C. increase   D. decrease
3. A. value   B. price   C. cost   D. spending
4. A. finance   B. offer   C. pay   D. fight
5. A. off   B. out   C. on   D. away
6. A. compensate B. accomplish   C. exchange   D. offset
7. A. spend   B. extend   C. expand   D. explore
8. A. mend   B. meet   C. respond   D. return
9. A. automatically B. timely   C. exceedingly D. excessively

10. A. If	B. Whether	C. Though	D. For fear that
11. A. as	B. of	C. like	D. except
12. A. satisfy	B. supply	C. plenty	D. comply
13. A. However	B. Otherwise	C. Nevertheless	D. Furthermore
14. A. interests	B. interesting	C. interested	D. interest
15. A. should	B. be increased	C. increase	D. increased
16. A. protest	B. impose	C. cover	D. restrict
17. A. consumer	B. controller	C. manager	D. employer
18. A. On	B. At	C. In	D. By
19. A. result	B. invent	C. discover	D. create
20. A. accessible	B. excessive	C. productive	D. processing

【例题解析】

1. B。根据句子结构判断,该缺项是一个引导定语从句的关系代词,选项 C "this"和选项 D"what"不能用于引导定语从句;选项 A"that"虽然可用 于引导定语从句,但不能放在前置介词之后。因此,只有选项 B 才符合 句意,应为正确答案。

2. C。根据句意,应为"消费者商品价格上升"。因此选项 C 应为正确答案。而 其他选项均不合句意。

3. A。通货膨胀其实就是物价上涨,货币贬值,因此选项 A 符合句意,应为正 确答案。

4. A。为了资助战争,政府才采取多发行纸币的措施从而造成物价上涨的后 果。因此,选项 A 符合句意。

5. B。该题主要测试动词词组搭配。carry out(实施);carry off(赢得);carry on (进行,经营);carry away(使失去理智)。根据句意,应为实施各种社会 计划,因此正确答案应为选择 B。

6. D。该句意为:为了弥补财政赤字,因此应选择 D"offset"(抵消,弥补)。而 选项 A"compensate"(赔偿,补偿);B"accomplish"(顺利完成);C "exchange"(交换,交流)皆不合句意。

7. C。该句意为:财政部加大货币供应量。选项 A 和选项 D 皆不合题意,应予 排除;选项 B"extend"主要用于指在数量、时间和空间上的扩大。 "expand"指在范围上的扩大、扩充,符合句意。

8. B。该句意为:政府发行纸币以满足政府债务的需求,meet need 的意思是 满足需要;符合题意。

9. A。该句意:纸币供应量的增长会引起美元自动贬值。根据上下文可以得知,纸币供应量的增加与美元的贬值联动。因此选项 A 符合题意,应为正确答案;选项 B"timely"(合时宜的)为形容词词性,选项 C"exceedingly"(极度地),选项 D"excessively"(过度地)皆不符合句意。

10. A。此处为条件状语从句,因此选项 A 应为正确答案。

11. C。根据上下文可知此填空之后所罗列的 television and computer 只是作者列举的几个例子。因此应选 like。该句意为:像电视、计算机这些广泛使用的商品,选项 A 中"as"虽有"像……"之意,但它一般用于引导一个状语从句或引导表示状态的补语,如:Why is he dressed as a woman?

12. A。satisfy demand 的意思是满足需要,为固定用法。因此,选项 A 符合题意。该句意为"由于物品缺乏,工业企业就会生产出更多产品以满足人们的需求。";而选项 B"supply"(供应);选项 C"plenty"(大量);选项 D"comply"(遵守)均不合题意。

13. D。根据上下文的逻辑判断,此处应为进一步说明,而不是转折,因此 A、B、C 三个表示转折的副词皆不合适,只有选项 D"further more"(更进一步地)符合句意。

14. D。该句意是:以高利率借款去买这些商品。interest 有"利息"之意,为不可数名词,选项 A 可排除;而选项 B"interesting"(有趣的);C"interested"(令人感兴趣的)如置于句中意思和用法上都不正确。因此,只有选项 D 符合句意。

15. B。表示命令、建议这类动词引导的宾语从句中的谓语动词应该用虚拟语气。由于此处是被动之意,因此应选 B。本句的谓语动词是 demand,因此,应使用虚拟语气。

16. C。该句意为:提高工人工资以支付过高的生活费用。cover(钱够……之用),符合题意。

17. A。该句意为:企业会把其他的生产费用转嫁到消费者身上。工业产品的最终用户是消费者,因生产而引起的费用自然会随着产品一起转嫁到消费者身上来。因此选项 A 应为正确答案。选项 B"controller"(审计官);C"manager"(经理);D"employer"(雇主)皆不合句意。

18. C。in summary 的意思是做出结论,其他三个选项和 summary 均不能搭配使用。

19. D。该句意为:所有这些原因都能引起通货膨胀的问题。选项 A"result"为不及物动词,与 in 搭配才可以表示导致的意思。因此,选项 D 应为正确答案。

20. B。excessive 的意思是"过度的"。该句意为:过多的政府开支是最重要的原

164

因。符合句意。

Exercise 1

Directions: *There are 20 blanks in the following passage. For each blank there are four choices marked A, B, C and D. You should choose the ONE that best fits into the passage.*

Cloze 1

About 485 years ago, a man stood alone on the coast of Spain. He looked towards the west and said to himself, "The earth cannot be flat. If I sail westward,   1   I shall hit land, India perhaps, and the queen will have a new and shorter   2   to the riches of that country."

Christopher Columbus sold his idea to Queen Isabella of Spain. She gave   3   men and three ships. And Columbus sailed westward for many weeks, through   4   seas.   5 , he saw land: a group of islands now called the West Indies. Columbus was sure it was India, and he called the natives "Indus".

Stories of what Columbus found quickly   6   across Europe. His word "Indus" became "Indiana" to the English   7   all the natives of the West Indies and Central America became known as "Indians".

Christopher Columbus   8   four trips to the New World. Yet, he died in Spain without knowing where he had been. He died   9   he had sailed to India.

It was soon learned that Columbus had made a mistake.   10   the word "Indian" was well established in Europe.

The first   11   who arrived in North Carolina and Virginia in the early 1600's called the natives Indians. This names spread north   12   the colonies of Maryland, New York, Pennsylvania and New land were settled.

Today the word is used to   13   the descendants of the first peoples of North and South America. In the far north they are called Eskimos. And in the far south   14   are the Patagonians and the Fuegians.

Students and scholars have long known   15   the American Indians were not really Indians   16 . And one scholar proposed a name that he believed would be better Amerinds. He made up this name by   17   American and Indian. This word is often used today by other scholars, but the general   18   has heard little of it.

Word experts say the name Indian may be wrong but we are stuck with it. It is too late to change it to Amerind. Most people would not __19__ the change. Besides, how could a movie of the old west be exciting if it concerned cowboys and Amerinds, __20__ cowboys and Indians?

1. A. then   B. sooner or later C. however   D. for instance
2. A. orbit   B. range   C. route   D. friction
3. A. him   B. her   C. them   D. his
4. A. high   B. calm   C. current   D. rough
5. A. In fact   B. Yet   C. Anyway   D. At last
6. A. set   B. undertook   C. spread   D. passed
7. A. well   B. but   C. luckily   D. and
8. A. made   B. declared   C. wished,   D. put
9. A. laughing   B. hoping   C. believing   D. suspecting
10. A. Nowadays   B. But   C. Incidentally   D. In short
11. A. Indians   B. explorers   C. settlers   D. Spanish
12. A. as   B. so that   C. if   D. even though
13. A. harm   B. describe   C. influence   D. serve
14. A. just   B. so   C. they   D. there
15. A. as   B. that   C. in order that   D. and
16. A. though   B. at all   C. either   D. now
17. A. joining   B. comparing   C. respecting   D. separating
18. A. public   B. idea   C. objective   D. inspector
19. A. confirm   B. receive   C. accept   D. permit
20. A. instead of   B. after   C. without   D. over

Cloze 2

There are many problems connected with space travel. The first and greatest of them is gravity. If you let your pencil drop to the floor, you can see gravity in __1__. Everything is held down to the earth __2__ magnetic force. A rocket must go at least 2,500 miles __3__ hour to take anyone beyond the gravity of the __4__ into space.

Another problem is the strain that a person is __5__ to when a rocket leaves the ground. Anything that is not moving __6__ to resist movement. As the rocket leaves the ground, it __7__ upward violently, and the person in the "nose cone" is pushed back against the chair. During this thrust, gravity __8__ a force on the body equal to, nine times its __9__ force.

__10__ out of the earth's gravity, an astronaut is affected by __11__ another problem—weightlessness. Here, if a pencil drops, it does not fall. If a glass of water is turned __12__, the water will not fall out. Our bodies, which are __13__ to gravity, tend to become upset in weightless conditions. Recent long flights have shown that the body needs special exercise in a __14__.

Astronauts could also be __15__ by boredom and loneliness. Same of them might have to sit in their spaceships for months with __16__ to do and no one to talk to. Space trips to __17__ planets or the nearest stars might take many years. It is possible that some trips might __18__ take a life time. So future astronauts must be trained to __19__ long periods of inactivity and solitude.

Cosmic rays and tiny dust __20__ also raise a problem. Outer space, which has no air, is filled with both of these. The dust particles can damage the front end of the rapidly moving spaceship. The cosmic rays, though they are invisible to the naked eye, can go through the ship and the astronauts themselves. No one is sure what damage the cosmic rays can do to a human being, but scientists feel that brief exposure is probably not very harmful.

1. A. reaction	B. density	C. action	D. inertia
2. A. of	B. by	C. from	D. through
3. A. every	B. half a	C. a	D. an
4. A. earth	B. sun	C. itself	D. rocket
5. A. equal	B. leading	C. subjected	D. suited
6. A. intends	B. tends	C. refers	D. serves
7. A. pulls	B. rushes	C. pushes	D. sweeps
8. A. exerts	B. imposes	C. disturbs	D. affects
9. A. required	B. abnormal	C. prime	D. normal
10. A. After	B. Although	C. Now that	D. Once
11. A. truly	B. merely	C. perhaps	D. still
12. A. away	B. out	C. upside down	D. tightly
13. A. suggested	B. accustomed	C. responded	D. suffered
14. A. spaceship	B. satellite	C. container	D. vehicle
15. A. anticipated	B. conquered	C. affected	D. guided
16. A. little	B. nothing	C. research	D. findings

17. A. uniform　　B. timely　　C. standard　　D. distant
18. A. typically　　B. also　　C. even　　D. yet
19. A. mind　　B. endure　　C. cover　　D. predict
20. A. molecule　　B. particles　　C. radiation　　D. planets

Cloze 3

For many people today, reading is no longer relaxation. To keep up their work they must read letters, reports, trade publications, inter-office communications, not to mention newspapers and magazines: a never-ending flood of words. In ___1___ a job or advancing in one, the ability to read and comprehend ___2___ can mean the difference between success and failure. Yet the unfortunate fact is that most of us are ___3___ readers.

Most of us develop poor reading ___4___ at an early age, and never get over them.

The main deficiency ___5___ in the actual stuff of language itself—words. Take individually, words have ___6___ meaning until they are strung together into phrases, sentences and paragraphs.

___7___, however, the untrained reader does not read groups of words. He laboriously reads one word at a time, often regressing to ___8___ words or passages. Regression, the tendency to look back over ___9___ you have just read, is a common bad habit in reading. Another habit which ___10___ down the speed of reading is vocalization—sounding each word either orally or mentally as ___11___ reads.

To overcome these bad habits some "reading clinics" use a device called an ___12___, which moves a bar (or curtain) down the page at a predetermined speed. The bar is set at a slightly faster rate ___13___ the reader finds comfortable, in order to "stretch" him. The accelerator forces the reader to read fast, ___14___ word-by-word reading, regression and sub-vocalization, practically impossible.

At first ___15___ is sacrificed for speed. But when you learn to read ideas, and concepts, you will not only read faster, ___16___ your comprehension will improve.

Many people, business managers, executives and engineers, have found ___17___ reading skill drastically improved after some training. ___18___ Charles

Au, a business manager, for instance, his reading rate was a reasonably good 172 words a minute __19__ the training, now it is an excellent words a minute. He is delighted that now he can __20__ a lot more reading.

1. A. applying   B. doing   C. offing   D. getting
2. A. quickly   B. easily   C. roughly   D. decidedly
3. A. good   B. curious   C. poor   D. urgent
4. A. training   B. habits   C. situations   D. custom
5. A. lies   B. combines   C. touches   D. involves
6. A. some.   B. a lot   C. little   D. dull
7. A. Fortunately   B. In fact   C. Logically   D. Unfortunately
8. A. reuse   B. reread   C. rewrite   D. recite
9. A. what   B. which   C. that   D. if
10. A. scales   B. cuts   C. slows   D. measures
11. A. some one   B. one   C. he   D. reader
12. A. accelerator   B. actor   C. amplifier   D. observer
13. A. then   B. as   C. beyond   D. than
14. A. enabling   B. leading   C. making   D. indicating
15. A. meaning   B. comprehension   C. gist   D. regression
16. A. but   B. nor   C. or   D. for
17. A. our   B. your   C. their   D. such a
18. A. Look at   B. Take   C. Make   D. Consider
19. A. for   B. in   C. after   D. before
20. A. master   B. go over   C. present   D. get through

Cloze 4

As you may have gathered from the above, in reading to learn English composition, you ought to regard the language as the main thing. To quote from my "A Word to the Wise".

"When you read a __1__ in English, do you read it for the story or for the English? This is a question that is not so foolish __2__ it may seem. For I find that many students of English __3__ far more attention to the story than to the English. They read and enjoy and for a long time __4__ remember the story, but do not care to study the use of words and __5__ in it. For instance, they cherish the memory of __6__ the mystery of the eternal triangles is solved, but do not remember a __7__ sentence in the story and can not tell what preposition is used before or __8__ a certain word in the speech of a certain __9__ .

"Of course, it is all right to read and __10__ and remember a story, and so long as one __11__ to know the story only, one need not __12__ about the language. But the case is quite different __13__ a student of English. I mean a student of English as distinguished from a student of stories or __14__ is called the general reader." As you may also have __15__ from the above, you ought to read very carefully. Not only very carefully but also aloud, and that again and again __16__ you know the passage by heart and can recite it as if it __17__ your own. Positively this will teach you many __18__ words and phrases; negatively it will help you to avoid many errors and faults in expression. __19__ , I have found from experience that intelligent copying is an aid to __20__ by heart.

1. A. writing   B. essay   C. story   D. survey
2. A. that   B. as   C. than   D. as if
3. A. take   B. suspend   C. give   D. pay
4. A. afterwards   B. towards   C. latter   D. merely
5. A. paragraphs   B. letters   C. terms   D. phrases
6. A. when   B. where   C. what   D. how
7. A. simple   B. long   C. single   D. compound.
8. A. prior to   B. after   C. over   D. due to
9. A. character   B. talk   C. dialogue   D. language
10. A. enjoy   B. ignore   C. comprehend   D. realize
11. A. recommends B. wants   C. assumes   D. fails
12. A. bother   B. bring   C. concern   D. talk
13. A. of   B. from   C. with   D. against
14. A. which   B. what   C. that   D. it
15. A. arrived   B. secured   C. thought   D. gathered
16. A. since   B. as   C. till   D. while
17. A. was   B. seems   C. is   D. were
18. A. useful   B. tough   C. desirable   D. available
19. A. Obviously   B. Briefly   C. Incidentally D. Immediately
20. A. hesitating B. learning   C. reading   D. viewing

Cloze 5

The first two stages in the development of civilized man were probably the invention of primitive weapons and the discovery of fire, although nobody knows exactly when he acquired the use of ___1___.

The ___2___ of language is also obscure. No doubt it began very gradually. Animals have a few cries that serve ___3___ signals, ___4___ even the highest apes have not been found able to pronounce words, ___5___ with the most intensive professional instruction. The superior brain of man is apparently ___6___ for the mastering of speech. When man became sufficiently intelligent, we must suppose that he ___7___ the number of cries for different purposes. It was a great day ___8___ he discovered that speech could be used for narrative. There are those who think that ___9___ picture language preceded oral language. A man ___10___ a picture on the wall of his cave to show ___11___ direction he had gone, or ___12___ prey he hoped to catch. Probably picture language and oral language developed side by side. I am inclined to think that language ___13___ the most important single factor in the development of man.

Two important stages came not ___14___ before the dawn of written history. The first was the domestication of animals; the second was agriculture. Agriculture was ___15___ in human progress to which subsequently there was nothing comparable ___16___ our own machine age. Agriculture made possible ___17___ immense increases in the number of the human species in the regions where it could be successfully practiced. ___18___ were, at first, only those in which nature fertilized the soil ___19___ each harvest. Agriculture met with violent resistance from the pastoral (畜牧的) nomads (游牧的), but the agricultural way of life prevailed in the end ___20___ the physical comforts it provided.

1. A. the latter B. the later C. the second D. the latest
2. A. source B. beginning C. start D. origin
3. A. like B. with C. as D. by
4. A. and B. but C. moreover D. for
5. A. even if B. even C. even though D. even as
6. A. a necessity B. necessities C. necessarily D. necessity
7. A. should gradually increase B. gradually increase
   C. gradually increased D. has gradually increased
8. A. that B. at which C. which D. when

9. A. with the respect　　　　　　　B. on this respect
　　C. in this respect　　　　　　　　D. at this respect
10. A. could draw　　B. should draw　　C. was able draw　D. was drawing
11. A. at which　　　B. in which　　　　C. on which　　　D. with which
12. A. of which　　　B. that　　　　　　C. which　　　　　D. what
13. A. is　　　　　　B. was　　　　　　C. has been　　　D. is being
14. A. too long　　　B. such long　　　　C. as long　　　D. so long
15. A. a stage　　　B. a step　　　　　　C. a development D. a way
16. A. until　　　　B. with　　　　　　C. for　　　　　D. to
17. A. the　　　　　B. an　　　　　　　C. that　　　　　D. one
18. A. Those　　　　B. These　　　　　C. There　　　　D. They
19. A. after　　　　B. with　　　　　　C. before　　　　D. at
20. A. since　　　　B. for　　　　　　　C. because　　　D. because of

第二节　改错

　　"改错"为大学英语综合测试部分供选择的考试形式之一,主要目的是测试考生综合运用语言的能力。该部分试题的主要选材范围是议论文、说明文、应用文等,共设有10道改错题,占试题总分值的10%,要求考生在指定的句子中借助上下文线索辨认错误并且加以纠正。

1."改错"题型的出题重点

　　"改错"题型的出题重点是测试考生在特定的语言环境条件下对语法、构词、语用、逻辑、惯用法等方面的掌握情况。

2."改错"题型的解题技巧

　　由于"改错"试题类属于综合测试范畴,所设计的试题基于语篇和语境环境。因此,解题时应通篇考虑,或根据相关语句的上下文使用排除法来确定需要纠正的病句并做出相应的纠正。具体解题步骤如下:

　　(1)通读短文以了解文章大意、布局和推展方式,为解逻辑型试题做准备。

　　(2)细读短文前三句以了解文章的句法、时态等基调,为解语法、时态类型试题做准备。

　　(3)根据上下文提示,采用排除法锁定错误并予以纠正。

（4）再次通读短文,复查试题,核对纠错部分是否正确。例如:

Many a young person tells me he wants to be a writer. I always encourage such people, but I also explain that there is a big difference between "being a writer" and writing. In most cases this individuals are dreaming of wealth and fame, not the long hours alone at typewriter. "You've got to want to write," I say to them, "not want to be a writer."

1. _____

2. _____

The reality is that writing is a alone, private and poor-paying affair. For every writer kissed by fortune, there are thousands more whose longing is never rewarded. When I leave a 20-year career in the U. S. Coast Guard to become a freelance writer, I had no prospects at all. That I did have was a friend who found me my room in a New York apartment builder. It didn't even matter that it was cold and had no bathroom. I immediately bought a used manual typewriter and felt as a genuine writer.

3. _____

4. _____

5. _____

6. _____

7. _____

After a year or so, however, I still hadn't gotten a break and began to doubt myself. It was so hard to sell a story that almost made enough to eat. But I knew I wanted to write. I had dreamed about it for years. I wasn't going to be one of those people who die wondering. What if? I would keep putting my dream to the test even though it meant living with uncertainty and fear of failure. This is the shadow land of hope, and anyone with a dream must learn to live there.

8. _____

9. _____

10. _____

【例题解析】

1. these individuals 改为 these。

这里指示代词修饰一个复数名词,因此应用 these。

2. 在 at typewriter 之前加 a。

补加不定冠词 a,因为 typewriter 是可数名词。

3. alone 改为 lonely。

此句中作者强调的是写作时的感受,而非是否一个人还是两个人在写作。

4. leave 改为 left。

作者在此句中陈述过去所发生的动作,因此应用动词 leave 的过去时 left。

5. That 改为 What。

此句中 What 引导的是一个主语从句,并在该从句中作宾语。That 也可用于引导主语从句时,但要求主语从句的意思必须完整,不需要关系代词做主语从句的任何成分。

6. builder 改为 apartment building。

building 意为"建筑物";builder 意为"建筑者"。根据上下文可知此句中 apartment building 指的是"公寓楼"。

7. as 改为 feel like。

feel like 意为"感觉像……一样"。这里 like 是介词,其后接名词或代词。

8. almost 改为 barely/hardly。

根据上半句"It was so hard to sell a story"可知能够挣出"足够吃的"应该是一件很困难的事。因此,此处应为 barely 或 hardly。

9. 无错。

10. 无错。

Exercise 2

Directions：*This part consists a short passage. In this passage, there are possibably 10 or less than 10 mistakes, one in each numbered line. You may have to change a word, add a word or delete a word. If you change a word, cross it out and write the correct word in the corresponding blank. If you add a word, put an insertion mark ( ) in the correct word in the corresponding blank. If you delete a word, cross it out and be sure to put a slash (/) in the blank.*

Passage 1

Every now and then, we come across a fact about our earth which no answer has yet been found. Such a fact is the existence of salt in the oceans. How did it get there?

The answer is we simply don't know how the salt got into the ocean! We do know, of course, that salt is water-soluble, and so passes into the oceans with rain water. The salt of the Earth's surface is constantly being dissolved and is passing into the ocean.

But we don't know whether this can account for the huge quantity of salt that is found in oceans. If all the oceans was 1. _____
dried up, enough salt would leave to build a wall 180 miles high 2. _____
and a mile thick. Such a wall would reach once around the

world at the Equator! Or put another way, the rock salt obtained if all the oceans dried up would have a bulk about 15 times as much as the entire continent of Europe.

The common salt which we all use is produced from sea water or the water of salt lakes, from salt springs, and from deposits of rock salt. The concentration of salt in sea water ranges about three percent to three-and-one-half percent.

Enclosed seas, such as Mediterranean and the Red Sea, contain more salt in the water open seas. The Dead Sea, which covers an area of about 340 square miles, contain about 11,600,000,000 tons of salt!

On the average, a gallon of sea water contains about a quarter of a pound of sale. The beds of rock salt that are formed in various part of the world were all originally formed by the evaporation of sea water millions of years ago. Since it is necessary for about nine-tenth of the volume of sea water to evaporate for rock salt to be formed, it is believed that the thick rock-salt beds that are found were deposited in what uses to be partly, enclosed seas. These evaporated faster than fresh water entered them, and the rock-salt deposits were thus formed.

Most commercial salt is obtained from rock salt. The usual method is to drill wells down to the salt beds. Pure water is pumped down through a pipe. The water solves the salt and it is forced through another pipe up to the surface.

3. _____

4. _____

5. _____
6. _____

7. _____

8. _____

9. _____

10. _____

Passage 2

Fostering economic growth will require a broader understanding of the environment than many environmental activists seem to appreciate. The most pressing environmental problems of the developing nations are related to poverty, not global climate change. Addressing these problem will require economic growth, and that will necessitate increasing, not decreasing, the use of fossil fuels. Such use does not mean evitable environmental degradation. New technologies have

1. _____

2. _____

allowed industrialized countries enjoy both economic growth and
environmental progress.

    Studies in the economic community support this idea. A
recent study at Princeton University find "no evidence that
environmental quality deteriorates steadily with economic
growth". And it found that after an initial decline, a nation's
environment improved as its economy growth.

    So the real secret to environmental improvement is
economic growth. And as this growth continues, the economies
of this region will need to import more oil, and, in a lesser
extent, gas.

    This growing reliance on petroleum imports will cause a
major eastward shift on the politics of energy. Nations may
form new alliances, are based on commercial interests, others
on geo-political considerations. The temptation may be strong
make these exclusive or restrictive, reversing recent trends
of more openness and harmony.

3. _____
4. _____
5. _____
6. _____
7. _____
8. _____
9. _____
10. _____

Passage 3

    Why do writers write? What makes them take a pen or
pencil and put their beliefs, ideas, and impressions on a piece of
paper?

    To answer this question is not easy. Motives are difficult
to fathom (看透，推想). But it is possible to suggest a few
tentative answer—answers, it should be remembered, that may
apply in some writers and not in others.

    One common reason for writing probably is concerned of
fame. A writer may want renown and money and prestige; he
may want to become famous. Another writer, however, may
simply enjoy the process of writing of putting words in paper
and seeing how they fit together. A third writer may want to
set down events as they happened just because of they
happened. A fourth may write to win his readers over to his
point of view.

1. _____
2. _____
3. _____
4. _____
5. _____

Influencing readers certainly is one important reason that
many writers do write. The urge to see one's ideas and opinions
accepting by others is strong in most writers. But telling others
your viewpoint may not win them over to your side. A writer
who wrote "I think baseball is a silly game and ought to be
abolished as soon as possible" may have wanted others to accept
his opinion, but would they do so? Might he have stated his
belief a few too bluntly? Might there be a better way—a less
subjective way—for him to get his opinion across without
alienating his readers or overwhelming them with his ideas?

6. _____

7. _____

8. _____

9. _____

10. _____

Passage 4

Globalization is often described as the process of increasing
the integration of the world economy of countries becoming
more interdependent and interconnected. As we embark on the
twenty-first century, advances in information and
communication technologies (ICT) are helping pave the way of
greater economic integration through unprecedented rapid flows
of goods, services, capital and ideas. Per day, more than US
$ I. 5 trillion is traded in the global currency markets; each
year nearly a fifth of the goods and services the world produce
are traded internationally. Much bas been said about how
globalization has helped to realize the benefits of free trade
through comparative advantage and division of labor. There are
also supporting, although not uncontroversial, evidence of a
link between external openness and economic growth via greater
access in technology.

As we enter the new millennium, we find us in an era of
knowledge-based economies where the possession, distribution
and consumption of knowledge play an important role in
economic growth. Competitiveness is becoming more dependent
in human capital and the acquisition of technology. In order
of least-developed countries (LDCs) and developing countries
to avoid falling further behind the more advanced economies,

1. _____

2. _____

3. _____

4. _____

5. _____

6. _____

7. _____

8. _____

9. _____

10. _____

they must be able to bring and apply information, ideas and innovations from abroad.

Passage 5

MVA here is 2.6 times higher than in the region, which is itself the most dynamic part of the world economy. MVA in the other giant economy in Asia, India, was 46 per cent of China's in 1990; it is now a mere 13 per cent. The three Latin American economies combined produce less than 60 per cent of China. The whole of SSA, including South Africa (which in turn accounts for nearly 60 per cent of the regional total), produces about 8 per cent of the total. If we project MVA in the basis of recent growth rates, by 2003 China will be larger than East Asia, South Asia and Sub-Saharan Africa combining. Of course, such simple projections are only illustrative—future performance may differ greatly from past.

China is not just the largest industrial economy in the developing world it is also the fastest growing. This combination may have significant implications for its competitive. Large size implies the ability to realize scale and scope economies, and so export products that are more difficult for smaller economies to provide. The later can set up large-scale facilities solely for export markets (for example, Singapore in petrochemicals), but this is more risky and does not allow a cushion for building local technological capabilities. It has to be handled by TNCs other than by local firms, which may restrict local linkages, spillovers (过多) and diversification (多样化). China can, by contrast, launch relatively capital-intensive and complex activities within local firms and gain export competence by learn in the domestic market. The additional advantage this provides is the associated learning and linkage benefits that entry into complex industries provides.

1. _____

2. _____
3. _____

4. _____

5. _____

6. _____

7. _____

8. _____
9. _____

10. _____

第三节　篇章问答（简短回答）

篇章问答又称"简短回答问题"（后称"简答"）是大学英语综合测试部分供选择的考试形式之一，占试题总分值的5％，主要选材范围是议论文、说明文、应用文等，旨在考查考生对英语书面材料的综合理解能力。该试题安排在"阅读理解"部分之后。每次考试为一篇文章，文章后设有5个问题或不完整的句子，要求考生在阅读之后用简短的英语（可以是句子，也可以是单词或短语）回答所提出的问题或补足不完整的句子。

大学英语四级考试对"简答"提出的具体要求是：

（1）语言表达必须正确。

（2）答案必须正确，答非所问不能得分。

（3）答案不能是直接照抄原文，或包含与问题无关的信息。

（4）答案的意思必须完整，字数不能超过规定的字数，通常不得超过10个字。

1. "简答"题型的出题重点

该题型的出题重点是回答"是什么"，"为什么"和"怎么样"的问题，要求考生快速阅读短文从中获取信息，回答问题或补足内容。该题的选材范围主要是科普性文章和社会生活方面的文章，多见说明文、应用文和议论文等。常见简短回答试题的类型有四种：

（1）主题思想问题。

（2）细节问题。

（3）词汇含义问题。

（4）作者意图、态度、观点问题。

2. "简答"题型的解题技巧

通常解答这类题目的方法是捕捉文章的大意，找出能够体现文章中心思想的句子。如有可能，通过从文章中找到作者阐述其论点所使用的具体论据和事实，以进一步领会文章作者的真实用意和写作目的，以帮助回答随后所提出的问题。注意在阅读过程中要对所涉及的具体细节做出标记，以便于在回答问题时回头查找。回答简短问题时，应掌握以下技巧：

（1）先看问题，再读文章。即在阅读文章的过程中，发现与问题有关的句子时，立刻做出标记，以备回答问题时查阅。

（2）先确定内容，再落笔行文。即找到问题的相关答案依据后，根据问题的内容，以贴切简洁的语句予以回答。

（3）保持问题与答案时态的一致性。原问题使用什么时态，回答问题时就要使用什么时态。

（4）注意答案前后不要矛盾。

注意，简答题的答案不是固定的，只要能够大致表述出问题的意思就算达到了做题的要求。例如：

The term "folk song" has been current for over a hundred years, but there is still a good deal of disagreement as to what it actually means. The definition provided by the International Folk Music Council states that folk music is the music of ordinary people, which is passed on from person to person by being listened to rather than learned from the printed page. Other factors that help shape a folk song include: continuity (many performances over a number of years); variation (changes in words and melodies either through artistic interpretation or failure of memory); and selection (the acceptance of a song by the community in which it evolves).

When songs have been subjected to these processes their origin is usually impossible to trace. For instance, if a farm laborer were to make up a song and sing it to a couple of friends who like it and memorize it, possibly when the friends come to sing it themselves one of them might forget some of the words and make up new ones to fill the gap, while the other, perhaps more artistic, might add a few decorative touches to the tune and improve a couple of lines of text. If this happened a few times there would be many different versions, the song's original composer would be forgotten, and the song would become common property. This constant reshaping and re-creation is the essence of folk music. Consequently, modern popular songs and other published music, even though widely sung by people who are not professional musicians, are not considered folk music.

The music and words have been set by a printed or recorded source, limiting scope for further artistic creation. These songs' origins cannot be disguised and therefore they belong primarily to the composer and not to a community.

The ideal situation for the creation of folk music is an isolated rural community. In such a setting folk songs and dances have a special purpose at every stage in a person's life, from childhood to death. Epic tales of heroic deeds, seasonal songs relating to calendar events, and occupational songs are also likely to be sung.

Questions:

1. What does the passage mainly discuss?

   _____   _____   _____   _____
   _____   _____   _____   _____

2. Why is it difficult to trace the folk songs' origin?

   _____   _____   _____   _____
   _____   _____   _____   _____

3. The author mentions that published music is not considered to be folk music because _____.

   _____   _____   _____   _____
   _____   _____   _____   _____

4. Why does the author mention the farm laborer and his friends in the passage?

   _____   _____   _____   _____
   _____   _____   _____   _____

5. According to the passage, why would the original composers of folk songs be forgotten?

   _____   _____   _____   _____
   _____   _____   _____   _____

【例题解析】

1. Elements that folk music has.
   参见全文。

2. Because they are often changed by the singers.
   参见第二段。

3. the songs are generally learned from the printed page
   参见第一段第二句。

4. Explain how a folk song evolves over time.
   参见第二段第一句。

5. Variations of folk songs come to exist side by side.
   参见第二段。

Exercise 3

Directions: *In this part there are three short passages with five questions or* *incomplete statements separately. Read the passages carefully. Then answer the questions or complete the statements in the fewest possible words.*

Passage 1

British Columbia is the third largest Canadian province, both in area and population. It is nearly 1.5 times as large as Texas, and extends 800 miles (1,280 km) north from the United States border. It includes Canada's entire west coast and the islands just off the coast.

Most of British Columbia is mountainous, with long, rugged ranges running north and south. Even the coastal islands are the remains of a mountain range that existed thousands of years ago. During the last Ice Age, this range was scoured by glaciers until most of it was beneath the sea. Its peaks now are islands scattered along the coast.

The southwestern coastal region has a humid mild marine climate. Sea winds that blow inland from the west are warmed by a current of warm water that flows through the Pacific Ocean. As a result, winter temperatures average above freezing and summers are mild. These warm western winds also carry moisture from the ocean.

Inland from the coast, the winds from the Pacific meet the mountain barriers of the coastal ranges and the Rocky Mountains. As they rise to cross the mountains, the winds are cooled, and their moisture begins to fall as rain. On some of the western slopes almost 200 inches (500 cm) of rain fall each year.

More than half of British Columbia is heavily forested. On mountain slopes that receive plentiful rainfall, huge Douglas firs rise in towering columns. These forest giants often grow to be as much as 300 feet (90 m) tall, with diameters up to 10 feet (3 m). More lumber is produced from these trees than from any other kind of trees in North America. Hemlock, red cedar, and balsam fir(香脂冰杉) are among the other trees found in British Columbia.

Questions:

1. In which part of British Columbia can a mild climate be found?

   ——————— ——————— ——————— ——————— ———————
   ——————— ——————— ——————— ——————— ———————

2. Why do winter temperatures average above freezing in the southwest coastal region of most of British Columbia?

   ——————— ——————— ——————— ——————— ———————

_____   _____   _____   _____   _____

3. What effect do the mountains have on winds?

_____   _____   _____   _____   _____

_____   _____   _____   _____   _____

4. Why is more than half of British Columbia heavily forested?

_____   _____   _____   _____   _____

_____   _____   _____   _____   _____

5. In British Columbia, what kind of timber are the main wooden products?

_____   _____   _____   _____   _____

_____   _____   _____   _____   _____

Passage 2

Global warming threatens to reverse human progress, and make unachievable all UN targets to reduce poverty, according to some of the world's leading international and development groups.

In a report published today, Oxfam, Greenpeace, Christian Aid, Friends of the Earth, WWF and 15 other groups say rich governments must immediately address climate change to avoid even worse levels of worldwide poverty.

"Food production, water supplies, public health and people's livelihoods are already being damaged," the report says. "There is no either/or approach possible. The world must meet its commitments to achieve poverty reduction and also tackle climate change. The two are complicatedly linked."

The report, which draws on UN predictions of the effects of climate change in poor countries over the next 50 years, says poor countries will experience more flooding, declining food production, more disease and the deterioration or extinction of entire ecosystems on which many of the world's poorest people depend.

"Climate change needs to be addressed now. The poor will be the first to suffer the impacts. The frontline experience of many of us working in international development indicates that communities have to combat more extreme weather conditions."

Climate change will severely affect agriculture and water supplies and will increase diseases. "By 2025 the proportion of the world's population living in countries of significant water stress will almost double, to 6 billion people.

Tropical and sub-tropical areas will be hardest hit—those countries already suffering from food insecurity."

Poor communities mostly do not need hi-tech solutions, but would most benefit from education, research and being shown how to farm better. The report says unchecked global warming, more than wars or political upheaval(动荡), will displace(迫使……离家) millions of people and destabilize many countries.

Questions:

1. What is made impossible by threats of global warming poses to human beings?

   _____ _____ _____ _____ _____

   _____ _____ _____ _____ _____

2. What are the two closely related problems the report mentions?

   _____ _____ _____ _____ _____

3. What will the growing population bring about?

   _____ _____ _____ _____ _____

4. What is favorable for poor communities apart from the techniques of effective farming?

   _____ _____ _____ _____ _____

   _____ _____ _____ _____ _____

5. What can displace people and destabilize countries?

   _____ _____ _____ _____ _____

   _____ _____ _____ _____ _____

Passage 3

Automobile drivers and passengers now face a new, unseen danger on the road: the users of cellular mobile telephones. Looking at the phone while dialing or speaking can prevent drivers from keeping their hands on the wheel and their eyes on the road; industry experts agree that drivers are more likely to have an accident while using their phones. That fact has excited concern among highway safety organizations in the United States, and some want to ban cellular phones altogether. While manufacturers have not yet come up with a cellular mobile phone that is completely "hands free", several companies have recently developed components that could make mobile phones less distracting—and their users less accident prone.

Voice Control Systems, Inc. , based in Dallas, Tex. , has developed a microprocessor unit that allows standard cellular telephones to "dial" numbers at the sound of a human voice. The Voice Dialer unit is attached to the phone's transmitter and receiver in the car's trunk. Programmed with a limited vocabulary, it can respond only to digits and specific control commands spoken by the users, who must pause a quarter of a second between each digit or command. (Frequently dialed numbers can be preprogrammed into simple, single command codes.) The driver picks up the handset, and begins calls by saying "Dial," followed by the number or command code; a synthesized voice will repeat the number sequence and place the call told to "Send." A unique aspect of the Voice Dialer is that its speaker is independent; the unit will respond to any voice regardless of gender, accent or tone.

Questions:

1. Drivers using cellular mobile telephones are prone to accidents because _____.

_____ _____ _____ _____ _____

_____ _____ _____ _____ _____

2. What is the purpose to invent a Voice Dialer according to the passage?

_____ _____ _____ _____ _____

3. Why do some people want to ban cellular phones altogether?

_____ _____ _____ _____ _____

4. The Voice Dialer unit is programmed to respond to _____.

_____ _____ _____ _____ _____

5. What is this passage mainly centers on?

_____ _____ _____ _____ _____

_____ _____ _____ _____ _____

Passage 4

Of all modern instruments, the violin is apparently one of the simplest. It consists in essence of a hollow, varnished(表面光泽的) wooden sound box, and a long neck, covered with a fingerboard, along which four strings are stretched at high tension. The beauty of design, shape, and decoration is no accident: the proportions of the instrument are determined almost entirely by acoustical(声学的,传音的) considerations. Its simplicity of appearance is deceptive. About 70 parts are involved in the construction of a violin. Its tone and outstanding range of expressiveness make it an ideal solo instrument. No less important, however, is its role as an orchestral and chamber instrument. In combination with the larger and deeper-sounding members of the same family, the violins form the nucleus of the modern symphony orchestra.

The violin has been in existence since about 1550. Its importance as an instrument in its own right dates from the early 1600's, when it first became standard in Italian opera orchestras.

In its early history, the violin had a dull and rather quiet tone resulting from the fact that the strings were thick and attached to the body of the instrument very loosely. During the eighteenth and nineteenth century, exciting technical changes were inspired by such composer-violinists as Vivaldi and Tartini. Their instrumental compositions demanded a fuller, clearer, and more brilliant tone that was produced by using thinner strings and a far higher string tension. Small changes had to be made to the violin's internal structure and to the fingerboard so that they could withstand the extra strain.

Accordingly, a higher standard of performance was achieved, in terms of both facility and interpretation. Left-hand technique was considerably elaborated, and new fingering patterns on the fingerboard were developed for very high notes.

Questions:

1. What does modern violin look like?

_____ _____ _____ _____

_____ _____ _____ _____

2. What is the main idea presented in paragraph 3?

_____ _____ _____ _____

_____ _____ _____ _____

3. According to the passage, how were early violins different from modern violins?

_____ _____   _____ _____

_____ _____   _____   _____ _____

4. When did the violins begin to be considered as an important musical instrument?

_____   _____   _____ _____   _____

_____   _____   _____   _____   _____

5. Why is the violin widely accepted as an ideal solo instrument?

_____   _____   _____   _____   _____

_____   _____   _____   _____   _____

Passage 5

In the North American colonies, red ware, a simple pottery fired at low temperatures, and stoneware, a strong, impervious (不渗透的) grey pottery fired at high temperatures, were produced from two different native clays. These kinds of pottery were produced to supplement imported European pottery. When the American Revolution (1775-1783) interrupted the flow of the superior European ware, there was incentive for American potters to replace the imports with comparable domestic goods. Stoneware, which had been simple, practical kitchenware, grew increasingly ornate (考究) throughout the nineteenth century, and in addition to the earlier scratched and drawn designs, three-dimensional molded relief decoration became popular.

As more and more large kilns (窑) were built to create the high-fired stoneware, experiments revealed that the same clay used to produce low-fired red ware could produce a stronger, paler pottery if fired at a hotter temperature. The result was yellow ware, used largely for serviceable items; but a further development was Rockingham ware—one of the most important American ceramics (陶器) of the nineteenth century. It was created by adding a brown glaze to the fired clay, usually giving the finished product a mottled (斑纹的) appearance. Various methods of spattering or sponging the glaze onto the ware account for the extremely wide variations in color and add to the interest of collecting Rockingham.

Articles for nearly every household activity and ornament could be bought in Rockingham ware: dishes and bowls, of course; also bedpans, foot warmers, lamp bases, doorknobs, molds, picture frames, even curtain tiebacks. All these items are highly collectible today and are eagerly sought. A few Rockingham specialties command particular affection among collectors and correspondingly high prices.

Questions:

1. Why were the red ware produced during the American Revolution?

   _____ _____ _____ _____ _____

   _____ _____ _____ _____ _____

2. What are the characteristics of the earliest stoneware according to the passage?

   _____ _____ _____ _____ _____

   _____ _____ _____ _____ _____

3. What kind of temperature is good for producing strong and paler stoneware?

   _____ _____ _____ _____ _____

   _____ _____ _____ _____ _____

4. How did yellow ware achieve its distinctive color?

   _____ _____ _____ _____ _____

   _____ _____ _____ _____ _____

5. Why do Rockingham's products interest people so much?

   _____ _____ _____ _____ _____

   _____ _____ _____ _____ _____

第三部分　综合训练

Test One

I Reading Comprehension

Section A　Passage Reading

Directions: *There are 2 passages in this section. Each passage is followed by some questions or unfinished statements. For each of them there are four choices marked A, B, C and D. You should decide on the best choice and mark the corresponding letter on Answer Sheet with a single line through the center.*

Passage One

Questions 1 to 5 are based on the following passage.

One hundred and thirteen million Americans have at least one bank-issued credit card. (They give their owners automatic credit in stores, restaurants and hotels, at home, across the country and even abroad and they make many banking services available as well.) More and more of these credit cards can be read automatically, making it possible to withdraw or deposit money in scattered locations, whether or not the local branch bank is open. For many of us the "cashless society" is not on the horizon—it's already here.

While computers offer these conveniences to consumers, they have many advantages for sellers, too. Electronic cash register can do much more than simply ring up sales, they can keep a wide range of records, including who sold what, when and to whom. This information allows businessmen to keep track of their list of goods by showing which items are being sold and how fast they are moving. Decisions to reorder or return goods by suppliers can then be made. At the same time these computers record which hours are busiest and which employees are the most efficient, allowing personnel and staffing assignments to be made accordingly. And they also identify preferred customers for promotional campaign. Computers are relied on by manufacturers for similar reasons. Computer-analyzed marketing reports can help to decide which products to emphasize now, which to develop for the future, and which to drop. Computers keep track of goods in stock, of raw materials on hand, and even of the production process itself.

1. What does the "cashless society" refer to in Paragraph One?

    A. It refers to the society without money.

    B. It refers to the society with many banks.

    C. It refers to the society with available bank-issued credit card.

    D. It refers to tile society in which all the Americans are given credit across the country and even abroad.

2. According to the passage, the credit card enables its owner to _____.

    A. cash money wherever he wishes to

    B. enjoy greater trust from the storekeeper

    C. obtain more convenient services than other people do

    D. withdraw as much money from the bank as he wishes

3. From the last sentence of the first paragraph we learn that _____.

    A. nowadays many Americans do not pay in cash

    B. in the future all the Americans will use credit cards

    C. it is now more convenient to use credit cards than before

    D. credit cards are mainly used in the United States today

4. The phrase "ring up sales" in Paragraph Two most probably means _____.

    A. make an order of goods   B. record sales on a cash register

    C. call the sales manager   D. keep track of the goods in stock

5. What is this passage mainly about?

    A. Conveniences brought about by computers in business.

    B. Advantages of credit cards in business.

    C. Significance of automation in commercial enterprises.

    D. Approaches to the commercial use of computers.

Passage Two

Questions 6 to 10 are based on the following passage.

Sometime in the next century, the familiar early-morning newspaper on the front porch will disappear. And instead of reading your newspaper, it will read to you. You'll get up and turn on the computer newspaper just like switching on the TV. An electronic voice will distribute stories about the latest events, guided by a program that selects the type of news you want. You'll even get to choose the kind of voice you want to hear. Want more information on the brief story? A simple touch makes the entire text appear. Save it in your own personal computer file if you like. These are among the predictions from communications experts working on the newspapers of the future. Pictured as part of broader home based media and entertainment systems, computer newspapers would unite print and broadcast reporting, offering news and analysis with video images of news events.

Most of the technology is available now, but convincing more people that they don't need paper to read a newspaper is the next step. But resistance to computer newspapers may be stronger from within journalism(新闻界). Since it is such a cultural change, it may be that the present generation of journalists and publishers will have to die off before the next generation realizes that the newspaper industry is no longer a newspaper industry. Technology is making the end of traditional newspapers unavoidable.

Despite technological advances, it could take decades to replace newsprint with computer screens. It might take 30 to 40 years to complete the changeover because people need to buy computers and because newspapers have established financial interests in the paper industry.

6. The best title for this passage is _____.

A. Computer Newspapers Are Well Liked

B. Newspapers of the Future Will Likely Be on Computer

C. Newspapers Are out of Fashion

D. New Communications Technology

7. It might take 30 to 40 years for computer newspapers to replace traditional newspapers, because _____.

A. it is technologically impossible now

B. computer newspapers are too expensive

C. there is strong resistance from both the general population and professional journalists

D. you can easily save information for future use

8. Which of the following is NOT an advantage of computer newspapers?

A. They are cheaper than traditional newspapers.

B. They are very convenient to us.

C. You can get more information from them quickly.

D. The saved information will have no use at all in the near future.

9. Journalists are not eager to accept computer newspapers, because _____.

A. they don't know how to use computers

B. they think computer newspapers take too much time to read

C. they think the new technology is bad

D. they have been trained to write for traditional newspapers

10. We can infer from the passage that _____.

A. all technological changes are good

B. all technologies will eventually replace old ones

C. new technologies will eventually replace old ones

D. traditional newspapers are here to stay for another century

Section B　Banked Cloze

Directions: *In this section, there is a passage with ten blanks. You are required to select one word for each blank from a list of choices given in a word bank following the passage. Read the passage through carefully before making your choices. Each choice in the bank is identified by a letter. Please mark the corresponding letter for each item on Answer Sheet with a single line through the center. You may not use any of the words in the bank more than once.*

Package holiday, covering a two weeks' stay in an attractive location, are increasingly popular, because they __1__ an inclusive price with few extras. __2__ you get to the airport, it's up to the tour operator to see that you get safely to your destination. Excursions, local entertainment, swimming, sunbathing, skiing—you name it—it's all well __3__ for you. There is, in fact, no reason for you to bother to arrange anything yourselves. You make friends and have a good time, but there is very little __4__ that you will really get to know the local people. This is even less likely on a coach tour, when you spend almost your entire time traveling. Of course, there are carefully __5__ stops for you to visit historic buildings and monuments, but you will probably be allowed only brief stay overnight in some famous city, with a polite reminder to be up and breakfast early in time for the coach next morning. You __6__ visit the beautiful, the historic, the ancient, but time is always at your elbow. There is also the added disadvantage of being obliged to ___7___ your holiday with a group of people you have never met before, may not like and have no reasonable ___8___ for getting away from. As against this, it can be argued that for many people, ___9___ the lonely or elderly, the feeling of belonging to a group, although for a short period on holiday, is an added benefit. They can sit safely ___10___ in their seats and watch the world go by.

A. arranged	E. realize	I. stranger	M. sometimes
B. back	F. Once	J. although	N. chance
C. scheduled	G. spend	K. offer	O. excuse
D. holiday	H. particularly	L. may	

Section C   Reading Comprehension (Skimming and Scanning)

Directions: *In this part, you will go over the passages quickly and answer the questions.*

For questions 1-7, mark

Y (*for YES*)   *if the statement agrees with the information given in the passage;*

N (*for NO*)   *if the statement contradicts the information given in the passage;*

NG (*for NOT GIVEN*)   *if the information is not given in the passage.*

For questions 8-10, complete the sentences with the information given in the passage.

It is estimated that on average, each airplane in the U. S. commercial fleet is struck lightly by lightning more than once each year. In fact, aircraft often trigger lightning when flying through a heavily charged region of a cloud. In these instances, the lightning flash originates at the airplane and extends away in opposite directions. Although record keeping is poor, smaller business and private airplanes are thought to be struck less frequently because of their small size and because they often can avoid weather that is conducive to lightning strikes.

The last confirmed commercial plane crash in the U. S. directly attributed to lightning occurred in 1967, when lightning caused a catastrophic fuel tank explosion. Since then, much has been learned about how lightning can affect airplanes. As a result, protection techniques have improved. Today, airplanes receive a rigorous(严格的) set of lightning certification tests to verify the safety of their designs. Nothing serious should happen because of the careful lightning protection engineered into the aircraft and its sensitive components. Initially, the lightning will attach to an extremity such as the nose or wing tip. The airplane then flies through the lightning flash, which reattaches itself to the fuselage(飞机机身) at other locations while the airplane is in the electric "circuit" between the cloud regions of opposite polarity(极性). The current will travel through the conductive exterior skin and structures of the aircraft and exit off some other extremity, such as the tail. Pilots occasionally report temporary flickering of lights or short-lived interference with instruments.

Most aircraft skins consist primarily of aluminum, which conducts electricity very well. By making sure that no gaps exist in this conductive path, the engineer can assure that most of the lightning current will remain on the exterior of the aircraft. Some modern aircraft are made of advanced composite materials, which by themselves are significantly less conductive than aluminum. In this case, the composites contain an embedded layer of conductive fibers or screens designed to carry lightning currents.

Modern passenger jets have miles of wires and dozens of computers and other instruments that control everything from the engines to the passengers' headsets. These computers, like all computers, are sometimes susceptible(敏感的) to upset from power surges. So, in addition to safeguarding the aircraft's exterior, the lightning protection engineer must make sure that no damaging surges or transients can reach the sensitive equipment inside the aircraft. Lightning traveling on the exterior skin of an aircraft has the potential to induce transients into wires or equipment beneath the skin. These transients(瞬变) are called lightning indirect effects. Careful shielding, grounding and the application of surge suppression devices avert problems caused by indirect effects in cables and equipment when necessary. Every circuit and piece of equipment that is critical or essential to the safe flight and landing of an aircraft must be verified by the manufacturers to be protected against lightning in accordance with regulations set by the Federal Aviation Administration (FAA) or a similar authority in the country of the aircraft's origin.

The other main area of concern is the fuel system, where even a tiny spark could be disastrous. Engineers thus take extreme precautions to ensure that lightning currents cannot cause sparks in 170 any portion of an aircraft's fuel system. The aircraft's skin around the fuel tanks must be thick enough to withstand a burn through. All of the structural joints and fasteners must be tightly designed to prevent sparks, because lightning current passes from one section to another. Access doors, fuel filler caps and any vents must be designed and tested to withstand lightning. All the pipes and fuel lines that carry fuel to the engines, and the engines themselves, must be protected against lightning. In addition, new fuels that produce less explosive vapors are now widely used.

The aircraft's radome—the nose cone that contains radar and other flight instruments—is another area to which lightning protection engineers pay special attention. In order to function, radar cannot be contained within a conductive enclosure. Instead, lightning diverter strips applied along the outer surface of the radome protect this area. These strips can consist of solid metal bars or a series of closely spaced buttons of conductive material affixed to a plastic strip that is bonded adhesively to the radome. In many ways, diverter strips function like a lightning rod on a building.

Private general aviation planes should avoid flying through or near thunderstorms. The severe turbulence found in storm cells alone should make the pilot of a small plane very wary. The FAA has a separate set of regulations governing the lightning protection of private aircraft that do not transport passengers. A basic level of protection is provided for the airframe, fuel system and engines. Traditionally, most small, commercially made aircraft have aluminum skins and do not contain computerized engine and flight controls, and they are thus inherently less susceptible to lightning; however, numerous reports of non-catastrophic damage to wing tips, propellers and navigation lights have been recorded.

The growing class of kit-built composite aircraft also raises some concerns. Because the FAA considers owner-assembled, kit-built aircraft "experimental" they are not subject to lightning protection regulations. Many kit-built planes are made of fiberglass or graphite (石墨)-reinforced composites. We routinely test protected fiberglass and composite panels with simulated lightning currents. The results of these tests show that lightning can damage inadequately protected composites. Pilots of unprotected fiberglass or composite aircraft should not fly anywhere near a lightning storm or in other types of clouds, because no thunderstorm clouds may contain sufficient electric charge to produce lightning.

1. This Passage tells the readers what happens when lightning strikes an airplane.

2. Large size airplanes are more in danger of being stricken by lightning than smaller ones.

3. It is a lightning striking airplane that reminds people to take some measures against it when the planes are designed.

4. Most aircraft's skins, fuel system, aircraft's radiomen, etc. are its sensitive parts.

5. Traveling by air is more dangerous than by sea.

6. General private aviation planes should avoid flying or near thunderstorms because of lack of air-supervision.

7. Because the materials used in kit-built composite aircraft are not good enough for flying through thunderstorm, they are banned to do so By FAA.

8. The commercial plane crash mentioned in the sentence was caused by _____.

9. The equipment inside the aircraft of the modern passenger jets are safely protected so that _____.

10. The fuel system should be given _____.

II Comprehensive Test

Section A   Cloze

Directions: *There are 20 blanks in the following passage. For each blank there are four choices marked A, B, C and D. You should choose the ONE that best fits into the passage. Then mark the corresponding letter on Answer Sheet with a single line through the center.*

Britain's secondary and primary schools will be able to exchange details of sports fixtures(定期的体育活动), general school activities, computer software lessons and personal messages through a new microcomputer-based network __1__ yesterday by The Times Network Systems, a subsidiary of News International.

The network, __2__ The Times Network for Schools (TTNS) has already attracted the interest of 80 local education authorities in the past few months during ___3___ development stage. The schools on the system link into the computers ___4___ by British Telecom's electronic mail service Telecom Gold（英国电信公司电子邮政服务黄金电信公司）. On these computers are more than 50 categories of ___5___ including a section on careers. The system will have more than 200,000 pages of information ___6___ the end of next year.

The network, designed for education, offers lessons on specific ___7___, and examinations can be conducted on it. The computer pages will he contributed by sources ___8___ local education authorities and industry and commerce. According to the creators of the network, Schools ___9___ the country will be able to exchange information at a fraction of the commercial price.

The network will also provide ___10___ links between education, industry, commerce and the professions by helping young people understand the requirements of their future and, ___11___, making them familiar with the new technology.

School using the system can transmit selected pages ___12___ telephone lines in second. Each school on the system will pay ￡69 for a 12-week term. An electronic "black Box" and the software ___13___ to link the "school micro"（校微机）to network will cost ￡152.

The aim is to attract ___14___ many of the country's 6,500 secondary schools and teacher training centers on to the network as possible. The next ___15___, within 12 months, will be to market（销售）the network to 27,000 primary schools.

The British network is the start of ___16___ could become a European operation. The designers want to ___17___ it to Holland, West Germany and France.

Computers will transform education by the end of the century, allowing more children to study ___18___, according to a book published yesterday (Colin Hughes writes).

Ray Hammond, the author, expects that, ___19___ schools will continue to exist, "they ___20___ be in the same form as they have been. "

1. A. launched   B. completed   C. removed   D. contributed
2. A. to be called   B. being called   C. so-called   D. to be known
3. A. it's   B. one's   C. their   D. its

4. A. supplied   B. required   C. operated   D. dreamed

5. A. cables   B. information   C. knowledge   D. program

6. A. on   B. by   C. for   D. within

7. A. tests   B. topics   C. weight   D. data

8. A. excluding   B. helping   C. including   D. threatening

9. A. under   B. for   C. from   D. throughout

10. A. vital   B. educational   C. apparent   D. net

11. A. at the same time   B. so far

    C. by the way   D. nevertheless

12. A. in   B. beneath   C. across   D. owing to

13. A. failing   B. required   C. having   D. attracted

14. A. with   B. so   C. as   D. also

15. A. measure   B. interval   C. time   D. phase

16. A. when   B. how   C. who   D. what

17. A. give up   B. concern   C. import   D. extend

18. A. in sequel   B. abroad   C. at home   D. outside

19. A. because   B. although   C. provided   D. since

20. A. won't   B. can't   C. couldn't   D. will

Section B   Error Correction

Directions: *This part consists a short passage. In this passage, there are possibably 10 or less than 10 mistakes, one in each numbered line. You may have to change a word, add a word or delete a word. If you change a word, cross it out and write the correct word in the corresponding blank. If you add a word, put an insertion mark ( ) in the correct word in the corresponding blank. If you delete a word, cross it out and be sure to put a slash (/) in the blank.*

It has been argued that socialization in the school is one of
the most powerful means of political control. The very fact of
having an entire generation within an institution where they are
required to cooperate and obey rules is considered by some
preparation to cooperate and obey the rules of the government.
Johann Fichte in Isrussia in the early nineteenth century
asserted that schools would prepare the individual to serve the
government and country with teaching obedience to the rules of   1. _____

the school and the development of a sense of loyalty the school.
He stated furtherly that students would transfer their obedience
to the laws of the school to obedience to the constitution of the
country. More important, according to Fichte, interaction
between students, as well loyalty and service to the school and
fellow students, would prepare the individual for service to the
country. The school was a miniature（缩影）community in
which children learned to adjust their individuality on the
requirements of the community. The real works of the school,
Fichte said, was in shaping this adjustment. The well-ordered
government required that the citizen go beyond mere obedience
to the written constitution and laws. Fichte believed that the
child must be adjusted to see the government of some thing
greater than the individual and must learn to sacrifice to the
good of the social whole.

2. _____
3. _____
4. _____
5. _____
6. _____
7. _____
8. _____
9. _____
10. _____

Section C   Short Answer Questions

Directions: *In this part there is a short passage with five questions or incomplete
statements. Read the passage carefully. Then answer the questions or complete
the statements in the fewest possible words.*

Americans in some states are already voting in the November second general
elections. Thousands of people lined up to vote in Florida, one of four states
where early voting began Monday. Election officials estimate that at least 20
percent of voters will vote before Election Day. Those votes, however, will be
counted at the same time as the others, on November second.

Since the 2000 election, many states have made it easier for people to vote
before Election Day. More and more people vote by mail. Absentee ballots（选
票）are meant for people who cannot go to their local voting station on Election
Day.

There is also a kind of ballot called a provisional ballot. These are given to
people who try to vote on Election Day but do not find their names on voter lists.
In 2002 Congress passed the Help America Vote Act. This law requires a
provisional（临时的）ballot to be counted if officials are able to later establish that

an individual could vote. Republicans and Democrats, however, are fighting over the rules for counting provisional ballots.

In the final days before the election, campaigning is aimed at several states known as swing states or battleground states. These are where Republican President George Bush and Democratic Senator John Kerry are closest in levels of support.

Ohio, Florida and Pennsylvania are considered the top three among these states. Some political experts say whichever candidate wins two of those three states will win the election.

Americans do not vote directly for their president. Instead, each of the 50 states represents a number of electoral votes. The number is related to population. A candidate must gain at least 270 out of 538 electoral votes to win.

Questions：(注意:答题尽量简短,超过10个词要扣分,每条横线限写一个英语单词,标点符号不占格。)

1. In what way can people vote easier?

   _____   _____   _____   _____

   _____   _____   _____   _____

2. What are given to those who cannot go to their local voting station on Election Day?

   _____   _____   _____   _____

3. What are given to those who cannot find their names on voter lists?

   _____   _____   _____   _____

   _____   _____   _____   _____

4. What are Republicans and Democrats arguing about?

   _____   _____   _____   _____

   _____   _____   _____   _____

5. What determines the number of electoral votes?

   _____   _____   _____   _____

   _____   _____   _____   _____

Test Two

I Reading Comprehension

Section A Passage Reading

Directions: *There are 2 passages in this section. Each passage is followed by some questions or unfinished statements. For each of them there are four choices marked A, B, C and D. You should decide on the best choice and mark the corresponding letter on Answer Sheet with a single line through the center.*

Passage One

Questions 1 to 5 are based on the following passage.

It has been thought and said that Africans are born with musical talent. Because music is so important in the lives of many Africans and because so much music is performed in Africa, we are inclined to think that all Africans are musician. The impression is strengthened when we look at ourselves and find that we have become largely a society of musical spectators. Music is important to us, but most of us can be considered consumers rather than producers of music. We have records, televisions, concerts, and radios to fulfill many of our musical needs. In most situations where music is performed in our culture it is not difficult to distinguish the audience from the performers, but such is often not the case in Africa. Alban Ayipaga, a Kasenta semi-professional musician from northern Ghana, says that when his flute(长笛) and drum ensemble(歌舞团) is performing, "Anybody can take part". This is true, but Kasenta musicians recognize that not all people are equally capable of taking part in the music. Some can sing along with the drummers, but relatively few can drum and even fewer can play the flute along with the ensemble. It is fairly common in Africa for there to be an ensemble of expert musicians surrounded by others who join in by clapping, singing, or somehow adding to the totality of musical sound. Performances often take place in an open area (that is, not on a stage) and so the lines between the performing nucleus and the additional performers, active spectators, and passive spectators may be difficult to draw from our point of view.

1. The difference between us and Africans, as far as music is concerned, is that _____.

   A. most of us are consumers while most of them are producers of music

   B. we are musical performers and they are semiprofessional musicians

   C. most of us are passive spectators while they are active spectators

   D. we are the audience and they are the additional performers

2. The word "such"(sentence 6) refers to the fact that _____.

   A. music is performed with the participation of the audience

   B. music is performed without the participation of the audience

   C. people tend to distinguish the audience from the performers

   D. people have records, television-sets and radios to fulfill their musical needs

3. The author of the passage implies that _____.

   A. all Africans are musical and therefore flute music is performed in Africa

   B. not all Africans are born with musical talent although music is important in their lives

   C. most Africans are capable of joining in the music by playing musical instruments

   D. most Africans perform as well as professional musicians

4. The word "nucleus"(last sentence) probably refers to _____.

   A. musicians famous in Africa

   B. musicians at the centre of attention

   C. musicians acting as the core in a performance

   D. active participants in a musical performance

5. The best title for this passage would be _____.

   A. The Importance of Music to African People

   B. Differences between African Music and Music of other Countries

   C. The Relationship between Musicians and Their Audience

   D. A Characteristic Feature of African Musical Performances

Passage Two

Questions 6 to 10 are based on the following passage.

Is it possible to persuade mankind to live without war? War is an ancient institution which has existed for at least six thousand years. It was always bad and usually foolish, but in the past the human race managed to live with it.

Modern ingenuity(独创性) has changed this. Either man will abolish war, or war will abolish man. For the present, it is nuclear weapons that cause the most serious danger, but bacteriological or chemical weapons may, before long, offer an even greater threat. If we succeed in abolishing nuclear weapons, our work will not be done. It will never be done until we have succeeded in abolishing war. To do this, we need to persuade mankind to look upon international questions in a new way, not as contests of force, in which the victory goes to the side which is most skillful in killing people, but by arbitration in accordance with agreed principles of law. It is not easy to change very old mental habits, but this is what must be attempted.

There are those who say that the adoption of this or that ideology would prevent a war. I believe this to be a big error. All ideologies are based upon dogmatic(教条主义的) statements which are, at best, doubtful, and at worst, totally false. Their adherents believe in them so fanatically that they are willing to go to war in support of them.

The movement of world opinion during the past few years has been very largely such as we can welcome. It has become a commonplace that nuclear war must be avoided. Of course very difficult problems remain in the world, but the spirit in which they are being approached is a better one than it was some years ago. It has begun to be thought, even by the powerful men who decide whether we shall live or die, that negotiations should reach agreements even if both sides do not find these agreements wholly satisfactory. It has begun to be understood that the important conflict nowadays is not between different countries, but between man and the atom bomb.

6. This passage implies that war is now _____.

    A. worse than in the past

    B. as bad as in the past

    C. not as dangerous as in the past

    D. as necessary as in the past

7. From paragraph 2 we learn that the writer of the passage _____.

    A. is an adherent of some modern ideologies

    B. does not think that the adoption of any ideology could prevent war

    C. believes that the adoption of some ideologies could prevent war

    D. does not doubt the truth of any ideologies

8. According to the writer, _____.

    A. a war is the only way to solve international disputes

    B. a war will be less dangerous because of the improvement of weapons

    C. it is impossible for people to live without war

    D. war must be abolished if man wants to survive

9. The writer believes that the only way to abolish wars is to _____.

    A. destroy nuclear weapons

    B. let the stronger nations control the world

    C. improve chemical weapons

    D. solve international problems through negotiations

10. The last paragraph suggests that _____.

    A. international agreements can be reached more easily now

    B. man begins to realize the danger of nuclear war

    C. nuclear war will definitely not take place

    D. world opinion welcomes nuclear war

Section B   Banked Cloze

Directions: *In this section, there is a passage with ten blanks. You are required to select one word for each blank from a list of choices given in a word bank following the passage. Read the passage through carefully before making your choices. Each choice in the bank is identified by a letter. Please mark the corresponding letter for each item on Answer Sheet with a single line through the center. You may not use any of the words in the bank more than once.*

    Those people who affect your life and the failure and the success you experience can ___1___ you to create who you are and who you become. Even the bad experiences can be learned from. In fact, they are the most important ones. If ___2___ breaks your heart, or hurts you, please ___3___ them, for they helped you to learn about the importance of being careful when you open your heart. If someone ___4___ you, love them back, because they are ___5___ you how to love and how to open your heart and eyes to things.

    You can make of your life anything you wish. Appreciate every moment and take everything from those ___6___ as possible as you can because you may never be able to ___7___ it again. Talk to people who you have never talked to ___8___, and when they talk, you'd better listen to them. Let yourself fall in love, then break free and set your sights high. Tell yourself you are a great person and believe in ___9___, for if you don't believe in yourself, it will be difficult for others to believe in you. Make every day meaningful and interesting. Create your own life and live without any regrets. Love your life ___10___ you may have some pleasant, cheerful and happy hours.

A. someone	E. open	I. and	M. moments
B. then	F. help	J. person	N. ago
C. loves	G. yourself	K. experience	O. before
D. teaching	H. forgive	L. success	

Section C   Reading Comprehension (Skinning and Scanning)

Directions: *In this part, you will go over the passages quickly and answer the questions.*

For questions 1-7, mark

Y (for YES)   *if the statement agrees with the information given in the passage;*

N (for NO)   *if the statement contradicts the information given in the passage;*

NG (for NOT GIVEN)   *if the information is not given in the passage.*

For questions 8-10, complete the sentences with the information given in the passage.

In case of Thailand, the recent financial crisis is different from the previous ones in that it was not only caused by factors related to economic cycle but also by structural weaknesses in the system. A significant cause of this crisis is the massive capital inflows into the economy without effective management mechanisms. Some examples of the weak initial conditions are ineffective corporate governance, inadequate supervision and regulation, and insufficient or in some cases inaccurate disclosure which resulted in lax(无常的) credit policies in banks and other financial institutions and misuses of funds in the corporate sector. Owing to the liberalization policy and the swift capital mobility in the integrated financial system, businesses had access to the overseas funds at relatively low cost and allocated such funds for rapid expansion and other purposes which were in general not subject to adequate monitoring and control mechanism. During a boom period, stakeholders including shareholders and creditors tended to neglect the soundness of the uses of funds; instead, they perceived that the ultimate economic benefits must outweigh the costs. Hence, in the downturn, the accumulation of these chronic(长期的) structural problems revealed serious symptoms.

To institute good corporate governance in Thailand, we will use the mixture of regulatory approach and voluntary approach, which seems to suit the Thai culture best.

Regulatory or Legislative Approach

Regulations in the area of corporate governance will be set up in accordance with four main principles namely, fairness, accountability, transparency and responsibility.

Fairness. Protection of shareholder rights is a primary aim of regulations. Shareholders especially minority ones need to be assured that their assets are protected against fraud(欺诈), managerial or controlling shareholder self-dealing and insider wrongdoing. In this regard, the SEC closely monitors and investigates suspicious cases of management wrongdoing and insider trading and consequently imposes both civil and criminal sanctions(制裁,处罚) against wrongdoers. Furthermore, we are now studying the possibility of bringing in the class action lawsuit in our law since it could be an effective mechanism for a broad class of shareholders to file a lawsuit against management for any conduct that unfairly disregards their interests.

Accountability. As the agency problem tends to divert(转移) managerial incentives from being accountable to shareholders, regulations could play a role in aligning(使一致) the interests of management with those of shareholders. The primary measure is to create the appropriate structure of the board of directors equipped with check and balance mechanisms to monitor management, guard against fraud and alleviate(减轻,缓和) other agency problems.

Second, the ownership and management structure should be designed to prevent the conflicts of interests. According to the Public Company Law, the cross-directorship between businesses, which have the same nature and directly compete with each other, is prohibited unless a director notifies the shareholder meeting prior to the resolution for his appointment. This provision serves to ensure the director will uphold the interests of his company.

Third, good internal control is another safeguard against management misconduct. Thus, the SEC and the SET include the establishment of an effective internal control system as a requirement for an applicant who wants to make public offering or to be listed on the exchange. In addition, an independent external auditor of the company granted such approval has to give his opinion in the annual financial statements as to the adequacy of and the compliance with the established internal control procedures.

Lastly, shareholders' voting rights must be protected and exercised in their best interests. One of the ongoing studies is to improve the proxy (代理) solicitation(恳求,恳请) process to furnish shareholders with a proxy statement, which contains sufficient information on the matters to be acted upon and allows a shareholder to specify his opinion regarding such matters.

Transparency. The disclosure of accurate and comprehensive information about corporate performance is a key to promote investor confidence and market efficiency. Provided with sufficient and timely information, investors incur (招致) lower cost in evaluating investment alternatives and monitoring the performance of companies in their portfolios (公事包). Market prices will incorporate complete information and reflect the actual picture of a company. Investors therefore have more confidence and are willing to commit greater capital to the more transparent market.

In terms of the ownership information, a company is required to disclose the names and stakes of major shareholders holding at least 10% of total shares. Besides, the information regarding the structure of the board of directors, total remuneration (报酬) of all directors, of all management team and of the top fifteen management staff as well as intercom any transactions must be disclosed.

Responsibility. Lastly, businesses have responsibilities to not only shareholders but also other stakeholders such as creditors, employees, government and society. Regulators therefore need to ensure that they abide by all relevant laws and regulations including those regarding tax, environmental protection, health and safety.

Voluntary Approach. The key to the voluntary approach is to change the mindset of the management, shareholders and related parties to be aware of the importance of good corporate governance and perform their duties accordingly. Businesses in particular need to realize their mission is to enhance long-term value to shareholders. To achieve such mission, they have to function in the larger society and thus bear responsibilities to all stakeholders.

First, we have motivated the private sector to realize their benefits from good corporate governance and merits of regulations in this area. For example, the compliance with regulations such as disclosure standards will enable the market to differentiate a company with good versus bad governance, thereby enhancing the competitiveness of a good company and facilitating its access to tap funds at lower cost.

Second, we have strongly encouraged the industries to set up their codes of conduct. In the securities business, broker-sales officers are required to have a license and to follow operating guidelines specified by the SET. Furthermore, many other industries have been increasingly aware of the importance of good governance and set up their codes of professional conduct such as the codes of the Association of Investment Management Companies, Association of Provident Fund Managers, Association of Securities Analysts, and Association of Valuers.

Lastly, on the shareholders side, the SEC and the SET have launched an educational campaign for shareholders to be increasingly aware of and better understand their rights as well as legal procedures available for the protection of their rights so that they will play a more active role in monitoring the management conduct.

In conclusion, the experiences from the past economic and financial crises have drawn greater attention to the quality aspect of investment alternatives. To recover from the crisis in the environment of the freely competitive and integrated market, we consider good governance a significant factor to improve the quality of our corporations and consequently enhance their competitiveness and access to the global financial market.

1. This passage is mainly concentrates on the economy and crisis in Thailand.

2. The recent financial crisis in Thailand is attributes to the unhealthy and inefficient management mechanisms in the Thailand Government.

3. Four main principles like fairness, accountability, transparency and responsibility would help the Thailand Government work effectively in finance.

4. Interest conflicts were widely existing in Thailand when the financial crisis broke out.

5. The Thailand Government is quite helpless in dealing with the financial crisis

there.

6. Both transparency and responsibility are served as the keys to promote investor confidence and market efficiency.

7. Four reasons are mentioned as the key to the voluntary approach to change the mindset of the management, shareholders, etc.

8. Good internal control like accountability is considered as _____.

9. Investor confidence is varied with the market prices and market prices will reflect _____.

10. The past economic and financial experiences have drawn greater attention to the _____.

II Comprehensive Test

Section A Cloze

Directions: *There are 20 blanks in the following passage. For each blank there are four choices marked A, B, C and D. You should choose the ONE that best fits into the passage. Then mark the corresponding letter on Answer Sheet with a single line through the center.*

Both skimming and scanning are specific reading techniques necessary for quick and efficient reading.

When skimming, we go through the reading material quickly in __1__ to get the gist of it, to know how it is organized, or to get an idea of the tone or the __2__ of the writer.

When scanning, we only try to __3__ specific information and often we do not even follow the linearity(线性) of the passage to do so. We simply let our eyes wander __4__ the text until we find what we are looking for, whether it be a name, a date, or a __5__ specific piece of information.

Skimming is __6__ a more thorough activity which requires an overall view of the text and implies a __7__ reading competence. Scanning, on the contrary, is far more limited __8__ it only means retrieving(检索) what information is relevant to our purpose. Yet it is usual to make use of these two activities together __9__ reading a given text. For instance, we may well skim through an article first just to know whether it is worth __10__, then read it through more carefully because we have decided that it is of interest. It is also possible afterwards to scan the same article in order to __11__ down a figure or a name which we particularly want to remember.

The first two exercises in the "skimming" section are training and preliminary exercises. Those that __12__ (exercises 3-10) try to recreate authentic reading situations. They should contribute to __13__ up the students' confidence by showing them how much they can learn simply by looking at some __14__ parts of an article, by catching a few words only, by reading a few paragraphs here and there in a story. Their aim is certainly not to encourage the students to read __15__ texts in such a superficial way that would be in contradiction with the principle of flexibility mentioned __16__ but they should make the students better readers, that is, readers who can decide quickly __17__ they want or need to read. So many students spend so much time carefully and thoroughly reading a newspaper (for instance) that by the time they find something of real interest, they no longer have time or energy __18__ to read it in detail.

The exercises suggested to practice scanning also try to put the students in an authentic __19__ where they would naturally scan the text rather than read it. The students are therefore asked to solve a specific problem as quickly as possible—which is only possible by means of __20__ .

1. A. case   B. time   C. order   D. favor
2. A. anticipation B. implication   C. idea   D. intention
3. A. introduce   B. locate   C. mention   D. go through
4. A. into   B. from   C. above   D. over
5. A. less   B. more   C. mere   D. somehow
6. A. therefore   B. however   C. no longer   D. even
7. A. inherent   B. definite   C. partial   D. sufficient
8. A. while   B. if   C. once   D. since
9. A. although   B. before   C. unless   D. when
10. A. studying   B. writing   C. reading   D. noting
11. A. shut   B. note   C. slow   D. scale
12. A. proceed   B. cover   C. follow   D. appear
13. A. giving   B. making   C. taking   D. building
14. A. prominent B. systematic   C. neutral   D. metric
15. A. such   B. all   C. whole   D. their

16. A. then   B. later   C. earlier   D. in time

17. A. what   B. that   C. as   D. when

18. A. needed   B. left   C. lost   D. pretended

19. A. text   B. article   C. situation   D. question

20. A. scanning   B. article   C. predicting   D. guessing

Section B   Error Correction

Directions: *This part consists a short passage. In this passage, there are possibably 10 or less than 10 mistakes, one in each numbered line. You may have to change a word, add a word or delete a word. If you change a word, cross it out and write the correct word in the corresponding blank. If you add a word, put an insertion mark ( ) in the correct word in the corresponding blank. If you delete a word, cross it out and be sure to put a slash (/) in the blank.*

Britain has widespread security and economic interests in other countries. She has extensive overseas trading links in terms of both visible and invisible trade: her overseas investments are substantial and British shipping and aviation have large international networks. To the extent that a beneficent attitude by overseas authorities towards Britain and her interests can be fostered by study opportunities in Britain, a

1. _____

considering "return" may be obtained from the continuing presence of foreign students in Britain. Many overseas governments do have a substantial identifiable part of their

2. _____

leadership—political, military, commercial—who have in the past been educating in the United Kingdom and the testimony

3. _____

of overseas British diplomatic and commercial representatives have been that such leaders have generally been helpfully

4. _____

oriented towards Britain by their study experiences here. (The possibility of a contrary affect—unhappy study experiences

5. _____

leading to negative attitudes towards Britain was one reason for

6. _____

the setting up of the Overseas Students Trust twenty years ago and for its early concern with overseas student welfare.) Of course, it is more difficult than hitherto(迄今) to identify the leaders of tomorrow, and it is to be expecting that the

7. _____

proportion of overseas leaders that is British trained will fall. Moreover, the direct benefit is hard to assess, and may equally be sought to other channels parallel to overseas study programs. If the experience of Britons working abroad is to be believed, study in Britain is a potent force in forming and maintained useful overseas relationships for this country and in securing our overseas interests. In this connection the links between educational exchange, the spread of the English language, and British commercial advantage is often stressed.

8. _____

9. _____

10. _____

Section C   Short Answer Questions

Directions: *In this part there is a short passage with five questions or incomplete statements. Read the passage carefully. Then answer the questions or complete the statements in the fewest possible words.*

It's never easy to admit you are in the wrong. Being human, we all need to know the art of apologizing. Look back with honesty and think how often you've judged roughly, said unkind things, pushed yourself ahead at the expense of a friend. Then count the occasions when you indicated clearly and truly that you were sorry. A bit frightening, isn't it? Frightening because some deep wisdom in us knows that when even a small wrong has been committed, some mysterious moral feeling is disturbed; and it stays out of balance until fault is acknowledged and regret expressed.

I remember a doctor friend, the late Clarence Lieb, telling me about a man who came to him with a variety of signs: headaches, insomnia(失眠症) and stomach trouble. No physical cause could be found. Finally Dr. Lieb said to the man, "Unless you tell me what's worrying you, I can't help you. "

After some hesitation, the man confessed that, as executor of his father's will, he had been cheating his brother, who lived abroad, of his inheritance. Then and there the wise old doctor made the man write to his brother asking forgiveness and enclosing a check as the first step in restoring their good relation. He then went with him to the mailbox in the corridor. As the letter disappeared, the man burst into tears. "Thank you," he said, "I think I'm cured. " And he was.

A heartfelt apology can not only heal a damaged relationship but also make it stronger. If you can think of someone who deserves an apology from you, someone you have wronged, or judged too roughly, or just neglected, do something about it right now.

Questions:（注意：答题尽量简短，超过10个词要扣分，每条横线限写一个英语单词，标点符号不占格。）

1. When we have done something wrong, we should _____ .

   _____ _____ _____ _____

   _____ _____ _____ _____

2. What will happen if we have done something wrong?

   _____ _____ _____ _____

   _____ _____ _____ _____

3. What exactly was the patient's trouble?

   _____ _____ _____ _____

   _____ _____ _____ _____

4. What should we do if we have done something wrong to others?

   _____ _____ _____ _____

   _____ _____ _____ _____

5. The patient was cured by _____ .

   _____ _____ _____ _____

   _____ _____ _____ _____

Test Three

I Reading Comprehension

Section A Passage Reading

Directions: *There are 2 passages in this section. Each passage is followed by some questions or unfinished statements. For each of them there are four choices marked A, B, C and D. You should decide on the best choice and mark the corresponding letter on Answer Sheet with a single line through the center.*

Passage One

Questions 1 to 5 are based on the following passage.

   Self-preservation is the most powerful of instincts. No greater force unthinkingly moves living beings. To deny it is to fight nature itself. To do so in the cause of preserving another person's life demands a super-human willingness to make the ultimate sacrifice—to accept consciously that an untimely death is possible, probable, and even inevitable.

Such was the unspeakable test confronting Seol Ik Soo. An Air China Boeing 767 passenger jet had turned the South Korean mountaintop where it smacked down into a wasteland of twisted metal, charred（把……烧成炭） fuselage and shattered trees. Aboard was Seol, a 25-year-old trainee for a tour company helping to bring South Korean tourists home from Beijing. The first indication anything was wrong came just minutes before the plane was due to touch down at Kimbae Airport near the southern city of Pusan. Sitting in his hospital bed three days after the crash, Seol recalls feeling the aircraft shudder twice, then hearing a crashing sound. The plane seemed to glide up the side of a mountain. The lights died and, sparks flashed up and down the cabin. He looked to his right and saw that rows of seats had simply vanished. Passengers were screaming in the darkness. Seol's first thought was: "I'm dead." When he saw a hole with light showing through, he made his way toward it and crawled through. Only then did he realize he had survived.

Seol knew the sparks inside the cabin could trigger an explosion and thought, "I have to run." But the other passengers who had followed out had collapsed beside the plane. He yelled at them to move, then hoisted（拎起） a survivor onto his back and carried him down a treacherously muddy slope to a flat clearing. He remembers hauling at least three or four injured people to safety, maybe as many as 10. "I don't know where the energy came from," he said later, "but it felt like I wasn't carrying anything at all."

1. What is the implication of the first paragraph?

    A. The hero survived an accident and tried to help other victims.

    B. The hero was willing to sacrifice his life.

    C. A superman accepts that death is possible and probable.

    D. Nature allows people to fight self-preservation.

2. What do you know about Seol according to the passage?

    A. He is an employer of a tour company.

    B. He is a tourist back from China.

    C. He is a trainee of a tour company.

D. He is a passenger back from South Korea.

3. What will our instinct tell us to do when we are in danger?
   A. To help others.   B. To escape from danger.
   C. To be on guard against it.   D. To report the danger.

4. Which is true according to the passage?
   A. Seol was strong enough to help others.
   B. There were more than just several survivors in the crash.
   C. Seol thought once and again before he went to help others.
   D. Self-preservation is the most powerful of instincts.

5. What will Seol talk about in the paragraphs that follow?
   A. Describe his experience of how he survived and helped other passengers.
   B. Explain his feeling as a superman.
   C. His complaint to the Airline.
   D. Recall what happened and what he thought about at the moment.

Passage Two
Questions 6 to 10 are based on the following passage.

The word "conservation" has a thrifty meaning. To conserve is to save and protect, to leave what we ourselves enjoy in such good condition that other may also share the enjoyment. Our forefathers had no idea that human population would increase faster than the supplies of raw materials; most of them, even until very recently, had the foolish idea that the treasures were "limitless" and "inexhaustible". Most of the citizens of earlier generations knew little or nothing about the complicated and delicate system that runs all through nature, and which means that, as in a living body, an unhealthy condition of one part will sooner or later be harmful to all the other.

Fifty years ago nature study was not part of the school work; scientific forestry was a new idea; timber was still cheap because it could be brought in any quantity from distant woodlands; soil destruction and river floods were not national problems; nobody had yet studied long term climatic cycles in relation to proper land use; even the word "conservation" had nothing of the meaning that it has for us today.

For the sake of ourselves and those who will come after us, we must now set about repairing the mistakes of our forefather. Conservation should, therefore, be made a part of everyone's daily life. To know about the water table(水位) in the ground is just as important to us as a knowledge of the basic arithmetic formulas. We need to know all watersheds(上游源头森林地带集水区) need the protection of plant life and why the running current of streams and rivers must be made to yield their full benefit to the soil before they finally escape to the sea. We need to be taught the duty of planting trees as well as of cutting them. We need to know the importance of big, mature trees, because living space for most of man's fellow creatures on this planet is figured not only in square measure of surface but also in cubic volume above the earth. In brief, it should be our goal to restore as much of the original beauty of nature as we can.

6. What does the author suggest by the first sentence in the first paragraph?

   A. Conservation is prevention of loss, waste, damage, etc.

   B. Conservation means thrift.

   C. Besides its common meaning of preservation, to conserve also means to save.

   D. Conservation has a special meaning of thrift nowadays.

7. Why is the conservation considered important nowadays?

   A. Resources are limited and exhaustible.

   B. We have to be long sighted for our future generations.

   C. Scientific studies on conservation have attracted much attention than before.

   D. Both A and B.

8. In order to use land properly we have to study _____.

   A. knowledge of watersheds   B. long-term climatic cycles

   C. scientific forestry   D. knowledge of water table

9. In the third paragraph the author compares the knowledge of water table with basic arithmetic formulas to _____.

   A. stress on the importance of learning basic arithmetic formulas

   B. suggest that knowledge of water table is essential for us

   C. show a close connection between water table and arithmetic

   D. explain that conservation of water is vital for mankind

10. What is the purpose of this passage?

   A. To introduce some basic knowledge of conservation.

   B. To trace out the development of the idea of "conservation".

C. To offer a fresh explanation of the word "conservation".

D. To advocate the importance of conservation.

Section B　Banked Cloze

Directions: *In this section, there is a passage with ten blanks. You are required to select one word for each blank from a list of choices given in a word bank following the passage. Read the passage through carefully before making your choices. Each choice in the bank is identified by a letter. Please mark the corresponding letter for each item on Answer Sheet with a single line through the center. You may not use any of the words in the bank more than once.*

More than two ___1___ people in Hong Kong live in overcrowded tenements, public housing units and boats. Not a pleasant sight—and an unending ___2___ that the Housing Department has to cope with ___3___ after year. The housing situation in the colony verges（边缘，界线，范围）almost the precarious. Alongside the squatters are the people who work for the hongs（商行），the government and multinationals who ___4___ the luxury of large flats, and the middle-income group who live in small and ___5___ comfortable flats.

Indeed the chronic problem of indefinite housing is not news ___6___ to any Hong Kong resident, not even the newcomer ___7___ has just arrived at Kal Tak Airport. Squatter areas are special in most ___8___ countries. Often huts sprout overnight, precious tiny shelters of a 100 150 square feet area or even less, offsetting public and temporary housing programs.

The task at hand is undeniably not at all easy for Government ___9___ sitting in the glass offices of some housing section nor the squatter control unit responsible for tearing down illegal huts in a bid to control and clear such areas. Thus, the government is caught between having to be the overlord for the poor as well as the administrator who has to ___10___ a fair economy for all.

A. in all	E. enjoyed	I. year	M. developing
B. section	F. at all	J. officials	N. million
C. problem	G. thousand	K. ensure	O. overnight
D. squatter	H. who	L. reasonably	

Section C　Reading Comprehension（Skinning and Scanning）

Directions: *In this part, you will go over the passages quickly and answer the* *questions.*

For questions 1-7, *mark*

Y (*for YES*)   *if the statement agrees with the information given in the passage;*

N (*for NO*)   *if the statement contradicts the information given in the passage;*

NG (*for NOT GIVEN*)   *if the information is not given in the passage.*

For questions 8-10, *complete the sentences with the information given in the passage.*

Find yourself in a hole where expenses exceed revenues? Thinking about layoffs and closing programs to make ends meet? It is cold comfort, but you're definitely not alone—many agencies are facing difficult times.

Here's a more or less sequential list of activities a chief executives can pursue to heal the financially sick organization, in no technical financial language.

The Right Mind-Set

First, you might need to re-adjust your thinking about the organization. Note the reference above about healing the organization. This is a critical mind-set for long-term success. Think of your agency as a living, breathing organism, not a machine. Make a deliberate effort to drop language like, "Get things back on track" or "Take it apart and put it back together." These tend to make you think you are merely operating a piece of machinery.

Here's some of what you need:

Timely monthly reports. To make progress, you absolutely must have monthly financial reports by the 15th of the subsequent month. For example, by May 15, you must have complete reports for all your financial activities in April. Why?

If you don't have at least two weeks each month to make changes that will impact next month, an effective turnaround is unlikely. Despite protests from the staff, this is a realistic timeframe. Much will be expected during difficult times, and your staff should expect overtime work.

Weekly cash-flow information. Monthly financial statements will report accrued data. This means you expect to receive certain payments, but you probably don't actually have the money yet. Meanwhile, you owe payroll and other bills, but you may not have enough cash to pay those bills. Organizations or businesses often have positive financial statements but experience cash-flow problems because one or more customers are late paying.

This is the one financial problem most often misunderstood by board and staff. It causes you to borrow money to pay your own bills, or delay paying them, in hopes that revenues will catch up. To monitor cash flow, have the accounting staff prepare a brief report every Monday morning that shows. The report doesn't have to be more than a half page. Every Monday morning, you and senior staff should have a 10-minute meeting to review this report. Everyone will know the week's critical issues.

Monthly trends of revenues and expenses. Every month, direct the accounting staff to prepare a 13-month rolling revenue and expense chart, exclusive of gift income. You want to see a set of green (revenues) and red (expenses) bars on a chart for each of the past 13 months. Since gift income is often restricted and relatively unpredictable, compared with revenue earned, exclude charitable receipts from this report.

Return on investment. For a really long-term view, ask the accounting staff to collect the organization's audits(经审核的账目) for the past 10 years. Take the total revenue for each year and subtract the gift income, resulting in the amount of revenue earned (RE). Next, determine the organization's total program and administrative staff (PAS)—take the number of employees for each year and subtract the number of development or fundraising staff. Divide RE by PAS for each year to calculate total dollars earned per staff member. Create a line graph for the 10 years to see if your staff has become more or less "productive" over the decade.

Keep in mind, the power vested(既定的) at the top of the organization can reduce expenses, but only the power at the bottom of the organization can maximize revenues. Unfortunately, as CEO, you probably don't know enough about all the operational details to make a difference. You will need the dedicated help of front-line staff to identify and exploit these seemingly small differences.

Engage Staff. When looking for ways to trim expenses, one of the first things on everyone's list is likely to be downsizing. Be very careful about jumping into this as a first action. Remember, the agency is a living organization. Layoffs are like surgery, and some surgery can put the patient in recovery well into the next year. Consider other alternatives first.

In nearly every organization, the CEO will need the help of every staff member to realize all the possible revenues and savings. Getting their help and support may be more difficult than you realize, and beginning the turnaround plan with layoffs can make collaboration much more difficult. Staff who are fearful of losing their jobs aren't eager to work collaboratively.

Engaging everyone in joint solutions means expanding participation. This requires letting go of the notion that financial information is confidential. As a matter of fact, you'll have to find ways to share fiscal data that everyone can easily understand, right down to the maintenance staff.

Here's one way to begin the process:

· Call a general staff meeting. Have more than one if shift work or geography requires it—make sure everyone attends. The CEO must lead this meeting.

· Create a half dozen or so large, poster-sized charts, and position them around the room. Possibilities include monthly trends of revenue and expenses, return on investment, utilization rates, increase or decrease in employees, increase or decrease in gift income, and number of referrals—all over the past 5-10 years.

· Divide employees into small groups and ask individuals to move from chart to chart, taking notes for discussion in their small groups.

· Each small group should discuss two questions:

· What does each chart mean individually?

· How do all charts relate to each other? Will change in one affect another?

· Consider asking the board of directors to go through this same process. When they've finished their discussions, describe how the staff reacted.

· Reassemble the full group and ask what they discovered and what surprised them.

· Take all questions, and try your best to answer them. Do more listening and paraphrasing of their thoughts than trying to explain finances. End with a plea: This organization we love is facing some very tough times. Each of us needs to help find ways to both make more money and save money. You will be meeting as work teams next week—every possible solution you find can be helpful.

In time for those team meetings, accounting staff should prepare, from the previous month's data, a revenues-versus-expenses graph for each team's individual unit. Each team will need to see this same chart by the 25th of each subsequent month. You'll be amazed how quickly these charts are posted on supervisor's walls and how quickly changes will take place.

A kind of magic happens when people clearly see an issue and realize they have friends and companions around to help work toward a solution. This turnaround process takes more than a good administrator; it takes a great leader to unleash the power of collaborative solutions.

1. The passage mainly provides some ways to balance the overdone expenses and exceeded revenues.

2. The agency should be treated and operated like a working machine.

3. Timely monthly reports is helpful for the manager to follow a realistic time frame.

4. Layoffs should be the priority to turn to when it is necessary to trim expenses.

5. When workers are overshadowed by the fear of losing jobs, they will not be willing to cooperate with their boss in a proper way.

6. Engaging everyone in joint solutions means to encourage them to find ways to solve the problems the company is face with.

7. By engaging everyone in joint solution, the boss can transfer the burden to his employees.

8. The positive financial statements of organization or business don't necessily mean they have no _____.

9. What unfortunately a CEO don't know enough is about _____.

10. If a CEO follows the suggestions mentioned here, _____.

II Comprehensive Test

Section A Cloze

Directions: *There are 20 blanks in the following passage. For each blank there are four choices marked A, B, C and D. You should choose the ONE that best fits into the passage. Then mark the corresponding letter on Answer Sheet with a single line through the center.*

One of the most widely discussed subjects these days is energy crisis. Automobile drivers cannot get gasoline; homeowners may not get enough heating oil; factories are __1__ by a fuel shortage.

The crisis has raised questions about the large oil companies and windfall(意外收获) __2__ . Critics of the oil industry charge that the major companies are getting richer because of the oil shortage. Shortage, of course, __3__ prices up. As oil prices rise, the critics say, the oil companies will make more and more money—windfall profits—without doing a thing to __4__ the extra cash. "windfall" profits are sudden unearned profit—profit made __5__ luck, or some special turn of events.

The word itself tells what "windfall" means—something blown __6__ by the wind, such as trees, or fruit blown from trees. But the word has taken on a special meaning. This meaning—getting something unearned—was first used in medieval __7__ .

This is how it started. At that time much of the land was in the hands of a __8__ barons(贵族). The rest of the people, commoners, lived and worked on their vast estates. They planted the seed, cared for the farm animals and harvested the crops. Not all the land, __9__ , was used for farming. Every land baron kept a large private forest for __10__ deer and "wind boar"(野猪).

When hungry, the people sometimes would kill the animals in the lord's forest for food. And there were times __11__ they might cut down trees for fuel. So, strong laws were passed to protect the forests and the animals. Violations were severely __12__ .

But there was one way people could get wood from the forest. __13__ they found trees blown down by the wind—"windfall"—they were free to take them for use as fuel in their homes. And __14__ is the meaning that has come down to us—something good gotten by luck or __15__ .

The common people of __16__ England, often hungry and cold, must often have prayed for a good strong wind. Critics today __17__ that the oil industry has also been praying for something just like it—some political or military __18__ that might produce a windfall—a rise in oil price and profits.

The oil companies deny that this is so. In Congress, critics of the oil companies have proposed a __19__ on such profits. The debate on rising oil prices will go on for some time, and __20__ likely we will hear more and more about windfall profits.

1. A. threatened   B. claimed   C. explored   D. narrowed
2. A. glimpse   B. sakes   C. trends   D. profits
3. A. exhaust   B. uncover   C. withstand   D. drive
4. A. waste   B. purchase   C. earn   D. omit
5. A. except   B. because of   C. beyond   D. for
6. A. up   B. down   C. off   D. away
7. A. Mediterranean   B. Europe   C. Rome   D. England
8. A. little   B. lot of   C. few   D. number of
9. A. therefore   B. indeed   C. however   D. of course
10. A. hunting   B. stopping   C. feeding   D. enduring
11. A. that   B. how   C. when   D. then
12. A. punished   B. diversed   C. neglected   D. misunderstood
13. A. while   B. If   C. As   D. Whenever
14. A. there   B. it   C. what   D. that
15. A. event   B. accident   C. satisfaction   D. worship
16. A. new   B. modern   C. old   D. young
17. A. suggest   B. confirm   C. realize   D. complain
18. A. storm   B. power   C. mixture   D. contrast
19. A. limit   B. tax   C. minimum   D. regulation
20. A. most   B. least   C. far   D. no longer

Section B Error Correction

Directions: *This part consists a short passage. In this passage, there are possibably 10 or less than 10 mistakes, one in each numbered line. You may have to change a word, add a word or delete a word. If you change a word, cross it out and write the correct word in the corresponding blank. If you add a word, put an insertion mark ( ) in the correct word in the corresponding blank. If you delete a word, cross it out and be sure to put a slash (/) in the blank.*

We found an enormous variety of circumstances in the
universities we visited and if we can generalize at all. That is to
say that the density of overseas students is fairly high in most
postgraduate courses in science and engineering. In no
university we visited would an undergraduate course close if no

overseas students came and most undergraduate courses had at least a little spare capacity. It appears then that the addition to costs or savings of more or fewer overseas students on this level would not be great.

1. _____

The opportunities for savings appear much greater at the postgraduate level, where indeed half of an all the overseas students in universities are to be found. Nevertheless, we found few case where the abandonment of a postgraduate course in case of a drastic fall in the numbers of overseas students applying was seriously contemplated. The common view was that staff development and "the educational profile" of the department required that courses be kept opened for home students even if only one or two students came.

2. _____

3. _____

4. _____

5. _____

Besides, even if certain courses were closed, staff were too specialized to be usefully redeployed in other departments or faculties; natural wastage could rarely cope off anything but small changes in staff in the right areas; early retirement was expensive and, moreover, the age profile of most departments showed a middle-age bulge; ancillary(助手) and part-time staff could of course be lay off but these involved very few numbers and so so. All these arguments led to the conclusion, heard almost everywhere, that there was little scope for savings even at the postgraduate level except in the very, very long run.

6. _____

7. _____

8. _____

9. _____

10. _____

Section C Short Answer Questions

Directions: *In this part there is a short passage with five questions or incomplete statements. Read the passage carefully. Then answer the questions or complete the statements in the fewest possible words.*

In only two decades Asian-Americans have become the fastest-growing US minority. As their children began moving up through the nation's schools, it became clear that a new class of academic achievers was emerging. Their achievements are reflected in the nation's best universities, where mathematics, science and engineering departments have taken on a decidedly Asian character. (This special liking for mathematics and science is partly explained by the fact that Asian-American students who began their education abroad arrived in the U. S. with a solid grounding in mathematics but little or no knowledge of English.) They are also influenced by the promise of a good job after college. Asians feel there will be less unfair treatment in areas like mathematics and science because they will be judged more immediate in something like engineering than with an arts degree.

Most Asian-American students owe their success to the influence of parents who are determined that their children take full advantage of what the American educational system has to offer. An effective measure of parental attention is homework. Asian parents spend more time with their children than American parents do, and it helps. Many researchers also believe there is something in Asian culture that breeds success, such as ideals that stress family values and emphasize education.

Both explanations for academic success worry Asian-Americans because of fears that they feed a typical racial image. Many can remember when Chinese, Japanese and Filipino immigrants were the victims of social isolation. Indeed, it was not until 1952 that laws were laid down giving all Asian immigrants the right to citizenship.

Questions：(注意：答题尽量简短，超过10个词要扣分，每条横线限写一个英语单词，标点符号不占格。)

1. While making tremendous achievements at college, Asian-American students feel they are mistreated because of _____.

   _____ _____ _____ _____

   _____ _____ _____ _____

2. What are the major factors that determine the success of Asian-Americans?

   _____ _____ _____ _____

   _____ _____ _____ _____

3. Why did academic success once worry Asian-Americans so much?

   _____ _____ _____ _____

   _____ _____ _____ _____

4. In what way do most Asian-American students' parents influence their children?

   _____ _____ _____ _____

   _____ _____ _____ _____

5. Why both explanations for academic success worry Asian-Americans?

_____ _____ _____ _____ _____

_____ _____ _____ _____ _____

Test Four

I Reading Comprehension

Section A Passage Reading

Directions: *There are 2 passages in this section. Each passage is followed by some questions or unfinished statements. For each of them there are four choices marked A, B, C and D. You should decide on the best choice and mark the corresponding letter on Answer Sheet with a single line through the center.*

Passage One

Questions 1 to 5 are based on the following passage.

Amongst the most popular books being written today are those which are usually classified as science fiction. Hundreds of titles are published every year and are read by all kinds of people. Furthermore, some of the most successful films of recent years have been based on science fiction stories.

It is often thought that science fiction is a fairly new development in literature, but its ancestors can be found in books written hundreds of years ago. These books are often concerned with the presentation of some form of ideal society, a theme which is still often found in modern stories.

Most of classics of science fiction, however, have been written within the last one hundred years. Books by writers such as Jules Verne and H. G. Wells have been translated into many languages.

Modern science fiction writers don't write about men from Mars or space adventure stories. They are more interested in predicting the results of technical developments on society and the human mind; or in imagining future worlds which are a reflection of the world which we live in now. Because of this their writing has obvious political undertones.

In an age where science fact frequently overtakes science fiction, the writers may find it difficult to keep ahead of scientific advances. Those who are sufficiently clear-sighted to see the way we are going, however, may provide a valuable lesson on how to deal with the problems which society will inevitably face as it tries to come to terms with a continually changing view of the world.

1. Which of the following statements is NOT true?

   A. Science fiction is fairly new in literature.

   B. Science fiction is rather popular with people today.

   C. Science fiction only deals with some form of ideal society.

   D. Hundreds of books classified as science fiction are printed every year.

2. Earliest science fiction was written _____.

   A. one hundred years ago

   B. by Jules Verne and H. G. Wells

   C. to tell people how to imagine future worlds

   D. hundreds of years ago

3. Modern science fiction writers are interested in _____.

   A. adventures in space

   B. some form of ideal world

   C. future worlds which have nothing in common with our present society

   D. predicting developments in technology and their efforts on society

4. In our present world, _____.

   A. science develops as fast as predicted by science fiction writers

   B. science develops faster than writers can imagine

   C. science fiction writers can always foresee what wonders science can do

   D. only science fiction writers can see the way science is going

5. Which of the following is NOT the conclusion that we can draw from this passage?

   A. Sensible science fiction writers may tell us what to do in future.

   B. We are bound to have problems as we try to make progress in science.

   C. No one knows anything about what to do with the problems we are to face.

   D. Our views of the world are subject to change.

Passage Two

Questions 6 to 10 are based on the following passage.

The liberal view of democratic citizenship that developed in the 17th and

18th centuries was fundamentally different from that of the classical Greeks. The pursuit of private interests with as little interference as possible from government was seen as the road to human happiness and progress rather than the public obligations and involvement in the collective community that were emphasized by the Greeks. Freedom was to be realized by limiting the scope of governmental activity and political obligation and not through immersion(沉浸) in the collective life of the polls. The basic role of the citizen was to select governmental leaders and keep the powers and scope of public authority in check. On the liberal view, the rights of citizens against the state were the focus of special emphasis.

Over time, the liberal democratic notion of citizenship developed in two directions. First, there was a movement to increase the proportion of members of society who were qualified to participate as citizens—especially through extending the right of voting and to ensure the basic political equality of all. Second there was a broadening of the legitimate activities of government and a use of governmental power to redress imbalances in social and economic life. Political citizenship became an instrument through which groups and classes with sufficient numbers of votes could use the state power to enhance their social and economic well-being.

Within the general liberal view of democratic citizenship, tensions have developed over the degree to which government can and should be used as an instrument for promoting happiness and well-being. Political philosopher Martin Diamond has categorized two views of democracy as follows. On the one hand, there is the "libertarian" perspective that stresses the private pursuit of happiness and emphasizes the necessity for restraint on government and protection of individual liberties. On the other hand, there is the "majoritarian" view that emphasizes the "task of the government to uplift and aid the common man against the malefactors of great wealth." The tensions between these two views are very clear today. Taxpayer revolts and calls for smaller government and less government regulation clash with demands for greater government involvement in the economic marketplace and the social sphere.

6. The author's primary purpose is to _____.

    A. study ancient concepts of citizenship

    B. contrast different notions of citizenship

  C. criticize modern libertarian democracy

  D. describe the importance of universal suffrage

7. It can be inferred from the passage that the Greek word polls means _____.

  A. family life   B. military service

  C. marriage   D. political community

8. The author cites Martin Diamond (Sentence 3. Para. 3) because the author _____.

  A. regards Martin Diamond as an authority on political philosophy

  B. wishes to refute Martin Diamond's views on citizenship

  C. needs a definition of the term "citizenship"

  D. wants voters to support Martin Diamond as a candidate for public office

9. According to the passage, all of the following are characteristics of the liberal idea of the government except _____.

  A. the emphasis on the rights of private citizens

  B. the activities government may legitimately pursue

  C. the obligation of citizens to participate in government

  D. the size of the geographical area controlled by a government

10. A majoritarian would be most likely to favor legislation that would _____.

  A. eliminate all restrictions on individual liberty

  B. be spending for social welfare programs

  C. provide greater protection for consumers

  D. raise taxes on the average worker and cut taxes on business

Section B Banked Cloze

Directions: *In this section, there is a passage with ten blanks. You are required to select one word for each blank from a list of choices given in a word bank following the passage. Read the passage through carefully before making your choices. Each choice in the bank is identified by a letter. Please mark the corresponding letter for each item on Answer Sheet with a single line through the center. You may not use any of the words in the bank more than once.*

  The Nile south of Khartoum is a complicated stream. For 500 miles it proceeds through the desert on a broad and fairly regular 1 , with trees and occasional low, bare hills on 2 bank. But at the point where the Sobat comes in from the Abyssinian mountains, a short distance above the present town of Malakal, the river turns west, the air grows more humid, the banks more green, and this is the first warning of the great obstacle of the Sudd that lies ahead. The Nile ___3___ itself in a vast sea of Papyrus ferns（蕨类植物）and rotting vegetation, and in that heat there is a spawning tropical life that can hardly have altered very much since the beginning of the world; it is as ___4___ and as hostile to man as the Sargasso Sea. Crocodiles（鳄鱼）and hippopotamuses（河马）flop ___5___ in the muddy water, mosquitoes and other insects choke the air, except ___6___ here there are no ordinary banks, merely chance pools in the forest of apple—green reeds that stretches away in a feathery mass to the horizon. This region is ___7___ land nor water. Year by year the current keeps bringing down more floating vegetation, and packs it into solid chunks perhaps twenty feet thick and strong enough for the elephant to walk ___8___ . But then this debris（碎岩）breaks ___9___ in islands and forms again in another place, and this is repeated in a thousand indistinguishable patterns and goes on ___10___ .

A. both	E. away	I. forever	M. for
B. course	F. primitive	J. neither	N. occasionally
C. on	G. about	K. that	O. either
D. loses	H. way	L. between	

Section C   Reading Comprehension （Skimming and Scanning）

Directions: *In this part, you will go over the passages quickly and answer the questions.*

For questions 1-7, mark

Y (*for YES*)　　　　　　*if the statement agrees with the information given in the passage;*

N (*for NO*)　　　　　　*if the statement contradicts the information given in the passage;*

NG (*for NOT GIVEN*)　*if the information is not given in the passage.*

For questions 8-10, complete the sentences with the information given in the passage.

Life in Finland, one of the world's best functioning welfare states and least known success stories, can be complicated. Consider the dilemma confronting parents looking for day care for a 4-year-old daughter in Kuhmo, a town of 10,000 near the middle of the country.

Should they put their child into the town nursery school, where she could spend her weekdays from 6:30 a. m. until 5 p. m. with about 40 other children, cared for by a 47-year-old principal with 20 years' experience, Mirsa Pussinen, as well as four teachers with master's degrees in preschool education, two teacher's aides and one cook? The girl would hear books read aloud every day, play games with numbers and the alphabet, learn some English, dig in the indoor sandbox or run around outside, sing and perform music, dress up for theatrical games, paint pictures, eat a hot lunch, take a nap if she wanted one, learn to play and work with others.

Or should that 4-year-old spend her days in home care? Most parents in Kuhmo choose this option, and put their children into the care of women such as Anneli Vaisanen, who has three or four kids in her home for the day. The 49-year-old Vaisanen doesn't have a master's, but she has received extensive training, has provided day care for two decades and has two grown children of her own. The kids in her charge do most of the things those at the center do, but with less order and organization. They also bake bread and make cakes.

How to decide? There's no financial difference; both forms of day care cost the parents nothing. There's no difference in the schooling that will follow day care—all the kids in Kuhmo (and throughout Finland) will have essentially identical opportunities in Finnish schools, Europe's best. There is no "elite" choice, no working-class choice; everyone is treated equally.

Finns have one of the world's most generous systems of state-funded educational, medical and welfare services, from pregnancy to the end of life. They pay nothing for education at any level, including medical school or law school. Their medical care, which contributes to an infant mortality rate that is half of ours and a life expectancy greater than ours, costs relatively little. (Finns devote 7 percent of gross domestic product to health care; we spend 15 percent.) Finnish senior citizens are well cared for. Unemployment benefits are good and last, in one form or another, indefinitely.

On the other hand, Finns live in smaller homes than Americans and consume a lot less. They spend relatively little on national defense, though they still have universal male conscription, and it is popular. Their per capita national income is about 30 percent lower than ours. Private consumption of goods and services represents about 52 percent of Finland's economy, and 71 percent of the

United States'. Finns pay considerably higher taxes—nearly half their national income is taken in taxes, while Americans pay about 30 percent on average to federal, state and local governments.

One fundamental Finnish value sounds a lot like an American principle—"to provide equal opportunities in life for everyone," as Pekka Himanen, a 31-year-old intellectual wunderkind(神童) in Helsinki, put it. Himanen, a product of Finnish schools who got his PhD in philosophy at 21, argues that Finland now does this much better than the United States, where he lived for several years while associated with the University of California in Berkeley.

In Finland, Himanen said, opportunity does not depend on "an accident of birth." All Finns have an equal shot at life, liberty and happiness. Yes, this is supposed to be an American thing, but many well-traveled younger Finns, who all seem to speak English, have a Finnish take on American realities. Miapetra Kumpula, a 32-year-old member of Parliament, volunteered this on the American dream: "Sure, anyone can get rich—but most won't."

Finns are enormously proud of their egalitarian(平等主义) tradition. They are the only country in Europe that has never had a king or a home-grown aristocracy(贵族统治的国家). Finland has no private schools or universities, no snooty clubs, no gated communities or compounds where the rich can cut themselves off from everyday life. I repeatedly saw signs of a class structure based on economics and educational attainment, but was also impressed by the life stories of Finns I met in prominent positions, or who had made a lot of money.

The Finnish educational system is the key to the country's successes and that, too, is a manifestation of egalitarianism. Surprisingly, it is a new system, created over the last generation by a collective act of will. The individual most responsible for it was Erkki Aho, director general of the National Board of Education from 1972 to 1992. Aho, now 68, was "a little bit of a radical," he told me with a smile—a Finnish Social Democrat who believed in trying to make his country fairer. The early '70s were a radical time in Finland. Change was in the air.

For reformers, education was the principal arena. The traditional Finnish system was conservative and divisive: Kids were selected for an academic track at the end of fourth grade. Those not chosen had no chance at higher education.

Universities were relatively few, and mostly mediocre.

Finland in the '90s became a high-tech powerhouse, led by Nokia, now the world's largest maker of cell phones. Finnish students have become the best in the world, as measured by an internationally administered exam that assesses the educational progress of 15-year-olds in all the industrial countries.

Aho's time in charge ended in the early '90s, when Finns turned against excessive centralization. After he left the Board of Education in 1992, power over the schools reverted to localities and the schools themselves.

1. Though Finland is a state of the world's best functioning welfare, it still has some problems.

2. Finns worry more about their choices for their children's education than the tuition fees concerned.

3. If Finns loss their jobs or fall ill, their government will be responsible for them.

4. Usually town nursery schooling is the priority for young children's education.

5. Some Finns give up their jobs just because their benefits are good and last.

6. Though Finns can enjoy very good welfare, but they can't offer larger homes than Americans do.

7. The values of Finns are the same as those of Americans'.

8. Finns take great pride in their system for their country is the only country in Europe without _____.

9. Education plays an extremely important role _____.

10. Finland excels in _____ and Finnish students have become _____.

II Comprehensive Test

Section A   Cloze

Directions: *There are 20 blanks in the following passage. For each blank there are four choices marked A, B, C and D. You should choose the ONE that best fits into the passage. Then mark the corresponding letter on Answer Sheet with a single line through the center.*

We all know whether we are left-handed or right-handed; hardly any of us know whether we are left-faced. Yet according to Professor Karl Smith of the University of Wisconsin we are all almost __1__ one or the other. Right-faced people are more __2__ than left-faced people, and there is a striking association between left-facedness and __3__ talent. Beethoven was left-faced(惯用左脸表情的). __4__ were Brahms(勃姆拉斯), Schubert(舒伯特), Wagner and Tchaikovsky(瓦格纳和柴可夫斯基). So __5__ the vast majority of well-known living __6__ of all kinds of music.

The idea of facedness __7__ from many years of computerized study of people's lip, tongue and jaw movements __8__ they were talking. Smith and his colleagues __9__ that in most people one side of the face was more active that the other. There are other signs of facedness, some of which can be __10__ in static pictures; in right-faced people the right-side of the face is less __11__ between jaw and brow; the right eyebrow __12__ to be higher; dimples and wrinkles are less marked than __13__ the left.

From a study of more than 500 people Smith found that the proportion of right-faced people __14__ about nine in 10 among Americans to two in three among Acapulco Mexicans. The fact that __15__ twins were always both right-faced or left-faced suggests a genetic origin for facedness.

The connection between left-faced and musical ability emerged by chance from a study of __16__ in different occupational groups. "Talented musical artists who perform classical, operatic, country and jazz music—are almost without exception __17__." Smith says in his report in the journal of the Acoustical Society of America.

Smith's findings fit in with theories that the right hemisphere(半球) of the brain (which controls the left side of the face) is __18__ for musical-performance, the left hemisphere for __19__. The idea of facedness, he says, "suggests new approaches __20__ the study of all aspects of cerebral(大脑的) dominance and its relation to handedness, speech disabilities, dyslexia(诵读困难) and perceptual disorders."

1. A. certain   B. certainly   C. accordingly   D. critically
2. A. indispensable B. preferable   C. common   D. desirable
3. A. musical   B. dance   C. cultural   D. instrumental
4. A. Neither   B. Nor   C. Rarely   D. So
5. A. are   B. were   C. was   D. does

6. A. programmers B. winners   C. reporters   D. performers

7. A. emerged   B. mentioned   C. outlined   D. remarked

8. A. why   B. where   C. while   D. now that

9. A. founded   B. found   C. forecast   D. simplified

10. A. signaled   B. recognized   C. matured   D. limited

11. A. generated   B. compressed   C. handled   D. governed

12. A. proves   B. remains   C. tends   D. grants

13. A. on   B. in   C. to   D. above

14. A. amounted   B. consisted of   C. varied with   D. ranged from

15. A. variable   B. similar   C. identical   D. punctual

16. A. customs   B. movements   C. handedness   D. facedness

17. A. left-faced   B. right-faced   C. left-handed   D. right handed

18. A. separated   B. revealed   C. specialized   D. tamed

19. A. music   B. language   C. symmetry   D. precaution

20. A. from   B. on   C. at   D. to

Section B　Error Correction

Directions: *This part consists a short passage. In this passage, there are possibably 10 or less than 10 mistakes, one in each numbered line. You may have to change a word, add a word or delete a word. If you change a word, cross it out and write the correct word in the corresponding blank. If you add a word, put an insertion mark (　) in the correct word in the corresponding blank. If you delete a word, cross it out and be sure to put a slash (/) in the blank.*

    To be fair, it is peculiarly difficult to define the objectives of cultural policy or to measure in any precise way how far those objectives achieved. The Plowden Report's definition, to give that impression of Britain and the British people which we would like foreigners to have, begs almost all the awkward and interesting questions: what impression it is possible to govern-　　　1. _____
ment activity of this sort to convey among the mass of other messages and images which other countries are simultaneously (同时) received, and how best to allocate priorities(优先权)　　　2. _____
among the various channels for influence within a limited budget(预算). Even with a substantial government budget for

overseas information and for cultural and educational inter-
change, there is severe limits on how far such activities can
counteract the impressions which foreign countries receive from
the far wider activities of British companies and their representatives, and so on. In best, the effects of the whole range of
government sponsored cultural activities by a relatively open
country such like the United Kingdom can only be marginal,
provide a useful marginal benefit when other developments are
going well, but able to do little to resist adverse(相反的)
trends. Matters are, of course, complicated still further by the
unavoidably long-term character of the investment. One cannot
expect an increased allocation of scholarship for study in Britain
to country X to bring either an increase in trade or a gain in
political relations within five years, perhaps even within ten
except in new nations in where the elite rises rapidly; other
factors being equal (which they rarely are), however, the hope
is that benefits will thereafter flow for many years.

3. _____

4. _____

5. _____

6. _____

7. _____

8. _____

9. _____

10. _____

Section C   Short Answer Questions

Directions: *In this part there is a short passage with five questions or incomplete
statements. Read the passage carefully. Then answer the questions or complete
the statements in the fewest possible words.*

The origins of nest-building remain obscure, but current observation of
nest-building activities provides evidence of their evolution. Clues to this
evolutionary process can be found in the activities of play and in the behavior and
movements of birds during mating, such as incessant(不停的) pulling at strips
of vegetation or scraping of the soil. During the early days of the reproductive
cycle, the birds seem only to play with the building materials. In preparation for
mating, they engage in activities that resemble nest-building, and continue these
activities throughout and even after the mating cycle. Effective attempts at
construction occur only after mating.

Although nest-building is an instinctive ability, there is considerable
adaptability in both site selection and use of materials, especially with those
species which build quite elaborate constructions. Furthermore, some element of

learning is often evident since younger birds do not build as well as their practiced elders. Young ravens(大乌鸦), for example, first attempt to build with sticks of quite unsuitable size, while a jackdaw's(穴鸟) first nest includes virtually any movable object. The novelist John Steinbeck recorded the contents of a young osprey(鱼鹰) nest built in his garden, which included three shirts, a bath towel, and one arrow.

Birds also display remarkable behavior in collecting building materials. Crows have been seen to tear off stout green twigs, and sparrow-hawks will dive purposefully onto a branch until it snaps(突然折断) and then hang upside down to break it off. Golden eagles, over generations of work, construct enormous nests. One of these, examined after it had been dislodged by high winds, weighed almost two tons and included foundation branches almost two meters long. The carrying capacity of the eagles, however, is only relative to their size and most birds are able to carry an extra load of just over twenty percent of their body weight.

Questions:（注意：答题尽量简短，超过10个词要扣分，每条横线限写一个英语单词，标点符号不占格。）

1. According to the passage, what activities are the characteristic of the early part of the reproductive cycle of birds?

   ＿＿＿＿＿ ＿＿＿＿＿ ＿＿＿＿＿ ＿＿＿＿＿

   ＿＿＿＿＿ ＿＿＿＿＿ ＿＿＿＿＿ ＿＿＿＿＿

2. How long will the activities of "nest-building" usually last?

   ＿＿＿＿＿ ＿＿＿＿＿ ＿＿＿＿＿ ＿＿＿＿＿

   ＿＿＿＿＿ ＿＿＿＿＿ ＿＿＿＿＿ ＿＿＿＿＿

3. Besides preparation for mating when the birds build their nests, what else do the activities suggest?

   ＿＿＿＿＿ ＿＿＿＿＿ ＿＿＿＿＿ ＿＿＿＿＿

   ＿＿＿＿＿ ＿＿＿＿＿ ＿＿＿＿＿ ＿＿＿＿＿

4. According to the passage, when gathering materials to build their nests, what sparrow hawks do?

   ＿＿＿＿＿ ＿＿＿＿＿ ＿＿＿＿＿ ＿＿＿＿＿

   ＿＿＿＿＿ ＿＿＿＿＿ ＿＿＿＿＿ ＿＿＿＿＿

5. What does the last paragraph suggest?

   ＿＿＿＿＿ ＿＿＿＿＿ ＿＿＿＿＿ ＿＿＿＿＿

Test Five

I Reading Comprehension

Section A   Passage Reading

Directions: *There are 2 passages in this section. Each passage is followed by some questions or unfinished statements. For each of them there are four choices marked A, B, C and D. You should decide on the best choice and mark the corresponding letter on Answer Sheet with a single line through the center.*

Passage One

Questions 1 to 5 are based on the following passage.

Before the 1850, the United States had a number of small colleges, most of them dating from colonial days. They were small church connected institutions whose primary concern was to shape the moral character of their students.

Throughout Europe, institutions of higher learning had developed, bearing the ancient name of university. In Germany a different kind of university had developed. The German University was concerned primarily with creating and spreading knowledge, not morals. Between mid-century and the end of the 1800, more than nine thousand young Americans dissatisfied with their training at home went to Germany for advanced study. Some of them returned to become presidents of venerable(古老的) colleges—Harvard, Yale, and Columbia—and transform them into modern universities. The new presidents broke all ties with the churches and brought in a new kind of faculty. Professors were hired for their knowledge of a subject, not because they were of the proper faith and had a strong arm for disciplining students. The new principle was that a university was to create knowledge as well as pass it on, and this called for a faculty composed of teacher scholars. Drilling and learning by rote(死背硬记) were replaced by the German method of lecturing, in which the professor's own research was presented in class. Graduate training leading to the PhD, an ancient German degree signifying the highest level of advanced scholarly attainment, was introduced. With the establishment of the seminar system, graduate students learned to question, analyze, and conduct their own research.

At the same time, the new university greatly expanded in size and course offerings, breaking completely out of the old, constricted curriculum of mathematics, classics, rhetoric, and music. The president of Harvard pioneered the elective system, by which students were able to choose their own courses of study. The notion of major fields of study emerged. The new goal was to make the university relevant to the real pursuits of the world. Paying close heed to the practical needs of society, the new universities trained men and women to work at its tasks, with engineering students being the most characteristic of the new regime. Students were also trained as economists, architects, agriculturalists, social welfare workers and teachers.

1. The word "this" (in line 12, paragraph 2) refers to which of the following?
   A. Creating and passing on knowledge.　　B. Drilling and learning by rote.
   C. Disciplining students.　　　　　　　　D. Developing moral principles.

2. According to the passage, the seminar system encouraged students to _____.
   A. discuss moral issues
   B. study the classics, rhetoric, and music
   C. study overseas
   D. work more independently

3. It can he inferred from the passage that before 1850 all of the following were characteristic of higher education EXCEPT _____.
   A. the elective system　　　　　　B. drilling
   C. strict discipline　　　　　　　D. rote learning

4. Those who favored the new university would be most likely to agree with which of the following statements?
   A. Learning is best achieved through discipline and drill.
   B. Shaping the moral character of students should be the primary goal.
   C. Higher education should prepare students to contribute to society.
   D. Teachers should select their student's courses.

5. The main idea of the passage is about _____.
   A. the characteristics of new higher education
   B. the origin and development of new university in America
   C. the influence of German college on the development of America higher

education

D. differences between two education systems

Passage Two
Questions 6 to 10 are based on the following passage.

It is all very well to blame traffic jams, the cost of petrol and the quick pace of modern life, but manners on the roads are becoming horrible. Everybody knows that the nicest men become monsters behind the wheel. It is all very well, again, to have a tiger in the tank, but to have one in the driver's seat is another matter altogether. You might tolerate the odd road-hog, the rude and inconsiderate drive, but nowadays the well-men-neared motorist is the exception to the rule. Perhaps the situation calls for a "Be kind to Other Drivers" campaign, otherwise it may get completely out of hand.

Road politeness is not only good manners, but good sense too. It takes the most cool-headed and good-tempered of drivers to resist the temptation to revenge when subjected to uncivilized behavior. On the other hand, a little politeness goes a long way towards relieving the tensions of motoring. A friendly nod or a wave of acknowledgement in response to an act of politeness helps to create an atmosphere of goodwill and tolerance so necessary in modern traffic conditions. But such acknowledgements of politeness are all too rare today. Many drivers nowadays don't even seem able to recognize politeness, when they see it.

However, misplaced politeness can also be dangerous. Typical examples are the driver who brakes violently to allow a car to emerge from a side street at some hazard to following traffic, when a few seconds later the road would be clear anyway: or the man who waves a child across a zebra(斑马) crossing into the path of oncoming vehicles that may be unable to stop in time. The same goes for encouraging old ladies to cross the road wherever and whenever they care to. It always amazes me that the highways are not covered with the dead bodies of these grannies.

A veteran driver, whose manners are faultless, told me it would help if motorists learnt to filter correctly into traffic streams one at a time without causing the total blockages that give rise to bad temper. Unfortunately, modern motorists can't even learn to drive, let alone master the subtler aspects of boatmanship. Years ago the experts warned us that the car ownership explosion would demand a lot more give and take from all road users. It is high time for all of us to take this message to heart.

6. According to this passage, troubles on the road are primarily caused by
_____.
   A. people's attitude towards the road hog
   B. the rhythm of modern life
   C. the behavior of the driver
   D. traffic conditions

7. The sentence "You might tolerate the odd road-hog..., the rule."(Para 1) imply _____.
   A. our society is unjust towards well-mannered motorists
   B. rude drivers can be met only occasionally
   C. the well-mannered motorist cannot tolerate the road-hog
   D. nowadays impolite drivers constitute the majority of motorists

8. By "good sense", the writer means _____.
   A. the driver's ability to understand and react reasonably
   B. the driver's prompt response to difficult and severe conditions
   C. the driver's tolerance of rude or even savage behavior
   D. the drive's acknowledgement of politeness and regulations

9. Experts have long pointed out that in the face of car-ownership explosion,
_____.
   A. road users should make more sacrifice
   B. drivers should be ready to yield to each other
   C. drivers should have more communication among themselves
   D. drives will suffer great loss if they pay no respect to others

10. In the writer's opinion _____.
   A. strict traffic regulations are badly needed
   B. drivers should apply road politeness properly
   C. rude drivers should be punished
   D. drivers should avoid traffic jams

Section B　Banked Cloze

Directions: *In this section, there is a passage with ten blanks. You are required to* *select one word for each blank from a list of choices given in a word bank following the passage. Read the passage through carefully before making your choices. Each choice in the bank is identified by a letter. Please mark the corresponding letter for each item on Answer Sheet with a single line through the center. You may not use any of the words in the bank more than once.*

Although the United States cherishes the tradition that it is a nation of small towns and wide open spaces, only one in __1__ eight Americans now lives on a farm. The recent population trend has been a double one, toward both urbanization and suburbanization.

Metropolitan areas have grown explosively in the past decade, and nearly half this __2__ has been in the suburbs. With the rapid __3__ of cities has come equally rapid decentralization. The flight of Americans from the central city to the suburbs constitutes __4__ of the greatest migrations of modern times; quiet residential sections outside cities have become collections of streets, split-level houses, and shopping __5__.

This sudden increase of suburban __6__, however, does not alter the basic fact that the United States has become one of the most urban nations on the face of the earth. When the United States became a __7__ it had no large cities at all; today some fifty cities have populations of more than 258,000. Large buildings of cities are developing in the __8__ of the East Coast and the east north-central states, __9__ the Pacific and Gulf coasts, and near the shores of the Great Lakes. Some sociologists now regard the entire 600-mile stretch between Boston and Washington D.C., an area holding a fifth of the country's population __10__ one vast city or, as they call it, megalopolis.

A. in	E. growth	I. expansion	M. like
B. every	F. decrease	J. nation	N. place
C. area	G. one	K. on	O. suburbs
D. increase	H. centers	L. as	

Section C   Reading Comprehension (Skimming and Scanning)

Directions: *In this part, you will go over the passages quickly and answer the questions.*

For questions 1-7, mark

Y (for YES)   *if the statement agrees with the information given in the passage*;

N (*for NO*)   *if the statement contradicts the information given in the passage*;

NG (*for NOT GIVEN*)   *if the information is not given in the passage.*

For questions 8-10, complete the sentences with the information given in the passage.

In looking at the issue of access to future telecommunication systems by people who have disabilities, it is useful to look at the different types of problems they may encounter and the different aspects of the infrastructure(基础设施) that might be involved. This document provides a first pass at this process. The goal here is not a comprehensive discussion of these points, but an enumeration (列举) of issues along with brief commentary to give them substance and clarity.

Interface—Individuals who are older or who have disabilities which limit their physical, sensory, or cognitive(认识的) abilities, may have difficulty operating the controls and seeing the displays necessary to use telecommunication equipment. A person who is blind, for example, may have no trouble in making a phone call, except that they are unable to find and identify a button on a business phone which would connect them to an unused phone line. A person with low vision may not be able to see the labels on the buttons of the phone, and may not be able to figure out how to use it as a result. A person with tremor (惊恐) may be unable to accurately dial a phone number. A person in a wheelchair may not be able to reach a phone, etc.

In the future, as we move to more advanced telecommunication systems, we may find the interface issues becoming more complex. We may also find that the "interface" actually emanates(起源) from many different sources. Some of it may be a function of the actual device in the person's hand. Other aspects of the interface may be generated by the local carrier, the "home" service provider the person contracted with, or the company or service being called, etc.

Transmission—A problem that has arisen in the past has been the ability of new technologies to successfully transmit signals generated by people with disabilities over the telecommunication network without undue(过分的) distortion. The major recent event was the problem generated by digital compression(压缩)(codecs) when trying to handle TTY signals. Since TTY signals were not used as samples when developing the compression standard, the compression technologies used in digital phones could not handle these common telephone signals without distorting them.

Content—Another area of difficulty may appear in the form of the actual telecommunication content. Today this content is largely auditory in nature and presents a problem only to individuals who are deaf or severely hard of hearing. To address the problem today, we have a telecommunication relay service which will convert the audio into text, which can be displayed on a TTY. In the future, telecommunications may involve visual as well as auditory information. This may pose problems for individuals with visual impairment or blindness.

Services—General—We already have some functions being carried out by telecommunications services that previously were carried out through direct conversation. The most obvious of these is the telephone receptionist. When calling a person at a company, one would previously first converse(谈话) with a secretary, who would then route the call to the person being called. Today, quite often, you will encounter an electronic "person," who would interact with you in the process of routing your call. Sometimes this is a computer system at the company. In other cases, it may be a telecommunications service run out of a central location or a service provider. If these "secretarial" services are not accessible it may not be possible to complete your call. With advances in speech recognition and speech synthesis(合成), we are more likely to see increased use of automated "people" mixed with live humans in the telecommunication system. We are also likely to see the way we communicate continually broaden.

Bridges and Translators—A key issue in accessibility will be the presence and functionality of bridges and translators between different telecommunication mechanisms. These bridges can provide the ability to have telecommunication which is sent in one form to be translated and delivered in another form.

The easiest type of bridge would be one that goes from one type of text communication system to another. For example, there are bridges today between TTY signals and text chat systems.

A bridge can also, however, be made between text and speech-based systems. The telephone relay service is an example of a bridge between voice communication and TTY text communication. There are also services which provide a bridge and translation service between voicemail and pagers.

Channeling—With multimedia communication, we are likely to see situations where an individual can access one type of information in a conversation, but not another. For example, an individual who is deaf may be able to see the other person talking but not understand what is being said. One mechanism for addressing this would be to split off the audio channel and have it routed through a special service which would translate it into text and send the text back to join the video signal being sent to the person. This could be done by routing the entire signal to the translation service. On the other hand, in a packet-based network, it might be more efficient to send the video information straight to its destination (which may be nearby) and to simply route the audio channel through the translation service. Such an approach would require a mechanism for routing and reassembling the signal at the receiving end. It would also require a mechanism for tracking the alternate routing and billing it (either to the person or to some third party payer).

Ancillary(辅助的) Signals—There also may be other types of information that needs to be conveyed outside of the standard channel. For example, when individuals who are deaf participate in an audio teleconference, they have a great deal of difficulty in jumping into the flow of conversation. Typically people wait for a pause and then jump into the conversation. However, an individual who is deaf is usually working through an interpreter, and so the conversation for them is always off by a second or two (or three). As a result, whenever they discover a pause in the conversation, it has already passed. If they jump in when they detect a pause, they in fact will jump in on top of somebody else who has already begun speaking. Some mechanism for electronically "raising your hand" in an audio conversation may be needed.

A second example would be a teleconferencing system that supported captioning. This would require an audio, a visual and a text channel as part of the standard telecommunication channel.

There may also be other interface or data components that might be required that are not currently part of all telecommunication systems.

1. The passage mainly focuses on the different problems the disabilities may encounter and the involved different aspect of the infrastructure.

2. Telephones are not convenient enough to all people who use them.

3. The transmission effect of telephone was not ideal when trying to handle

TTY signals.

4. So far the actual telecommunication content hasn't be solved at all.

5. When calling a person at a company, one has to be transferred from a secretary to the target person.

6. There is still a long way to go for telephone to be further improved.

7. The problems of functionality of bridges and transistors between telecommunication mechanism haven't solved yet.

8. Multimedia communication can possibly become a very helpful audible means _____.

9. It's usually difficult to find a chance to break in _____.

10. It is very necessary to invent a certain mechanism like electronically "raising your hand" in _____.

II Comprehensive Test

Section A Cloze

Directions: *There are 20 blanks in the following passage. For each blank there are four choices marked A, B, C and D. You should choose the ONE that best fits into the passage. Then mark the corresponding letter on Answer Sheet with a single line through the center.*

The Industrial Revolution began sometime in the eighteenth century. It __1__ greater changes in technology than there had been in all the __2__ history of mankind. By the mid-1800s the revolution had run its __3__, and advanced countries began to enjoy such __4__ as railways, steamships, electricity and a variety of steam-driven __5__ that increased production tremendously and made the industrial countries richer and more powerful.

Technology, also enriched, was __6__ refined to produce the telephone, wireless telegraphy, the automobile and the airplane. Improvements __7__ mass production soon made these new things __8__ to ordinary people, and by the 1930's new entertainment industries, __9__ the radio and sound motion pictures, __10__ the age of mass consumption.

All of this took about 200 years, __11__ in the later stages the pace of development __12__. If the First World War __13__ up the pace of industrial development dramatically, the second global __14__ was the catalyst (催化剂)

for a real __15__ of technology. It __16__ to us the __17__ blessings of nuclear energy and weapons, space travel and intercontinental ballistic (弹道的) missiles, automation and petrochemicals. Some inventions changed the face of industry, while others began to __18__ the character of society and family life.

__19__, the process of technology made life more productive, safer and more agreeable, but also more __20__.

1. A. brought up   B. brought forward C. brought out   D. brought about
2. A. preceding   B. proceeding   C. processing   D. presenting
3. A. course   B. way   C. route   D. road
4. A. discoveries   B. novelties   C. equipment   D. techniques
5. A. devices   B. facilities   C. appliances   D. machinery
6. A. quite   B. further   C. rather   D. already
7. A. in   B. for   C. of   D. with
8. A. accessible   B. available   C. adaptable   D. additional
9. A. excluding   B. concluding   C. including   D. comprising
10. A. enlivened   B. enriched   C. enhanced   D. enlightened
11. A. otherwise   B. therefore   C. but   D. moreover
12. A. slowed   B. enlarged   C. accelerated   D. stepped
13. A. made   B. turned   C. picked   D. stepped
14. A. conflict   B. confusion   C. conquest   D. conduct
15. A. destruction   B. deterioration   C. devotion   D. explosion
16. A. provided   B. furnished   C. introduced   D. supplied
17. A. changed   B. affected   C. mixed   D. confused
18. A. differ   B. vary   C. alternate   D. alter
19. A. In particular B. In short   C. In consequence D. In the end
20. A. fascinating   B. challenging   C. amusing   D. overwhelming

Section B   Error Correction

Directions: *This part consists a short passage. In this passage, there are possibably 10 or less than 10 mistakes, one in each numbered line. You may have to change a word, add a word or delete a word. If you change a word, cross it out and write the correct word in the corresponding blank. If you add a word, put an insertion mark ( ) in the correct word in the corresponding blank. If you delete a word, cross it out and be sure to put a slash (/) in the blank.*

Other Americans, especially those concerned about the Cold War with the Soviet Union, argued that the public schools were the weakest link in national defense because they did not produce enough scientists and engineers to win the technological race with our rivals.

The problem, as it was stated by military leaders such as Hyman Rickover, was that the schools were controlled by professional educators who had no respectful for the life of the mind and had produced an anti-intellectual weather in the United States. Government organization such as the National Science Foundation tried to correct this situation by enlisting scientists and engineers to the business of creating new mathematic and science programs for the public schools.

The concern about the domination of education by professional educators can best be understood by looking at the inter-linkages between educational policy-making groups at the state level. As discussed in earlier sections of this chapter, educational policy at the state level tends to be dominated by the state department of education and educational lobbying groups. The positions within these organizations are primarily held by professional educators who moves from one organizational setting to another. In other words, a member of an educational lobbying group one year might be on the staffs of the state department of education the next year. In fact, many members of state departments of education hold membership in state educational associations that have lobbyists at the state capital.

1. _____
2. _____
3. _____
4. _____
5. _____

6. _____

7. _____

8. _____

9. _____
10. _____

Section C   Short Answer Questions

Directions: *In this part there is a short passage with five questions or incomplete statements. Read the passage carefully. Then answer the questions or complete the statements in the fewest possible words.*

One of the most exciting attempts to find the source of the Mississippi was made by the Italian Constantino Beltrami. Aged 41, in Italy he had been a magistrate(地方法官) and student of the classics. In the New World, however, he was interested in exploration—not so much for reasons of scientific curiosity but in response to romantic dreams nourished by literary and mythological study. Setting out from St. Louis in 1823, he traveled as far as Fort Snelling by boat and then proceeded up rivers by canoe, accompanied by three Indians. The journey was an adventurous one. On August 23, 1823, Beltrami came to a small lake in what is now northern Minnesota, which he called Lake Julia in memory of a woman he had loved, and which he proclaimed to be the source of the Mississippi. His romantic self-comparison to Icarus, the Phoenicians(菲尼基人), Marco Polo and Columbus, however, was not calculated to satisfy geographers, for he had no compass with which to determine his location. When he returned to New Orleans, he related his travels and as a result, he was welcomed in Europe and became a member of several academies, while Lafayette and Chateaubriand honored him with their friendship. In America, on the other hand, many regarded him as an imposter(江湖骗子).

Nine years after Beltrami, Henry Rowe Schoolcraft, the United States Superintendent(负责人) of Indian Affairs proclaimed "Itasca"—a lake in Minnesota—the true source of the Mississippi.

His claim that Lake Itasca was the source of the Mississippi was accepted for many years, but many geologists now disagree. Accurate recent surveys show that a spring flows into it from Elk Lake, and that this in turn is linked with yet other lakes, which may be collectively regarded as the source of the great river.

Questions：(注意：答题尽量简短，超过10个词要扣分，每条横线限写一个英语单词，标点符号不占格。)

1. Beltrami liked to explore because _____.

   _____ _____ _____ _____ _____

   _____ _____ _____ _____ _____

2. How did he travel throughout his journey?

   _____ _____ _____ _____ _____

   _____ _____ _____ _____ _____

3. Who name the Lake Julia?

   _____ _____ _____ _____ _____

   _____ _____ _____ _____ _____

4. Why did he fail to tell the exact location the source of the Mississippi River?

   _____ _____ _____ _____ _____

5. What does the passage mainly tell us?

_____ _____ _____ _____ _____

_____ _____ _____ _____ _____

_____ _____ _____ _____ _____

Test Six

I Reading Comprehension

Section A   Passage Reading

Directions: *There are 2 passages in this section. Each passage is followed by some questions or unfinished statements. For each of them there are four choices marked A, B, C and D. You should decide on the best choice and mark the corresponding letter on Answer Sheet with a single line through the center.*

Passage One

Questions 1 to 5 are based on the following passage.

Many United States companies have, unfortunately, made the search for legal protection from import competition into a major line of work. Since 1980 the United States International Trade Commission (ITC) has received about 280 complaints alleging(指控) dam age from imports that benefit from subsidies by foreign governments. Another 340 charge that foreign companies "dumped" their products in the United States "at less than fair value. " Even when no unfair practices are alleged, the simple claim that an industry has been injured by imports is sufficient grounds to seek relief.

Contrary to the general impression, this quest for import relief has hurt more companies than it has helped. As corporations begin to function globally, they develop an intricate web of marketing, production, and research relationships. The complexity of these relationships makes it unlikely that a system of import relief laws will meet the strategic needs of all the units under the same parent company.

Internationalization increases the danger that foreign companies will use import relief laws against the very companies the laws were designed to protect. Suppose a United States-owned company establishes an overseas plant to manufacture a product while its competitor makes the same product in the United States. If the competitor can prove injury from the imports and that the United States received a subsidy from a foreign government to build its plant abroad the United States Company's products will be uncompetitive in the United States, since they would be subject to duties.

Perhaps the most brazen case occurred when the ITC investigated allegations that Canadian companies were injuring the United States salt industry by dumping rock salt, used to deice(除冰) roads. The bizarre aspect of the complaint was that a foreign conglomerate(大型联企业) with United States operations was crying for help against a United States company with foreign operations. The "United States" company claiming injury was a subsidiary of a Dutch conglomerate, while the "Canadian" companies included a subsidiary of a Chicago firm that was the second-largest domestic producer of rock salt.

1. The passage is chiefly concerned with _____ .

   A. arguing against the increased internationalization of United States corporations

   B. warning that the application of laws affecting trade frequently has unintended consequences

   C. demonstrating that foreign based firms receive more subsidies from their governments than United States firms receive from the United States government

   D. advocating the use of trade restrictions for "dumped" products but not for other imports

2. It can be inferred from the passage that the minimal basis for a complaint to the International Trade Commission is which of the following?

   A. A foreign competitor has received a subsidy from a foreign government.

   B. A foreign competitor has substantially increased the volume of products shipped to the United States.

   C. A foreign competitor is selling products in the United States at less than fair market value.

   D. The company requesting import relief has been injured by the sale of imports in the United States.

3. The last paragraph performs which of the following functions in the passage?

   A. It cites a specific case that illustrates a problem presented more generally in the previous paragraph.

B. It introduces an additional area of concern not mentioned earlier.

C. It discusses an exceptional case in which the results expected by the author of the passage were not obtained.

D. It presents a recommendation based on the evidence presented earlier.

4. The passage suggests that which of the following is most likely to be true of United States trade laws?

A. They will eliminate the practice of "dumping" products in the United States.

B. They will enable manufacturers in the United States to compete more profitably outside the United States.

C. They will affect United States trade with Canada more negatively than trade with other nations.

D. Those that help one unit within a parent company will not necessarily help other units in the company.

5. According to the passage, companies have the general impression that International Trade Commission import relief practices have _____.

A. caused unpredictable fluctuations in volumes of imports and exports

B. achieved their desired effect only under unusual circumstances

C. actually helped companies that have requested import relief

D. been opposed by the business community

Passage Two

Questions 6 to 10 are based on the following passage.

Many critics of the current welfare system argue that existing welfare regulations foster family instability. They maintain that those regulations, which exclude most poor husband and wife families from Aid to Families with Dependent Children assistance grants, contribute to the problem of family dissolution. Thus, they conclude that expanding the set of families eligible(合格 的) for family assistance plans or guaranteed income measures would result in a marked strengthening of the low-income family structure. If all poor families could receive welfare, would the incidence of instability change markedly? The unhappily married couple, in most cases, remains together out of a sense of economic responsibility for their children, because of the high costs of separation, or because of the consumption benefits of marriage. The formation, maintenance, and dissolution of the family are in large part a function of the relative balance between the benefits and costs of marriage as seen by the individual members of the marriage. The major benefit generated by the creation of a family is the expansion of the set of consumption possibilities, the benefits from such a partnership depend largely on the relative dissimilarity(不同,不相似) of the resources or basic endowments(捐款,捐赠) each partner brings to the marriage. Persons with similar productive capacities have less economic "cement" holding their marriage together. Since the family performs certain functions society regards as vital, a complex network of social and legal buttresses(支撑) has evolved to reinforce marriage. Much of the variation in marital stability across income classes can be explained by the variation in costs of dissolution(分解,分离) imposed by society, e. g. division of property, alimony (丈夫在分居或离婚后付给妻子的赡养费), child support, and the social stigma(耻辱) attached to divorce.

Marital stability is related to the costs of achieving an acceptable agreement on family consumption and production and to the prevailing social price of instability in the marriage partners-social-economic group. Expected AFDC income exerts pressures on family instability by reducing the cost of dissolution. To the extent that welfare is a form of government subsidized alimony payments, it reduces the institutional costs of separation and guarantees a minimal standard of living for wife and children. So welfare opportunities are a significant determinant of family instability in poor neighborhoods, but this is not the result of the regulations concerned that exclude most intact families from coverage. Rather, welfare-related instability occurs because public assistance lowers both the benefits of marriage and the costs of its disruption by providing a system of government-subsidized alimony payments.

6. Some criticize the current welfare regulations because _____.

   A. those regulations encourage family dissolution

   B. the low-income families are not given enough the family assistance grants

   C. they expand the set of families eligible for family assistance

   D. the guaranteed income measures are increased

7. According to this passage, family stability depends on _____.

   A. the couples earning ability

B. the relative balance between the benefits and costs of marriage

C. how much possessions the couple have before marriage

D. a network of social and legal support

8. All of the following are mentioned by the author as factors tending to perpetuate a marriage EXCEPT _____.

A. the stigma attached to divorce

B. the social class of the partners

C. the cost of alimony and child support

D. the loss of property upon divorce

9. The author argues that _____.

A. the agreement between couples reinforce marital stability

B. expected AFDC income helps to strengthen family stability

C. AFDC regulations are to blame for family instability

D. public assistance upsets the balance between benefit and cost of marriage

10. The tone of the passage can best be described as _____.

A. confident and optimistic   B. scientific and detached

C. discouraged and alarmed   D. polite and sensitive

Section B Banked Cloze

Directions: *In this section, there is a passage with ten blanks. You are required to select one word for each blank from a list of choices given in a word bank following the passage. Read the passage through carefully before making your choices. Each choice in the bank is identified by a letter. Please mark the corresponding letter for each item on Answer Sheet with a single line through the center. You may not use any of the words in the bank more than once.*

English colonists got on well together, sharing the __1__ spirit of independence. They were both fiercely separatist in the American Revolution and fought __2__ by side against the British. After the war, New York became the first capital of the United States, being already the largest city in North America. By the end of the 18th century it had a __3__ of 60 thousand, but it grew rapidly during the 19th century __4__ the millions of immigrants who landed there.

However, New York did not __5__ the capital for long. In 1793, the foundation of a new capital city was laid by Washington and the Americans called their new capital ___6___ after their great leader. New York, however, became one of the largest and most powerful cities in the western ___7___ and has at present a population of more than 9 million.

Modern New York is an exciting city. The architecture of Manhattan, with its soaring skyscrapers, is not dull, as many foreigners imagine. The ___8___ used—copper, stainless steel, concrete and glass—give the buildings a striking ___9___. The long avenues, broad and straight, lined with expensive stores and massive apartment houses, impress people by their scale alone. Its museums and numerous art galleries, the concerts, opera and ballet ___10___ at the Lincoln Center, the theaters on and off Broadway and in Greenwich Village, make it one of the world's centers of the arts.

A. because	E. remain	I. world	M. performed
B. New York	F. Washington	J. materials	N. ugly
C. side	G. exciting	K. population	O. scale
D. thanks to	H. same	L. beauty	

Section C Reading Comprehension (Skinning and Scanning)

Directions: *In this part, you will go over the passages quickly and answer the questions.*

For questions 1-7, mark

Y (*for YES*) *if the statement agrees with the information given in the passage;*

N (*for NO*) *if the statement contradicts the information given in the passage;*

NG (*for NOT GIVEN*) *if the information is not given in the passage.*

For questions 8-10, complete the sentences with the information given in the passage.

While many U. S. college students spent their fall weekends cheering for their school's football team, Jonathan Jackson took in his first rugby match, cycled across the spectacular landscape in New Zealand and learned to pronounce "good on you" Kiwi-style. A junior at Rice University, Jackson studied Maori culture last summer and fall at the University of Otago.

And as he immersed himself in a foreign culture and earned credits toward his college degree, Jackson ended up ahead on the deal. His financial-aid package, which went with him, amounted to more than the cost of the Otago program. Jackson, who lives in Ben Wheeler, Tex. , used the surplus for travel and other expenses.

Not every kid is so lucky. But colleges and universities have made international study more attainable by beefing up（加强）financial aid, offering summer and between-term sessions, and accepting credits from a wider pool of institutions, some of which charge less for tuition and fees. As a result, student participation has jumped almost 20% since 2000.

But before your kids start dreaming of springtime in Prague, they should check with their adviser. They could feel pretty dumb if the credits they earn abroad don't transfer and they need an extra semester to score that sheepskin. "Integrating the program into your major can be tricky," says John Duncan, of StudyAbroad. com, a clearinghouse for international study. "To make this a reality, you should start planning as a freshman."

Study-abroad offices can guide you to programs whose credits should transfer, but students still need their adviser's sign-off. "We may approve a university in Australia, but that doesn't mean you can take tap dancing," says Daisy Fried, of Syracuse University's study-abroad program.

Kids can hit the books at an institution with which their school has a direct relationship or go through a program run by another U. S. university or outside organization, such as the Council on International Education Exchange. Rice University lets students choose among more than 500 study-abroad options; Jackson organized his Kiwi adventure through the Arcadia University Center for Education Abroad.

Financial aid. With so many choices, comparing prices is like playing translator in the Tower of Babel. Some schools, including Syracuse, require that you pay at-home tuition no matter where you go; others have you pay the sponsoring group or foreign school.

That's a big distinction. At Northwestern University, for instance, students who study this year through an affiliated（附属的）program at the Universidad Nacional de Cuyo, in Argentina, will pay $12,000, plus a $3,200 administrative fee, compared with the $32,000 tuition they would have owed Northwestern. As with Rice, Northwestern students who attend Northwestern's program or affiliated programs can keep the change if their financial-aid package exceeds the program's cost.

In addition to tuition, you must factor in the cost of transportation, health insurance, books and orientation, which some programs cover and others don't. Expect to spend more to study in big cities, in developed countries and at private universities. Even with the strengthening dollar, there are no more bargains in Western Europe, says Fried.

Some awards encourage students to travel to certain destinations. Marlena Del Hierro, a student at the University of Texas at Austin, used a scholarship from the Institute of International Education to study Kiswahili and conservation in Tanzania. The IIE also administers the Freeman-Asia Award, which pays up to $7,000 to students who head to the Far East.

Paying for the program is only the beginning. Whether kids are traveling abroad for an entire semester or just over spring break, you also need to get them to their destination, replenish(补充) their funds once they're there, and have a way to stay in touch with them.

Generally, programs will either make travel arrangements for you or guide you to group rates. Arcadia tipped off Jackson to a $1,000 round-trip fare between Auckland, New Zealand, and Los Angeles (he got to and from L. A. on his own). It's usually cheaper to buy a round-trip ticket than two one-way fares, even if you have to pay a surcharge to change the date for the return trip. Students who plan to roam after the program—and many do—should check out open-jaw fares, which allow departures from cities other than the arrival point.

Cost versus convenience. Students can use domestic credit or debit cards to exchange currency and get cash, especially in an emergency, but they'll be nailed on usage charges, which may add as much as 5% to each transaction (check the bank's policy). Jackson swallowed the cost and used ATMs affiliated with Chase Manhattan so that his mother could manage his account from back home. The Visa Buxx prepaid card lets you reload the account and track your child's spending (a plus from some perspectives), but banks that issue the cards also tack on significant fees. If your scholar spends an extended time abroad, the least expensive option might be to open a local account.

Staying in touch. Almost every country outside the U. S. uses GSM cell-phone technology. Your kid can buy a GSM phone before leaving home, but it may not accept a SIM card—the chip that activates local service—from other companies, and roaming charges can add up to dollars a minute. It would be less expensive to buy a phone abroad, or through www. telestial. com, whose SIM cards come with low-rate prepaid airtime for the country you're visiting. GSM operates on different frequencies around the world. The more frequency bands your phone works on, the more flexibility you'll have.

Remember land lines? They work, too. Check out low rates on prepaid phone cards at www. speedypin. com.

Finally, the Internet offers a dandy way for kids to check in with the rents. They can stop in at Internet cafés, which charge by the minute for Web access, from Paris to Peru. Or they can download free software from Skype, an online phone company, to tell Mom in their own voice how much they miss her.

1. The passage is mainly served as an introduction to those who are interested in studying abroad.
2. Not every student is so lucky as to get financial aid for his or her international study.
3. Before sending kids abroad to study, one had better consult some professional agency concerned for necessary information.
4. Nobody wants to study in such a college or university which doesn't transfer the credits gained there.
5. The tuition fees vary from university to university because of world's economic fluctuation.
6. The expenses of studying abroad may be much larger than one has expected.
7. Overseas students are expected to learn something more from outside university.
8. If overseas students are in need of exchanging currency, or getting cash, they can use their _____.
9. It's not a good idea to use SIM card to have a phone call because of _____.
10. More information about low rates on prepaid phone card can be got from _____.

II Comprehensive Test

Section A Cloze

Directions: *There are 20 blanks in the following passage. For each blank there* *are four choices marked A, B, C and D. You should choose the ONE that best fits into the passage. Then mark the corresponding letter on Answer Sheet with a single line through the center.*

Checks have largely replaced money as a means of exchange, for they are widely accepted everywhere. Though this is very __1__ for both buyer and seller, it should not be forgotten that checks are not real money: they are quite __2__ in themselves. A shop-keeper always runs a certain __3__ when he accepts a check and he is quite __4__ his rights if, __5__ he refuses to do so.

People do not always know this and are shocked if their good faith is called __6__. An old and very wealthy friend of mine told me he had an extremely unpleasant __7__. He went to a famous jeweler shop which keeps a large __8__ of precious stones and asked to be shown some pearl necklaces. After examining several trays, he __9__ to buy a particularly fine string of pearls and asked if he could pay __10__ check. The assistant said that this was quite __11__, but the moment my friend signed his name, he was invited into the manager's office.

The manager was very polite, but he explained that someone with __12__ the same name had presented them with a __13__ check not long ago. He told my friend that the police would arrive __14__ any moment and he had better stay __15__ he wanted to get into serious trouble. __16__, the police arrived soon afterwards. They apologized to my friend for the __17__ and asked him to __18__ a note which had been used by the thief in a number of shops. The note __19__: I have a gun in my pocket. Ask no questions and give me all the money in the safe. __20__, my friend's handwriting was quite unlike the thief's.

1. A. complicated   B. trivial   C. bearable   D. convenient
2. A. valueless   B. invaluable   C. valuable   D. indefinite
3. A. danger   B. change   C. risk   D. opportunity
4. A. within   B. beyond   C. without   D. out of
5. A. in general   B. at the least   C. on occasion   D. in short
6. A. in difficulty   B. in doubt   C. in earnest   D. in question
7. A. accident   B. experience   C. event   D. incident
8. A. amount   B. stock   C. number   D. store
9. A. considered   B. thought   C. conceived   D. decided
10. A. by   B. in   C. with   D. through
11. A. in order   B. in need   C. in use   D. in common

12. A. largely   B. mostly   C. exactly   D. extremely

13. A. worth   B. worthy   C. worthwhile   D. worthless

14. A. for   B. at   C. until   D. during

15. A. whether   B. if   C. otherwise   D. unless

16. A. Really   B. Sure enough   C. Certainly   D. However

17. A. treatment   B. manner   C. inconvenience   D. behavior

18. A. write off   B. write out   C. copy out   D. make out

19. A. read   B. told   C. wrote   D. informed

20. A. Especially   B. Fortunately   C. Naturally   D. Basically

Section B   Error Correction

Directions: *This part consists a short passage. In this passage, there are possibably 10 or less than 10 mistakes, one in each numbered line. You may have to change a word, add a word or delete a word. If you change a word, cross it out and write the correct word in the corresponding blank. If you add a word, put an insertion mark (　) in the correct in the corresponding blank. If you delete a word, cross it out and be sure to put a slash (/) in the blank.*

Copyright in works of art was born with the idea of "substantial taking," or "colourful imitation." To "copy" a work of art has always implied total as well as partial copying. However, the concept of copying has undergone various other developments since the fine arts came under copyright in Britain in 1862. For the beginning, the legal concept of copying was   1. _____
tied to the technological process of printing.   2. _____

Copying meant mechanical replication and multiplication; substitution as the purpose of dissemination. But this changed   3. _____
into an understanding of copying, in relation as art, which   4. _____
entailed (限定,法律用语) also a judgment of artistic dependency. Secondly, courts have practised a form of aesthetic
analysis in which art has been conceived into a "representation   5. _____
of nature." As a result, works of art that do not in any obvious way use this formula of representation, have been judged to be "copies" rather than "originals." To prevent such an analytical confusion, it is suggesting in the thesis that the critical concept   6. _____

of "framing", taking from art theory, is applied. Rather than
viewing art through the dichotomy(二分法) of art versus
nature, a work of art can be viewed as a "framing." The
"framing" is the artistic vision that an artist shares of us
through his work. Legitimate copying occurs when a person
presents his audience with the artistic vision of another artist,
and this should be indicated by elements of framing such as
composition, perspective and selection of material.

7. _____

8. _____
9. _____

10. _____

Section C   Short Answer Questions

Directions: *In this part there is a short passage with five questions or incomplete
statements. Read the passage carefully. Then answer the questions or complete
the statements in the fewest possible words.*

Because the low latitudes(纬度) of the Earth, the areas near the equator,
receive more heat than the latitudes near the poles, and because the nature of
heat is to expand and move, heat is transported from the tropics to the middle
and high latitudes. Some of this heat is moved by winds and some by ocean
currents, and some gets stored in the atmosphere in the form of latent(潜在的)
heat. The term "latent heat" refers to the energy that has to be used to convert
liquid water to water vapor. We know that if we warm a pan of water on a
stove, it will evaporate, or turn into vapor, faster than if it is allowed to sit at
room temperature. We also know that if we hang wet clothes outside in the
summertime they will dry faster than in winter, when temperatures are colder.
The energy used in both cases to change liquid water to water vapor is supplied
by heat-supplied by the stove in the first case and by the Sun in the latter case.
This energy is not lost. It is stored in water vapor in the atmosphere as latent
heat. Eventually, the water stored as vapor in the atmosphere will condense to
liquid again, and the energy will be released to the atmosphere.

In the atmosphere, a large portion of the Sun's incoming energy is used to
evaporate water, primarily in the tropical oceans. Scientists have tried to
quantify this proportion of the Sun's energy. By analyzing temperature, water
vapor, and wind data around the globe, they have estimated the quantity to be
about 90 watts per square meter, or nearly 30 percent of the Sun's energy. Once
this latent heat is stored within the atmosphere, it can be transported, primarily

to higher latitudes, by prevailing, large-scale winds. Or it can be transported vertically to higher levels in the atmosphere, where it forms clouds and subsequent storms, which then release the energy back to the atmosphere.

Questions：(注意:答题尽量简短,超过10个词要扣分,每条横线限写一个英语单词,标点符号不占格。)

1. How is heat transported from the tropics to the middle and high latitudes according to the passage?

   _____ _____ _____ _____

2. How do the tropics differ from the Earth's polar regions?

   _____ _____ _____ _____

3. Why does the author mention "the stove" in the first paragraph?

   _____ _____ _____ _____

4. According to the passage, where does most ocean water evaporation occur?

   _____ _____ _____ _____

5. According to the passage, 30 percent of the Sun's incoming energy _____ .

   _____ _____ _____ _____

Test Seven

I Reading Comprehension

Section A Passage Reading

Directions： *There are 2 passages in this section. Each passage is followed by some questions or unfinished statements. For each of them there are four choices marked A, B, C and D. You should decide on the best choice and mark the corresponding letter on Answer Sheet with a single line through the center.*

Passage One

Questions 1 to 5 are based on the following passage.

Teaching children to read well from the start is the most important task of elementary schools. But relying on educators to approach this task correctly can be a great mistake. Many schools continue to employ instructional methods that have been proven ineffective. The staying power of the "look-say" or "whole-word" method of teaching beginning reading is perhaps the most flagrant(臭名昭彰的) example of this failure to instruct effectively.

The whole-word approach to reading stresses the meaning of words over the meaning of letters, thinking over decoding, developing a sight vocabulary of familiar words over developing the ability to unlock the pronunciation of unfamiliar words. It fits in with the self-directed, "learning how to learn" activities recommended by advocates(倡导者) of "open" classrooms and with the concept that children have to be developmentally ready to begin reading. Before 1963, no major publisher put out anything but these "Run-Spot-Run" readers.

However, in 1955, Rudolf Flesch touched off what has been called "the great debate" in beginning reading. In his best-seller *Why Johnny Can't Read*, Flesch indicted(控诉) the nation's public schools for mis-educating students by using the look-say method. He said—and more scholarly studies by Jeane Chall and Rovert Dykstra later confirmed—that another approach to beginning reading, founded on phonics(语音学), is far superior.

Systematic phonics(声学) first teaches children to associate letters and letter combinations with sounds; it then teaches them how to blend these sounds together to make words. Rather than building up a relatively limited vocabulary of memorized words, it imparts a code by which the pronunciations of the vast majority of the most common words in the English language can be learned. Phonics does not devalue the importance of thinking about the meaning of words and sentences; it simply recognizes that decoding is the logical and necessary first step.

1. The author feels that counting on educators to teach reading correctly is
   _____.
   A. only logical and natural　　B. the expected position
   C. probably a mistake　　D. merely effective instruction
2. The author indicts(指控) the look-say reading approach because _____.
   A. it overlooks decoding
   B. Rudolf Flesch agrees with him

C. he says it is boring

D. many schools continue to use this method

3. One major difference between the look-say method of learning reading and the phonics method is _____.

A. look-say is simpler

B. Phonics takes longer to learn

C. look-say is easier to teach

D. phonics gives readers access to far more words

4. The phrase "touch off" (Sentence 1, Para 3) most probably means _____.

A. talk about shortly   B. start or cause

C. compare with   D. oppose

5. According to the author, which of the following statements is true?

A. Phonics approach regards whole-word method as unimportant.

B. The whole-word approach emphasizes decoding.

C. In phonics approach, it is necessary and logical to employ decoding.

D. Phonics is superior because it stresses the meaning of words thus the vast majority of most common words can be learned.

Passage Two

Questions 6 to 10 are based on the following passage.

Green-space facilities are contributing to an important extent to the quality of the urban environment. Fortunately, it is no longer necessary that every lecture or every book about this subject have to start with the proof of this idea. At present it is generally accepted, although more as a self-evident statement than on the base of a closely-reasoned scientific proof. The recognition of the importance of green-spaces in the urban environment is a first step on the right way; this does not mean, however that sufficient details are known about the functions of green-space in towns and about the way in which the inhabitants are using these spaces. As to this rather complex subject I shall, within the scope of this lecture, enter into one aspect only, namely the recreative function of green-space facilities.

The theoretical separation of living, working, traffic and recreation which for many years has been used in town-and-country planning, has in my opinion resulted in disproportionate attention for forms of recreation far from home, whereas there was relatively little attention for improvement of recreative possibilities in the direct neighborhood of the home. We have come to the conclusion that this is not right, because an important part of the time which we do not pass in sleeping or working, is used for activities at and around home. So it is obvious that recreation in the open air has to begin at the street-door of the house. The urban environment has to offer as many recreation activities as possible, and the design of these has to be such that more obligatory(应尽的,强制性的) activities can also have a recreative aspect.

The very best standard of living is nothing if it is not possible to take a pleasant walk in the district, if the children cannot be allowed to play in the streets, because the risks of traffic are too great, if during shopping you can nowhere find a spot for enjoying for a moment the nice weather, in short, if you only feel yourself at home after the street-door of your house is closed after you.

6. According to the author, the importance of green spaces in the urban environment _____.

    A. is still unknown   B. is usually neglected

    C. is being closely studied   D. has been fully recognized

7. The theoretical separation of living, working, traffic and recreation has led to _____.

    A. the disproportion of recreation facilities in the neighborhood

    B. the location of recreation facilities far from home

    C. relatively little attention for recreative possibilities

    D. the improvement of recreative possibilities in the neighborhood

8. The author suggests that the recreative possibilities of green-space should be provided _____.

    A. in special areas   B. in the suburbs

    C. in the neighborhood of the house D. in gardens and parks

9. According to the author, green-space facilities should be designed in such a way that _____.

    A. more obligatory activities might take on a recreative aspect

    B. more and more people might have access to them

    C. an increasing number of recreative activities might be developed

    D. recreative activities might be brought into our homes

10. The main idea of this passage is that _____.

A. better use of green-space facilities should be made so as to improve the quality of our life

B. attention must be directed to the improvement of recreative possibilities

C. the urban environment is providing more recreation activities than it did many years ago

D. priority must be given to the development of obligatory activities

Section B   Banked Cloze

Directions: *In this section, there is a passage with ten blanks. You are required to select one word for each blank from a list of choices given in a word bank following the passage. Read the passage through carefully before making your choices. Each choice is the bank is identified by a letter. Please mark the corresponding letter for each item on Answer Sheet with a single line through the center. You may not use any of the words in the bank more than once.*

Artists and scientists both make valuable contributions to our society. It may seem sometimes that artists are   1   valued. That's because those artists who are famous make a lot of money. However, they are relatively few. The fact is that scientists are more valued. They get more   2   from society for the work they do.

  3   reflect their times and their culture. A painter or a writer shows us in pictures and words what we're like as a people. They record our culture for future generations. Actors and other   4 , like singers and dancers,   5   us. They take our minds off our troubles, and   6   us how beautiful and exciting our imaginations can be. Artists also help keep their societies mentally and emotionally healthy. For example, children who participate in the arts, such as painting or music in school do better in their other studies. Art of all types is necessary to the   7 .

The contributions scientists make to society are more obvious. They include the cars we drive, the computers we use at home and at work, and the appliances that help us cook our   8   and clean our houses. All of these come from the ideas and hard work of   9 . Because of scientific discoveries, we're living longer and more healthful lives. Scientists also contribute to the arts. Movies are the result of   10 . So are television, radio, and the recording of music on CDs.

A. materials	E. remind	I. appliances	M. contributions
B. respect	F. more	J. Artists	N. participate
C. performers	G. human spirit	K. scientists	O. generations
D. entertain	H. meals	L. science	

Section C   Reading Comprehension (Skimming and Scanning)

Directions: *In this part, you will go over the passages quickly and answer the questions.*

For questions 1-7, mark

Y (*for YES*)   *if the statement agrees with the information given in the passage*;

N (*for NO*)   *if the statement contradicts the information given in the passage*;

NG (*for NOT GIVEN*) *if the information is not given in the passage.*

For questions 8-10, complete the sentences with the information given in the passage.

Radiation from the sun is the earth's primary source of energy. More than 99 per cent of the processes that are happening on earth are energized by the sun either directly or indirectly. As solar radiation is a permanent and renewable source of energy, why, then, do we have an "energy crisis"? The problem, of course, lies in how to utilize this energy. It is diffuse and intermittent(断断续续的) on a daily and seasonal basis, thus collection and storage costs can be high. But we already have at our disposal a means of capturing and storing a proportion of this energy, and we have always had such a means. It is plant life—the "biomass". The process involved is photosynthesis(光合作用).

This capture of solar energy and conversion into a stored product occurs, with only a low overall efficiency of about 0. 1 per cent on a world-wide basis but because of the adaptability of plants, it takes place and can be used over most of the earth.

We should remember two things about this energy source. First, the world's present and precarious(靠不住的) dependence on fossil fuels—first coal, and then oil—is only about two hundred years old. Before that, most of the energy required by human beings for heating, cooking and industrial purpose was supplied from biological sources. By this, we mean mainly wood, or its derivative(衍生的) charcoal. Secondly, wood still accounts for one sixth of the world's fuel supply. In the non-OPEC developing countries, which contain 40 per cent of the world's population, non-commercial fuel often comprises up to 90 per cent of their total energy use. With the increasingly doubtful future of fossil fuel supplies, fuel from biological sources may have to become even more important.

Traditional fuels of biological origin include wood, charcoal, agricultural residues such as straw and dried animal dung. With the growth in world population, there has been increasing pressure on these resources, leading to what is sometimes called the "second energy crisis". This is more drastic for mankind than the "first", or oil crisis. It takes the form of deforestation, with loss of green cover in hot lands, leading to desiccation(脱水) and the loss of fertile land to desert.

The threat from both energy crises can be partly met by utilizing the enormous supply of energy built up annually in green plants. The question is, how should this be done? In the past, photosynthesis has given us food, fuel wood, fiber and chemicals. It has also, ultimately, given us the fossil fuels— coal, oil and natural gas, but these are not renewable while the other products are. Recently, however, with abundant oil, the products of present-day photosynthesis are mainly evident to the developed world as food.

We should re-examine and, if possible, re-employ the previous systems; but, with today's increased population and standard of living, we cannot revert to old technology and must instead develop new means of using present-day photosynthetic systems more efficiently.

Fortunately for us, plants are very adaptable and exist in great diversity— they could thus continue indefinitely to supply us with renewable quantities of food, fibre, fuel and chemicals. If the impending(迫近的) fuel problem which is predicted within the next ten to fifteen years comes about, we may turn to plant products sooner than we expect. Let us be prepared!

Some basic research can be done centrally, without reference to the conditions in any one country. For example, all plant energy storage depends ultimately on the process of photosynthesis. Experiments are being made to see whether this process can either be speeded up, or even reproduced artificially, in order to produce a higher efficiency in energy extraction. Most research should be done locally, however, because of climatic and vegetation differences, and also because of the difference in needs and emphasis in varying countries. Such research and development is an excellent opportunity to encourage local scientists, engineers and administrators in one field of energy supply. Even if biomass systems do not become significant suppliers of energy in a specific country in the future, the spin-off in terms of benefits to agriculture, forestry, land use patterns and bioconversion technology is certain to be valuable.

What are the methods currently in use or under trial for deriving energy from biomass? The first is the traditional use outlined in paragraph 3, which may be termed the "non-commercial" use of biomass energy. The second also has a long traditional history: the use of wood-fuel under boilers to generate steam. This has now been revised on an intensive scale. In a study from the Philippines, it has been estimated that a 9100 hectare fuel wood plantation "would supply the needs of a 75 megawatt steam power station if it were not more than fifty kilometers distant". Such a plantation would use a species of fast-growing tree—leucaena leucocephala, or the giant "ipil-ipil". The investment requirements and cost of power produced looks favorable and competitive with oil-fired power stations of similar capacity. In addition, residues from crop land after harvest and from sawmills(锯木厂) could be used as steam-producing fuel. The steam could then be used to generate electricity.

There are also bioconversion processes to produce liquid fuels such as oil and alcohol. Some fuel oils can be pressed directly from certain crops. Alcohols, on the other hand, can be produced by converting plant material by fermentation (发酵). Ethanol (ethyl alcohol) can be extracted from growing plants such as sugar cane, from waste plant material, or from whole grain. Methanol (methyl alcohol) can be produced from coal, wood, sewage and various waste products. These alcohols have several industrial uses and can also be used as fuels in the internal combustion engines of vehicles. Technology is already advanced, and the main problem is devising ways of collecting enough organic material to make the installations commercially viable. Some crops can be grown specifically for this purpose. In other cases the installations can make use of the residue, or "trash" produced in the large-scale plantation farming of such crops as sugar cane and pineapple. Another fuel product produced by a fermentation process is fuel gas of various kinds, including a biogas called methane. Several of these processes can be applied to household or municipal wastes and refuse—a large and concentrated source in all big towns and cities.

1. Practically all the plant biomass produced by farmers around the world is a potential source of energy, whether the crop is grown for food, fuel or fibre.

2. Sugar cane is an important crop that can be used to produce ethanol for motor fuel.

3. Only developing countries that have large areas of agricultural or forest land can benefit from biomass sources of energy.

4. The use of charcoal for cooking has been a common practice for hundreds of years.

5. Systematic deforestation to supply steam-producing fuel serves to improve the fertility of the land and reduce desiccation(干燥).

6. OPEC countries use more fuel from non-fossil biological sources than the developing world in general.

7. Traditional use of biomass material for fuel caused no serious problems when popular levels were low.

8. With today's increased population and standard of living we cannot revert to _____.

9. Not all of research can be done centrally without reference to _____.

10. Some crops can be grown specifically for the purpose of producing organic material to _____.

II Comprehensive Test

Section A Cloze

Directions: *There are 20 blanks in the following passage. For each blank there are four choices marked A, B, C and D. You should choose the ONE that best fits into the passage. Then mark the corresponding letter on Answer Sheet with a single line through the center.*

Comparisons were drawn between the development of television in the 20th century and the diffusion of printing in the 15th and 16th centuries. Yet much had happened __1__. As was discussed before, it was not __2__ the 19th century that the newspaper became the dominant pre-electronic __3__, following in the wake of the pamphlet（小册子）and the book and in the ___4___ of the periodical. It was during the same time that the communications revolution ___5___ up, beginning with transport, the railway, and leading ___6___ through the telegraph, the telephone, radio, and motion pictures ___7___ the 20th century world of the motor car and the airplane. Not everyone sees that process in ___8___ . It is important to do so.

It is generally recognized, ___9___ , that the introduction of the computer in the early 20th century, ___10___ by the invention of the integrated circuit during the 1960s, radically changed the process, ___11___ its impact on the media was not immediately ___12___ . As time went by, computers became smaller and more powerful, and they became "personal" too, as well as ___13___ , with display becoming sharper and storage ___14___ increasing. They were thought of, like people ___15___ generations, with the distance between generations much ___16___ .

It was within the computer age that the term "information society" began to be widely used to describe the ___17___ within which we now live. The communications revolution has ___18___ both work and leisure and how we think and feel both about place and time. But there have been ___19___ views about its economic, political, social and cultural implications. "Benefits" have been weighed ___20___ "harmful" outcomes. And generalizations have proved difficult.

1. A. between   B. before   C. since   D. later
2. A. after   B. by   C. during   D. until
3. A. means   B. method   C. medium   D. measure
4. A. process   B. company   C. light   D. form
5. A. gathered   B. speeded   C. worked   D. picked
6. A. on   B. out   C. over   D. off
7. A. of   B. for   C. beyond   D. into
8. A. concept   B. dimension   C. effect   D. perspective
9. A. indeed   B. hence   C. however   D. therefore
10. A. brought   B. followed   C. stimulated   D. characterized
11. A. unless   B. since   C. lest   D. although
12. A. apparent   B. desirable   C. negative   D. plausible
13. A. institutional B. universal C. fundamental D. instrumental
14. A. ability   B. capability   C. capacity   D. faculty
15. A. by means of B. in terms of C. with regard to D. in line with

16. A. deeper   B. fewer   C. nearer   D. smaller

17. A. context   B. range   C. scope   D. territory

18. A. regarded   B. impressed   C. influenced   D. effected

19. A. competitive   B. controversial   C. distracting   D. irrational

20. A. above   B. upon   C. against   D. with

Section B   Error Correction

Directions: *This part consists a short passage. In this passage, there are possibably 10 or less than 10 mistakes, one in each numbered line. You may have to change a word, add a word or delete a word. If you change a word, cross it out and write the correct word in the corresponding blank. If you add a word, put an insertion mark ( ) in the correct word in the corresponding blank. If you delete a word, cross it out and be sure to put a slash (/) in the blank.*

Truth is, I'm just not interested in it anymore. Knowledge, on the other hand, there's still a desire for knowledge. It's a curious thing, the thirst for knowledge very few people have it, you know, even among scientists. Most of them are happy to make a career for themselves and move into management, but it's incredibly important to the history of humanity. It's easy to imagine a fable of which a small group of   1. _____

men a couple hundred, at the most, in the whole world work   2. _____

intensively on something very difficult, very abstract, completely incomprehensible to the uninitiated. These men remain completely unknown to rest of the world; they have no   3. _____

apparent power, no money, no honors; nobody can understand the pleasure they get from their work. In fact, they are the most powerful men in the world, for one simple reason: they hold the keys of rational certainty. Everything they declare to   4. _____

be true will be accepted, soon or later, by the whole   5. _____

population. There is no power in the world economic, political, religious, or social that can compete for rational certainty.   6. _____

Western society is interested beyond all measure in philosophy and politics, and the most vicious, ridiculous conflicts have been about philosophy and politics; it has also had a passionate love affair with literature and the arts, but nothing in its   7. _____

history has been as important so the need for rational certainty.   8. _____

The West has sacrificed everything of this need: religion,   9. _____

happiness, hope—and, finally, its own life. You have to

remember this when passing judgment on Western civilization.   10. _____

Section C   Short Answer Questions

Directions: *In this part there is a short passage with five questions or incomplete statements. Read the passage carefully. Then answer the questions or complete the statements in the fewest possible words.*

Generally, in order to be preserved in the fossil (化石) record, organisms must possess hard body parts such as shells or bones. Soft, fleshy structures are quickly destroyed by predators (食肉动物) or decayed by bacteria. Even hard parts left on the surface for a length of time will be destroyed. Therefore, organisms must be buried rapidly to escape destruction by the elements and to be protected by agents of weathering and erosion (腐蚀). Marine organisms thus are better candidates for fossilization than those living on the land because the ocean is typically the site of sedimentation (沉积), whereas the land is largely the site of erosion.

The beds of ancient lakes were also excellent sites for rapid burial of skeletal (骸骨的) remains of freshwater organisms and skeletons of other animals, including those of early humans. Ancient swamps were particularly plentiful with prolific (多产的,丰富的) growths of vegetation, which fossilized in abundance. Many animals became trapped in bogs overgrown by vegetation. The environment of the swamps kept bacterial decay to a minimum, which greatly aided in the preservation of plants and animals. The rapidly accumulating sediments in flood plains, deltas (三角洲), and stream channels buried freshwater organisms, along with other plants and animals that happened to fall into the water.

Only a small fraction of all the organisms that have ever lived are preserved as fossils. Normally, the remains of a plant or animal are completely destroyed through predation and decay. Although it seems that fossilization is common for some organisms, for others it is almost impossible. For the most part, the remains of organisms are recycled in the earth, which is fortunate because otherwise soil and water would soon become depleted of essential nutrients. Also, most of the fossils exposed on Earth's surface are destroyed by weathering processes. This makes for an incomplete fossil record with poor or no representation of certain species.

Questions：（注意：答题尽量简短，超过10个词要扣分，每条横线限写一个英语单词，标点符号不占格。）

1. According to the passage, an organism without hard body parts _____ .

   _____ _____ _____ _____ _____

   _____ _____ _____ _____ _____

2. Why are marine organisms good candidates for fossilization?

   _____ _____ _____ _____ _____

   _____ _____ _____ _____ _____

3. Why is land largely the site of erosion according to the passage?

   _____ _____ _____ _____ _____

   _____ _____ _____ _____ _____

4. According to the passage, why were the remains of organisms trapped in swamps better preserved for the fossil record than those that were not?

   _____ _____ _____ _____ _____

   _____ _____ _____ _____ _____

5. Why some organisms can't be fossilized?

   _____ _____ _____ _____ _____

   _____ _____ _____ _____ _____

Test Eight

I Reading Comprehension

Section A Passage Reading

Directions: *There are 2 passages in this section. Each passage is followed by some questions or unfinished statements. For each of them there are four choices marked A, B, C and D. You should decide on the best choice and mark the corresponding letter on Answer Sheet with a single line through the center.*

Passage One

Questions 1 to 5 are based on the following passage.

Every year television stations receive hundreds of complaints about the loudness of advertisements. However, federal rules forbid the practice of making ads louder than the programming. In addition, television stations always operate at the highest sound level allowed for reasons of efficiency. According to one NBC executive, no difference exists in the peak sound level of ads and programming. Given this information, why do commercials sound so loud?

The sensation of sound involves a variety of factors in addition to its peak level. Advertisers are skilful at creating the impression of loudness through their expert use of such factors. One major contributor to the perceived loudness of commercials is that much less variation in sound level occurs during a commercial. In regular programming the intensity of sound varies over a large range. However, sound levels in commercials tend to stay at or near peak levels.

Other "tricks of the trade" are also used. Because low-frequency sounds can mask higher frequency sounds, advertisers filter out any noises that may drown out the primary message. In addition, the human voice has more auditory impact in the middle frequency ranges. Advertisers electronically vary voice sounds so that they stay within such a frequency band. Another approach is to write the script so that lots of consonants are used, because people are more aware of consonants than vowel sounds. Finally, advertisers try to begin commercials with sounds that are highly different from those of the programming within which the commercial is buried. Because people become adapted to the type of sounds coming from programming, a dramatic change in sound quality draws viewer attention. For example, notice how many commercials begin with a cheerful song of some type.

The attention getting property of commercials can be seen by observing one to two year old children who happen to be playing around a television set. They may totally ignore the programming. However, when a commercial comes on, their attention is immediately drawn to it because of its dramatic sound quality.

1. According to the passage, the maximum intensity of sound coming from commercials _____.

   A. does not exceed that of programs

   B. is greater than that of programs

   C. varies over a large range than that of programs

D. is less than that of programs

2. Commercials create the sensation of loudness because _____.

   A. TV stations always operate at the highest sound levels

   B. their sound levels are kept around peak levels

   C. their sound levels are kept in the middle frequency ranges

   D. unlike regular programs their intensity of sound varies over a wide range

3. Many commercials begin with a cheerful song of some kind because _____.

   A. pop songs attract viewer attention

   B. it can increase their loudness

   C. advertisers want to make them sound different from regular programs

   D. advertisers want to merge music with commercials

4. One of the reasons why commercials are able to attract viewer attention is that _____.

   A. the human voices in commercials have more auditory impact

   B. people like cheerful songs that change dramatically in sound quality

   C. high frequency sounds are used to mask sounds that drown out the primary message

   D. they possess sound qualities that make the viewer feel that something unusual is happening

5. In the passage, the author is trying to tell us _____.

   A. how TV ads vary vocal sounds to attract attention

   B. how the loudness of TV ads is overcome

   C. how advertisements control the sound properties of TV ads

   D. how the attention getting properties of sounds are made use of in TV ads

Passage Two
Questions 6 to 10 are based on the following passage.

If women are mercilessly exploited year after year, they have only themselves to blame. Because they tremble at the thought of being seen in public in clothes that are out of fashion, they are always taken advantage of by the designers and the big stores. Clothes which have been worn only a few times have to be put aside because of the change of fashion. When you come to think of it, only a woman is capable of standing in front of a wardrobe packed full of clothes and announcing sadly that she has nothing to wear.

Changing fashions are nothing more than the intentional creation of waste. Many women spend vast sums of money each year to replace clothes that have hardly been worn. Women who cannot afford to throw away clothing in this way, waste hours of their time altering the dresses they have. Skirts are lengthened or shortened; neck lines are lowered or raised, and so on. No one can claim that the fashion industry contributes anything really important to society. Fashion designers are rarely concerned with vital things like warmth, comfort and durability. They are only interested in outward appearance and they take advantage of the fact that women will put up with any amount of discomfort, as long as they look right. There can hardly be a man who hasn't at some time in his life smiled at the sight of a woman shaking in a thin dress on a winter day, or delicately picking her way through deep snow in high heeled shoes.

When comparing men and women in the matter of fashion, the conclusions to be drawn are obvious. Do the constantly changing fashions of women's clothes, one wonders, reflect basic qualities of inconstancy and instability? Men are too clever to let themselves be cheated by fashion designers. Do their unchanging styles of dress reflect basic qualities of stability and reliability? That is for you to decide.

6. Designers and big stores always make money _____.

   A. by mercilessly exploiting women workers in the clothing industry

   B. because they are capable of predicting new fashions

   C. by constantly changing the fashions in women's clothing

   D. because they attach great importance to quality in women's clothing

7. To the writer, the fact that women alter their old-fashioned dresses is seen as _____.

   A. a waste of money   B. a waste of time

   C. an expression of taste   D. an expression of creativity

8. The writer would be less critical if fashion designers placed more stress on the _____ of clothing.

   A. cost   B. appearance

   C. comfort   D. suitability

9. According to the passage, which of the following statements is TRUE?

   A. New fashions in clothing are created for the commercial exploitation of women.

B. The constant changes in women's clothing reflect their strength of character.

C. The fashion industry makes an important contribution to society.

D. Fashion designs should not be encouraged since they are only welcomed by women.

10. By saying "the conclusions to be drawn are obvious"(Sentence 1, Para. 4) the writer means that _____.

A. women's inconstancy in their choice of clothing is often laughed at

B. women are better able to put up with discomfort

C. men are also exploited greatly by fashion designers

D. men are more stable and reliable in character

Section B Banked Cloze

Directions: *In this section, there is a passage with ten blanks. You are required to select one word for each blank from a list of choices given in a word bank following the passage. Read the passage through carefully before making your choices. Each choice in the bank is identified by a letter. Please mark the corresponding letter for each item on Answer Sheet with a single line through the center. You may not use any of the words in the bank more than once.*

In many countries it is common for teenagers to take part-time jobs when they are still in high school, while in other societies this is virtually unheard of. In the __1__ situation, students are expected to __2__ all of their time on their studies and consider schoolwork their "job".

While it is true that a student's most important __3__ must be to learn and to do well at his studies, it does not need to be the only goal. In fact, a life which consists of only study is not __4__ and may cause the student to miss out on other valuable learning experiences. In addition to bringing more balance to a student's life, part-time work can __5__ his range of experience. He will have the __6__ to meet people from all walks of life and will be faced with a wider variety of __7__ to solve. Furthermore, work helps a student to develop greater independence, earning his own __8__ money and teaching him how to handle his finances. Finally, a part-time job can help a student to develop a greater __9__ of responsibility, both for his own work and for that of the team he works with. As a result of those, most students would __10__ from taking a part-time job while they are in high school.

A. former	E. spend	I. sense	M. develop
B. take	F. goal	J. problems	N. questions
C. opportunity	G. balanced	K. pocket	O. tuition fee
D. latter	H. broaden	L. benefit	

Section C Reading Comprehension (Skimming and Scanning)

Directions: *In this part, you will go over the passages quickly and answer the questions.*

For questions 1-7, mark

Y (*for YES*)   *if the statement agrees with the information given in the passage;*

N (*for NO*)   *if the statement contradicts the information given in the passage;*

NG (*for NOT GIVEN*) *if the information is not given in the passage.*

For questions 8-10, complete the sentences with the information given in the passage.

An upstart Internet venture calling itself http://www. student. com is hiring students this semester and paying them to take notes in as many as 50 core courses per campus.

The note-takers post their jottings(简短笔记) electronically, within 24 hours, on a central website. Among the dozens of notes already listed are those taken Tuesday during Professor John Syer's course on world politics at California State University in Sacramento and on Aug. 94 during Professor Robert Schwebach's lecture on financial markets at Colorado State University.

The service, which first went on-line Wednesday, is free. And the stenographers(速记员), most of them hired through their fraternities(同行朋友) and enrolled in the courses, are paid $ 300 a semester to open their notebooks to the world.

The creator of the site, Oran Wolf, a 27-year-old graduate of the University of Texas at Austin, who hopes to earn a profit partly through advertising, said he started the service to help students augment their own notes or to help them catch up after a sick day.

But he conceded that his offerings could be abused by those with less legitimate excuses, like chronic oversleeping or lingering hangovers(宿醉).

"I definitely don't believe students should skip class," Mr. Wolf said this week from his Houston office, as he admitted that he, too, on occasion, had done just that.

"It is important for them to attend the class, use this information as supplements to the course and if they do that, they are going to get A's."

There is no shortage of critics who believe that the arrival of Mr. Wolf's venture—along with other web sites that sell sample term papers and synopses of great books—signals nothing less than the erosion(侵蚀) of liberal education, if not civilization.

But Mark Edmundson, a professor of English at the University of Virginia, one of the schools where Mr. Wolf has set up shop, thinks the problem lies more with universities—and their reliance, often for financial reasons, on 300-student lecture courses—than on those trying to beat the system.

"There's something sleazy(卑劣的) about students taking notes and selling them on the web," Mr. Edmundson said.

"But if you can buy the notes and satisfy the course requirements, maybe the course should have been distributed as a book, rather than having this charade(荒谬的借口) of somebody standing up and going through a lecture that, for all purposes, doesn't change from year to year, and doesn't allow students the possibility of discussion."

Peter Wood, a professor of anthropology and the associate provost at Boston University, which is also on Mr. Wolfs list, said the university might consider taking legal action once notes from the school appear on the site—which, as of Wednesday, they had not.

"I am troubled by it because I, like thousands of faculty members, spent a great deal of time developing my courses within a specific intellectual context, a context that I control," he said.

Mr. Wolf said the seeds of his idea were first sown while he was studying economics at Austin, when he had occasionally taken advantage of a similar service there: For $30 per class, a private note-taking firm would arrange for him to get paper copies of any notes that he might have missed.

After graduating in 1995 and moving to Houston, he learned that the university there had no such service, and so he founded his own. Initially taking

10 hours of notes a day himself, he quickly expanded his operation to include about 3,000 subscribers—they, too, paid $30 for each of 120 classes—and about 40 note-takers.

Mr. Wolf said professors at the University of Houston were initially wary of helping him and his note-takers gain access to classes, if they were not enrolled.

But he said he won them over when they realized that attendance did not drop as a result.

When Mr. Wolf discovered that such services were rare on other campuses, he said he decided to take his operation national.

With an investment from New Strategy, a Houston company that has nurtured other web companies, and rolling banner of advertisements that includes the Capital One Visa Platinium Card, Mr. Wolf began recruiting note-takers at fraternities at 62 of the largest colleges and universities throughout the United States.

Because he has assembled his operation so quickly, using students already in courses, Mr. Wolf said he would not be asking professors for permission to broadcast their notes.

Thus, many are likely to be as surprised as Professor Syer at Sacramento who learned from a reporter Wednesday that his introduction to the world's 10 largest countries had been reproduced by an anonymous note-taker for all to see.

"I'm not unalterably opposed to this dissemination(普及,宣传)," he said.

"I'd just like to know how wide my audience is. I'm going to get up there and take on the policies of the U.S. government, the policies of the Indonesian government and the policies of the Chinese government. "

"If I think this is something that is going to be quoted globally," he said, "it may change what I say. "

1. Students who wish to visit the web site offering notes of major college courses must pay a fee.
2. Mr. Wolf used to over-sleep chronically(积习成癖地).
3. Many people believe that the kind of service offered by Mr. Wolf is detrimental(有害的,不利的) to the education of arts.
4. Professor Mark Edmundson believes that such web sites pose a major threat to the present educational system.
5. Students who take notes for Mr. Wolf were denied access to classes.

6. By broadcasting notes without permission from the professors, Mr. Wolf might get involved in lawsuits.

7. Professor Syer was indignant when he learned that notes of his lecture were posted on the Internet.

8. Mr. Wolf set up the web shop not for the purpose of helping those _____.

9. Peter Wood possibly takes legal action against Mr. Wolf's doing if _____.

10. In order to let more campuses to get such service, Mr. Wolf decided to _____.

II Comprehensive Test

Section A Cloze

Directions: *There are 20 blanks in the following passage. For each blank there are four choices marked A, B, C and D. You should choose the ONE that best fits into the passage. Then mark the corresponding letter on Answer Sheet with a single line through the center.*

What does the future hold for the problem of housing? A good __1__ depends, of course, on the meaning of "future". If one is thinking in __2__ of science fiction and the space age __3__ at least possible to assume that man will have solved such trivial and earthly problems as housing. Writers of science fiction have __4__ the suggestion that men will live in great comfort, with every __5__ device to make life smooth, healthy and easy, __6__ not happy. But they have not said what his house will be made of.

The problems of the next generation or two can more readily be imagined, Scientists have already pointed out that __7__ something is done either to restrict the world's rapid growth in population or to discover and develop new sources of food (or both), millions of people will be dying of starvation or, __8__, suffering from under-feeding before this __9__ is out. But nobody has worked out any plan for housing these growing populations.

Admittedly the worse situations will occur in the __10__ parts of the world, where housing can be of light structure, or in backward areas where standards are __11__ low. But even the minimum shelter requires materials of __12__ kind, and in the crowded, bulging towns the low-standard "housing" of flattened petrol cans and dirty canvas is far more wasteful __13__ ground space than can be tolerated.

Since the war, Hong Kong has suffered the kind of crisis which is likely to __14__ in many other places during the next generation. __15__ millions of refugees arrived to __16__ the already growing population and emergency steps had to be taken to prevent squalor (污秽,肮脏) and disease and the __17__ of crime. Hong Kong is only one small part of what will certainly become a vast problem—and not __18__ a housing problem, because when population grows at this rate there are __19__ problems of education, transport, water supply and so on. Not every area may have the same resources as Hong Kong to __20__ and the search for quicker and cheaper methods of construction must never cease.

1. A. transaction   B. deal   C. definition   D. assumption
2. A. reference   B. respect   C. terms   D. consequence
3. A. he is   B. one is   C. it is   D. we are
4. A. conveyed   B. conceived   C. deduced   D. formulated
5. A. conceptual   B. considerate   C. conceivable   D. complimentary
6. A. if   B. but   C. yet   D. although
7. A. only if   B. even if   C. in case   D. unless
8. A. for the better B. in the least C. at the most   D. at the best
9. A. age   B. resource   C. century   D. problem
10. A. hottest   B. coldest   C. poorest   D. richest
11. A. customarily   B. habitually   C. conventionally D. traditionally
12. A. every   B. some   C. this   D. certain
13. A. of   B. on   C. for   D. with
14. A. rise   B. raise   C. arise   D. arouse
15. A. Precisely   B. Numerically   C. Literally   D. Previously
16. A. swell   B. diverge   C. inflate   D. delete
17. A. extension   B. disposal   C. spread   D. expansion
18. A. likely   B. certainly   C. merely   D. necessary
19. A. accompanying B. associating   C. escorting   D. attaching
20. A. stretch out   B. stick to   C. take in   D. draw upon

Section B Error Correction

Directions: *This part consists a short passage. In this passage, there are possibably 10 or less than 10 mistakes, one in each numbered line. You may have to change a word, add a word or delete a word. If you change a word, cross it out and write the correct word in the corresponding blank. If you add a word, put an insertion mark ( ) in the correct word in the corresponding blank. If you delete a word, cross it out and be sure to put a slash (/) in the blank.*

America has been called a democracy since its independence more than 200 years ago. However, at that time, only
men were permitted for voting. Only men could own land and   1. _____
practiced most professions. Women could not get a   2. _____
high education and hold public office. The woman's place was   3. _____
considered to be at home. Working women were not common.   4. _____
They usually had poor jobs and a little respect. Throughout the   5. _____
history of our country, many American women worked to   6. _____
reduce the restriction that society placed on them. They have
met opposition. Slowly, however, the opportunities for women
have increased. Colleges and universities were established for
women. Later women were admitted to schools originally
establishing only for men. In the early part of this century,   7. _____
American women were finally allowed to vote. During and
since World War Two, American women have become a
considerable part of the American work force.

Today, many women in America hold important positions
or are pursuing careers that they could not pursue in the past.
But many women are dissatisfied about the current situation.   8. _____
They point out that women are often paid fewer than men for   9. _____
the same work they do. The top positions in nearly all fields are
still overwhelming held by men. In many ways, a woman's life   10. _____
is still dominated by her father and her husband.

Section C Short Answer Questions

Directions: *In this part there is a short passage with five questions or incomplete* *statements. Read the passage carefully. Then answer the questions or complete the statements in the fewest possible words.*

Ours has become a society of employees. A hundred years or so ago only one out of every five Americans at work was employed, i. e, worked for somebody else. Today only one out of five is not employed but working for himself. And when fifty years ago "being employed" meant working as a factory laborer or as a farmhand, the employee of today is increasingly a middle-class person with a substantial formal education, holding a professional or man agement job requiring intellectual and technical skills. Indeed, two things have characterized American society during those last fifty years: middle class and upper class employees have been the fastest growing groups in our working population—growing so fast that the industrial worker, that oldest child of the Industrial Revolution, has been losing in numerical importance despite the expansion of industrial production.

Yet you will find little of anything written on what it is to be an employee. You can find a great deal of very dubious advice on how to get a job or how to get a promotion. You can find a great deal of work in a chosen field, whether it is the mechanist's trade or bookkeeping. Every one of these trades requires different skills, set different standards, and requires a different preparation. Yet they all have employeeship in common. And increasingly, especially in the large business or in government, employeeship is more important to success than the special professional knowledge or skill. Certainly more people fail because they do not know the requirements of being an employee than because they do not adequately possess the skills of their trade; the higher you climb the ladder, the more you get into administrative or executive work, the greater the emphasis on ability to work within the organization rather than on technical ability or professional knowledge.

Questions：(注意：答题尽量简短,超过10个词要扣分,每条横线限写一个英语单词,标点符号不占格。)

1. What about the the percentage of intellectuals working as employees fifty years ago?

　　_____ _____ _____ _____ _____
　　_____ _____ _____ _____ _____

2. What happened to the factory laborers in the total employee population with

the development of modern industry?

_____ _____ _____ _____ _____

_____ _____ _____ _____ _____

3. What kinds of have did people usually get?

_____ _____ _____ _____ _____

_____ _____ _____ _____ _____

4. According to the writer, professional knowledge or skill is _____.

_____ _____ _____ _____ _____

_____ _____ _____ _____ _____

5. From the passage it can be seen that employeeship helps one _____.

_____ _____ _____ _____ _____

_____ _____ _____ _____ _____

Test Nine

I Reading Comprehension

Section A Passage Reading

Directions: *There are 2 passages in this section. Each passage is followed by some questions or unfinished statements. For each of them there are four choices marked A, B, C and D. You should decide on the best choice and mark the corresponding letter on Answer Sheet with a single line through the center.*

Passage One

Questions 1 to 5 are based on the following passage.

Long before they can actually speak, babies pay special attention to the speech they hear around them. Within the first month of their lives, babies' responses to the sound of the human voice will be different from their responses to other sorts of auditory stimuli. They will stop crying when they hear a person talking, but not if they hear a bell or the sound of a rattle. At first, the sounds that an infant notices might be only those words that receive the heaviest emphasis and that often occur at the ends of utterances. By the time they are six or seven weeks old, babies can detect the difference between syllables pronounced with rising and falling inflections. Very soon, these differences in adult stress and intonation can influence babies' emotional states and behavior. Long before they develop actual language comprehension, babies can sense when an adult is playful or angry, attempting to initiate or terminate new behavior, and so on, merely on the basis of cues such as the rate, volume, and melody of adult speech.

Adults make it as easy as they can for babies to pick up a language by exaggerating such cues. One researcher observed babies and their mothers in six diverse cultures and found that, in all six languages, the mothers used simplified syntax(句法), short utterances and nonsense sounds, and transformed certain sounds into baby talk. Other investigators have noted that when mothers talk to babies who are only a few months old, they exaggerate the pitch, loudness, and intensity of their words. They also exaggerate their facial expressions, hold vowels longer, and emphasize certain words.

More significant for language development than their response to general intonation is observation that tiny babies can make relatively fine distinctions between speech sounds. In other words, babies enter the world with the ability to make precisely those perceptual discriminations that are necessary if they are to acquire aural language.

Babies obviously derive pleasure from sound input, too: even as young as nine months they will listen to songs or stories, although the words themselves are beyond their understanding. For babies, language is a sensory-motor delight rather than the route to prosaic(如实的) meaning that it often is for adults.

1. What does the passage mainly discuss?

A. How babies differentiate between the sound of the human voice and other sounds?

B. The differences between a baby's and an adult's ability to comprehend language.

C. How babies perceive and respond to the human voice in their earliest stages of language development?

D. The response of babies to sounds other than the human voice.

2. Why does the author mention a bell and a rattle in the first paragraph?

A. To contrast the reactions of babies to human and nonhuman sounds.

B. To give examples of sounds that will cause a baby to cry.

C. To explain how babies distinguish between different nonhuman sounds.

D. To give examples of typical toys that babies do not like.

3. The word "noted" in sentence 3, paragraph 2 is closest in meaning to
_____.

    A. theorized   B. requested

    C. disagreed   D. observed

4. Which of the following can be inferred about the findings described in paragraph 2?

    A. Babies who are exposed to more than one language can speak earlier than babies exposed to a single language.

    B. Mothers from different cultures speak to their babies in similar ways.

    C. Babies ignore facial expressions in comprehending aural language.

    D. The mothers observed by the researchers were consciously teaching their babies to speak.

5. What point does the author make to illustrate that babies are born with the ability to acquire language?

    A. Babies begin to understand words in songs.

    B. Babies exaggerate their own sounds and expressions.

    C. Babies are more sensitive to sounds than adults.

    D. Babies notice even minor differences between speech sounds.

Passage Two
Questions 6 to 10 are based on the following passage.

Increasingly, over the past ten years, people—especially young people—have become aware of the need to change their eating habits, because much of the food they eat, particularly processed food, is not good for the health. Consequently there has been a growing interest in natural foods: foods which do not contain chemical additives(添加剂) and which have not been affected by chemical fertilizers, widely used in farming today.

Natural foods, for example, are vegetables, fruit and grain which have been grown in soil that is rich in organic matter. In simple terms, this means that the soil has been nourished by unused vegetable matter, which provides it with essential vitamins and minerals. This in itself is a natural process compared with the use of chemicals and fertilizers, the main purpose of which is to increase the amount but not the quality of foods grown in commercial farming areas.

Natural foods also include animals which have been allowed to feed and move freely in healthy pastures. Compare this with what happens in the mass production of poultry: there are battery(笼式的) farms, for example, where thousands of chickens live crowded together in one building and are fed on food which is little better than rubbish. Chickens kept in this way are not only tasteless as food; they also produce eggs which lack important vitamins.

There are other aspects of healthy eating which are now receiving increasing attention from experts on diet, Take, for example, the question of sugar. This is actually a nonessential food! Although a natural alternative, such as honey, can be used to sweeten food if this is necessary, we can in fact do without it. It is not that sugar is harmful in itself. But it does seem to be addictive: the quantity we use has grown steadily over the last two centuries and in Britain today each person consumes an average of 200 pounds a year! Yet all it does is to provide us with energy, in the form of calories. There are no vitamins in it, no minerals and no fiber.

It is significant that nowadays fiber is considered to be an important part of a healthy diet. In white bread, for example, the fiber has been removed. But it is present in unrefined flour and of course in vegetables. It is interesting to note that in countries where the national diet contains large quantities of unrefined flour and vegetables, certain diseases are comparatively rare. Hence the emphasis is placed on the eating of whole meal bread and more vegetables by modern experts on "healthy eating".

6. People have become more interested in natural foods because _____.
   A. they want a change of diet
   B. they want to eat food that is better for them
   C. they no longer like processed foods polluted by chemical additives
   D. they want to be fashionable
7. Soil that is rich in organic matter _____.
   A. has had nothing added to it
   B. provides vegetable matter with vitamins and minerals
   C. contains unused vegetable matter
   D. has had chemicals and fertilizers added to it
8. Battery chickens cannot be called "natural food" because _____.
   A. they live in crowded conditions

B. they are tasteless

C. their eggs have no vitamins

D. they are not allowed to move about and eat freely

9. According to experts on diet _____.

A. sugar is bad for the health

B. the use of sugar is habit forming

C. people need sugar to give them energy

D. sugar only sweetens food

10. If we ate more food containing fiber, _____.

A. our diet would be healthier

B. we would be as healthy as people in other countries

C. our diet would be more interesting

D. we would only eat whole-meal bread and vegetable

Section B   Banked Cloze

Directions: *In this section, there is a passage with ten blanks. You are required to select one word for each blank from a list of choices given in a word bank following the passage. Read the passage through carefully before making your choices. Each choice in the bank is identified by a letter. Please mark the corresponding letter for each item on Answer Sheet with a single line through the center. You may not use any of the words in the bank more than once.*

Office calls are, perhaps, the most difficult and the most important part of a secretary's work. The first impression that a client receives about a business is very often through a ___1___ contact. A caller who is left hanging on "hold" will get the ___2___ that he or she has been forgotten or ignored. If a call is answered rudely, the ___3___ may become angry. And ___4___ the call is routed directly to the right person, the caller may feel that he or ___5___ is getting the "runaround" (推诿).

Judy Miller is a secretary in the executive offices of a large manufacturing company. As a good office ___6___, Judy knows that all phone calls must be answered promptly and handled ___7___. She knows that a secretary must be pleasant and helpful, no matter how busy she is or what kind of mood she may be in. She knows she must keep calm if a caller gets ___8___ or become angry; also, of course, she knows she can never allow herself to lose her temper. If she does not have the ___9___ the caller asks for, she must know who does have the information.

Finally, she knows that one of her most important responsibilities is to "screen" telephone calls and to know which ___10___ to refer to her boss, which calls to refer to other people, and which calls to handle herself.

A. caller	E. she	I. feeling	M. lose
B. helpful	F. impatient	J. calls	N. secretary
C. information	G. efficiently	K. telephone	O. people
D. if	H. impression	L. angry	

Section C   Reading Comprehension (Skimming and Scanning)

Directions: *In this part, you will go over the passages quickly and answer the questions.*

For questions 1-7, mark

Y (*for YES*)   *if the statement agrees with the information given in the passage;*

N (*for NO*)   *if the statement contradicts the information given in the passage;*

NG (*for NOT GIVEN*)   *if the information is not given in the passage.*

For questions 8-10, complete the sentences with the information given in the passage.

Educational and propagandist uses of television have become increasingly possible with the development of closed circuit TV technology and greater freedom of access by private individuals and groups to the public television networks. In the present chapter we discuss the growth of "access television" and educational technology specifically.

Our definition of persuasion on television has implied a style of use whereby the medium serves interests other than those of the viewer. Definitions of education, on the other hand, imply the use of communication channels in the recipient's interest specifically. The educational use of television may therefore be defined as that which intends to serve the viewer's interests by providing him with specific benefits. Of course, the definition of educational benefit will ultimately be subjective; and a working distinction between persuasion and education need not concern us in this any other context, since it is found to be elusive. At the nexus（联系）between forms of persuasion and education as commonly understood，however，we may observe numerous communication forms. A leading example of television's use to communicate material of this intermediate（中间的）type during the 1970s has been apparent in the "access" to the medium by amateur users. Political and popular pressures on the broadcasting organizations to provide public airtime on demand have been described by Groom bridge (1972)，while the case for democratic participation in the media was espoused（支持，拥护）by Anthony Wedgwood Benn，then Minister of Technology in 1968："Broadcasting"，he said，"is really too important to be left to the broadcasters." This maxim has been held as the origin for the flood of popular access activities that has followed. Most of the British television companies have in one way or another made available their facilities to individuals or to minority social groups appealing for it. The request for airtime is now not only seen as acceptable，but also as a necessary way in which the media can display a social conscience and responsibility. Whether the broadcasters like it or not，the effort is on to "demystify the medium" as surely as the Emperor was denuded（剥光，使赤裸）of his new clothes.

But in view of the extent to which the properties of television as a communication tool are an unknown quantity even to those whose skill in its use are maximal，access to the medium by amateur users likely to have any unpredicted effects? At a time when the potency（潜力）of television effects is only gradually becoming apparent，is general access to media techniques a premature and rather dangerous development? The beneficial effects of experimentation with television in therapeutic work are considerable (Brenes，1975). Through objectifying personal and group problems in a media context，strategies may be organized and a solution arrived at. The process is nonetheless a hesitant one，for however persuasive the use of television，it still readily arouses suspicion. A two-year old child，on seeing its father depicted there，will retreat from its initial recognition to cling to the real image for assurance. An active relationship between viewers and the medium must be established if actual reorganization is to result.

In the Canadian pioneering work with access television，its particular strength in community contexts has been observed. Through gradual access to production skills and persistence in bringing them to the notice of authorities， radical local reforms are obtained. The effects are achieved ill camera, closed circuit; access to the airwaves is unnecessary if the intended audience can be identified and isolated. The broadcast use of access is justified if the audience is diffuse; and recent examples of the vogue in Britain have achieved notable results in transmitting advice on general themes of political and medical self-help. The purpose of much other access broadcasting has been less clearly defined; Edward Goldwyn (1974), producer of the BBC-TV Open Door series, acknowledges that few single programs probably have any real effect. Indeed, in aiming the production at an audience far broader than required, it is possible that many groups achieve far less of an effect through access than they might have done. Are there other dangers? In the hands of the semi-skilled media worker, can television serve to damage his cause, frustrating the attempt at self-expression rather than creating new opportunities as expected?

From the immense complexity of the production and viewing processes indicated earlier it is clear that the possibilities for undesired effects when television is used by amateurs are infinite. Variations in production, editing and performance technique are each shown to exert potentially far-reaching effects on the way the television message is interpreted. The extent to which total freedom should be granted to the amateur user to produce, edit and present his own material should therefore certainly be questioned.

Since television's powers of imagery derive mainly from implication and inference rather than from logical argument, skills of verbal persuasion are inadequate when used on their own. If an image is to be changed through argument rather than by example, the techniques of media control must first be learned. The risks of any total access to the medium are clear from the evidence that even experienced media controllers may not realize all the psychological effects their techniques exert. Since much of televised content seems to receive our less than total attention, often failing to register in a conscious fashion at all, the chance of achieving a positive effect on the basis of isolated transmissions is in any case slender and in the preparations for any access venture this should be the first warning.

Indeed, as a safeguard in the provision of media access generally, the present firm stipulations that the facility shall not be used to advertise defame or incite should be extended. The aim of an access project must be clearly defined, and the advantages of broadcast vs. closed circuit transmission carefully weighed. If broadcasting organizations really want to display a social responsibility they might encourage use of their facilities on a closed circuit basis where appropriate.

The problem of control over television's dynamics is the prime question which must be tackled before its future development as a socially valuable tool may be ensured. From a basis of ignorance as to its properties, as we have seen, the use of television for social benefit may be offset by a number of negative effects. The problem is even more apparent when television is used for overt educational effects than it is in its campaigning usage. In the next section we examine the uses to which television has been put in education proper during the revolution in educational technology that has taken place since the early 1960s.

1. This passage is expected to discuss the growth of access television and educational technology mainly.
2. The definition of persuasion on television is different from that of education.
3. Nowadays people tend to television education rather than campus education.
4. Television media can help people to solve all of problems by objectifying personal and group problems.
5. The effort to demystify the medium is easily affected by people's performance.
6. The producers of the BBC-TV Open Door series was very successful as soon as it started.
7. People had no confidence in BBC-TV program at first.
8. The educational use of television is to serve the viewers' interest by _____.
9. When television is used by non-professionals, it is possible to create _____.
10. A social responsibility display might be encouraged to put on a closed circuit basis _____.

II Comprehensive Test

Section A   Cloze

Directions: *There are* 20 *blanks in the following passage. For each blank there* *are four choices marked A, B, C and D. You should choose the ONE that best fits into the passage. Then mark the corresponding letter on Answer Sheet with a single line through the center.*

Teachers need to be aware of the emotional, intellectual, and physical changes that young adults experience. And they also need to give serious __1__ to how they can best __2__ such changes. Growing bodies need movement and __3__, but not just in ways that emphasize competition. __4__ they are adjusting to their new bodies and a whole host of new intellectual and emotional challenges, teenagers are especially self-conscious and need the __5__ that comes from achieving success and knowing that their accomplishments are __6__ by others. However, the typical teenage lifestyle is already filled with so much competition that it would be __7__ to plan activities in which there are more winners than losers, __8__, publishing newsletters with many student written book reviews, __9__ student art-works, and sponsoring book discussion clubs. A variety of small clubs can provide __10__ opportunities for leadership, as well as for practice in successful __11__ dynamics. Making friends is extremely important to teenagers, and many shy students need the __12__ of some kind of organization with a supportive adult __13__ visible in the background.

In these activities, it is important to remember that young teens have __14__ attention spans. A variety of activities should be organized __15__ participants can remain active as long as they want and then go on to __16__ else without feeling guilty and without letting the other participants __17__. This does not mean that adults must accept irresponsibility.

__18__, they can help students acquire a sense of commitment by __19__ for roles that are within their __20__ and their attention spans and by having clearly stated rules.

1. A. thought   B. idea   C. opinion   D. advice
2. A. strengthen   B. accommodate   C. stimulate   D. enhance
3. A. care   B. nutrition   C. exercise   D. leisure
4. A. If   B. Although   C. Whereas   D. Because
5. A. assistance   B. guidance   C. confidence   D. tolerance
6. A. claimed   B. admired   C. ignored   D. surpassed
7. A. improper   B. risky   C. fair   D. wise
8. A. in effect   B. as a result   C. for example   D. in a sense

9. A. displaying   B. describing   C. creating   D. exchanging

10. A. durable   B. excessive   C. surplus   D. multiple

11. A. group   B. individual   C. personnel   D. corporation

12. A. consent   B. insurance   C. admission   D. security

13. A. particularly   B. barely   C. definitely   D. rarely

14. A. similar   B. long   C. different   D. short

15. A. if only   B. now that   C. so that   D. even if

16. A. everything   B. anything   C. nothing   D. something

17. A. off   B. down   C. out   D. alone

18. A. On the contrary   B. On the average

     C. On the whole   D. On the other hand

19. A. making   B. standing   C. planning   D. taking

20. A. capabilities   B. responsibilities   C. proficiency   D. efficiency

Section B   Error Correction

Directions: *This part consists a short passage. In this passage, there are possibably 10 or less than 10 mistakes, one in each numbered line. You may have to change a word, add a word or delete a word. If you change a word, cross it out and write the correct word in the corresponding blank. If you add a word, put an insertion mark ( ) in the correct word in the corresponding blank. If you delete a word, cross it out and be sure to put a slash (/) in the blank.*

Large companies need a way to reach the savings of the
public at large. The same problem, on a smaller scale, faces
practically every company trying to develop new products and
create new jobs. These can be little prospect of raising the sort
of sums needing from friends and people we know, and while   1. _____
banks may agree to provide short-term finance, they are
generally unwilling to provide money in a permanent basis for   2. _____
long-term prospect. So companies turn to the public, invited   3. _____
people to lend them money, or take a share in the business in
exchange for a share in future profits. This they do by issuing   4. _____
stocks and shares in the business through the Stock Exchange.
By doing so, they can put into circulation the savings of
individuals and institutions, both in home and overseas. When   5. _____

the saver needs his money back, he does not have to go to the company with whom he originally placed it. Instead, he sells his shares through a stockbroker to some saver who is seeking to invest his money.

6. _____

Many of the services needed both by industry and by each of us is provided by the Government or by local authorities. Without hospitals, roads, electricity, telephones, railways this country could function. All these require continuous spending on new equipment and new development if they are to serve us properly, requiring more money than is raised through taxes lonely. The Government, local authorities, and nationalized industries therefore frequently need to borrow money to finance major capital spending, and they, too, come to the Stock Exchange.

7. _____

8. _____

9. _____

There is hardly a man or woman in the country whose job or whose standard of living does not depend on the ability of his or her employers to raise money to finance new development. In one way or another, this new money must come from the savings of the country. The Stock Exchange exists to provide a channel through which these savings can reach those who need finance.

10. _____

Section C　Short Answer Questions

Directions: *In this part there is a short passage with five questions or incomplete statements. Read the passage carefully. Then answer the questions or complete the statements in the fewest possible words.*

Much of the excitement among investigators in the field of intelligence derives from their trying to determine exactly what intelligence is. Different investigators have emphasized different aspects of intelligence in their definitions. For example, in a 1921 symposium(座谈会) on the definition of intelligence, the American psychologist Lewis M. Terman emphasized the ability to think abstractly, while another American psychologist. Edward L. Thorndike, emphasized learning and the ability to give good responses to questions. In a similar 1986 symposium, however, psychologists generally agreed on the importance of adaptation to the environment as the key to understanding both what intelligence is and what it does. Such adaptation may occur in a variety of environmental situations. For example, a student in school learns the material that is required to pass or do well in a course; a physician treating a patient with an unfamiliar disease adapts by learning about the diseases; an artist reworks a painting in order to make it convey a more harmonious impression. For the most part, adapting involves making a change in oneself in order to cope more effectively, but sometimes effective adaptation involves either changing the environment or finding a new environment altogether.

Effective adaptation draws upon a number of cognitive processes, such as perception. learning, memory, reasoning, and problem solving, The main trend in defining intelligence, then, is that it is not itself a cognitive or mental process, but rather a selective combination of these processes purposively directed toward effective adaptation to the environment. For examples, the physician noted above learning about a new disease adapts by perceiving material on the disease in medical literature, learning what the material contains, remembering crucial aspects of it that are needed to treat the patient, and then reasoning to solve the problem of how to apply the information to the needs of the patient. Intelligence in sum has come to be regarded as not a single ability, but an effective drawing together of many abilities. This has not always been obvious to investigators of the subject, however, and, indeed, much of the history of the field revolves around arguments regarding the nature and abilities that constitute intelligence.

Questions:

1. What does the passage mainly discuss?

   _____ _____ _____ _____ _____

   _____ _____ _____ _____ _____

2. Which aspect of intelligence has been emphasized most recently?

   _____ _____ _____ _____ _____

   _____ _____ _____ _____ _____

3. According to the passage, effective adaptation _____ .

   _____ _____ _____ _____ _____

   _____ _____ _____ _____ _____

4. What processes does cognition consist of?

   _____ _____ _____ _____ _____

5. What does the second paragraph imply?

_____ _____ _____ _____ _____

_____ _____ _____ _____ _____

_____ _____ _____ _____ _____

Test Ten

I Reading Comprehension

Section A   Passage Reading

Directions: *There are 2 passages in this section. Each passage is followed by some questions or unfinished statements. For each of them there are four choices marked A, B, C and D. You should decide on the best choice and mark the corresponding letter on Answer Sheet with a single line through the center.*

Passage One

Questions 1 to 5 are based on the following passage.

Beauty has always been regarded as something praiseworthy. Almost everyone thinks attractive people are happier and healthier, have better marriages and have more respectable occupations. Personal consultants give them better advice for finding jobs. Even judges are softer on attractive defendants. But in the executive circle, beauty can become a liability.

While attractiveness is a positive factor for a man on his way up the executive ladder, it is harmful to woman.

Handsome male executives were perceived as having more integrity than plainer men; effort and ability were thought to account for their success.

Attractive female executives were considered to have less integrity than unattractive ones; their success was attributed not to ability but lo factors such as luck.

All unattractive women executives were thought to have more integrity and to be more capable than the attractive female executives. Interestingly, though, the rise of the unattractive overnight successes was attributed more to personal relationships and less to ability than was that of attractive overnight successes.

Why are attractive women not thought to be able? An attractive woman is perceived to be more feminine and an attractive man more masculine(男性的) than the less attractive ones. Thus, an attractive woman bas an advantage in traditionally female jobs, but an attractive woman in a traditionally masculine position appears to lack the "masculine" qualities required.

This is true even in politics. "When the only clue is how he or she looks, people treat men and women differently." says Anne Bowman, who recently published a study on the effects of attractiveness on political candidates. She asked 125 undergraduate students to rank two groups of photographs, one of men and one of women, in order of attractiveness. The students were told the photographs were of candidates for political offices. They were asked to rank them again, in the order they would vote for them.

The results showed that attractive males utterly defeated unattractive men, but the women who had been ranked most attractive invariably received the fewest votes.

1. The word "liability"(Last sentence, Para. 1) most probably means _____.
   A. misfortune　　　　　　　　B. instability
   C. disadvantage　　　　　　　 D. burden

2. In traditionally female jobs, attractiveness _____.
   A. reinforces the feminine qualities required
   B. makes women look more honest and capable
   C. is of primary importance to women
   D. often enables women to succeed quickly

3. Bowman's experiment reveals that when it comes to politics, attractiveness _____.
   A. turns out to be an obstacle to men
   B. affects men and women alike
   C. has as little effect on men as on women
   D. is more of an obstacle than a benefit to women

4. It can be inferred from the passage that people's views on beauty are often _____.
   A. practical　　　　　　　　　B. prejudiced
   C. old fashioned　　　　　　　 D. radical

5. The author writes this passage to _____.
   A. discuss the negative aspects of being attractive

B. give advice to job-seekers who are attractive

C. demand equal rights for women

D. emphasize the importance of appearance

Passage Two

Questions 6 to 10 are based on the following passage.

A new era is upon us. Call it what you will: the service economy, the information age, the knowledge society. It all translates to a fundamental change in the way we work. Already we're partly there. The percentage of people who earn their living by making things has fallen dramatically in the Western World. Today the majority of jobs in America, Europe and Japan (two thirds or more in many of these countries) are in the service industry, and the number is on the rise. More women are in the work force than ever before. There are more part time jobs. More people are self-employed. But the breadth of the economic transformation can't be measured by numbers alone, because it also is giving rise to a radical new way of thinking about the nature of work itself. Long-held notions about jobs and careers, the skills needed to succeed, even the relation between individuals and employers—all these are being challenged.

We have only to look behind us to get some sense of what may lie ahead. No one looking ahead 20 years possibly could have foreseen the ways in which a single invention, the chip, would transform our world thanks to its applications in personal computers, digital communications and factory robots. Tomorrow's achievements in biotechnology, artificial intelligence or even some still unimagined technology could produce a similar wave of dramatic changes. But one thing is certain: information and knowledge will become even more vital, and the people who possess it, whether they work in manufacturing or services, will have the advantage and produce the wealth. Computer knowledge will become as basic a requirement as the ability to read and write. The ability to solve problems by applying information instead of performing routine tasks will be valued above all else. If you cast your mind ahead 10 years, information services will be predominant. It will be the way you do your job.

6. A characteristic of the information age is that _____.

   A. the service industry is relying more and more on the female work force

   B. manufacturing industries are steadily increasing

C. people find it harder and harder to earn a living by working in factories

D. most of the job opportunities can now be found in the service industry

7. One of the great changes brought about by the knowledge society is that
_____.

A. the difference between the employee and the employer has become insignificant

B. people's traditional concepts about work no longer hold true

C. most people have to take part-time jobs

D. people have to change their jobs from time to time

8. By referring to computers and other inventions, the author means to say that_____.

A. people should be able to respond quickly to the advancement of technology

B. future achievements in technology will bring about inconceivable dramatic changes

C. the importance of high technology has been overlooked

D. computer science will play a leading role in the future information services

9. The future will probably belong to those who _____.

A. possess and know how to make use of information

B. give full play to their brain potential

C. involve themselves in service industries

D. cast their minds ahead instead of looking back

10. Which of the following would be the best title for the passage?

A. Computers and the Knowledge Society.

B. Service Industries in Modern Society.

C. Features and Implications of the New Era.

D. Rapid Advancement of Information Technology.

Section B   Banked Cloze

Directions: *In this section, there is a passage with ten blanks. You are required to select one word for each blank from a list of choices given in a word bank following the passage. Read the passage through carefully before making your choices. Each choice in the bank is identified by a letter. Please mark the* *corresponding letter for each item on Answer Sheet with a single line through the center. You may not use any of the words in the bank more than once.*

Long bus rides are like television shows. They have a beginning, a middle, and an end—with commercials thrown in every three or four minutes. The __1__ are unavoidable. They happen whether you want them or not. Every couple of minutes a billboard glides by outside the bus window. Only if you sleep, which is equal to turning the __2__ set off, are you spared the unending cry of "You Need It! Buy It Now!"

The beginning of the ride is __3__ and somewhat exciting, even if you've traveled that way before. Usually some things have changed—new houses, new buildings, sometimes even a __4__ road. The bus drivers have a style of driving and it's to try to figure out the first hour or so. If the __5__ is particularly reckless or daring, the ride can be as thrilling as a suspense story. Will the driver pass the truck in time? Will the driver move into the right or the left-hand __6__? After a while, of course, the excitement dies down. Sleeping for a while helps __7__ the middle hours of the ride. Food always makes bus rides more interesting. But you've got to be careful of what kind of food you eat. Too much salty __8__ can make you very thirsty between stops.

The end of the ride is somewhat like the __9__. You know it will soon be over and there's a kind of expectation and excitement in that. The seat, of course, has become harder as the hours have passed. By now you've sat with your legs crossed, with your hands in your laps, with your hands on the arm rests—even with your __10__ crossed behind your head. The end comes just at the right time. There are just no more ways to sit.

A. lane	E. passed	I. expectation	M. crossed
B. television	F. hands	J. food	N. thrilling
C. comfortable	G. driver	K. beginning	O. suspense
D. new	H. pass	L. commercials	

Section C   Reading Comprehension (Skimming and Scanning)

Directions: *In this part, you will go over the passages quickly and answer the questions.*

For questions 1-7, mark

Y (for YES)   *if the statement agrees with the information given* in the passage;

N (for NO)   if the statement contradicts the information given in
                                 the passage;

NG (for NOT GIVEN)   if the information is not given in the passage.

For questions 8-10, complete the sentences with the information given in the
passage.

Wave energy research in Britain is under threat again following a report
which argues that public funding for large offshore projects should be restricted
to a token sum. The report, by the government's Renewable Energy Advisory
Group, calls instead for more government investment to develop ways of
generating electricity from hydroelectric plants, wind, waste and crops:
technologies which have existing markets.

The decision is complicated by the publication of a review of wave energy by
the government's Energy Technology Support Unit, which shows that the cost
of electricity generated from wave devices has fallen considerably in recent years,
and that new designs could make even greater savings.

The wave energy review was not completed in time for the renewable group
to consider it. Nevertheless, the group gives offshore wave machines the thumbs
down on economic grounds, and suggests that they should be given "no further
significant research and development expenditure".

Stephen Salter, professor of engineering design at the University of
Edinburgh and a pioneer of wave power, described the group's conclusions as
"nonsense". Improvements made over the past decade have brought down the
theoretical costs of producing electricity from his departments device, the
Edinburgh Duck, to about 16p per kilowatt-hour. A radical redesign to
overcome technical problems highlighted by ETSU has further reduced the cost.

Salter is reticent（有保留的）about the scale of these reductions, but
ETSU's own computer models are believed to put the cost at around 4p/kWh,
similar to the cost of energy from coal and gas.

ETSU's estimates are based on the assumption that all technical problems
with a wave device are solved. It stresses that wave energy technology is
"relatively immature", and that a great deal of R&D will be needed before a
practical offshore machine is built. The best prospects, it says, may lie with
radical redesigns of older ideas, such as Salter's Duck, or one of several new

designs which promise electricity "at substantially lower costs".

The renewable group makes no recommendations about the most developed wave energy devices—those sited on the coastline. One such machine has been built on the island of Islay by researchers from Queen's University of Belfast. ETSU estimates that it could produce electricity at 6p/kWh.

Trevar Whittacker, who manages the wave energy program at Queen's, believes that the market for shoreline machines must be developed now. Offshore devices will not be needed for 20 years, he says, but "if you're going to go for serious energy production you've got to go offshore". He warns that if the basic research is not done now, "you're going to grind to a halt in 10 to 15 years".

A theme running through the group's report is the need to bolster(支持) the industries that have grown up over the past two years for generating electricity from, for example, wind and biomass. These markets have grown chiefly because regional electricity companies have been forced to buy electricity from Nuclear Electric and renewable energy producers at an inflated price under the non-fossil fuel obligation.

The NFFO was conceived as a means to keep Nuclear Electric "cash rich", but is proving to be "a useful mechanism" for creating markets in new technologies, says the report. Twidell says that by accident the government has found an ingenious way offering the pace of technology. Companies receive a return on their wind turbines, or chicken litter furnaces only when they begin producing electricity. "Once the companies are generating, they want to make the plant more efficient, so the research is very applied and market-oriented", he says.

According to Martin Holdgate, director of the World Conservation Union, and chairman of the renewables group, "the hope is that as the technology becomes proven, it will become an increasingly attractive investment".

The group argues that by 2025, renewables should contribute about 60 terawatt-hours of electricity a year, which is equivalent to one-fifth of present annual production. To reach this goal, it says "the government must intervene in the market".

Holdgate argues that Britain's commitment to the Climate Change Convention, signed at the Earth Summit last June, is reason enough for the government to give extra support to technologies that produce no polluting gases. Renewables are also at a disadvantage because the full environmental damage of fossil fuels is not taken into account in their costs.

Despite its optimistic view, the group calls on the government to increase the amount of renewable energy bought under the NFFO to around 1 500 megawatts over the next seven years. This would still leave renewables with only 0.1 per cent of Britain's electricity supply. Environmentalists say this is a pitiable increase.

1. Wind energy is more cost-effective than tidal power.
2. The Edinburgh Duck is not as viable (可行的) as the machine built by researchers from Queen's University.
3. Producing electricity at the cost of 4p/kWh is the aim of scientists studying wave power.
4. The Renewable Energy Advisory Group feels that the government should give more support to efforts to use renewable energy.
5. Renewable energy includes nuclear energy and energy from wave, biomass and wind.
6. Currently, electricity from renewable resources accounts for 0.1% of the total electricity generated in Britain.
7. Scientists from the University of Strathclyde have been working on a pilot project for a number of years.
8. The NFFO means to generate electricity using _____.
9. Chicken litter is used to _____.
10. In order to increase the provision of electricity out of renewable materials in the future the government must _____.

II Comprehensive Test

Section A Cloze

Directions: *There are 20 blanks in the following passage. For each blank there are four choices marked A, B, C and D. You should choose the ONE that best fits into the passage. Then mark the corresponding letter on Answer Sheet with a single line through the center.*

Having passed what I considered the worst obstacle, our spirits rose. We __1__ towards the left of the cliff, where the going was better, __2__ rather steeper. Here we found little snow, __3__ most of it seemed to have been __4__ off the mountain. There was no __5__ of the mountain in the distance because the clouds were forming all round us.

About 1 o'clock a storm __6__ suddenly. We ought to have __7__ its approach but we were concentrating on cutting steps, and __8__ we had time to do anything, we were blinded by snow. We could not move up or down and had to wait __9__ , getting colder and colder.

__10__ my hood（兜帽）, my nose and cheeks were frostbitten and I dared not take a hand out of my glove to warm them.

After two hours of this, I realized we would have to do __11__ to avoid being frozen to death where we stood. From time to time through the mist I had __12__ the outline of a dark buttress（扶壁）just above us, to descend in the wind was __13__ question; our only hope was to scramble（攀爬）up to this buttress, and dig out a platform at the foot of it on which we could __14__ our tent.

We climbed to this place and started to __15__ the ice. At first my companion seemed to regard the __16__ as hopeless but gradually the wind __17__ and he cheered up. __18__ we had made a platform big enough to put up the tent, and we did this as __19__ we could. We __20__ into our sleeping bags and fell asleep, feeling that we were lucky to be still alive.

1. A. set   B. got   C. made   D. took
2. A. even   B. though   C. so   D. if
3. A. when   B. where   C. as   D. so that
4. A. fallen   B. flown   C. split   D. blown
5. A. view   B. vision   C. look   D. glimpse
6. A. came up   B. came out   C. came over   D. came on
7. A. viewed   B. noticed   C. notified   D. glanced
8. A. after   B. before   C. unless   D. until
9. A. motionlessly B. constantly C. steadily   D. continually
10. A. In spite of B. In relation to C. In case of D. In the event of
11. A. anything B. nothing   C. something   D. everything
12. A. laid out B. made out   C. drawn out   D. marked out
13. A. without   B. in   C. beyond   D. out of the
14. A. wrench   B. wedge   C. pad   D. pinch

15. A. cut down　　B. cut away　　C. cut out　　D. cut off

16. A. position　　B. situation　　C. occupation　　D. orientation

17. A. died out　　B. died off　　C. died back　　D. died down

18. A. Instead　　B. Furthermore　　C. Indeed　　D. At last

19. A. well　　B. good　　C. best　　D. better

20. A. climbed　　B. crashed　　C. crept　　D. crawled

Section B　Error Correction

Directions: *This part consists a short passage. In this passage, there are possibabl y 10 or less than 10 mistakes, one in each numbered line. You may have to change a word, add a word or delete a word. If you change a word, cross it out and write the correct word in the corresponding blank. If you add a word, put an insertion mark (　) in the correct word in the corresponding blank. If you delete a word, cross it out and be sure to put a slash (/) in the blank.*

A survey is a study, generally in the form of an interview
or a questionnaire that provides information concerning how
people think and act. In the United States, the best-known
surveys are the Gallup poll and the Harris poll. As anyone who
watches the news during campaigns residents know these polls
have become an important part of political life in the United
States.

North Americans are familiar with the many "persons on
the street" interviews on local television news shows. While
such interviews can be highly entertained, they are not　1. _____
necessary an accurate indication of public opinion. First, they　2. _____
reflect the opinions of only those people who appear at a certain
location. Thus, such samples can be biased in favor of　3. _____
commuters, middle-class shoppers, or factory workers,
depending on whose area the news-people select. Second,　4. _____
television interviews tend to attract ingoing people who are　5. _____
willing to appear on the air, while they frighten away others　6. _____
who may feel intimidated(害怕的) by a camera. A survey must
be based on a precise, representative samples if it is to genuinely　7. _____
(真实地) reflect a broad range of the population.

In preparing to conduct a survey, sociologists must exercises great care in the wording of questions. An effective survey question must be simple and clear enough for people to understand it. It must also be specific enough so that there is no problems in interpreting the results. Even questions that are less structured must be carefully phrased in order to elicit (引出，探出) the type of information desiring. Surveys can be indispensable sources of information, but only if the sampling is done properly and the questions are worded accurately.

8. _____

9. _____

10. _____

Section C   Short Answer Questions

Directions: *In this part there is a short passage with five questions or incomplete statements. Read the passage carefully. Then answer the questions or complete the statements in the fewest possible words.*

For centuries men dreamed of achieving vertical flight. In 400 A. D. Chinese children played with a fan-like toy that spun upwards and fell back to earth as rotation ceased. Leonardo da Vinci conceived the first mechanical apparatus, called a "Helix", which could carry man straight up, but was only a design and was never tested.

The ancient-dream was finally realized in 1940 when a Russian engineer piloted a strange looking craft of steel tubing with a rotating fan on top. It rose awkwardly and vertically into the air from a standing start, hovered a feet above the ground, went sideways and backwards, and then settles back to earth. The vehicle was called a helicopter.

Imaginations were fired. Men dreamed of going to work in their own personal helicopters. People anticipate that vertical flight transports would carry million of passengers as do the airliners of today. Such fantastic expectations were not fulfilled.

The helicopter has now become an extremely useful machine. It excels in military missions, carrying troops, guns and strategic instruments where other aircraft cannot go. Corporations use them as airborne offices, many metropolitan areas use them in police work, construction and logging companies employ them in various advantageous ways, engineers use them for site selection and surveying, and oil companies use them as the best way to make offshore and remote work stations accessible to crews and supplies. Any urgent mission to a hard-to-get-to place is likely task for a helicopter. Among their other multitude of uses: deliver across town fly to and from airports, assist in rescue work, and aid in the search for missing or wanted persons.

1. People expect that helicopters would someday be able to _____.

_____ _____ _____ _____ _____

_____ _____ _____ _____ _____

2. Helicopters work with the aid of _____.

_____ _____ _____ _____ _____

_____ _____ _____ _____ _____

3. What was said about the expectation of people for the helicopter?

_____ _____ _____ _____ _____

_____ _____ _____ _____ _____

4. How has the use of the developed helicopters?

_____ _____ _____ _____ _____

_____ _____ _____ _____ _____

5. Under what conditions are helicopters found to be absolutely essential?

_____ _____ _____ _____ _____

_____ _____ _____ _____ _____

第四部分　参考答案与解析

第一部分

Exercise 1

1. D。这是一道难度较大的篇章主旨题。选项 A 和 D 的内容很相似,文章的很多地方讲的都是 computer criminals escape punishment,但这仅是表层意思,是为了说明主题的一种表面现象。正是因为他们容易逃脱惩罚,所以文章在最后一句"And so another computer criminal departs with just the recommendations he needs to continue his crimes elsewhere."中说他们可以到一个新地方继续从事犯罪活动,其结果自然是计算机犯罪消除不了。因此,本题的正确选项应为 D。

2. D。本文的主旨体现在各个段落的大意中。第一段第一句"Any talk of the energy needs of the United States should include a discussion of the Tennessee Valley Authority, a successful but sometimes quiet federal agency."充分说明了 TVA 在美国能源问题方面的重要地位,而第一段接下来的三句话则介绍了最初修建 TVA 的初衷;文章的第二段具体讲述的是在几十年的发展过程中 TVA 都进行了哪些建设和针对出现的一些问题采用了什么样的对策;文章的最后一句话"The TVA will then be once again producing a cheaper source of energy and helping solve the nation's problems, several at a time."表明,TVA 将会再一次制造出更加便宜的能源,从而在很多方面帮助解决美国的能源问题—这与选项 D 中所说的 the TVA has always been a pioneer in the energy field 的意思相吻合,因此选项 D 应为正确答案。

3. C。根据第一段第一句即其主题句"Basic to any understanding of Canada in 20 years after the Second World War is the country's impressive population growth."可知,第一段主要谈论的将是加拿大在二战后二十年来的人口增长问题。在通常情况下,一篇阅读材料的第一段的主题句同时也是全文的主题句。所以考生通过略读(skimming)其余三个段落,可以得知第二、三、四段分别具体谈论了二战后加拿大人口增长的特点与趋势，因此选项 C 符合题意。选项 B 的意思过于笼统，不能准确地概括全文的大意；选项 A 仅在第二段提到一句"Young people were staying at school longer，"并未展开论述，因此可以排除；选项 D 在文章中也只是在第二段提到一句"rising living standards were cutting down the size of families，"也未展开论述，因此也不应视作正确答案。

4. C。根据第一段第一句即其主题句"Orchids are unique in having the most highly developed of all blossoms，"可知，本文主要谈论的对象是 orchids。即使考生不认识这个生词，根据后面的 blossoms（花朵），也可以推断出 orchids 是一种花的名称，即正确答案应为选项 C。此外考生还可通过略读（skimming）全文，总结出每段的大意（第一段，描述 orchids 的特殊之处——其复杂的花朵内部的构造；第二段，描述为了吸引昆虫帮助其完成授粉作用，orchids 采取的种种办法；第三段，描述 orchids 如何进一步采取措施以防止昆虫在尚未完成授粉作用时离开它的花朵。然后综合三个段落的大意）得出结论（全文都是围绕 orchids 这种花朵展开的描述）。

5. A。纵览全文，文章的第二、三、四段都是围绕着第一段的第一句（主旨句）（American women experience a great variety of lifestyle. ）进行拓展说明的，即美国妇女在不同时期所采取的不同生活方式；选项 B、C 和 D 均为该主题句的具体拓展内容。只有选项 A 的意思才与第一段的主题句，也是全文主旨句的意思相吻合，因此，应为正确答案。

6. A。本文的主旨也是开篇的第一句话，合作是防止神经性疾病蔓延的惟一安全措施（Cooperation is the only safeguard we have against the development of neurotic tendencies），以说明合作的重要性。文章的第二、三段分别论述的是缺乏合作精神会导致的严重后果及我们对待生活所应持有的态度。作者在文章的最后指出，合作对人类进步的重要性。由此可见，A 项的意思可以涵盖文章的这一大意。因此应为是正确答案。选项 B、C 和 D 只是作者为说明合作的重要性而进行拓展说明的几个方面或某个例子，不具有概括力。

7. C。文章在开首段先谈到了着装在生意场合的重要性，然后分两段介绍了在生意场合中着装所应遵循的原则，所以文章的中心内容是怎样才能做到着装得体。选项 C 所总结的内容与其吻合，应为正确答案。

8. B。本文在开首段通过讲述因游客对科罗拉多大峡谷形成的原因和过程可能产生的误解，引出其真正的原因：漫长有序的侵蚀的过程。接着作者便在下面几段中对这一过程进行了具体的阐述。可见,本文讨论的主题是促使科罗拉多大峡谷形成的力量,因此与选项 B 所描述的内容相一致。

9. C。文章在句首点题:Most people... the level of the day dream. 大部分人都承认广告中的功能只能在想象中实现。因此,选项 C 符合题意,应为正确答案。

10. B。本文在第一段首句中谈到哈得逊流派这个术语时说它是19世纪北美最具代表性风景画流派,接着指出哈得逊流派出现是由于新老艺术家斗争的结果。随后在第二段中又讲述了这个名字的由来。因此综合这两段的信息可知,本文的主旨是描述哈得逊流派的出现以及名字的由来。这些与选项 B 所陈述的细节相吻合,应为正确答案。

Exercise 2

1. C。根据第一段第一句即其主题句"In a time of low academic achievement by children in the United States, many Americans are turning to Japan, a country of high academic achievement and economic success, for possible answers."可知,由于孩子们在学业方面几乎没有什么作为,许多美国家长正在转向日本————一个在学术和经济方面高度发达的国家,寻求帮助。而接下来的 However, the answers provided by Japanese preschools are not the ones Americans expected to find. 说明美国家长发现日本的学前教育并非其想象的那么强调学业成绩。也就是说,现实与美国家长所想象的不符。选项 C 准确地描述了美国家长对于日本学龄前教育的错误认识,与段落原意相吻合。因此,正确答案应为 C。选项 A 就美国和日本家长在孩子的学习中的参与程度进行了比较,这一点在文章中根本没有提到。选项 B 把日本的经济发展成功归功于其科学成就,这一点文中也没提到。选项 D 说日本的教育比其他国家的教育水平都高,语气过于绝对,并且文章并未提及,不足为答案。

2. A。该段通过比较调查结果说明日本人对于团队经历教育看得比美国人更重。这一点是可通过对此调查结果的比例得以印证:日本人与美国人对于这种教育的认可度的比例是91%:64%。该段落虽然提到了美国人更强调个性发展(more individually oriented),但是,这只是用来说明普通美国人对教育的一种观念,而不是对此项调研的结果。因此,选项 B 和 C 均不符合段意。选项 D 的语气太绝对,且本段落中只把这句话当作说明现今美国人对教育态度的反衬,而非段落的主旨。所以不可为正确答案。

3. B。根据第二段第一句即其主题句"There are three main types of galaxy：spiral，elliptical，and irregular."可知，本段落将主要谈论星系的三种主要类型：螺旋形、椭圆形和不规则形。而接下来的 The Milky Way is a spiral galaxy，a flattish disc of stars with two spiral arms emerging from its central nucleus. 提到银河系(The Milky Way)是为了将其作为螺旋形星系的一个具体例子而出现的，并非本段落探讨的主要对象，因此可以排除选项 A。事实上，第二段除主题句外，其余的句子都是推展句。虽说选项 C 和 D 的内容在文章中都提过，但都不够全面，不能概括整个段落的大意。因此，只有选项 B 符合题意，应为正确答案。

4. C。文章第二段的大意是"家长对孩子要求的严格程度差异很大，有些家长在钱上对孩子管束十分的严格，有些家长则严格地要求孩子晚上何时回家或是要求他按时吃饭。总而言之，家长对孩子的管束不仅是为了孩子的幸福，也表明父母的需要和社会的价值观"。段落的前三句显然是以实例来说明不同家长对教育孩子所持的不同态度，藉此为最后的结论句作铺垫。选项 A 涵盖面太宽。此外，本段落只陈述事实，而没说家长是否应该对孩子严格要求；选项 B 和 D 的意思太偏，不能作为答案。只有选项 C 与段落大意相吻合，因此应为正确答案。

5. B。作者在第一段第二句中提到，许多论述采访的书籍把重点放在新闻报道的方法方面，而不是放在采访本身、采访环境及其内涵的概念方面(Most of these books，as well as several chapters，mainly in，but not limited to，journalism and broadcasting handbooks and reporting texts，stress the "how to" aspects of journalistic interviewing rather than the conceptual aspects of the interview，its context，and implications.)，作者在本段最后两句中指出"新闻领域和其他领域一样，许多知识可以从系统研究该职业的实际工作中学到。这样的研究能汇集可靠的信息，由此可以制定出总的原则"。由此可以推导出作者对此问题的基本观点"应该重视新闻采访的系统研究"。因此，选项 B 应是正确答案，而其他选项意思均不符合题意。

6. C。实际上，第二段的第一句为段落的主题句，大致意思是新闻与广播方面的研究文献越来越多。然而人们却很少问津对采访本身的研究。可见作者对当前新闻界的研究状况不甚满意。此后的句子为段落的推展句，主要是进一步说明令人不满的具体现状，以支持该段落的主题句。选项 C 的意思与主题句的意思相吻合，因此，应为正确答案。其他选项的意思要么太偏,要么太广,与原文不符,所以不可为答案。

7. A。该段落首先提到,教育的重要性与教师的待遇之间的矛盾,指出为解决这个问题,州长提出了免征教师个人所得税;然后又评说,州长的提案是一个 bad public policy 从而道出了作者自己的观点。所以,选项 A"免征教师个人所得税考虑不周"符合段落大意,应为正确答案。其他选项内容均与段意不符,不可为该题的正确答案。

8. C。文章第一句是该段落的主题句。潘多拉是主神宙斯命火神用粘土制成的人类第一个生命。据希腊神话,宙斯命潘多拉带着一个盒子下凡,但却不许打开那只盒子。潘多拉没有按照神的旨意去做,私自打开盒子,于是里面的疾病、罪恶、疯狂等各种祸害全跑出来散布到世界上。这里打开潘多拉的盒子暗含为教师免除税收确实是为教师免除了一些经济负担,但却会因此引发许多麻烦的意思。因此,选项 C 符合段意,应为正确答案。

Exercise 3

1. C。文章的第一段就提出了全文要探讨的问题:摩天大楼对环境的负面影响。第二段的主题句 Skyscrapers are also lavish consumers, and wasters, of electric power. 指出,摩天大楼还是电力的巨大消费者与浪费者;第三段具体陈述 Glass-walled skyscrapers 与 mirror-walled skyscrapers 对能源的浪费与对周边环境的影响;第四段第一句 Skyscrapers put a severe strain on a city's sanitation (卫生,卫生设施) facilities, too. 说的是摩天大楼对城市卫生设施造成严重压力;第五段第一句 Skyscrapers also interfere with television reception, block bird flyways, and obstruct air traffic. 指出摩天大楼阻碍了电视信号的接收、鸟类的飞行线路,而且阻断了空气的流通。最后一段话题一转,讲到尽管摩天大楼有以上这么多缺点与弊端,但是由于种种原因,人们仍在继续建造摩天大楼。综合各段内容,可以看出全文作者的思路:提出问题,总述(第一段)——具体阐述问题(第二到第五段);第六段相对独立,并由此可以判定,选项 C 最为符合题意。

2. D。文章第一段第一句中指出长期保体重的积极因素为数不多,体育锻炼是其中之一。"这句话是该段落主题句,也是全文的主题句。接下来第二句语气一转,指出了问题的症结所在:美国老百姓对于体育锻炼的重要性还不甚了解,他们宁可改喝"淡"啤酒、吃低卡面包而不会增加运动量(Unfortunately, that message has not gotten through to the average American, who would rather try switching to "light" beer and low-

calorie bread than increase physical exertion.)。第二段讲述了体育锻炼的艰苦性；第三段讲述的是体育锻炼的重要性；最后一段讲述的是坚持体育锻炼的效果与好处。综合各段大意，全文遵循了传统的"提出问题—解决问题"的写作模式。以此为据可以推出作者的写作目的是想告诉读者体育锻炼是一种减肥的有效方式，即选项 D 所表述的意思。而选项 A 和 C 过于细节化，不能概括全文的内容；选项 B 的内容文章中并未提及。

3. D。文章第一段并没有明确的主题句，而是具体地介绍了 Joyce Carol Oates 的文学生涯；第二段则通过将 Joyce Carol Oates 与 John Barth, Donald Barthelme, and Thomas Pynchon 进行对比，着重介绍了 Joyce Carol Oates 的写作特点。在第二段的最后一句话中"Whatever the source and however shocking the events or the motivations, however, her fictive world remains strikingly akin to that real one reflected in the daily newspapers, the television news and talk shows, and the popular magazines of our day. "作者又总结了 Joyce Carol Oates 贴近现实生活的写作特点。由此可知，本文作者的写作目的是在向读者介绍 Joyce Carol Oates，作为一位作家的文学生涯与写作特点，这与选项 D 的意思最为贴近。而选项 C 的内容文中根本没有提及；选项 A 中的 By The North Gate 仅仅在文章第一行中提及，并未展开介绍，因此不足为答案；选项 B 过于宽泛，作者在第二段中拿 Joyce Carol Oates 与 John Barth, Donald Barthelme, and Thomas Pynchon 进行对比，其目的还是为了突出 Joyce Carol Oates 的写作特点，而非为了对比某些现代作家。

4. A。本文先是论述文化冲击(culture shock)的种种现象及影响，然后话锋一转，转向了 future shock，并将两者进行比较，指出前者是较温和的社会疾病，旨在说明后者更应受到重视，尤其在结尾处更是点明了作者的忧虑"This is the prospect that man now faces. Change is avalanching upon our heads and most people are absurdly unprepared to cope with it. ""这就是人类所面临的未来。我们身边正发生着巨大的变化。而大多数人们对此并无任何应付它们的准备。"由此可以推断出本文作者的写作目的：警示今天的读者防止未来可能发生的危险。因此，选项 A 符合题意，应为正确答案。

5. D。本考题为段落概括题。在第一段第二句中，作者提到 Power 这个词很容易使人们产生误解。然后作者通过说明不应该理解成什么，而应该怎样理解等情况，澄清了对 Power 的误解。因此，给 Power 下定义是作者有意为避免人们产生此种误会而为的。

6. B。通读全文可知,作者主要论述的是美国"一个教室的学校"正面临逐渐被关闭的现状,同时指出这种学校所拥有的自己独特的优点。由此可见选项 B 应为正确答案。选项 C 与原文意思相悖。选项 D 所涉及的内容虽在文中提到过,但是总结美国教育历史却不是本文作者的真实写作目的。因此,不可为正确答案。

7. A。文章首先在首段点了题,描述了三种基本经济体制,接下来各用一段分别地进行了具体的介绍。因此,选项 A 符合题意,应为正确答案。

8. B。文章在第一段中讲述的是荷尔蒙在人成长的不同阶段所起的作用;第二段讲述的是激素的分泌机制;第三段讲述的是内、外分泌的区别。选项 A、C、和 D 分别概括文中所提到的关于荷尔蒙的一个方面,不足于说明作者的写作目的。只有选项 B 才与问题相吻合,因此应为正确答案。

9. A。文章第一段是全文的中心句,主要讲述的是慢跑的积极作用与方法。随后几段又从各方面阐述了慢跑所存在的问题。文章在第四段所谈到慢跑时的着装问题,只是为主题服务的一个细节,不是文章的写作目的。此外,文中所提到的慢跑好处的科学证据,也只是文章的一个细节信息,不具有概括性。只有选项 A 才最符合题意,应为正确答案。

10. C。文章首句就是本文的中心思想,第一段最后一句与句首遥相呼应从而构成了一篇完整的文章,凸显了写作目的"A study of art history might be a good way to learn more about a culture than is possible to learn in general history classes. ""In short, art expresses the essential qualities of a time and a place, and a study of it clearly offers us a deeper understanding than can be found in most history books. "这点可见与选项 C 的意思相吻合,而其他段落均为这一写作目的服务。

Exercise 4

1. A。文章的第一段主要讲述的是太空中存在的大量碎片对空中飞行物所产生的威胁性。作者在第二段中又谈到太空卫星泛滥成灾致使人们不得不采取措施加以控制等。可见,该文章谈论的中心议题始终是太空垃圾问题。因此,选项 A 符合题意,应为正确答案。而选项 B,C 和 D 中所提到的内容虽然在文章中都曾提到,但由于太偏不足于涵盖短文的全部内容,所以不能为正确答案。

2. C。通过阅读全文可知:该文主要讲述的是学龄前教育的发展历程。即始于公元前4世纪,17世纪得到长足发展,20世纪得到补充,现在蓬勃发展。由此可知选项 C 是本文的最佳标题。因此,应为正确答案。选项 B 的内容虽然在文中提到,但不是文章的中心议题。选项 D 涵盖面太偏,文章只在的最后一段中才提到美国的幼儿园,也不是文章的中心议题,不可视为正确答案。

3. B。本文第一段主要谈的是做广告的社会效益。第二、三段的中心意思是广告使物有所值,因而贡献巨大;最后两段论述的是广告的促销做法。总之这一切都在说明广告所能带来的许多益处。据此可见,选项 B 的意思与文章的大意吻合,应为正确答案。选项 A,C 和 D 的涵盖面太偏,不能视作正确答案。

4. A。作者在本文一开始就指出:"如果你要在谈话中利用幽默而使人发笑,你必须知道如何去确定具有相同感受的经历和困扰(If you intend using humor in your talk to make people smile, you must know how to identify shared experiences and problems.)",紧接着在第二段中举例加以说明作者的这一观点;第三段转向如何选择幽默的对象;第四段指出幽默故事应如何讲才能取得预想的结果。综上所述,可见选项 A 概括了本文的中心思想。因此,应为正确答案。

5. D。文章说,千百年来,人类在地球上生存栖息,据地球上的资源为己所用,并且对此加以评论:All this is good—up to a point. But it has gone too far. We ourselves have increased until the sheer numbers of people on Earth have upset the balance of nature,并由此道出了文章的主旨——大自然的生态平衡被打破了。选项 D 作为文章的标题与文章的内容大致吻合,因此应为正确答案。其他选项的意思太偏,不可为答案。

Exercise 5

1. D。选项 D 应为正确答案。本文主要介绍了亚裔学生在学业上所取得的成就以及他们取得成就的原因,同时作者也指出亚裔美国人对一些问题的担忧,如亚裔种族再度成为美国社会隔离、歧视的牺牲品。作者在陈述中自始至终没有使用明显表现个人态度、情感的词汇。由此可以断定作者在文中的语气是客观的,而非同情、怀疑或批评的。

2. A。综览全文,可见作者想通过引用一个接一个的遭遇,先是修理工不守时,好不容易盼来之后又一个接一个的抢用主人家的电话;最后终于要干活了又告诉主人他们修理不好,劝作者重新买新的使用法,在说明作者对这类事情的不满。遇见这样的事儿,没有人会不生气,更没有人会不在意,因此选项 C 显然不正确。另外,文章开头说"If I sounded all out of breath,it's because I had three repairmen here this afternoon."在这句话中,out of breath 本意是"气喘吁吁,上气不接下气",这里是一种比喻用法,意为"怒不可遏"。即表达了作者非常愤怒的心情。因此,选项 A 符合文章述说自己遭遇的语气,应为正确答案。选项 B 的意思是"讽刺",选项 D 意为"幽默",显然都与原文不符。

3. D。该题为语气题。作者对于家庭妇女为了全家人的安逸生活所做出的牺牲和默默奉献简明扼要地给予了充分的肯定,指出没有家庭妇女的这种自我牺牲和无私奉献的精神,全家人的生活就会一团糟糕。这一点从文中的每个段落都可找到证据。可见通篇文章都在充分地肯定家庭妇女的不平凡的境界。因此,选项 A 应为正确答案。critical 的意思是"批评的";indifferent 意为"漠不关心的";ironical 的意思是"讽刺的";appreciative 的意思是"表示感激的",符合行文语气。

4. B。文章在第一句中就指出,人的学习潜能是无限的(So far there have been discovered no limits to man's capacity to learn.),在第三段的第一句中又重复了这个论点(These findings have led educators to be much more modest and less hasty in their labeling and classifying procedures.),在最后一段的最后一句又说,人们只动用了自己全部能力的一小部分意思是说人们的能力潜力大得很(It seems that, in customary educational settings, one habitually uses only a tiny fraction of one's learning capacities.)。由此可以得出一个结论:作者的语气是乐观的。因此,选项 B 应为正确答案。

5. B。第一段提到,网络空间、数据高速公路、多媒体——在那些能够预测未来的人看来,计算机联网、电视、电话将改变我们的生活。但是,尽管人们在大谈未来技术上的理想王国,却很少有人关注这些穷国。像对待其他新技术一样,西方国家只关心"如何发展",而对于"为谁而发展"却置之不理。可见,这里作者认为技术的开发对富国的益处大于穷国。第四段中提到,发展中国家如何掌握自己的命运的问题,其中提到的一种方式是购买最先进的计算机和通讯设备,即所谓的"发展通信"现代化。对此,作者认为这样做会使发展中国家长期或永久依赖(发达国家)。由此,可以看出作者对于 communications revolution 所持有的态度显然是批评的。因此,选项 C 符合题意,应为正确答案。

Exercise 6

1. D。根据第一段第四句的解释(The decimum was the wife's right to receive a tenth of all her husband's property.)可知这里 decimum 指的是妻子有权利分享丈夫十分之一的财产。选项中只有选项 D 符合上述定义。因此,应为正确答案。

2. C。作者在第一段的最后两句中指出"And more than just a right: the documents show that she enjoyed a real power of decision, equal to that of her husband. In no case do the documents indicate any degree of difference in the legal status of husband and wife."选项 C 准确地表达了这一观点。因此,应为正确答案。

3. A。参阅第二段倒数第二句。

4. B。作者在该段中采用了反衬的写作手法,即以三位在美国现代历史、文学诗歌以及政治方面做出巨大贡献的女士为例,说明美国的女士在当时所处的地位是何等的低下,即便是做出这么大的贡献者也不能例外,不能在历史的史册中占一席地位。这一点在第一段第三句在中就明确地作了说明。此外,该段的最后两句话"But little or no notice was taken of these contributions. During these centuries, women remained invisible in history books."实际上就是对上述的客观事实所做出的结论。因此,选项 B 符合题意,应为正确答案。

5. C。该选项答案的参考依据是最后一句中的后半句"and they were uncritical in their selection and use of sources"。uncritical 的意思是"对……不予置评的",也就是说对资料来源不予考证,照单全收,因而不一定准确。因此,选项 C 符合题意,应为正确答案。选项 A 或 B 或 D.中所涉及的内容文中均未提及。

6. C。该选项的参考依据是第二句"Personal correspondence, newspaper clippings, and souvenirs were saved and stored."选项 C 中所说的来自母亲写给女儿的信函显然与句中的 Personal correspondence 相对应。因此,应为正确答案。其他选项如 A,虽然 Newspaper accounts 一词确在文中提过,但是选项中对该词的界定范围是"对总统选举结果",这点显然与原文不符,因此,不可视作正确答案。

7. C。该选项的参考依据为第三段最后一句"Such sources have provided valuable materials for later generations of historians."虽然文中并没有提到这篇文章的具体写作时间,无法准确地推断出选项 C 中所提到的时间是否正确,但是至少说选项C的意思与原句意思相吻合,而其他选项均与问题不沾边。因此,选项C应为正确答案。

8. A。本题答案的依据是第二段第一句(Numerous youth organizations give young people a chance to develop and broaden their interests, and to gain experience in working with others.)。选项B、C、D的内容分别是以下各段中所涉及的内容,同时也是student's interests and social abilities的一部分,相比较可见只有选项A所涵盖的内容相对比较全面,因此,应为正确答案。

9. B。本文第三段说的是学生到农场劳动的事,其中第一句就谈到了这种劳动的目的:learn to work together。用排除法进行筛选,选项A虽然与本段的最后一句youths compete for prizes in raising farm animals and growing crops意思接近,但细加推敲可以发现这种competition不是"唯一的",因此,不能视作正确答案;选项C显然不符合文章所说的事实;而选项D则是关于学生对农场劳动的看法,这在文中并未提及,所以也不能做正确答案。

10. C。本题是关于student government的活动,相关内容见文章第五段。根据段意可知学生同校方之间的态度是合作的。因此,选项A不符合此意;该段的最后一句说明,学生们除了组织校内活动,还组织一些社会活动并参与一些社区工程,如为了公共利益的集资活动等。因此,选项B和D均不符合题意,不可视作正确答案。

11. D。该试题问的是"When and where did Baptists possibly start as a branch of the Protestant church?"根据第一段第三句:自17世纪伊始浸礼教徒就已经在英格兰小规模存在,占那里总人口的1%。(From a beginning in 17th century England, the Baptists have continued on a small scale in England where they are about 1% of the population.)可知该教会成立的具体时间很可能早于17世纪,其发源地肯定不是美国,而唯一的可能追溯到的时间与地点应是在17世纪的英国。因此,选项D应为正确答案。

12. D。该细节题属于句子层面上的理解,根据文中第一段第四句:"some white Baptists... stand up courageously in difficult circumstances for their belief in the equality of all human beings before God, whatever their color"可知选项D的内容是对此句的高度概括,因此,符合句意,应为正确答案。

13. C。本题属于句群理解题。答案的依据是第一段最后三句:一方面,从"有些白人信奉宗教平等"句意可以推导出,有些白人仍存歧视观念;另一方面,黑人在寻找自己的活动空间方面受到的歧视现象说明这种歧视现象确实存在。因此,选项 C 符合题意,应为正确答案。

14. C。该细节题属于句子层次上的理解。由文章第三句"The majority of the Catholics are descendants of immigrants from Ireland, Italy and Poland" 可知多数天主教徒来自所提到的三个国家。因此,选项 C 应为正确答案。

15. B。本题答案的参考依据在第五、六句中。其中前者是观点,后者为例证。选项 A 为主体错误,选项 C 的范围过窄,选项 D 的语气表达强度不到位,不可视作正确答案。

16. A。本题是句子层次上的理解题,答案的依据在第八句"By 1960, however, John F Kennedy's presidential election victory put to rest the Catholic religion as an issue in national politics. 中。根据此句意可推知 John F Kennedy 把 Catholics 的宗教问题列入国家的问题中意味着美国的新一届政府对待这个问题很认真。这一点无疑对保证该宗教不受歧视有百利而无一害。因此,选项 A 符合句意,应为正确答案。

17. C。本题测试的是对 But Catholic institutions, especially in large cities, still serve large numbers of Catholics and a growing number of non-Catholics, who are attracted by the discipline and education offered in these schools 句子的理解,属于句子层次上逻辑角度变换型题。既然这些学校的学科与教育竟然吸引越来越多的 non-Catholics,说明该校办得非常成功。因此,选项 C 符合逻辑,应为正确答案。

18. D。作者在第二段第六句中说:a close analysis of the use of credit cards for heavy purchases will show that the buyer has added to the cost of making these purchases. 紧接着在第七、八、九句中对其作了具体说明,即用信用卡购物的付款中还应包括两笔费用:利息和处理信用卡的费用。选项 D 总结归纳了上述的句意,因此应为正确答案。

19. D。本文在第二段第五句中写道:Interest is the price of using money over a long period of time. 随后又在第七、八两句作了具体阐述:每月透支的钱和购物时所没有支付的现金都应付利息(It must also be kept in mind that unpaid monthly balances mean added interest charges. Furthermore, the use of credit cards will add to the cost of the product since the shopkeeper does not receive the money at the time of purchase.)由此可见利息是长时间使用钱所应付出的代价。因此,选项 D 符合句意,应为正确答案。

20. C。在第二段中作者提醒使用信用卡购物的消费者要知道用信用卡购物是要支付附加费用,所以应该谨慎购物。因此,选项 C 符合题意,应为正确答案。

21. C。本题属于篇章层次的信息理解,而答案依据的重点则在第一段的前三句,后面内容实际上只是例证而已。因此,选项 C 符合句意,应为正确答案。

22. B。本题属于句子理解。答案的依据在 Disney refused to put up signs asking his "guests" not to step on them 一句。Disney 既然不愿禁止"客人"踩踏草坪,visitors 当然可以自由践踏了。因此,选项 B 应为正确答案。其他选项意思太窄,不能涵盖所应涵盖的信息。

23. D。本题属于句群理解题。只要看完第二段,又能理解 Finally there is Frontierland which represents the Old West,即 One can get some knowledge of the American history,就可以得出此答案。

24. C。由文章最后一段第二句 Walt Disney World designed to thrill east-coast visitors as Disneyland has thrilled those in the west 可知,Walt Disney World 同 Disneyland 相比毫不逊色。因此,选项 C 符合段意,应为正确答案。

25. C。本题属于篇章层次的理解题。在文章的前三段中每一段都具体说明了一种测量方法,第一段 using ropes,第二段 using sound,第三段 under water photograph,正好是三种方法,而从第四段开始说的则是另外的东西。因此,正确答案应为 C。

26. C。从文章最后一段可知,环绕地球的巨大海底山脉刚刚被发现不久,由此可见,对于广袤的海洋世界,人类目前所知之甚少。因此,正确答案应为选项 C。

27. D。本段第一句说的是 marine life,第二句说的是 minerals,第三句说的是 deep hollows hold most of the world's water,由此可以得出结论,本段主要讲的是 marine resources 的问题。因此,选项 D 符合此意,应为正确答案。

28. C。本题属于词义推测题。文章第三句说明了针灸(acupuncture)的用途即 the use of needles for treating disease,而由第四句可知针灸治疗起源于中国(acupuncture originated from China),由此可知答案应为选项 C。

29. A。文章二、三两段详细地描述了记者所见证的 acupuncture 的实际过程和病人的反应,旨在说明在此过程中病人并无痛苦,因此,正确答案应为选项 A。

30. C。第一段第二句话中提到只要病人愿意死的话,可以允许医生终结那些患有无法治愈疾病的病人生命(After six months of arguing and final 16 hours of hot parliamentary（议会的）debates，Australia's Northern Territory became the first legal authority in the world to allow doctors to end the lives of incurable ill patients who wish to die.)。所以选项 C 符合题意,应为正确答案。

31. B。第一段第二句话说澳大利亚的 Northern Territory 是全球第一个可以实施安乐死的合法机构。所以选项 B 应为正确答案。

32. D。第一段最后一句话说,这不仅仅是发生的澳大利亚的事实,这也关系到全球历史。所以选项 D 符合题意,应为正确答案。

Exercise 7

1. D。其参考依据在本文的最后一段。该段落虽然也提到 better food 作为吸引乘客的一种手段,但是这并不意味着飞机上所提供的好食物都是免费的。因此,选项 D 不在此列。

2. D。参见第三自然段。

3. D。选项 A、B 和 C 分别在文中的第二、三段里提到过,只有选项 D 文中没有提及。因此,应为正确答案。

4. D。由第一段第一句中的"small birds that typically nest on beaches or in open fields，their nests merely scrapes in the sand or earth."一语可以推知选项 D 应为正确答案。选项 A 的意思显然与第一句话的意思不一致,因为任何一种筑在空旷地面上或者是海滩上的鸟巢想不被飞禽走兽发现的可能性是极小的。另外,根据短文可知,当这类海鸟发现食肉爬行动物威胁鸟巢时会想方设法地把它们引开这一行为本身就是该鸟的一种防御行为,因此选项 B 的说法不正确。此外,此鸟遇到不同情况所做出的相应反应说明,当该鸟遇到危险时的反应十分机敏,由此选项 C 也应排除。

5. C。选项 A、B 和 D 的内容分别在第三段第一句,第一段最后一句话和第二段倒数第三句中提及。只有选项 C 的内容文中没有提及。因此,该选项应为正确答案。

6. C。该题的参考依据为倒数第二自然段。

7. D。选项 A 的参考依据见第二自然段的第二、三句;选项 B 的参考依据见第三自然段第二句话;选项 C 的参考依据见第三自然段的倒数第二句。

8. C。第一段第二句"Not long after the last Ice Age，around 7，000 B. C.

(during the Neolithic period), some hunters and gatherers began to rely chiefly on agriculture for their sustenance. "的意思是"最后一个冰河时代不久之后,大约在公元前7000年前的新石器时代期间,一些猎人和采集者就主要依靠农业维持生计了。"这句话意味着在这个时期之前人们的生存主要依靠打猎和采集为生的。因此,选项 C 应为正确答案。

9. A。文章的第三段最后一句 "Now WTO is also pledged to reduce tariffs and other barriers and to eliminate discriminatory treatment in international trade. "(目前世贸组织也致力于减少关税和其他障碍以及消除国际贸易中的不平等待遇。)涵盖了选项 B、C、D 的全部内容,只有选项 A 该句中未被提及。此外,短文的其他段落中也未提及"To strike balance of payment. "之事。因此,正确答案应为选项 A。

10. D。第一段最后一句话的原句是"WTO has a wider role than GATT, covering commercial activities beyond the operational scope of the latter body. "意思与选项 D 正相反。选项 A 参见第一段第二句话中;选项 B 参见倒数第二段第一句话;选项 C 参见最后一段第一句话。

11. C。选项 A 在第二段第三条中提及;选项 B 在第一段第一句中提及;选项 D 在第二段第三条中提及。只有选项 C 文中没有提及。所以,应为正确答案。

Exercise 8

1. B。第一段指出,在国与国之间以及每个国家内部,两个差别正在加大,一是贫富差别,二是每个国家内部老年人和年轻人之间的差别。这两个差别都具有着深远影响。贫富差别是人们反对全球化的根本原因。全球化指跨国公司(multilateral corporation)在世界范围内寻找最佳生产环境的趋势:尽量少的(投资)环境法规限制,尽量低的劳动力成本。贫困国家的人认为这将能给他们带来就业机会,而富裕国家的人却认为全球化减少了他们的就业机会。

2. B。第二段第一句提到,对劳动力和环境的担忧被认为是旧贸易保护主义论调的现代翻版。这里所谓"对劳动力和环境的担忧"当然指的是前一段中提到的 popular opposition to globalization。

3. A。第三段提到了美洲的例子,如果像中美洲那样涉及很多国家,这些国家就会展开竞争,通过宽松的环境和劳动力法规——如果制定什么法规的话,来吸引国外企业投资。在美国,在联邦政府实施统一的环境和劳工标准之前,贫困州也是这个样子。如果能达成协议,制定一些国际范围内的(投资环境和劳工)标准还是有必要的(make sense)。由此可知选项 A 应为正确答案。

4. B。最后一段提到世界贸易(此处应该理解为全球化)的增长会伤害很多人,这些人将继续表达自己的反对意见——或者利用民主国家的民意测验方式,或者像在其他国家一样上街游行。同时,另外一些(从全球化中)受益者也会利用同样方式表达自己的支持,多数情况下,天平可能倾向于受益者一边,即支持者占了上风。但是,政府应该听一听那些合理的批评,应该限制一下公司贪婪本能的进一步膨胀。最后一句的含义是:国家应该就海外投资事宜做出一些严格的规定。由此可见选项 B 与该段的意思吻合,因此应为正确答案。

5. B。参阅第2、第3题题解。

6. D。第一段指出,孩子在很小的时候,既不能进行抽象思维(abstract thinking),也不能做客观性思维。他对于自己的经历仅限于极其主观化的(personalized)认识。比如,正如母亲哺育他一样,地球上的植物也哺育着他,这样,他会很自然地将地球看作母亲或某个女性的神,或至少把地球看作女神的住所。第三段第一句指出,儿童对世界的认识是他对父母及家庭活动的认识的反应,是一种由内向外的、主观的认识过程。由此可知选项 D 符合题意,应为正确答案。

7. B。正如第二题题解所分析的,孩子通过对家庭关系的认识来认识世界。第二段第二句指出,由于孩子知道自己受父母保护(watch over),因此他认为:在世界上也有一个像他们这样的保护神(a guardian angel),而且比他们更强大、睿智、可靠。这种认识不仅不会影响人们对将来世界的理性认识,反而会为他们提供必要的安全感,随着孩子走向成熟,这一安全感最终有助于一个真正的理性的世界观(world view)的形成(参阅第三段第三句)。由此可知选项 B 符合题意,应为正确答案。

8. D。文章在第一段中指出,能源危机表明,人类肆无忌惮地使用地球资源已使世界处于灾难的边缘(brink);现代交通运输的过度发展使城市濒临毁灭,使家庭解体,污染了城市的空气和大气层。因此,选项 D 符合题意,应为正确答案。

9. B。第三段指出,现在,许多道德的伦丧和腐败现象被揭露出来,甚至国家的最高层也不依法办事。这些现象的存在使国家岌岌可危。所以,道德需要新生,人需要新的奉献精神等。由本段第二、第三句可以看出,第一句主要是指人们缺乏奉献精神,意思是解决目前的危机还需要人们做出奉献。选项 A 之所以不正确是因为原文中所说的“违法”

(lawbreaking)主要得是指腐败,即高级官员们不能尽职尽责相反却以权谋私。而选项 C 和 D 与 loss of moral integrity 无关。因此,选项 B 应为正确答案。

10. C。作者在文章的最后一段中提出了应付危机的对策,指出人们都应充分理解(a widespread understanding)我们目前所面临的危机的性质——它绝不是暂时的(passing),我们所需要的是一种以科学技术为基础的新的生活方式(a transformed life style),指出要接受它需要人们真诚的奉献,以便使我们的子孙后代生活得更美好。作者的这一观点恰好与选项 C 的意思相吻合。因此,应为正确答案。其他选项均与段意不符。

11. A。根据第七句(All the men described in this book were sad as they stood their trials, not only because they were going to be punished.)可以推知,这篇文章是选自一本书的前言。因此,选项 A 应为正确答案。

12. A。文章在第一句中指出,如果一个人的观念比他的祖国的观念更先进或者是更落后的话,他就不可避免要与其祖国发生冲突(The relationship between a man and fatherland is always disturbed by conflict if either man or fatherland is highly developed.)。因此,选项 A 符合题意,应为正确答案。

13. A。第三句指出,如果他想继承国家的传统,他们不得不同一些人做斗争:这些人自认是传统的代表,他们想把前一代人所达到的文化传统固定下来(If he is to carry on the national tradition, he must wrestle with those who, speaking in its name, desire to crystallize it at the point reached by the previous generation.);第五句指出,如果国家不像熟烂的梨子一样疲软,每个国民的血脉中都应该有一两滴反抗精神(All men should have a drop or two of resistance spirit in them, if the nations are not to go soft like so many sleepy pears.)。由此可知作者虽然对当前人们的表现不甚满意,但却暗示对这种反抗现象的首肯。因此,选项 A 符合题意,应为正确答案。

14. B。文章在第八、第九句中指出,即使不面对审判,他们也会同样感到悲伤,因为他们抛弃了熟悉的媒介即:第三句所说的"If he is to carry on the national tradition, he must wrestle with those who, speaking in its name, desire to crystallize it at the point reached by the previous generation."寄希望于不会关心他人的怜悯;在感觉到其保护者的漠不关心后,他们生活在恐惧之中;他们不再对那些本来可以热爱他们的人抱有幻想。可见,这些人有一种被抛弃的绝望感。由此可知选项 B 符合题意,应为正确答案。

15. A。文章在第一段第二句中提到,今天的妇女雄心勃勃,决心在职业和做家长之间重新做出选择,以便担任两种角色时所做出的牺牲不会太大,或者被搞得筋疲力尽。最后一段也说,每个妇女都面临着自己的困境,如如何协调家庭和工作的关系问题。对此,她们都必须自行解决。然而,她们经常会感到力不从心,无法在二者之间找到满意的平衡。由此可见,妇女目前最想解决的问题恐怕就是平衡工作与家庭之间的关系了。因此,正确答案应为选项 A。

16. A。文章第二段的大意是妇女在时间、精力、个人所做的牺牲上都做出了力所能及的调整,但是,她们还是不能够全身心地投入到工作中去。由于一系列复杂的原因——许多因素是她们无法控制的,她们感到在工作和照料孩子之间存在着矛盾,除了为数不多的人外,几乎所有的人都不再相信存在着女超人。由此来看,这里所谓的"女超人",显然是指既能做好工作,又能同时照料好孩子的女人。因此,正确答案应为选项 A。

17. C。文章在第三段第五、第六句的大意是今天,妇女发现自己与社会处于激烈的斗争中,因为社会对于工作道德还抱着狭隘的认识,她们没意识到,支持这种道德的那种家庭结构几十年来已经消亡。但是,人们还抱着这样的认识,认为家里应该总得有一个女人照料孩子、做家务。因此,正确答案应为选项 C。

Exercise 9

1. C。本文第一句"I'm usually fairly skeptical about any research that concludes that people are either happier or unhappier or more or less certain of themselves than they were 50 years ago."首先示明作者对于大量关于人们心理状态研究持有怀疑态度,随后话题一转,在第三句"Still, I was struck by a report, which concluded that today's children are significantly more anxious than children in the 1950s."中提到一篇令作者大为惊讶的报告:现今美国的孩子比50年代的孩子更加焦虑不安。随后又在第三段到第六段中具体说明家长应该如何做来帮助孩子应对压力与焦虑。由此可以得出结论,家长的关心与帮助可以减轻孩子的焦虑,即选项 C 为正确答案。选项 A 过分空泛;选项 B、D 内容文中没提到,不足为答案。

2. D。本文中,作者主要描述了垒球的特征,也论述了如何对其欣赏。指出只有根据垒球的特征来欣赏它,才能真正体会到它的魅力。根据第三段第二句"You will contemplate the game from one point as a painter does his

subject; you may, of course, project yourself into the game." 可知，作者认为，观察到垒球比赛中运动员的各种动作、垒球位置之间的关系等是欣赏的关键。只有从整体来把握它，才能不放过每一个微小的动作及每一个眼神乃至"静止"的含义。也只有这样，才能全身心地投入到比赛中去，更真切地欣赏它的魅力。由此可以断定，作者对垒球有着很深的理解而且非常喜爱垒球。因此，正确答案应是选项 D。

3. D。选项 A 的意思是核武器在把小行星推离运行轨道的同时会毁灭地球。这个结论下得过于武断。因为文章只说这个办法利大于弊而没有说会毁灭地球。选项 B 说"在夜空中游弋的小行星在不久的将来有可能与地球相撞"，这种说法也不正确。因为在文章第五段中指出，"Experts think an asteroid big enough to destroy lots of life might strike Earth once every 500,000 years." 也就是说发生这种碰撞的可能性很小，约五十万年一次。选项 C 显然走向另一个极端。让我们的后代去考虑两者能否碰撞，因为在我们这一代中，小行星撞击地球的事情是不会发生的。从文中 "Buy $50 million worth of new telescopes right now. Then spend $10 million a year for the next 25 years to locate most of the space rocks. By the time we spot a fatal one, the scientists say, we'll have a way to change its course." 可见危险还是有的。选项 D 说还有待于找到一个切实可行的办法来阻止小行星撞击地球。从对全文的分析来看，唯一提出的办法就是用核武器，而用这种办法弊又大于利，可见这并不是切实可行的办法。因此，选项 D 是正确结论。

4. A。文章最后一句写道：如果没有具有亲和力的领导，大规模的变革也可能会发生，但变革的步伐要缓慢得多，人们看不清变革的方向，领导小组没完没了地开会商讨。该句话是段落的结论句，同时也是该段落前几句话的归纳总结，与选项 A 的意思吻合，应为正确答案。

5. A。根据文章的第二段可知，耐克利用名人来做广告，获取巨大利润；同时乔丹也赚了大钱。作者在文章结束时提到，麦当劳和可口可乐公司的商业广告提升了乔丹的公众形象而他们也依靠名人效应刺激了广大消费者的购买欲。由此可知这对双方来说都是受益的。因此，选择 A 应为正确答案。

Exercise 10

1. D。文章一开头就提出了这个问题："Are organically grown foods the best food choices?"（有机食物/绿色食物是最佳的食物选择吗？）通常情况下,作者对某事提出质疑,其后没有马上给出肯定的答案,就意味着作者对这个问题持有怀疑的态度(skeptical)。对于这个问题,作者的处理方法恰好如此,符合这一写作规律。此外,作者紧接着在第二句中又说"The advantages claimed for such foods over conventionally grown and marketed food products are now being debated."讲到有机食品所宣称的优点正在"争论"之中(advantages are being debated),显然是在暗示作者本人对此问题所持的怀疑态度。因此,选项 D 符合题意,应为正确答案。

2. B。做好本题的关键是对全文有一个整体的理解。虽然作者一开始就指出了计算机的不足之处,但在第二段中却又说"I like computers..."这就意味着作者还是喜欢计算机的,也正是因为喜欢才建议应本着以人为本的原则去改造、利用计算机。因此,选项 B 符合题意,应为正确答案。

3. A。本文驳斥了有关神话故事对小孩有害的观点。认为应该给孩子讲神话故事。可见作者对这个问题的态度是肯定的。因此,选项 A 符合题意,应为正确答案。

4. B。从第二段最后一句"and we find that mixed-ability teaching contributes to all these aspects of learning"得知,作者对多种能力混合教学班所持的态度是赞同的,因为这种混合班有助于各个方面能力的培养。选项 A 意为"质疑的",选项 C"客观的",选项 D"挑剔的"均不合原意。只有选项 B 才符合题意。因此,应为正确答案。

5. B。该题为事实分析题。本文客观地描述了一个社会调查情况,对任何一种生活模式都没有给予褒贬。这一点恰好与选项 B 的意思相吻合,因此应为正确答案。

6. B。作者写该文的目的是告诉人们:批评会给孩子们造成各方面的负担和压力,积极鼓励才会对孩子的成长有益,因此,选项 B"强调积极鼓励对孩子成长的重要性"符合题意,应为正确答案。

7. D。作者在文章第一段中批驳了对标准化测试的否定看法,认为标准化测试的价值在于对测试结果的正确分析和评价,并提出在什么情况下测试的结果最为有效。由此可见作者对标准化测试所持的态度是肯定的。

8. D。作者在文中描述冰山时所使用的单词大多是褒义词,如:spectacular(壮观的,引人注目的),creation(创举),graceful(优美的,优雅的),stately(堂煌的,壮观的),inspiring(振奋人心的)等。由此可以看出作者对冰山所持的态度是肯定的。wonder 的意思是"惊叹",符合文章的语调,因此选项 D 应为正确答案。

9. B。从篇章内容的组织情况来看,作者先道出了工业化时代中各阶层人们的焦虑感,紧接着在最后一段中又提出了改变这种模式的建议,可见作者对工业化现象所持的态度是极其不满的。

10. B。根据文章第二段第四句可以看出作者对压力所持的肯定态度,第五句表明作者对压力持否定态度。肯定和否定态度既有积极的一面又有消极的一面,所以选项 B 与之意思相吻合,应该为正确答案。选项 A 之所以不正确的原因是作者在第一段最后一句提到放松对身心健康很重要,但并没说精神压力问题。所以选项 A"压力和放松对健康身心很重要"的说法不确切;选项 C"压力不能完全从生活中除掉"所涉及的内容只是作者所谈的枝节问题,而且还是很不现实的一种说法,选项 D 也是如此。

Exercise 11

1. D。文章第五段第一句 "Most colleges believe students should contribute to tuition costs." 中 contribute to tuition costs 的意思是"为学费出一份力,起一份作用";句中 should 表示虚拟。这正好与选项 D 所表达的意思相吻合,因此,应为正确答案,即英国的学生可能在不久的将来要为其所受的高等教育付费。

2. A。根据第三段的第一句"Another machine measures any dangerous features of tools,thus proving information upon which to base a new design。"中的 a new design 可知,第二句中提到的 a tripod ladder 就是一种 a new design,而四条腿的梯子便就成了 an old design 了。也就是说,过去用的梯子都是是四条腿的。选项 A 的意思与之相吻合,应为正确答案。

3. B。第五段第一句提到,Starway 是一个(春兰摩托车的)独家(exclusivity)供应商。没有"中间人"这一环节使得 Starway 能以无与伦比的低价格(unbeatable value)提供各型号的春兰摩托车。第四段第二句也提到了 Starway 直销(direct)春兰摩托车。因此,选项 B 与段意相吻合,应为正确答案。

4. C。作者在最后一段第一句中写道:Incidents of this kind will continue as long as sport is played competitively rather than for the love of the game. 在结论段中作者以两次比赛为例,说明体育运动比赛中竞争性造成了这类事件,因而有损于国家与国家间的友好关系。选项 A"虚伪的国家尊严是如何引起国际比赛中不尽如人意的事件的"有较大的干扰性。但选项 A 主要谈的是"how"。这点作者文中并没有谈及，所谈的是竞争性的消极一面。因此，选项 C 符合题意，应为正确答案。

5. B。这是一道论点与论据之间的逻辑关系题。作者在第一段第三句中先说：By opening vast areas of unoccupied land for residential expansion, the omnibuses, horse railways, commuter trains, and electric trolleys pulled settled regions outward two to four times more distant from city centers than they were in the pre modern era.（由于使用公共汽车、公路运输、市郊往返火车以及电车使居住区离市中心的距离比过去远了2～4倍。）紧接着用"for example"举出了波士顿和芝加哥由于公交系统的发展使城区不断向四周扩展的事实。可见选项 B"表明公共交通改变了许多城市"反映了论点与论据之间的逻辑关系。因此，应为正确答案。

Exercise 12

1. A。选项 A 的意思是"完全"。因为该词在句中所修饰的是 accurately，显然是表示一种程度。因此，选项 A 符合题意，应为正确答案。当然，altogether 还有其他几种含义，如"一共"、"总之"等。在下例中所采取的词义显然不同于文章中所采用的词义，如：There were five people altogether. /Lots of sunshine, wonderful food, and amazing nightlife—altogether a great vacation!

2. B。该词所在的句子是一个由让步状语从句加主句构成的复合句。主句的意思是：涉及到这一过程的相互关系还会常常被误解。由此逆向推导可知让步状语从句中所表述的一切努力都是积极和肯定的。即深入细致的研究与大力发展。据此可知选项 B 符合句意，应为正确答案。该词修饰的是 research，意思是集中研究。decrease 意为"减少"，creative 意为"具有创造性的"，advanced 意为"先进的"，与语境意思不相符，不能视作正确答案。

3. C。根据 list 所在句的上一句 Until late in the nineteenth century only a few industries could use... 可以推知此处 list 是承接上句而来的，指的是上文中所指的"为数不多的行业"。

4. B。assumption 后面接的是一个同位语从句。根据该句的意思：科学在工业用途上的应用是一个线性过程……，可知这一说法是对 assumption 的详细展述，也是一种观点或看法。因此，选项 B 的意思是一种"假设的看法"，符合题意，应为正确答案。

5. C。句中 coarse 修饰的是 fiber，也是短文中谈论的主题。文章的第二段倒数第二句"By the mid-1870's, however, the best glass fibers were finer than silk and could be woven into fabrics or assembled into imitation ostrich(鸵鸟) feathers to decorate hats."使用了描述玻璃纤维特点的形容词比较级,由此反衬可以推知早期的玻璃纤维是很粗糙的。因此,选项 C 应为正确答案。其他选项均不符合文章的上下文的意思。

6. A。该词上文谈的是 "Wandering trades-people began to spin glass fibers...",紧接着作者又指出"but this material was of little practical use",由此以推知 this material 指代的显然是 glass fibers。因此,选项 A 应为正确答案。

7. A。玻璃纤维本身的特点就是脆,加之当时的工艺不够完美,这一特点肯定会对其质量产生影响。文中用 ragged, and no longer than ten feet 来描述玻璃纤维的特点,可知其韧度也不怎么样。因此 easily broken 就不可避免的了。因此,选项 A 符合题意,应为正确答案。

8. D。文中"The glacier had formed as layer upon layer of snow accumulated year after year."一句的意思是"冰川是由年复一年积累起来的一层层雪构成的"。由此可知选项 D 的意思与该词相吻合,应为正确答案。

9. B。前文说的是"冰川是由年复一年积累的一层层雪构成的",后文句中引用了 through time 一词暗指钻探进入冰层和从冰层退出的时间。从逻辑的角度来看,选项 B 与之吻合,因此,应为正确答案。

10. C。根据 remarkable 所处的上下文可以得知,该词应取"异常的"这一层含义,因为 Almost every time the chill of an ice age descended on the planet, carbon dioxide levels dropped. 即"几乎在冰河时期的每一个时代中,当寒冷降临星球时,二氧化碳的含量都会随之下降"。由此可见温度和二氧化碳含量在大气层中的完整记录这一结果自然应是非同寻常了。选项 C 意同 remarkable;选项 A"genuine"的意思是"真实的,真正的";选项 B"permanent"的意思是"永久的"。因此,均不符合题意。

11. A。句中两个动词 start 和 resume 是由连结词 or 联系在一起的,意思是"或者",即要么这样,要么那样,由此可以推断若不是开始一个 additional newspapers,就得恢复 the daily weather map。因此,选项 A 应为正确答案。

12. D。该词意思的推导须建立在上一段信息和下一个句子意思的基础上。在倒数第二段中,作者大谈于70和80年代中天气图在报纸上所起的重要作用以及报主为了更具有竞争性所采取的相应措施。进入最后一段,作者通过过度句,即先对前一段的陈述予以肯定之后,再提出一个具有转折性的信息,在这种情况下过度句所表述的意思必定要与其前一段落中所表述的意思保持一致。因此,正确答案应是选项 D。选项 A"makes up for"的意思是"弥补";选项 B"combines with"的意思是"与……相结合";选项 C"interferes with"的意思是"干预",均不合题意。

13. D。根据该词的所处的语言环境"while others dropped the comparatively drab satellite photos"(而另一些报刊却扔掉了那些乏味的卫星图像)可以推知 drab 的意思就是 dull 的意思,否则报纸是不会扔掉那些卫星图片的。可见,选项 D 符合句意,应为正确答案。

14. B。ironically 在句中所起的作用是转折。根据句意,报纸上的天气图标信息最丰富,最有指导性,然而却占得版面很小,很不引人注目。由此可知这种现象在作者眼里是很不正常的事。对于这种现象唯一能解释通的原因就是报主对天气图不够重视。可见,选项 B 符合题意,应为正确答案。

15. B。这句话的大致意思是"除了一些共同的特征外,没有两课彗星在外观上一模一样……"。该句子的前半部分采用了全否定的表达方法,而在后半句中又对彗星的外观作了部分肯定。根据逻辑,在这种情况下句子前半部分的界定词应与后半句的意义上一致。因此,选项 B 符合题意,应为正确答案。

16. A。heart 一词的基本意思是"心脏"。通常人们总是把心脏认定为于人体的中心。这里 heart 使用的是比喻的意思,意同中心位置。因此,选项 A 符合题意,应为正确答案。

17. D。graphic 的意思是"生动的,如画的"。流星在天空中划过时的情景非常壮观,用此词来修饰流星所留下的 proof 显然应该是 vivid。因此,选项 D 与该词义相吻合,应为正确答案。

18. A。这里 distinct 的意思是 something visible。根据后文对彗星形状的描述可知它的形状是可视的。否则没人会知道彗星究竟是个什么样子。

19. C。该题为词义辨析题。schism 一词的含义须根据上下文的意思来判断。本篇开头作者提到:科学与文化的其他方面一直就存在着极不和谐的关系。在随后的几个段落中,我们又看到:自然科学与人文科学之间的分歧不但没有消除,反而更加严重,以至于分裂成科学与反科学两大阵营。由此可以推断,文章首段第四行中的 schism 一词应理解为"不和"或"分裂"选项 C"separahon"正为此意。其他选项 A 对抗、B 不满、D 貌视,均与原文在意思上有出入。

20. D。该题为词义辨析题。该词所在句的意思是:斯坦福大学的 Paul Ehrlich,

环境科学的开拓者认为,科学上的真正敌人是那些质疑支持全球变暖的证据的人,即臭氧层损耗及其他工业发展所引起的后果(The true enemies of science, argues Paul Ehrlich of Stanford University, a pioneer of environmental studies, are those who question the evidence supporting global warming, the depletion of the ozone layer and other consequence of industrial growth.)从句子的结构来分析 the depletion of the ozone layer and other consequence of industrial growth 是 global warming 的同位语,起着解释作用的。根据常识可知气候变暖的原因就是由大气臭氧层的减少所致。因此,正确答案应为选项 D。repletion 的意思是“充足的,充足供应的”;completion 意为“完成”;reception 的意思是“接待”,均不合逻辑。

21. D。上文说到哈佛大学校园里争论的焦点问题是:大学应该遵从什么样的价值和理想标准以及如何进行度量。接着提出了大学是应该远离政治和社会变革,还是要充当政治和社会变革的试验田甚至发动机的问题?可见,这里的“知识分子庇护所”是指不受外界影响、专门从事学术研究与教学的高等学府。因此,选项 D 与短语意思相吻合,应为正确答案。

22. B。在第四段中,Walter Lippmann 指出,如果大学要想发挥自己的作用,就必须独立于任何党派或社会利益团体之外,不参与政治和社会变革运动或从中谋利,这样才能对事物做出独立的、客观的判断,大学秉承这样的理念才会办学成功。因此选项 B 符合题意,应为正确答案。

Exercise 13

1. D。One of the best-known examples of mass extinction occurred 65 million years ago with the demise of dinosaurs and many other forms of life. 的意思是“随着恐龙和许多其他种类生命死亡,著名的集体灭绝例子之一就发生在六千五百万年前。”恐龙的灭绝是人尽所知的,根据普通常识便可推出 demise 的基本含义,加之句子的前半部分讲著名的集体灭绝是随着恐龙的灭绝而发生的,更加印证了这一词义在此句中意思。因此,mass extinction 与 demise 的意思应该是相同的,都意味着 death。

2. A。该答案须由 plankton 与其他生物等的相互依存关系的进行逻辑推导。如由此句的后半句 affecting even organisms not living in the oceans 可以推知 plankton 与海洋中的 organisms 构成相互间的直接依存关系,即小生物与有机物之间的关系。因此,选项 A 符合这一逻辑,应为正确答案。

3. B。从 stigma 所在句“Divorce rates can be expected to be higher in groups that

attach less stigma to divorce than in those that attach more."(在一些认为离婚不光彩的社会群体中,其离婚率比那些认为离婚不大会影响名声的社会群体高)及上下文的意思可以判断出,此处,stigma 的意思应为 dishonor。

4. C。作者在此段中指出离婚率的变化取决于家庭周期。许多研究都指向了一个事实:婚姻存续时间越长就越容易保持长久的婚姻状况。这一结论显然不是一时兴起,或者是建立在某个人的亲身经历的等基础上而得出的,而是研究多年的婚姻状况才得出的,即根据以往的经验而得出的。因此,正确答案应为选项 C。(empirical:经验主义的)。

5. A。文章在开首部分说信息系统是改进社会投资成本效益的一种主要工具。在经济领域期望能够取得更高的生产效率,这一点无论是工业还是服务行业都是如此。所不同的是使用的手段。随后继续推展说,认识到拥有信息等同于拥有竞争优势这一事实,激发人们收集公司和国家技术与经济情报(Awareness that possession of information is tantamount to a competitive edge is stimulating the gathering of technical and economic intelligence at the corporate and national levels)。由此可知选项 C 符合题意,应为正确答案。

6. D。从第二段第四行的"That country's economic recession... jobs relinquished most permanently..."中的 economic recession(经济衰退),所导致的后果及紧接其后的 most permanently 可以推断出,relinquished'的意思应为 given up 因此,选项 D 应为答案。其他三个选项 A"given away"(泄露,分送);选项 B"given in"(交上,投诉,屈服);选项 C"given out"(分发,放出)均与原文上下文的意思不符,不能视作答案。

7. C。dubious 作为超纲生词,直接判断其含义通常会有一定的困难,因此首先应在原文中找到其所在的句子 You can find a great deal of very dubious advice on how to get a job or how to get a promotion. 以其为立足点,然后参考前一句 Yet you will find little if anything written on what it is to be an employee. 进行分析,可发现该句使用了表示转折的特征词 yet 和表示否定含义的词 little,由此可以判定,dubious 一定是一个具有负面的含义。而选项 A"valuable"(有价值的)、选项 B"useful"(有用的)、选项 D "helpful"(有帮助的),都是具有肯定含义的词,只有选项 C"doubtful""可疑的,不确定的"的意思与之吻合,因此应为正确答案。

8. D。本文主要谈论的是美国家长如何把自己的风俗习惯与价值观念教授给孩子们,以具体的实例陈述了家长是如何从小就开始培养孩子们的独立精神,以使他们不要依赖父母,而是要做一个独立自主的人。在这种前提下,作者使用了这两个词语。cut the cord 的字面意思为"割断脐带",其隐含的喻义为"不再让孩子依附母亲";而 not to be tied to the apron strings 字面意思是"不要把孩子系在围裙带上",其隐含的喻义也是"不要让孩子总跟着大人寸步不离,要放开手脚,让他们学会照看自己"。也就是说,要让孩子从小养成独立性,不依赖父母。因此,选项 D 符合题意,应为正确答案。

Exercise 14

1. A。第五段共三句话。第一句说"Surgery is also valuable as a preventive measure in controlling cancer."(外科手术作为控制癌症的预防手段也很有价值)。第二句"It may be used..."和第三句"It may be used..."是对第一句的详细说明;而且,两句的结构相似。其中的 It 所指代的都是 surgery。因此,选项 A 符合题意,应为正确答案。

2. B。"今日世界"体现在文中第一段中"the universe in which they lived was made up of three separate, but related, worlds: In the last there lived humans..."由此可以得出 the last 和 this World 是相对应的。所以,选项 B 符合题意,应为正确答案。选项 A"所有的星体"显然是不正确的;选项 C"整个宇宙"更是超出了"今日世界"的范围"今日世界"只是其中之一,因此可以排除;选项 D"上个世界"也不正确。

3. C。that 所在句"The carcinogenic potential of radioactive elements and ultraviolet light has been established, while that of highly energetic cosmic radiation remains to he documented"中 The carcinogenic potential...established 是主句;其中,The carcinogenic potential 是主语。while 引导了一个让步状语从句;其中,代词 that 指代的是 The carcinogenic potential。因此,选项 C 符合题意,应为正确答案。

4. A。this 指代的是第二段中有关英国工人"工作节奏慢,不卖力气"这一现象(...the pace of work is much slower here. Nobody tries too hard)。实际上 this(Para 3,Line 1)在文章后面的语句中(缓慢的工作节奏英国成了一个轻松惬意的,令人向往的国家)也暗示了 this 所指代的内容。因此,正确答案应为选项 A。

5. B。根据文章第五段最后一句所提到 young Xer 说的话,可以推断正确答案应为选项 B。此外,最后一段讨论了工作满意度的问题,重点提到的是年轻工人大多在寻找满意的职位,最后一句说 Xer 占了65%,所以据此也可以推断山 Xer 指的是年轻人。因此,选项 B 符合题意,应为正确答案。

6. C。文章第五段首先点明了主题,政治家道德和伦理水准下降,同样,国会也做的不到位,所以 screw up 意同选项 C"搞得"一团糟;"弄得一塌糊涂",与选项 C 的意思相吻合,因此应为正确答案。

7. C。文章第五段第四句里谈到"……议会成员考虑得更多的是自己的政治前途",意指"寻求更高身份的职业"。所以,选项 C 的意思与之相吻合,应为正确答案。其他选项之所以不正确的原因是(根据原文)议员们只考虑自己的前途,对国家和人民的前途不太关心。因此,若说议员"考虑整个民族的前途"或"人民将来的富有"是不切合实际的。

Exercise 15

Passage 1

1. B。该句使用了一个让步状语从句"比起10年以前,我更善于倾听,但是……",由此可以推断出说话者对现状并不十分满意。因此"我得承认"实属无奈。

2. D。该句的大致意思是有效地倾听别人的意见不只是避免经常打断别人的讲话,这种做法虽算不上什么错误至少也是一种非常突出的不良表现。由此可知,在作者的眼里经常打断别人的讲话绝非一种良好的习惯。因此,该词符合上下文逻辑。

3. M。这里 thought 意为"想法,思路"。听别人讲话,显然是在听取别人的想法,而非别人所发出的声音。

4. E。rather than 意为"而非",用在此处恰好使该词组的前后句子的意思形成正反两种不同的具有对比性的行为,符合题意。

5. F。此处,该词意为"回答,反应",与句中的 listen 相对应。

6. K。从结构上讲,句中空格6 "symbolic of the ___6___ we live"与"the way we fail to listen is"中的 the way 相一致。

7. L。speaking with 意为"与……交谈"。

8. H。意为"在……周边"。

9. N。instead 前后的两种谈话方式绝然不同。因此,由该词来成全两种截然不同的谈话方式。

10. J。在对话过程中,应减缓的显然应该是对对方讲话所做出的反应。

Passage 2

1. B。此句意由 dress-down Friday 一词推导而知,如果这种办公室工作人员的衣着习惯不是一种习俗的话是很难蔚然成风的。另外,第二段第三句中明确地指出这种穿戴是一种习俗。因此,该词符合逻辑。

2. C。interpret 意为"理解,释义"。该句在段首使用了一个表示转折的词 yet 及 unsure,显然是指人们对这种衣着不甚了解,或者是说不出个所以然来。因此选 C 符合逻辑。

3. D。"Many people want to know if they actually have to dress down.""Some people are uncomfortable doing so or don't think they look their best in casual clothes."这两句话尽管是相互独立的,但是就逻辑而言却构成了内在的让步关系。即"(尽管)许多人想知道他们是否真的要穿着随便一些""(但是)有些人仍然认为穿着随便会感到很不舒服或者是不能体现出他们的最好形象"。因此,符合逻辑。

4. F。wearing 为持续性的动作,意思是"穿着"。该空格的之后是 T-shirt and jeans,而且用的是现在进行时,显然是指人们当时的穿着了。此外,wear 是持续性的动作,而 put on 是一时性的动作。由此可见该选词符合逻辑。

5. G。dressed up 意思是"(把)打扮得漂漂亮亮,身着盛装,穿着考究"。根据该句后的 nice shirt 可以推知作者认为这身打扮会使自己看起来很漂亮。

6. J。comfortable 在此句中与前文"因穿着随便而感觉不适"相对应。

7. E。either 用在否定句中表示"也"的意思。前一句说"you won't stand out...",第三段第一句承接上文,用的也是否定句,因此,此句顺理成章也应填入 either 一词以使之符合上下文的逻辑。

8. L。in 意思是"身着"。

9. M。meant 意为"意思是"。

10. I。left 意为"留在,扔在"。休闲衣服等显然不适合在正式场合中穿戴,应搁在家里是最好的主意。

Passage 3

1. K。from generation to generation 是"一代又一代"的意思,为固定用法。

2. F。比较级。

3. B。"花钱"应为 spend money。

4. C。前文"他们有很多钱可花,非常自由自在"。由此必然的逻辑走向应是"不依赖于父母"。

5. M。blindly 意思是"盲目地"。根据逻辑,既然很独立,不依赖他人,那么自然就不会盲目的接受他人的观点了。

6. G。比较级。

7. H。根据后文中的 that preceded it 可知,这里的一代人应该是一代新人。

8. J。根据上文的口气可以推知,老一代人的看法可能是建立在主观的臆断基础上。因此,应填入该词。

9. I。what 在此句中引导了一个宾语从句。

10. L。older 指老的一代人。

Passage 4

1. K。raise 的意思是"提高(收入)"。根据逻辑推理可知,家长之所以让子女接受教育的目的是提高他们将来的收入。

2. A。此句的意思是"他们的真正的意图是⋯⋯"

3. L。根据前文"他们的真正的意图是为社会提供劳动力,而非⋯⋯",其后半句显然也是针对社会而言。因此,应选填 L。

4. B。George Bernard Shaw 或 Thomas Alva Edison 是世界上两大名人。现实是并非人人都能够像他们那样成功,即便是碰巧叫这个名字,也未见得会有同样的命运。因此,这里蕴含了极大的否定意思。

5. I。make sure 意思是"务必"。目前,最火的一种学位就是"MBA"。在人们的心目中,只要拿到这个学位,就能成功。

6. N。take effect 的意思是"起作用,奏效",为固定词组。

7. M。except for 作为词组,其意思是"除了",即在说明基本情况后加以补充。根据上文,由该词组所引导的下文显然是对上文给予补充。

8. F。该词在此句中引导了一个定语从句,指在某个学科方面。

9. G。unemployed 意思是"找不到工作"。根据上下文可以推知,即使拿到博士学位,也不一定会找到理想的工作。

10. E。part 意思是"地方"。该句使用了一个形容词比较级,其比较的范围是该国与除该国以外的世界其他国家或地方。因此,符合句意。

Passage 5

1. K。according to 是词组,意为"根据"。该答案是根据上下文逻辑和空格后的介词 to 的提示推导出的。

2. A。take its course 为固定搭配,意为"走上了正轨"。

3. C。此句中,该词与上文的 rush 相呼应。

4. L。灾害有两种,如果不是人为的灾害,那就是自然的灾害。人为的灾害文中已出现，所剩下的自然就应该是自然灾害了。

5. D。more or less 为固定词组，意思是"或多或少的"。

6. F。repaired 意思是"修理"。该空格后面的 fire hydrants to be reconnected 实际上是 to be required 的并列结构。

7. G。根据后文，the blank slate is no longer blank 可知，再作新计划显然为时太晚。因此，符合逻辑。

8. H。site 意为"工地，地方"。根据上下文可知，此语指的是世贸中心的具体场地。

9. M。point out 为词组，意为"指出"。

10. I。immediate 意为"直接的"。

Exercise 16

Passage 1

1. Y。参见第一段。

2. NG。参见全文。

3. Y。参见第四段标题。

4. Y。参见第五段最后一句。

5. N。参见第七段标题。

6. Y。参见第九段。

7. Y。参见第十三、十四段。

8. his negative attitude to it。参见第二段。

9. his problem discussion with certain students。参见第八段。

10. they give the instructor some useful information。参见第十一段。

Passage 2

1. Y。参见全文标题。

2. Y。参见第一段倒数第二句。

3. Y。参见第三段最后一句。

4. Y。参见第五段第一句。

5. Y。参见全文。

6. NG。参见全文。

7. Y。参见第四段。

8. culture background knowledge。参见第四段。

9. natural condition and geographical environment of an area。参见第六段第一

句。

10. as a social culture influence on reading comprehension。参见第七段。

Passage 3

1. Y。参见全文。
2. Y。参见第一段第三句。
3. Y。参见第一、二段句。
4. N。参见第一段。
5. Y。参见第一段。
6. N。参见第四段第五句。
7. Y。参见最后一段倒数第二句。
8. showing its first signs of weakness。参见第一段最后一句和第二段第一句。
9. 4.8%。参见第四段第二句。
10. opportunities for readjustment and reform。参见最后一段倒数第二句。

Passage 4

1. Y。参见第二段第三句。
2. N。参见第二段第二句。此句不是作者的观点，而是 James Braid 的观点。
3. N。参见第三段第一句。
4. N。参见第三段。
5. N。参见第五段。
6. Y。参见第六段。
7. NG。文中没提。
8. psychological，social and/or physical experiences。参见第三段。
9. to repeat continuously simple suggestion in the same tone of voice。参见第四段第二句。
10. the use of hypotism is legal situation is not reliable。参见第十一段第二句。

Passage 5

1. Y。参见第二段第三句。
2. NG。参见全文。
3. Y。参见第四段最后一句。
4. Y。参见全文各例，尤其是第六段。
5. N。参见第六段 Lou Gemtner 例子。

6. Y。参见第六段。

7. NG。参见全文。

8. to look for an outsider with inside knowledge of the business。参见第十一段第一句。

9. an MBA and four years experience with Mckinsey。参见第二段倒数第二句和第三段最后一句。

10. identical social, cultural and demographic characteristics。参见第九段第二句。

第二部分

Exercise 1

Cloze 1

1. B。选项 B"sooner or later"(迟早)。根据上下文可知驾船行驶碰到陆地是那个人想象中可能发生的事。至于究竟在何时,到那时为止无法断定。因此,符合题意。

2. C。route 的意思是"路线",该句意为:女王将会有一条新的更短的途径到达……。符合题意。选项 A"orbit"(轨道);选项 B"range"(范围);选项 D"friction"(摩擦)均不可用于指"路线"。

3. A。him 在这里作句子的宾语。该词在句中指代的是 Christopher Clumbers。

4. D。在哥伦布漂洋过海,行驶多周期间不可能总是风平浪静。更何况,他所路经的途径通常凶险多桀。因此,选项 D"rough"(汹涌的)符合题意,应为正确答案。选项 C"current"的意思是"水流,当前"。

5. D。根据前文可知那段海上的航行是十分艰辛而漫长的。当哥伦布到达群岛时必定历经千辛万苦,at last 的意思是"最后,终于",常用于指经过一番努力而最终完成某事,符合题意。

6. C。该句意为:哥伦布的故事很快就传遍了欧洲。词组 spread across 意为"传播",符合句意。

7. D。and 在此句中起着承上启下的作用。

8. A。词组 make a trip to 的意思是"去……旅行",符合题意。

9. C。believing 为现在分词,在句中用作伴随状语,意为"认为"。

10. B。根据前一句"很快得知哥伦布弄错了。但 Indian 一词却在欧洲扎下了根。",可以推知该句子在逻辑上与前一句形成转折。因此,but 用在此句中,符合逻辑。

11. C。根据定语从句"who arrived in North Carolina and Virginia in the early 1600s called the natives Indians"可知这里 native Indians 指的就是那里的定居者,即"第一批定居者"。因此,选项 C 符合题意。选项 A"Indians"语句中的"Indians"重叠;选项 B"explorers"(开拓者),不符合题意。

12. A。as 的意思是"作为"。这里 the names 指的就是 the colonies of Maryland,New York 和 Pennsyania。

13. B。describe(描述,说),符合题意。

14. D。there be 表示(存在有),符合题意。

15. B。known as 为词组,意为"被称作"或"以……而出名",符合题意。

16. B。though 为副词,在句中表示让步。

17. A。该句意为:他把美国和印度的名字和并在一起,创造了这个名字。

18. A。根据前半句"This word is often used today by other scholars"及转折词后的"but the general public has heard little of it"可以推知,这一名字只有某些学者才知道,而其他平民百姓并不知道。即 public 在句中的与 scholars 形成对照,符合题意。

19. C。此句实际上是前一句:It's too late to change it to Amerind 的进一步推展说明。据此推知该句的意思应该是:most people would not accept the change。

20. A。instead of(而非,而不是)在句中起着排除的作用,符合题意。

Cloze 2

1. C。该句意为:如果你让笔落在地上,你就会看见是地球的吸引力在起作用。in action 意为"在起作用";reaction、density 不可与介词 in 一起搭配使用。inertia 意为"惯性",不符合题意。

2. B。by 意为"被、由",符合题意。

3. D。hour 是以元音开首的,因此其前面须用 an。

4. A。本文主要谈的就是关于地球的吸引力的问题。此句主要谈的是火箭进入太空中需要摆脱地球吸引力所需要的速度。因此,选项 A 符合题意,应为正确答案。

5. C。be subjected to 的意思是"易受……的"。该句意为:当火箭离开地面时易受张力的影响。符合题意。be equal to 的意思是"与……平等";suit 的意思是"适合于"。

6. B。该答案是经逻辑推理而得出来的。此外,根据常理,移动不动的东西大多是因阻力太大所至。tend to 意为"往往,趋向于",符合题意。refer to 意思是"谈到,参考";serve 与 as 搭配使用;intend"意图"。

7. C。该句意为:当火箭离开地面时,会猛烈地向上推进,坐在驾驶舱里的人则被推向椅背方向。

8. A。exert a force on 意为"为……施加压力",符合题意。选项 B"impose"(把……强加于);选项 C"disturb"(打扰);选项 D"affect"(影响),常含有产生不良影响的内涵。

9. D。此句显然是指两种不同的力,一种是地球吸引力,另一种是非正常的力。因为非正常力是没有特定的标准的。

10. D。该句意为:一旦摆脱了地球的引力,宇航员又会受到另一个问题的影响。紧接着下一句又谈到了一个新的问题,可见上文所提到的问题并非唯一。

11. D。参见第10题。

12. C。该句意为:如果把一杯水倒过来,水不会从杯子中洒出来。这显然是一个非正常现象的实例。turn upside down 的意思是"倒置",符合题意。

13. B。be accustomed to 为词组,意为"习惯于……",符合题意。

14. A。spaceship 意同 a vehicle for carrying people through space,而 satellite 相当于 a machine that has been sent into space and goes around the Earth, moon etc。container(容器);vehicle 为车辆的总称。

15. C。该句意为:宇航员还会受到厌倦和孤独的影响。affect(影响)符合题意。anticipate(预期);conquer(征服);guide(引导)。

16. A。此句中 with little to do 意为"无所事事"。上句中提到厌倦和孤独显然是因为宇航员并不总是很忙,由此而引出下文"无所事事"一说,因此,选项 A 符合题意。

17. D。句中与 the nearest stars 相对应的星星显然是相距遥远的星星了。因此,选项 D 符合题意。

18. C。这里 even 表示程度,为副词。

19. B。该句意为:所以未来的宇航员必须长时间地忍受没有活动的生活和寂寞。选项 endure(忍受),符合题意。

20. B。tiny dust particles 意为"宇宙尘埃",符合题意。

Cloze 3

1. D。get a job 意为"找到一份工作",符合题意。申请工作应是 apply for a job。

2. A。read and comprehend quickly 意为"快速阅读理解",因此,选项 A 符合题意。

3. C。该句意为:不幸的是我们大多数人都是阅读能力不强的人。既然"不幸"自然阅读能力就不会太强了。因此,选项 C 符合这一逻辑。

4. B。reading habits 意为"阅读习惯",符合句意。

5. A。lie in 为固定词组,意为"在于",符合题意。combine 应与介词 with 搭配使用,意为"与……结合";touch(触摸,感动);involve 常与介词 in 连用,意为"涉及到"。

6. C。该句意为:只有把单词组合成短语、句子和段落才会有意义。

7. D。Unfortunately 在句中表示转折,因为下文主要谈的是未受过训练的读者效率不高的原因——不会按词群来读,这点恰好与上文形成对照。

8. B。reread 意为"重读"。re-为英语前缀,表示再一次的意思。

9. A。what 在此句中引导了一个介词宾语从句。that 虽然也可以用于引导从句,但不可以用在介词后面。

10. C。slow down 为词组,意为"使缓慢下来",符合题意。

11. B。此句中 one 为不定代词。

12. A。accelerator(加速器);amplifier(放大器);observer(观察员)。根据上下文可知,阅读训练班的目的是提高阅读速度,培养阅读能力。因此,选项 A 符合题意。

13. D。此处为比较级。根据空格前的 faster 一词可知此句为比较级,因此应在空格内填入 than。

14. C。making word-by-word reading...practical impossible 意为"使逐字阅读……根本不可能",符合题意。enable 的用法是 enable sb to do sth。

15. B。从其后一句"当你学会阅读观点和概念时,你不但会读得更快,而且阅读理解能力也会随之改进。"可知初学阅读时,要想达到理想的目的是要付出努力的。

16. A。参见15题。

17. C。此句中 their 指代的是句中所提到的 people,business managers 等。

18. B。take...for instance 意同 take...for example(举……为例)。

19. D。从文中所引用的数字来看,作者显然是想说明训练前和训练后阅读速度的变化。

20. D。get through(浏览),符合句意。

Cloze 4

1. C。从该句的下文"do you read it for the story or for the English?"可以推出作者说此话不是针对某个阅读对象的,用英语写的东西也不应限制在某个方面,而是泛指任何一种可能用英语写出的东西。因此,选项 C 应为正确答案。选项 B"essay"(小品文,短论);选项 D"survey"(概括,调查)。

2. B。so...as...为惯用语,意为"如此……以致"。该句意:"这个问题并不像看起来那么愚蠢。"

3. D。pay attention to 为词组,意为"注意,关注",符合题意。

4. A。afterward(以后,随后),符合题意。

5. D。phrase 意为"短语",符合题意。

6. D。how 在此句中引导了一个表示方式的介词宾语从句。

7. C。single 表示"一个"的意思时,语气比 one 或 a 更强。这里作者强调说某些读者读过小说后,居然竟一个句子也记不住。

8. B。此句中 after 与 before 相对应。

9. A。character 在此句中指故事中的"人物",符合题意。

10. A。该句首先对阅读方式予以肯定,enjoy 为褒义词,符合逻辑。

11. B。recommend(推荐);assume(假设)。

12. A。bother about(为某事而烦心);bring about(带来);concern about/for/over(关心,担心,挂念)。

13. B。be different from(与……不同),为固定词组。

14. B。what 在此句中引导一个介词宾语从句。

15. D。这里 gather 转意为"得出"。其他选项如用在此句中逻辑不通。

16. C。till(直到),符合题意。

17. D。were 在这里用作虚拟语气,由 as if 引导。

18. A。在此句开首使用了一个 positively(积极地,肯定地),恰好与 useful 相对应。

19. C。选项 C"Incidentally"(碰巧,意想不到地),符合题意。选项 A"Obviously"(明显地);选项 B"Briefly"(简要地,简单地);选项 D"Immediately"(立刻,马上),均不合题意。

20. B。learn by heart 为词组,意为"记住",相当于 keep in mind。

Cloze 5

1. A。the latter 指的是两者中的后者,因此符合题意。the later 的意思是"后来的",the latest 意为"最近的",均不符合句意。

2. D。从下文逆向推导可知,此处指的是语言发展的起源,因此选 D"origin"（起源,出身）符合题意。而 source（源泉）,beginning（开始）和 start（开端,开始）均不可用于指"起源"。

3. C。该句的意思是:动物能发出呼叫信号的声音来。serve as 为固定搭配,意思是"当作,用作"。

4. B。此句与上半句构成一种转折关系,动物的呼叫可用作信号,但高级动物猩猩尚未发现能发出单词的声音来,因此,选项 B 应为正确答案。

5. B。根据逻辑推理,even 在此处所起的作用是加强语气,意为"甚至";even if,even though 通常用于引导一个状语从句;even as 没有进一步说明之意。

6. A。necessity（必要之物）可用作可数名词,此处应用其单数形式。

7. C。该句意为人类出于不同的目的而增加了呼叫次数,因此选项 C 应为正确答案。

8. D。根据句子结构可知,when 在此句中引导一个表示时间的状语从句,而不是定语从句,因此应选择 D。

9. C。in this respect 的意思是"在这一方面",起着承接上句作用。with the respect 虽有此短语,但其意为"充满尊敬",句意不同。选项 B 和 D 均无此搭配。

10. A。could 在此句表示可能性。

11. B。in which 在此句中引导了一个宾语从句。

12. D。该句意为:人们在洞穴上做标记来表明他希望捕获什么。what 在句中引导了一个宾语从句,与前一句相并列,what 还同时担当该从句 catch 的宾语。

13. C。此句应使用现在完成时,表示动作的一种持续与完成的状态。

14. A。long before 意为"以前很久",not too long before 意为"不久就……",符合句意。

15. B。该句意是:农业是人类进步过程中所迈出的一步。此处 a step 与 progress 相对应,因此应选 B。

16. A。该句的意思是:直到机器时代。这一进步（农业）才是无可比拟的,因此选 until 符合句意。介词 to 虽有"到……"之意,但不强调持续性。

17. B。该句意为:此处 one 用于指所提及的诸多事物之一,而在本句中没有提及因其他的因素所造成的人口增长,故 A、C 和 D 项应予以排除。

18. B。上句中作者提到 in the regions,此处作者从 the regions' 这一概念出发对其进行具体的描述,与后面的 those 相对应,因此应选用 these,其他三个选项皆不合句意。

19. A。该句意为：在每次丰收之后，大自然便会使土壤肥沃。因此，选项 A 符合句意。选项 B、C、D 均不合句意。

20. D。该句意为：由于它提供的在物质方面的舒适，才使农业生活方式最终才得以流行起来。该填空引导的部分是一个名词性短语，因此选项 D 符合句意。

Exercise 2

Passage 1

1. was 改为 were。
   此句为虚拟语气，因此应为 were。

2. leave 改为 be left。
   此句的主语是 salt，是"物"，与动词之间的关系是被动的。因此，应为 be left。

3. 无错。

4. about 改为 from。
   range from...to... 为动词词组，也是固定搭配，意为"（范围）从……到……"，而不可与介词 about 一起连用。

5. open 前加 than。
   此句使用了形容词的比较级。因此应补入 than。

6. contain 改为 contains。
   contain 的主语为 the Dead Sea。因此，其动词应用单数第三人称。

7. part 改为 parts。
   通常 various 修饰名词时后跟名词的复数形式。

8. nine-tenth 改为 nine-tenths。
   分数的表示方法是：当分子等于1时，分母用单数形式；当分子大于1时，分母用复数形式。

9. 无错。

10. solves 改为 dissolves。
    solve 的意思是"解决"，如 solve problems；dissolve 的意思是"溶解"。根据句意可知，water 与 salt 之间的关系应是"水溶入盐"。

Passage 2

1. problem 改为 problems。

根据上文可知,要面对的问题不止一个。因此,此处 problem 必须要用复数形式。

2. evitable 改为 inevitable。

   该句意"这种使用方法并不意味着不可避免的环境恶化。"此句为双重否定句,表示肯定的意思。根据上下文逻辑,此句应对前面的观点表示肯定。

3. enjoy 改为 to enjoy。

   allow sb to do sth 为动词固定用法。

4. find 改为 found。

   陈述过去发生的事情,应该用过去式。

5. And 改为 Instead。

   此句所表达的意思,恰好与上文相反。

6. growth 改为 grew。

   as 为关系代词,引导状语从句。句中 growth 是名词,不能用作动词与 as 构成从句。

7. in 改为 to。

   to an extent 为惯用语,意为"在某种程度上"。

8. on 改为 in。

   指在某个方面时,应使用介词 in。

9. make 改为 to make。

   be 之后的动词不定时不能省略 to。

10. of 改为 toward/to。

    trend to/toward 为固定搭配,意为"趋向于"。

Passage 3

1. answer 改为 answers。

   根据上文 a few 和下文破折号后/前的 answers 可知,这里的答案决不止一个。因此应用复数形式。

2. in 改为 to。

   并列结构,与 apply to some writers 结构相并列。

3. of 改为 with。

   be concerned with 为固定搭配,意为"关系,与……有关"。

4. in 改为 on。

   put words on paper 为固定用法,意为"把字写在纸上"。

5. because of 改为 because。

because of 为介词短语,不能用于引导原因状语从句。

6. that 改为 why。

   修饰 reason 的定语从句应由 why 引导;that 引导同位语从句。

7. accepting 改为 accepted。

   accept 所修饰的词是 one's ideas and opinions,表示被动的意思,应用过去
   分词。

8. 无错。

9. a few 改为 a little。

   a few 用于修饰可数名词。此句 bluntly 应由可表示程度的 a little 来修饰。

10. 无错。

Passage 4

1. of 改为 for。

   pave the way for 为动词词组,是固定用法,意为"为……铺平道路"。

2. Per day 改为 Each day。

   通常每一天用 each day 来表达。each 强调个体,而 per 则多用于计量单位。
   如:3 miles per hour。

3. produce 改为 produces。

   此句谓语动词的主语是 world。因此,谓语动词应使用单数第三人称。

4. There are 改为 There is。

   此句中的主语是 supporting evidence 是单数的概念。因此,应使用 there be
   的单数表达形式。

5. /。

6. in 改为 to。

   access 之后应跟介词 to。

7. us 改为 ourselves。

   find oneself in 为固定用法,意为"发现自己已在(某个地方,某种状况)"。

8. /。

9. in 改为 on。

   be dependent on 为固定用法,意为"依靠,依赖"。

10. of 改为 for。

    此句中,for 所引导的是一个动词不定时的逻辑主语。

Passage 5

1. in 改为 on。

    on the basis of 为词组，意为"根据……"。

2. combining 改为 combined。

    此句中 combine 暗含着被动和完成的意思。因此应用过去分词。

3. past 改为 the past。

    the past 为形容词加定冠词的用法，意为"过去，过去的事"。其他具有同类
    用法的形容词还有 the old，the aged 等。

4. competitive 改为 competitiveness。

    代词所有格用于修饰名词。

5. The later 改为 Latter。

    the latter 意为两者之间的"后者"；later 为副词，意为"以后"，且不跟定冠
    词一起使用。根据上下文可知，此句主要谈论的是上文所提到的两件事的
    后者。因此，应用 latter。

6. 无错。

7. other than 改为 rather than。

    rather than 意为"而不是"；other than 意为"除了"。根据逻辑此句并不表
    示排除，而是对前文的否定。

8. 无错。

9. learn 改为 learning。

    by 为介词，其后应跟名词或动名词。

10. 无错。

Exercise 3

Passage 1

1. In the southwest.

    参见第三段第一句。

2. Because the sea winds blow inland from the west.

    参见第二段第二句。

3. Make them weak.

    参见第四段第一句。

4. Because of plentiful rainfall.

    参见最后一段第二句。

5. Firs timber.

    参见第五自然段第二、三句。

Passage 2

1. Human progress and poverty reduction.
   参见第一段第一句。
2. Poverty (reduction) and climate change.
   参见第二段。
3. Food insecurity and water shortage/stress.
   参见倒数第二段。
4. Education and research.
   参见最后一段。
5. Global warming, wars and political upheaval.
   参见最后一段最后一句。

Passage 3

1. telephone conversation distracts users from driving.
   参见第一段第二句。
2. To avoid traffic accident caused by distraction when drivers drive.
   参见第一段最后一句。
3. Because of greater possibility of traffic accidents caused by cellular phones.
   参见第一段第三句。
4. only the telephone numbers and specific control commands.
   参见第二段第二句。
5. A new hazard on the road.
   参见全文。

Passage 4

1. They are beautiful in design and shape.
   参见第一段第五句。
2. The violin has been modified to fit its evolving musical functions.
   参见第三段第二、三句。
3. They produced a dull and rather quiet tone/softer tones.
   参见第一段倒数第三句。
4. Since the early 1600's.
   参见第二段第二句。
5. Because of its tone and outstanding range of expressiveness.

参见第一段第六句。

Passage 5

1. To make up the shortage of imported European pottery.

   参见第一段第二句。

2. Simple and practical for kitchen use.

   参见第一段最后一句。

3. High temperature.

   参见第一段第一句。

4. By brown-glazing.

   参见第二段倒数第二句。

5. Because of particular affection among collectors and correspondingly high prices.

   参见最后一段最后一句。

第三部分

Test One

I Reading Comprehension

Section A   Passage Reading

1. C。本题为词意推导题。参阅第一段可知,由于信用卡所能提供的诸多方便,每个美国人都至少拥有一张信用卡。这就意味着,美国人使用现金交易的情况相对大大地减少,而使用信用卡的机会则人人有之。据此进一步推导可知,美国人之所以喜欢使用信用卡的原因应是信用卡所带来的方便以及使用信用卡的方便条件,所以"无现金社会"应该指 C 项包含的内容。

2. C。本题为细节题。参阅第一段第二句"They give their owners automatic credit in stores, restaurants and hotels, at home, across the country and even abroad and they make many banking services available as well." 选项 A、D 意思太绝对,任何人都不可能从银行想取多少钱就取多少钱,也不能在任何地方都能任意兑换现金,选项 B 文中未提及。

3. A。本题为细节推导题。第一段中说"无现金社会"不是 on the horizon,意即

不是远在天边的事,而是已经到来了,因此选项 A 应为正确答案。其他
选项均不符题意。

4. B。本题为词义推导题。文中谈到电子现金出纳机,其主要功能自然具有记
录销售金额的功能。

5. A。本题为主旨题。本文主要介绍信用卡的使用给人们带来了许多便利(参
阅第一段),而第二段第一句又说是电脑将这些方便带给销售商的。因
此,选项 A 符合题意,应为正确答案。

6. B。本题为标题主旨题。本文第一段对下世纪有关计算机报纸的情况作了
种种推测;第二段描述了技术的发展将使计算机报纸取代传统报纸;第
三段主要论述这一转变需要几十年的时间及其原因。文章的主旨是:将
出现计算机报纸。因此,选项 B 符合题意,应为正确答案。

7. C。本题为推导题。文章第二段段首说"Most of the technology is available
now, but convincing more people that they don't need paper to read a
newspaper is the next step.(想让人们相信他们不再需要借助于纸张来
读报是下一步的事。但来自新闻界的阻力会更大)"。第三段最后一句说
"It might take 30 to 40 years to complete the changeover because people
need to buy computers and because newspapers have established financial
interests in the paper industry.(这一转变需要三四十年时间的原因:一
是人们需要购买计算机,二是报纸在报业中奠定了经济利益的基础)"。
选项 C"general population"和"professional journalists"对实现计算机报
纸有很大的阻力。因此,应为正确答案。

8. A。本题为排除型试题。文章第一段第三句说"You'll get up and turn on the
computer newspaper just like switching on the TV.(早晨起床后,你打开
计算机报纸就会像打开电视一样方便)",与选项 B 句意一致。第一段
第四句说"An electronic voice will distribute stories about the latest
events, guided by a program that selects the type of news you want.(电
子声音会向你发送最新消息)",与选项 C 意思相符。第一段第八句说
"Save it in your own personal computer file if you like.(如果需要,可以
将新闻内容存入个人电脑文件中)",与选项 D 意思相符。而选项 A 计
算机报纸比传统报纸便宜,这与事实不符,更谈不上优点了,因此,应为
正确答案。

9. D。本试题为原因题。文章第二段第三句说"Since it is such a cultural
change, it may be that the present generation of journalists and
publishers will have to die off before the next generation realizes that the

newspaper industry is no longer a newspaper industry.（由于这是一个巨大的文化转变,所以,当这一代记者和发行者消失后,下一代人或许才会意识到报业再也不是报业了。)"由此可以推断出,现在的记者们所能做的只是为传统的报纸进行写作,因此,选项 D 符合题意,应为正确答案。

10. C。本试题为推导题。文章在第二段最后一句中说"Technology is making the end of traditional newspapers unavoidable.（科学技术正使传统报业的消亡成为必然)"。选项 A 则说所有的技术变化都是好的。这一点根据文章的内容是推导不出的。选项 B,所有的技术将最终取代旧技术,意思不明确。因为所有的技术与旧技术概念不清,不符合文章的意思。选项 D 说传统报纸的存在将会延长一个世纪,本文并没这个意思。选项 C"新技术最终将取代旧技术"的意思符合原文旨意,因此应为正确答案。

Section B　Banked Cloze

1. K。offer a price 意思是"报价"。

2. F。once 意为"一旦,一经,只要"。即一旦到了机场,一切都由操办人去处理。

3. A。根据上文可知,所有的活动均由专人为你排妥当,因为该旅游的性质是 Package holiday。

4. N。chance 在此句中的意思是"可能性"。

5. C。scheduled 意思是"计划的(停留)"。

6. L。根据上下文可知,这些观光安排只是为了举例说明这种性质的旅游特点。并非都是如此。

7. G。spend 意为"花(时间)"

8. O。excuse 意为"理由,借口",... have no reasonable excuse for getting away from 是一种典型的广告用语。

9. H。根据上下文可知,这里使用具体的实例来说明前者。

10. B。sit safely back 为词组,意思是"安适地静观"。

Section C　Reading Comprehension

1. Y。参见全文。

2. Y。参见第一段。

3. Y。参见第二段。

4. Y。参见第三、五、六段第一句。

5. NG。参见全文。

6. N。参见第七段。

7. NG。参见第八段第一、二句。

8. catastrophic fuel tank explosion because of lightning
   参见第二段第一句。

9. no damaging surges transients can reach them
   参见第四段。

10. extreme precautions to
    参见第五段。

II Comprehensive Test

Section A Cloze

1. A。launch 意为"发起,着手进行"。根据上文可知英国所举办的活动显然是一项常规性校园活动。对于一项活动来讲,要么是"开展",要么是"举办"或"发起",而不能一开始就"完成"(complete)或者是"去掉"(remove)等。

2. A。这里涉及到动词不定式和现在分词的用法问题。一般来讲动词不定式强调具体的动作,其一般时态通常用于指发生在谓语动词之后的动作,而现在分词则强调动作发生的时间与谓语动词同时性。这里 network 既然将被称作 TTNS,选项 A 符合题意,应是最佳选择。

3. D。这里 its 指代的是 network。

4. C。operated 意为"操作",符合题意。

5. B。根据后文 including section on careers 可以推知,此处应指有关方面的信息。因此,选项 B 应为正确答案。

6. B。此处 by 为"到某时之前"的意思。

7. B。根据前文 education,加上其后的 offer lessons on specific topics,可以得知,这里应指的是"具体课程专题",而非 tests 或 data。

8. C。The computer pages will he contributed by sources 与 local education authorities and industry and commerce。之间的关系为"总"与"分"的关系。

9. D。schools throughout the country 的意思是"全国各地的学校"。

10. A。这里 vital 意为"极其重要的"。这里用于强调教育、工业、商业等之间联系的重要性。education,net 均有重复之嫌。

11. A。从结构上讲 making them familiar with the new technology 与 helping young people... 为并列结构。

12. C。此处 across 意为"越过"的意思,符合题意。

13. B。required 为过去分词,表示被动的意思,即"被要求"。

14. C。这里使用的是 as...as... 结构。

15. D。phase 意为"阶段"。这段主要指事情发展的步骤或阶段。

16. D。这里 what 引导了一个介词宾语从句,并在该从句中起着一个主语的作用。

17. D。extend 意为"延伸",其后跟介词 to,即"延伸到……"。

18. C。在通常情况下,学生是在学校里学习的,有了计算机的帮助,学习地点就有可能改在家里了。

19. B。这里 although 引导了一个让步状语从句。

20. A。根据上句 although schools will continue to exist 及填空所在句中的 the same form as they have been 推知该句应使用将来时态。

Section B　Error Correction

1. with 改为 by。

   by 意为"凭借手段",相当于 by means of。

2. loyalty 后加 to。

   to 为介词,是 loyalty 所要求的。意思是"忠于……"。

3. furtherly 改为 further。

   该词本身就可用作副词。因此,不需要在其后加-ly。

4. important 改为 importantly。

   more importantly 为成语,意为"更为重要的是",在句中用作状语。

5. as well 改为 as well as。

   as well as 意为"和,以及",相当于 and;as well 表示此意时,必须与 and 一起连用:and...as well。

6. on 改为 to。

   该句中使用的动词是 adjust,其后应跟介词 to,为固定用法。

7. works 改为 work。

   works 的意思是"作品";work 意为"工作"时,为不可数名词。

8. 无错。

9. of 改为 as。

   see as 意为"视作",为固定用法。

10. to 改为 for。

    "为……做出牺牲"应为 sacrifice for。

Section C　Short Answer Questions

1. By mail.

参见第二段第一、二句。

2. Absentee ballots.

参见第二段第三句。

3. Provisional ballots.

参见第三段第四句。

4. The rules for counting provisional ballots.

参见第三段第五句。

5. Population.

参见最后一段第三、四句。

Test Two

I　Reading Comprehension

Section A　Passage Reading

1. C。本题为指代题。文章第四句指出"Music is important to us, but most of us can be considered consumers rather than producers of music. (音乐对我们来说非常重要,但我们大多数人应该被看作是音乐的消费者而非创作者)"。倒数第二句还指出"It is fairly common in Africa for there to be an ensemble of expert musicians surrounded by others who join in by clapping, singing, or somehow adding to the totality of musical sound. (以专业音乐家为核心,其他人拍手,唱歌或以其他方式汇入乐声)"。由此可见,我们大多数人是被动消极的观众而他们大多数人则是积极活跃的观众,这正是选项 C 的内容,故为答案。由此亦可排除选项 D。第四句指出"This is true, but Kasenta musicians recognize that not all people are equally capable of taking part in the music. ... and so the lines between the performing nucleus and the additional performers, active spectators, and passive½ spectators may be difficult to draw from our point of view. (我们大多数人应该被看作是音乐的消费者而非音乐的创作者)",单凭这句话得不出大多数非洲人是音乐创作者这一结论,所以选项 A 不正确;选项 B 与文章内容也不符。

2. B。本题为指代题。such 作为代词,在句中指代上文的整个句子,即:在音乐表演中,很容易分清谁是观众,谁是表演者。也就是说,观众就是不参与表演的旁观者,这正是 such 的意义,因此,应为正确答案。

3. B。本题为推导题。文章第一句指出"It has been thought and said that Africans are born with musical talent.（人们一直认为非洲人生来具有音乐天赋）"。文章最后四句指出,并非所有的(非洲)人都有同等能力参与音乐表演。一些人只能跟着鼓手唱,少部分人能击鼓,只有更少的人能随着歌舞吹奏长笛。以专业音乐家为核心,其他人击掌打拍子,歌唱或以其他方式汇入乐声。所以选项 B 与题意相符,应为正确答案。选项 A、C 和 D 均与上述内容不符。

4. C。本题为词意题。nucleus 意为"中心,核心"。本文中的 nucleus 指代的是上句中的 expert musicians surrounded by others who。因此,选项 C 应为正确答案。

5. D。本题为标题主旨题。全文主要围绕非洲人在音乐方面与我们大多数人不同的特点而写的,因此,选项 D 符合题意,应为答案。文章确实提及音乐对非洲人的重要性,但并不是全文的中心思想,因此,选项 A 不对。

6. A。本题为推导题。根据文中第一段的前五句话可知,战争已存在至少6千年,过去一直被认为是件坏事,是愚蠢的,但那时人类能与它并存。现代社会改变了这一点。要么是人类废除战争,要么是战争毁灭人类。由此可推断出,目前战争带给人类的东西要远比过去可怕。因此选项 A 应为正确答案。

7. B。本题为段落大意题。从文中第二段可知,作者对于某些人的看法——采用这样或那样的思想教育可以防止战争是个大错误(those who say that the adoption of this or that ideology would prevent war.)。因为他认为所有的思想体系都是建立在教条的陈述基础上的,而这些陈述是令人怀疑的,或者说是完全错误的。由此可见作者对这些思想意识是持否定态度的。因此选项 B 符合题意,应为正确答案。

8. D。本题为观点推导题。纵览全文不难看出作者的观点。人类要想生存下去,必须废除战争。文中更有类似的句子来表达这一观点。如第一段第六、七句话"For the present, it is nuclear weapons that cause the most serious danger, but bacteriological or chemical weapons may, before long, offer an even greater threat. If we succeed in abolishing nuclear weapons, our work will not be done.（若我们成功地废除了核武器,我们的工作还没有完成。我们的工作永远不会做完,直到我们成功地废除战争）"。再如文中最后一段最后一句话:"It has begun to be understood that the important conflict nowadays is not between different

countries, but between man and the atom bomb. (人们已经开始认识到，目前重要的冲突不是不同的国家之间的冲突，而是人和原子弹之间的冲突)。"因此，选项 D 应为正确选项。

9. D。本题为观点推导题。从文中第一段倒数一、二句话可知，为了做到这一点(消除战争)，我们需要说服人类以一种新的方式来看待国际问题。我们不要把它看作是以判断哪一方更会杀人为衡量胜利的标准的军事竞赛，而要根据已获批准的法律原则来进行仲裁。因此可看出，作者认为废除战争的惟一可行之法就是通过协商解决国际间的争端。因此选项 D 符合题意，应为正确选项。

10. B。本题为段落推导题。从文中最后一段不难看出这一点。此段第二句话告诉我们，核战争必须避免发生，对这一点人们已经达成共识。最后一句话说，人们已经开始认识到，目前重要的冲突不是发生在不同的国家之间而是人类和原子弹之间的冲突。因此可知，人类开始认识到核战争带给人类的危险。因此选项 B 应为正确选项。

Section B　Banked Cloze

1. F。help 意为"有助于"。

2. A。someone 在此句中用于泛指某人。

3. H。根据后文"因为他们会帮助你知道……"，可以得出一个结论，那并非一件坏事，所以应该原谅他们。

4. C。根据后文 love them back，前文显然应该是 If someone loves you，否则，就不会有 love them back 之说。

5. D。teaching 在此句中的意思是"教导"。

6. M。此处的 moments 与前半句的 every moment 相并列。

7. K。experience 意思是"经历"。

8. O。ago 虽然与 before 同义，但是 ago 所在句子的时态必须是过去时。

9. G。后文 for if you don't believe in yourself，显然是在承接前半句的话，需要保持前后一致。

10. I。此句为特殊结构，相当于 if 引导的条件句加主句。

Section C　Reading Comprehension

1. Y。参见全文。

2. Y。参见第一段。

3. Y。参见 I Regulatory or Legislative Approach。

4. N。参见第六段。

5. NG。参见全文。

6. N。参见第九、十一段。

7. N。参见倒数第五段。

8. another safeguard against management misconduct
   参见第五段。

9. the actual picture of a company
   参见第九段。

10. quality aspect of investment alternatives
    参见最后一段。

II Comprehensive Test

Section A Cloze

1. C。in order to 为短语,意为"为了……",用于引导表示目的的状语短语。

2. D。根据句意可知阅读的目的除了了解文章的大意、文章的结构和语气外,作者的写作意图也是一个重要的目的。虽然选项 A"anticipation"(预期),选项 B"implication"(内含)有可能是写作目的之一,但并不总是如此;选项 C"idea",与前一个 idea 重叠。因此,均不能为答案。

3. B。这里 locate 的意思是"找到",符合题意。

4. D。wonder over 为词组,意为"浏览",符合句意。

5. A。前文提到名字、日期等,这些信息都是非常具体的。与之相对应的应是一些不太具体的东西。因此,选项 A 符合题意,应为正确答案。

6. A。从逻辑上讲,这一句应该是对上文的一个总结。因此,应该选择 A。

7. B。definite 在此句中的意思是"明确的",即蕴含着明确的阅读能力。

8. D。since 为连接词,在句中起着一个解释和说明的作用。

9. D。该句意是:在阅读指定的文章时,这两种活动通常同时进行。句中 when 引导了一个现在分词短语。

10. C。文章谈论的主题是阅读。因此,worth reading 应与主题保持一致。

11. B。note down 意为"写下来,记下来",相当于 write down 或 put down。

12. C。前文讲到"前两个练习",在其后一句话的破折号中列出 exercise 3-10 由此可知,此句自然指的就是其后的练习。因此,选项 C 符合题意,应为正确答案。

13. D。build up,意为"建立(信心)",符合题意;give up 意为"放弃"。

14. A。prominent 意为"突出的、显眼的"。但凡要求学生学习点什么,自然要从好的读物或者是优秀的读物中学习。因此,选项 A 符合题意,应为正确答案。

15. B。从后文中所说的优秀的读者能够知道该读什么、不该读什么一句可以推知,不应该鼓励学生阅读全文。

16. C。这里 earlier 指的是早先/前面提到的东西。

17. A。参见第15题。

18. B。这里 left 为过去分词,意为"剩下的"。

19. C。text, article 和 question 均不存在是否 authentic 的问题。

20. A。本段落谈论的主题是 scanning,因此,前后应该保持一致。

Section B   Error Correction

1. considering 改为 considerable。

considerable 意为"相当大/多的,不可忽视的",此句部分的意思是"从……中可以获得大量的回报";considering 意为"鉴于,考虑",不符合题意。

2. 无错。

3. educating 改为 educated。

根据上下文推知,此句应使用现在完成时的被动语态,因此应使用 educate 的过去分词形式。

4. have 改为 has。

该句的逻辑主语是 the testimony,为单数,所以其谓语也应使用单数第三人称。

5. affect 改为 effect。

effect 为名词,contrary 是形容词,其后应跟名词;affect 为动词,不可以被形容词所修饰。

6. 无错。

7. to be expecting 改为 to be expected。

此处 to be expected 意为"预期",表示被动的意思,expect 应用过去分词形式。

8. sought to 改为 sought through。

这里 sought through 的意思是"通过",与后文的 other channels 相搭配,意为"通过其他渠道",符合句意。

9. maintained 改为 maintaining。

在此句中 maintain 表示的是主动的意思,因此应用-ing 形式。此外,maintain 与 forming 并列,必须使用同等结构。

10. exchange 改为 exchanges。

两者之间进行交换显然不能一次或由一方来单独完成。因此,exchange 必须要用复数形式。

Section C   Short Answer Questions

1. admit the fault and express the regret

   参见最后一段最后一句。

2. Our moral balance will be disturbed. / We will feel uneasy.

   参见第二、三段。

3. Something wrong with his conscience.

   参见第三段第一句。

4. To apologize for it right away.

   参见最后一段。

5. sending a check by post and asking his brother to forgive him

   参见第三段第二句。

Test Three

I   Reading Comprehension

Section A   Passage Reading

1. B。本题为段意推导题。文章的第一段看似与全文没有太大关系,实际上它正是全文的引子,又是全文的归纳。故事的主人公为了他人性命而与自我保护的本能相对抗,去接受那可能到来的死亡威胁。正是 B 项的意思。

2. C。本题为细节推导题。根据文章第二段第三句话"Aboard was Seol, a 25-year-old trainee for a tour company helping to bring South Korean tourists home from Beijing."便可知选项 C 是正确答案。

3. B。本题为细节推导题。文章第一段告诉我们:自我保全是生物最大的本能,危急情况下,人的本能即是逃避,而不是其他,Seol 的经历也在说明这一点,他先是逃开,后来又清醒了,意识到怎么回事后再去帮助别人。因此,正确答案为 B。

4. B。本题为排除题。根据文章最后一段可知,Seol 作为一位幸存者,也救助了其他几位乘客,由此可知,选项 B 符合题意,为正确答案。

5. D。本题为推测题。本文已经讲到了 Seol 活下来并救助了其他人,所以,下文不会再讲他幸存并救人的经历,根据文章首段含义,也可推知本文并不是讲述 Seol 在飞机失事后投诉航空公司或讲述他因救人而成为超人的那种感受,所以 D 最合理。

6. C。本题为段落推导题。根据第一句话后面的解释可知 conservation 不仅有

"保存、保护"的意思,本文还特别指出应从"节俭"的角度来认识它(To conserve is to save and protect, to leave what we ourselves enjoy in such good condition that other may also share the enjoyment.)。因此,正确答案应为选项 C。

7. D。本题为原因题。根据短文可知我们的祖先错误地认为资源是无限的,过去人们对于环境资源没有长远打算(Our forefathers had no idea that human population would increase faster than the supplies of raw materials; most of them, even until very recently, had the foolish idea that the treasures were "limitless" and "inexhaustible".)。如今,我们应改正这些错误认识,这也是我们认为节俭重要的原因所在。因此,正确答案应为选项 D。

8. B。本题为细节题。作者在第一段中叙述了50年代在研究如何合理利用土地时没有人研究长期气候循环产生的影响,这种做法是不正确的。因此,正确答案为选项 B。

9. B。本题为段落细节题。作者的目的在于论述 conservation 的重要性。在此领域中的基础知识如水位等与数学中的基本算术公式同样重要,因此,正确答案为选项 B。

10. D。本题为目的题。本文的中心意思是提醒大家共同保护我们有限的资源,尽量维护我们原有的美丽家园。因此,正确答案为 D。

Section B　Banked Cloze

1. N。香港作为一个大都市,其所拥有的人口通常是以百万论计的。因此,符合题意。

2. C。根据上下文可知,作为一个大都市,令人不愉快的景象和没完没了的问题是不可避免的。因此,此处应填 problem。

3. I。year after year 为固定用法,意思是"年复一年"。

4. E。根据其后文 the luxury of large flats 这里显然应该是说人们所喜欢的东西。因此,选填 enjoy 符合逻辑。

5. L。在 group who live in small and reasonable comfortable flats 句子中,该词的意思是"说得过去地"。即虽然公寓不太大,但却也说得过去,很舒适。

6. F。not...at all 为习语短语,意思是"一点也不,根本不"。

7. H。who 在句中引导了一个定语从句,修饰先行词 newcomer。

8. M。因为这种现象大多发生在发展中国家,而在发达国家却很少见。

9. J。该段的写作目的显然是为了与前文所描述的景象形成鲜明的对照。一方面是平民百姓所面对的尴尬情况,另一方面是政府官员高高在上地享用着舒适的环境。

10. K。ensure 意思是"保证,确保"。

Section C   Reading Comprehension

1. Y。参见一段及全文小标题。

2. N。参见第三段。

3. Y。参见第五段。

4. N。参见第十段(Engage staff)。

5. Y。参见第十一段。

6. Y。参见第十二段。

7. NG。参见全文。

8. cash-flow problems (because one or more customers are late paying)
   参见第六段。

9. all the operational details to make a difference
   参见第九段。

10. a kind of magic happens
    参见最后一段。

II   Comprehensive Test

Section A   Cloze

1. A。工厂面临燃料短缺显然是对工厂生存的一种威胁。因此,选项 A 符合题意,应为正确答案。

2. D。从上下文可知,一家石油公司的意外收获首先应该是"利润";而不是 glimpse 或者是 sakes 等。

3. D。drive prices up 意为"使得价格上涨"。其他的几个词均不可与 up 一起搭配使用。

4. C。文章先提到...companies will make more and more money,然后解释道到前者是一种 windfall profits,而且获得这些意外的利润是 without doing a thing to earn the extra cash。所以,earn money,earn cash 都是可以的。因此,选项 C 符合题意,应为正确答案。

5. B。从逻辑的角度讲 profit made because of luck,一语在句中所起的作用是解释说明 sudden unearned profits。因此,选项 B 符合题意,应为正确答案。

6. B。词组 blow up 意为"吹起",符合题意。blow down 的意思是"吹掉";blow

off；blow away"吹走"。因此，选项 B 符合题意，应为正确答案。

7. D。此文是以英国为背景而写的，这一点在第二段第一句中点明。

8. C。该句中 much of the land 与 a few of batons 形成对照，旨在说明那时的土地主要集中在少数人的手中。因此，选项 C 符合题意，应为正确答案。

9. C。however 在此句中表示转折。

10. A。hunting deer 意为"捕猎鹿"。

11. C。此句中 when 引导了一个修饰时间的定语从句。

12. A。该句的意思是：违反行为会受到严厉的惩罚。既然是"违反行为"，而且还要受到"严厉的……"，结果予以惩罚是顺理成章的事。此句实际上也是上一句话的进一步推展：法律效力的具体体现的重要表现之一就是惩罚。因此，选项 A 应为正确答案。选项 B"diverse"意为"不同的"；选项 C"neglect"意为"疏忽"，均不合题意。

13. B。此句中 if 引导了一个条件状语从句。

14. D。这里 that 指的是上文中所提到的事。因此，选项 D 符合题意，应为正确答案。

15. B。by accident 为词组，意思是"偶然"，与 by luck 形成对照。

16. C。这一段主要回顾以前英格兰普通老百姓的生活状况。因此，old 在这里主要用于指旧时代的英格兰。因此，选项 C 符合题意，应为正确答案。

17. D。该句话的意思是：如今批评家抱怨石油公司也在祈求诸如此类的事——某些政治或者是军事方面的动荡是会促成一些意外的收获——石油价格的上涨和增加利润。从语气上可以明显地感受到批评家对那些人的这种心态强烈不满。因此 complain 适合此语境。

18. A。参见第17题。

19. B。空格19之后的介词 on 是 tax 所要求的。

20. A。most 在此句中这里用作程度副词，意思是"很，非常"。因此，选项 A 应为正确答案。

Section B　Error Correction

1. on 改为 at。

   students at this level 的意思是"在这个层次的学生"。介词 at 常用于指程度、比例、时间、地点等的一个具体的点。

2. 去掉 an。

   这里 an 是多余的，应去掉。half 在 half of all the overseas students 的短语中用作名词，表示部分与整体的关系。

3. case 改为 cases。

尽管 few 在数量上表示否定的意思,但是被该词修饰的名词一定要用复数形式。

4. 无错。

5. opened 改为 open。

open 在此句中的词性是形容词,用作主语补足语。

6. 无错。

were 为系动词的虚拟语气表达形式。根据上下文可以推知学校里某些课程是不可能不开的,因为如果不开课,就会造成人力资源的浪费,于事无补。

7. off 改为 with。

cope with 相当于 deal with successfully,为固定搭配。

8. lay off 改为 laid off。

lay off 意为"下岗"。lay 的过去式和过去分词均是 laid,而 lie 的过去式和过去分词才是 lay,lain。

9. so so 改为 so forth。

and so forth 相当于 and so on,意为"等等"。

10. 无错。

Section C   Short Answer Questions

1. limited knowledge of English.

参见第一段倒数第三句和最后一句。

2. Asian culture and the American educational system.

参见第二段第一句。

3. Because they had no right to citizenship then.

参见最后一段最后一句。

4. Concern a lot of their homework.

参见第二段第二句。

5. Because they worried to be isolated from American society in general.

参见最后一段第一句。

Test Four

I   Reading Comprehension

Section A   Passage Reading

1. A。本题为排除题。首先应注意的问题是 not true,由第二段第一句话 It is

often..., but...中的关键词 but 构成转折,表示后面所表述的意思与前面的不同。因此,选项 A 的内容是错误的,选项 B 内容正确,选项 C 所表述的意思可从第二段第二句可找到,选项 D 的意思可从第一段第二句找到。

2. D。本题为细节题。第二段第一句"Its ancestors can be found...hundreds of years ago""hundreds of years ago"的意思是数百年以前,而并非一百年以前。而 Jules Verne and H. G. Wells 写的科幻小说是在过去一百年里写的,因此,选项 A、B 和 C 均不正确。

3. D。本题为细节题。由第四段可知,现代科幻小说家对科学技术的发展,对人类思想和社会的影响感兴趣。根据第四段中第一句的意思可以断定选项 A 是错误的,根据 reflection of the world which we live in now 可以得知选项 B 中 ideal 是错误的。选项 C 中 have nothing in common with our present society 意思与原文不符。

4. B。本题为细节题。最后一段的第一句应译为"在科学经常把科幻小说变成现实的时代",其中 keep ahead of scientific advance 是句中的关键词,意为"科幻小说家感到很难站在科技发展的前沿",即科学技术的发展比科幻小说家想象的快得多,因此,选项 B 符合题意,应为正确答案。

5. C。本题为排除题。选项 A 的参考依据在最后一段第二句,选项 B 的意思与原文的意思相符,选项 C 中 No one...是错误的,因为并不是没有人知道怎样处理我们将要面对的问题。据最后一段的最后一句...changing view of the world 可知选项 D 的意思与原文相符,是正确的。

6. B。本题为目的推导题。这篇短文主要围绕着公民权这个概念展开,比较了有关公民权的不同概念。(首先文章从17和18世纪的民主公民权与古希腊的民主公民权的实质性的不同说起。紧接着又论述了公民权发展史上表现出来的两个不同方向。最后论述了公民权范围内政府作为推动人民幸福的工具应当起多大作用。)其目的显然是通过陈述"不同性"、"不同方向"和"作用",客观地比较对照不同的公民权的观点。因此,选项 B 符合题意,应为正确答案。选项 A、C 和 D 所涵盖的面太偏,且均不是文章的主要写作目的。

7. D。本题为推导题。polls 一词使用在古希腊的民主政治中的一个术语。古希腊人的民主公民权是围绕着参与集体议政展开的,他们不像近代人那样看重个人利益,强调政府干预越少越好。因此,由此可以推出它的意义是"政治团体"。

8. A。本题为原因题。相关内容见文章最后一段。在民主公民权的概念中,对于政府作为推动人民幸福的工具应当起多大作用存在着争论。文章引用了政府哲学家 Martin Diamond 关于民主看法的两种分类,指出了这种观点上的分歧确实存在,即使是在今天,这种争论也更加明显。

9. D。本题为细节推导题。文章在一开始就提出了17和18世纪公民权差异首先表现在公民的私有权方面(The liberal view of democratic citizenship that developed in the 17th and 18th centuries was fundamentally different from that of the classical Greeks.)。近代的观点认为政府应当尽可能少地干涉私人利益。第二段中提出,公民权的发展经历了两个方向,其一是扩大社会成员行使公民权的人数,特别是扩大投票人的资格,其二是扩大政府合法行为的范畴(Over time, the liberal democratic notion of citizenship developed in two directions. First, there was a movement to increase the proportion of members of society who were qualified to participate as citizens... Second there was a broadening of the legitimate activities of government and a use of governmental power to redress imbalances in social and economic life.)。由此可见,前三个选项均是文中所提及的内容。选项D"the size of the geographical area controlled by a government"未在文中提及。因此,正确答案应为选项 D。

10. C。本题为细节推导题。文章最后一段的结尾部分谈到 Martin Diamond 提出两种关于民主的观点,其一是"自由主义者",他们强调个人对幸福的追逐,主张有必要对政府进行限制,对个人自由主义者进行保护。而"多数派"的观点则强调政府的任务是帮助普通人不受富人的侵害。选项 C "provide greater protection for consumers"符合多数派的主张,为正确答案。

Section B   Banked Cloze

1. B。course 在此句中指河流的"航道"。

2. O。河流只有两个岸边,由于句中的河岸 bank 用的是单数,可见这里所指的河岸必定是某一侧的河岸。

3. D。lose oneself in 为成语,意味"消失在……之中",符合题意。

4. F。根据后文的描述,眼前的这一片景象显然是一种非常原始的景象。因此,应该选填该词。

5. G。about 为"到处,四处"的意思。

6. K。这里 that 引导了一个从句。实际上,that 也是 except 所要求的,即 except that(除了)。

7. J。neither ... nor 为一组关联词,表示两者都不的意思。

8. C。on 指"在……表面上"。

9. E。从后半句 and forms again in another place 来推导，尼罗河每逢小岛便分成支流，随后又在另一个地方汇合在一起。

10. I。此空格前的动词词组 go on 说明这一大自然的行为的持续不断性。因此 forever 在此处为最恰当的选词。

Section C Reading Comprehension

1. Y。参见第一段第一句。

2. N。参见第四段第一句。

3. Y。参见第五段。

4. N。参见第二段。

5. NG。参见全文。

6. N。参见第六段。

7. Y。参见第七段。

8. a king or a home-grown aristocracy
参见第九段第一、二句。

9. in the country's successes
参见第十段。

10. high-tech/the best in the world
参见第十二段。

II Comprehensive Test

Section A Cloze

1. B。该句意：根据 Karl U Smith 教授的观点几乎我们所人要么习惯用左侧脸做表情，要么惯用右侧脸做表情，两者必取其一。句中作者只用了两个表示肯定意思的词，一个是 all，另一个是 almost，以强调肯定的观点。此外，紧随其后的一句话，从作用上讲是对前一句的推展，进一步加强了他的观点。因此，选项 B 符合句意，应为正确答案。

2. C。这里 common 意为"普遍的"。这里"左脸"、"右脸"之说是对一种现象的观察结果，而非主观的某种意愿。因此，选项 C 符合题意，应为正确答案。

3. A。从下一句中所列举的人名可以反推出用"右侧脸"做表情的人大多是在音乐方面具有才分的人。

4. D。实际上该句与下一句之间的关系是一个并列的关系。从逻辑的角度来看两句话中分别所提出的内容是分层递进。因此，选项 D 符合题意，应为正确答案。

5. A。该句为倒装句,其主语是 the vast majority of...,是复数。

6. D。performers 意为"演奏者",符合题意。

7. A。emerge...from 意为"从……出现"。其他的单词不能与介词 from 一起连用。

8. C。while 的意思是"当……时候",强调由该词所引导的从句的动作与主句的动作同时发生。即用计算机研究人们在谈话时,唇、舌头与下颌的运动。

9. B。found 为 find 的过去时;founded 则是 found(创建)的过去时。

10. B。这里 recognized 的意思是"辨识出";signal 的意思是"发信号";mature 意为"使成熟";limit 意为"限制"。

11. B。这里 compress 的意思是"眉眼与下颌之间的挤皱"。其他选项均不合题意。

12. C。tend to 意为"往往,趋向于"。即上述情况常常是这样的,而非已经证明了的事。

13. A。人的脸部上的皱纹通常是呈现在表面上的,所以应该选择 A。

14. D。range from... 指"从……到……"的一个范围,与其后的介词 to... 相衔接。

15. C。由于基因的原因,通常单卵双胞胎的外貌会长得一模一样。因此,选项 C 应为正确答案。

16. D。facedness 是本文的谈论主题,也是该段落的谈论主题。这一点从后文中可以得到证实。

17. A。参见第 16 题。

18. C。be specialized for 意思是"专长于",为固定搭配。separate 则与介词 from 一起连用;reveal 为及物动词,意为"揭示,揭露"。

19. B。the left hemisphere for language 的意思是"大脑左半球的作用主语言。"选项 A 与 musical performance 有重叠之嫌;symmetry 意为"对称",不合题意。

20. D。to 为介词,是名词 approaches 所要求。

Section B   Error Correction

1. to 改为 for。
   此句中 for 用于引导动词不定式的逻辑主语,其结构为:for sb to do sth。

2. received 改为 receiving。
   此句中使用的是现在进行时,而非被动语态。

3. there is 改为 there are。

此句中 there be 的主语是 severe limits 为复数。因此,be 应是用复数形式。

4. 无错。

5. In best 改为 At best。

at best 意为"充其量",是成语。其他类似用法还有:at least, at most 等。

6. such like 改为 such as。

such as 通常用于列举事例,是固定搭配,不可以与 like 连用,但 like 在非正式表达中也可以单独使用,意同 such as。

7. provide 改为 providing。

这里 providing 为现在分词,起着一个进一步解释说明的作用。

8. scholarship 改为 scholarships。

scholarship 为可数名词。此外,但凡要增加奖学金的分配,就意味着不止提供一个奖学金。

9. 无错。

10. in where 改为 where。

此句中 where 引导一个定语从句,修饰 nations。where 相当于 in which,其前面不加介词 in。

Section C   Short Answer Questions

1. Collecting nest-building materials

参见第一段第三句。

2. It will last throughout and even after the mating cycle.

参见第一段倒数第二句。

3. Instinctive ability, adaptability in site selection and use of materials.

参见第二段第一句。

4. Break down the branch to make it hang upside down purposefully.

参见第三段第二句。

5. To show the birds' remarkable behavior in collecting building materials.

参见最后一段第一句。

Test Five

I   Reading Comprehension

Section A   Passage Reading

1. A。本题为指代题。参见第二段第八句。该句的意思是新的原则是大学要去创造和传播知识,这要求一个由学者组成的教师群体。很显然,从上下文可知 this 指代的是 create knowledge as well as pass it on。

2. D。本题为推导题。参见第二段最后一句:With the establishment of the seminar system, graduate students learned to question, analyze, and conduct their own research. 该句对讨论课体制的作用进行了说明。即学生能够提出问题,分析问题并自己去作研究。因此,正确答案应为选项 D。

3. A。本题为排除题。根据第二段第七句"Professors were hired for their knowledge of a subject, not because they were of the proper faith and had a strong arm for disciplining students"可以推出以前的大学看中的是教授的信仰和是否对学生严格。根据第二段第九句"Drilling and learning by rote were replaced by the German method of lecturing..."可以推断出以前大学的特点是 drilling and learning by rote(灌输和死记硬背)。所以选项 B、C 和 D 都是1850年前大学的特点。而第三段第二句表明是哈佛大学校长首先推行了选课系统。因此,选项 A 符合题意,应为正确答案。

4. C。本题为推测题。最后一段倒数第二句表明新型的大学密切关注社会的实际需求,以学生适应将来作为目标。因此,选项 C 符合题意,应为正确答案。选项 A 和 B 是1850年前大学的特点。选项 D 的意思和文中原意相反。根据最后一段,应是学生自己选择选修课。

5. B。本题为主旨题。全文主要叙述的是受德国大学影响,美国新型大学的兴起和迅速发展,以及其特点。选项 A、C、和 D 都是文章的细节和分论点。

6. C。本题为细节题。本文的第一段和以后的几段都谈到了由于司机的不礼貌、不体谅人的行为引起交通事故,所以选项 C 应为正确答案,因为选项 A、B 和 D 都不是引起交通事故的主要原因。

7. D。本题为句意推导题。"You might tolerate the odd road-dog...the rule"一句意同选项 D"现今不礼貌的司机占大多数"。选项 A"我们的社会对礼貌的司机不公"和选项 C"有礼貌的司机不容忍没礼貌的司机"与原文无关;选项 B 的意思与原文相反,均不可为正确答案。

8. A。本题为词意推导题。本文第二段谈到,司机在遇到不文明的行为时,只有头脑冷静,脾气温和才能抵制进行报复的诱惑。另一方面,礼貌可以缓和开车时的紧张气氛。所以,good sense 指司机不仅自己要有礼貌,而且对别人的礼貌也要做出反应,这与选项 A"司机的正确理解能力和理智地做出反应的能力"的意思相符。选项 B"司机对困难和严重情况的迅速反应",原文中没有提到;选项 C 和 D 的意思涵盖不全,不可作为正确答案。

9. B。本题为细节题。专家很久之前就指出,面对汽车拥有量的爆炸,应该互相照顾。选项 B"司机应时刻想到彼此让步"的意思与之相吻合,应为正确答案;选项 A"道路使用者做出更多的牺牲"与原文内容不符;选项 C "司机彼此之间应有更多的交流"和选项 D"若司机不能彼此尊敬,他们会有很大损失"都不是专家提到的内容。

10. B。本题为观点推导题。根据第三段"However, misplaced politeness can also be dangerous.(然而,不适当的礼貌也可能是危险的)",说明司机不仅要有礼貌,而且礼貌行为要适时、得当。否则,有可能会产生危险的后果。因此,选项 B 符合题意,应为正确答案。选项 A、C 和 D 不符合题意。

Section B   Banked Cloze

1. B。one in every eight 的意思是"每八个中就有一个",为习惯表达语。

2. D。该句的后半部分实际上是进一步解释说明前半句 Metropolitan areas have grown explosively in the past decade(爆炸式地增长)的意思的。

3. E。此句是承接上文而来。

4. G。one 是"……之一的意思"。

5. H。shopping center 是"购物中心"的意思。

6. I。expansion 意思是"扩张,扩展"。即城市在不断地向周边郊区扩展。

7. J。nation 虽然意指国家,但却侧重该国家的"人民"。如果强调一个国家的政体,则多用 state。

8. C。东部沿岸实际上是一个地区。因此,此处应该选填该词。

9. K。在沿岸应用介词 on。

10. L。as 是动词 regard 所要求的。

Section C   Reading Comprehension

1. Y。参见第一段第一句。

2. Y。参见第二段。

3. Y。参见第四段。

4. N。参见第五段。

5. N。参见第六段第三、四句。

6. NG。参见全文。

7. N。参见第九段。

8. for the deaf

参见第十段。

9. during an audio teleconference

参见第十一段。

10. an audio conversation

参见第十一段。

II Comprehensive Test

Section A Cloze

1. D。本题主要测试由动词 bring 所构成的词组。bring about 意为"产生"；bring up"培养,养大"；bring forward"提出"；bring out"使出现,公布,出版"。

2. A。该题为词意题。preceding 意为"先前的,前面的"符合句意；proceeding "进行的"；processing"加工的"；presenting"呈现的"。

3. A。run its course 为词组,意为"自然地发展,经历其发展过程"。

4. B。novelties 的意思相当于 previously unknown thing, idea, etc.; sth. strange or unfamiliar（新奇的事物、观念；奇怪或不成熟的事物）；equipment"设备"；technique"技术,方法"。

5. D。machinery 为"机器,机械"的总称；device,主要用于指装置,设备,仪表,方法等；facility"（复数）设施",常指电话、图书馆、邮局等公用设施。appliance"用具,器具"。如：home appliances"家用电器"。

6. B。选项 Further 意为"进一步"。

7. A。结构搭配题。improvement in sth. 意为"在……方面改进"。如：There has been improvement in the weather. 注意：improvement on sth. 的意为"对……是一大改进；对……的改造"。

8. B。available to 意为"可得到的"；accessible"易接近的,能进去的；可以理解的"常与介词 to 一起连用；adaptable"善于适应环境的,适应性强的"；additional"附加的,另外的,更多的"。

9. C。include 意为"包括"；exclude"排除"；conclude"得出,结论"；comprise"包含,由……组成"。根据题意选项 C 应为正确答案。

10. A。enliven 的意思相当于 make sb/sth more lively and cheerful（使更活跃或更愉快）,符合句意；enrich"使丰富"；enhance"增进,促进"；enlighten"启迪,启发,启蒙,教导"。

11. C。but 在此处表示语气转折,符合题意。

12. C。accelerated 意为"加速",相当于 speed up,而 step up 则相当于 increase,

accelerate"增加,提高,加速"。

13. D。step up 意为"增加,加速";make up"编造,构成;弥补;化妆";turn up"开大",如:turn up the radio。

14. A。conflict 意为"冲突"。此处意指"第二次世界大战"。

15. D。explosion 意为"爆炸,突然增加",如:real explosion of technology"技术的真正大发展"。

16. C。本题主要测试词义的搭配。introduce sth to sb 的意思是"把……介绍给某人"。

17. C。本题主要测试同义搭配。mixed blessing 意为"悲喜交集的事情"。

18. D。alter 的意思是"(部分地)改变,修改";differ 与介词 from 搭配使用,意为"与……不同";differ...in...指"在……方面不同";alternate (with)"与……交替";vary 相当于 be different (from)"与……不同"。

19. B。in short 的意思是"总之"为特征词。在此句中起着总结归纳的作用;in particular"特别是";in consequence"因此";in the end"最终",符合题意。

20. B。本句中 but 表示语气转折。故应选 challenging 以与 more productive, safer and more agreeable 形成对照。

Section B Error Correction

1. respectful 改为 respect。

   have respect for 为固定用法,意为"尊重……;对……给予尊重"。respectful 意为"尊重的"。

2. weather 改为 climate。

   climate 意为"气候,气氛",在此句中取第二层意思;weather 意为"天气"。

3. organization 改为 organizations。

   该词的意思是"组织机构"。从下文由 such as 引导的列举可以判断,这里所指的组织机构决不止一个,而是诸多之一。因此,应用复数形式。

4. to 改为 into。

   给介词是动词 enlist 所要求的。enlist sb into...意为"征募某人加入某组织"等固定搭配。

5. mathematic 改为 mathematics。

   mathematics 意为"数学"。该词虽以-s 结尾,但是仍是单数名词。具有这种特点的同类的学科名称还有:physics, statistics 等。

6. 无错。

7. moves 改为 move。

   虽然 move 的主语为 who,但是其先行词却是 educators。因此,应用复数形式。

8. staffs 改为 staff。

该词为集合名词,单复数同型。

9. 无错。

10. 无错。

Section C   Short Answer Questions

1. he wanted to make his dreams come true

参见第一段第三句。

2. By boat first and then by canoe.

参见第一段第四句。

3. The Italian Constantino Beltrami.

参见第一段第六句。

4. Because he had no compass then.

参见第一段第七句。

5. The History of the Mississippi.

参见全文。

Test Six

I   Reading Comprehension

Section A   Passage Reading

1. B。该题为细节推导题。告诫人们申请"进口救济"会影响企业,常带来意想不到的后果。这回答了"文章主要涉及到什么?"的问题。文章第一段只讲了"投诉"情况。第二段涉及文章实质性问题:"进口救济"对公司的作用伤害多于帮助(第二段第二句)。随着大公司展开全球性业务……救济法不一定能满足同一公司下所有单位的战略需要。第三段进一步论证这一点:国际化增加了外国公司利用进口救济法来对付法律力图保护的本国公司。最后一段举实例证明这一点。所以选项 A 反对美国公司国际化的争论;选项 C 论证的是外企从他们政府接受的津贴多于美国公司从本国政府接受的津贴;选项 D 鼓吹行业限制倾销产品。三项意思都不正确。

2. D。该题为推导题。公司受到进口商品伤害,要求进口救济。这在文章第一段最后一句话"只要工业受到进口伤害这样一个简单的声明就有足够的理由寻求救济。(Even when no unfair practices are alleged, the simple

claim that an industry has been injured by imports is sufficient grounds to seek relief.)所以选项 D 回答第二题的提问"向国际贸易委员会提出申诉的最小理由是哪一项？"选项 A 外国竞争对手从外国政府接受津贴。选项 B 外国竞争对手增加运入美国的商品量；选项 C 外国竞争对手在美国以低于市场价卖产品。三项都和问题无关。

3. A。该题为段落分析题。最后一段引用了一个实例来证明在上一段中所述的问题。文章在最后一段中引用一个实例，以证明第二段中所述的"公司的国际化会使外国公司可能利用进口救济法来对付法律想要保护的（本国）公司"。所以下边三个选项都和问题无关。（选项 B 介绍了上面没有提及的另一关注领域。选项 C 讨论了一个特别事件，并没有达到作者预期的结果。选项 D 提出基于上述证据的推荐书。）

4. D。该题为推导题。能帮助同一母公司下的某一个单位的美国法律制度不一定就能帮助公司的其他单位。这在第二段最后一句话："这些关系错综复杂，救济法不一定能满足同一母公司下所有单位的战略要求。"(The complexity of these relationships makes it unlikely that a system of import relief laws will meet the strategic needs of all the units under the same parent company.)回答了第四题的提问"下面有关美国贸易法哪一项可能是正确的？"而选项 A,B,C 的内容文内根本没涉及。

5. C。该题为细节题。该选项确实帮助了寻求进口救济的公司。这在第二段第一句话"和一般的印象正相反，这种进口救济对公司伤害多于帮助。"中(Contrary to the general impression, this quest for import relief has hurt more companies than it has helped.)回答了本题所问的"根据文章所述，普遍认为国际贸易委员会的进口救济具有（什么作用）"的问题。选项 A、B 和 D 这三项内容，文内没有涉及。

6. A。本题为原因题。选项 A 与第一段第一句话意思相符。根据第一段第二句，大多数没有小孩的贫困家庭被排除在这些福利规定之外，而不是选项 B 中所说的"未获得足够的资助"。选项 C 和 D 的解决方案是批评家提出的。因此，不是正确答案。

7. B。本题为细节题。作者在第二段第一句明确地指出了婚姻稳定的决定因素：与实现家庭消费与支出平衡的成本有关，而其他选项内容与之不相关。因此，选项 B 符合题意，为正确答案。

8. B。本题为排除题。作者在第一段后半部分中提出了影响婚姻家庭稳定的因素。而选项 A、C 和 D 均有提到。

9. D。本题为细节推导题。根据第一段"The formation, maintenance, and

dissolution of the family are in large part a function of the relative balance between the benefits and costs of marriage as seen by the individual members of the marriage"得知，作者认为婚姻家庭的稳定与婚姻的获益和成本间的平衡有关。而最后一段末句指出公共福利的资助既降低了婚姻的获益，也减少了其解体的成本。因而导致了由于福利而引起的婚姻的不稳定。因此，选项 D 符合题意，应为正确答案。选项 A 的意思不明确，只是说 agreement，而文中指出的是 agreement on family consumption and production，选项 B 与文章观点相悖，而选项 C 的意思则过于绝对。因此，均不可为正确答案。

10. B。本题为语气判断题。作者理性客观地分析了造成家庭婚姻解体的诸多因素。选项 B 的内容与文章的主旨相吻合，因此，应为正确答案。

Section B　Banked Cloze

1. H。根据前半句 English colonists got on well together，所以"共有相同的独立精神"，是顺理成章的事，符合逻辑。

2. C。side by side 为成语，意思是"肩并肩"。

3. K。根据后半句意思可知此句主要谈的是当时的人口问题。

4. D。thanks to 意思是"由于"，引导此句的目的是用于说明发展之快的原因。

5. E。根据本句开首的 However 一词可知，这一现状不会持续太久。该词在此句中用作系动词，意为"保持"。

6. F。是以"华盛顿"的名字命名的。这里 after their great leader 指的就是其半句中所提到的 Washington。

7. I。这里 world 指的是"西方世界"。

8. J。根据后文 copper, stainless steel, concrete and glass 可知，这些东西都是用于建筑的材料。

9. L。beauty 意指"美色"。

10. M。指在林肯中心(at the Lincoln Center)演出的音乐会、歌剧和芭蕾舞(the concerts, opera and ballet)。

Section C　Reading Comprehension

1. Y。参见全文。

2. Y。参见第三段。

3. Y。参见第四、五段。

4. NG。参见第四段。

5. NG。参见全文。

6. Y。参见第九段。

7. Y。参见第十段。

8. domestic credit or debit cards
   参见第十三段。

9. incontinence and high cost
   参见第十四段。

10. land line：www. speedypin. com
    参见第十五段。

II   Comprehensive Test

Section A   Cloze

1. D。上一句讲的是支票如何作为一种交换手段而备受欢迎,随后就此句话进行进一步推展。从逻辑的角度讲,此处指"支票对买卖双方均很方便",因此正确答案为选项 D。其他选项词 complicated"复杂的";trivial"琐碎的,无足轻重的";bearable"可忍受的",均不合题意。

2. A。valueless 的意思是"无价值的"。从上下文看,支票不是真正的钱,因为支票本身是无价值的。invaluable"无法估计的,非常宝贵的",不符合上下文逻辑。

3. C。本题测试惯用搭配。run a risk 是固定搭配词组,意为"冒风险"。

4. A。本题测试惯用搭配。within one's rights 的意思是"有权……,在某人的权限内"。

5. C。on occasion 意为"偶尔"。根据上下文逻辑选项 C 应为正确答案。因为"当店主接受支票时,他总是要冒点的风险。因此,如果他偶尔拒绝收支票,也是完全有权这样做的。" in general"一般来说";at the least"至少";in short"总之",均不合题意。

6. D。call sth in question 为惯用语,意思是"对……表示怀疑",相当于 raise doubt about sth。in earnest 意为"认真地",不符合题意。

7. B。have an extremely unpleasant experience 意为"有一次非常不愉快的经历";accident 意为"事故";event"重大事件";incident"事件,事变,附带的事",如：border incident(边界事件)。相比之下 experience 最适合上下文的语境。因此,为正确答案。

8. B。keep a large stock of 的意思是"备有大量……的现货供应"。这里 stock 指的是商店里供出售的现货。a large store of sth 指"大量贮藏某物"。根据题意,此处是指商店。商店不是仓库,商店的现货是供出售的,而不是储存的。因此,如在此句选 store 不合题意。a number of 之后接可数名词复数。此处如选择 number 虽不算错,但不是最佳答案。an amount of 后接单数形式的不可数名词。

9. D。本题主要测试结构型词义搭配。decide 后可接动词不定式,而 consider 之后接动名词。如:consider changing one's plan。如果 consider 后接不定式,则必须与连接代词或连接副词一起连用。如:consider how to change the plan。think 和 conceive 在语法结构上均不合适。

10. A。pay by check 为惯用搭配,意为"用支票支付";pay in cash 或 pay cash 意为"付现金"。

11. A。be in order 为惯用搭配,在此句中的意思是"合适、恰当、符合规定"。另如:Is your passport in order?(你的护照符合规定吗?);in need 意为"在逆境中"。如:A friend in need is a friend indeed. (患难之交才是真正的朋友。);in use"在使用",其反义词是 out of use"(现在)不使用";in common"共同的"。

12. C。exactly 的意思是"正确地,完全地",相当于 correctly,quite;extremely 意为"极度地,极端地"如用在本句,有言过其实的感觉;largely"主要地";mostly"主要地"。均不合题意。

13. D。worthless 的意思是"毫无价值的",符合题意。

14. B。at any moment 意为"即刻,随时"。

15. D。unless 意为"除非,如果不",用于连接反意条件句。

16. B。sure enough 的意思是"果然,果然不出所料",符合上下文的逻辑。really (真正地,实在),但该词放在句首,作插入语并用逗号分开时,意为"确实,实际上";certainly 放在句首,并用逗号分开用作插入语时,一般用于问答句中,意为"当然"。注意:在选择承上启下的过渡词时,必须纵览上下文。切勿断章取义。

17. C。inconvenience 意为"不便,麻烦";treatment"对待,处理";manner"(做事情的)方式,方法";behavior"举止,品行,行为"。根据题意选 C 应为正确答案。本句译文:由于给我的朋友带来麻烦,他们向他表示歉意,并请他抄写那个诈骗犯在几家商店里曾经用过的条子。

18. C。copy out 的意思是"抄写",为固定搭配,符合句意。write off 意为"报废,勾销(债务)";write out"开出(药方,支票等),写出";make out"弄懂,辨认,开出等"。

19. A。此句中 read 的意思是"上面写道",符合题意。再如:The ticket reads "From New York to Boston". (票上写着从纽约到波士顿。)

20. B。fortunately"很幸运"。根据句意:我朋友的书写字体与贼的书写字体不一样,因而没受到惩罚自然是一件很幸运的事。因此,符合上下文逻辑。

Section B   Error Correction

1. For 改为 In/At。

   in/at the beginning 为词组,意为"在开始,一开始"。注意 from the beginning 意为"从一开始"。

2. 无错。

3. as 改为 for。

   for the purpose of 为词组,意为"为了……目的"。

4. as 改为 to。

   in relation to 意为"关于,与……有关"。

5. into 改为 of as。

   conceive of as 动词词组,意为"视作",相当于 think of as 或 consider as。

6. suggesting 改为 suggested。

   It is suggested that...,固定句型,意为"据建议……",其宾语从句应用虚拟语气。

7. taking 改为 taken。

   take 的逻辑主语是 the critical concept of "framing",因此,必须要使用被动形式。

8. of 改为 with。

   share with,动词词组,含义为"与……共享",相当于 have in common。

9. Legitimate 改为 Illegitimate。

   该句的"... when a person presents his audience with the artistic vision of another artist,..."的意思是"当某个人把别的艺术家的艺术品(当作自己的作品)提交公众时……",可以推知这种作法显然是非正当的行为。

10. 无错。

Section C   Short Answer Questions

1. Some is transformed by winds and some by ocean currents.

   参见第一段第二、三句。

2. The tropics get larger amount of heat than the polar.

   参见第一段第一句。

3. To illustrate how water vapor is stored.

   参见第一段倒数第二、三、四句。

4. In the tropical oceans.

   参见第二段第一句。

5. gets stored as latent heat

参见第三段倒数第二句。

Test Seven

I Reading Comprehension

Section A Passage Reading

1. C。本题为细节理解题。其线索是第一段的第二句话,其中的 relying on educators 与题干中的 counting on educators 意思完全吻合。

2. A。本题为意愿推导题。作者先在第一段的最后一句说 look-say 或 whole-word 的阅读教学方法是失败的,第二段分析了这种方法失败的原因,是因为它 "stresses the meaning of words over the meaning of letters, thinking over decoding..."

3. D。本题为细节理解题。文章在最后一段谈到了 phonics method 的特点和好处。鉴于该段的第二句话 "Rather than building up a relatively limited vocabulary of memorized words, it imparts a code by which the pronunciations of the vast majority of the most common words in the English language can be learned",可见这种方法能使学习者获得更大的词汇量。

4. B。本题为词意推测题,要求利用上下文线索猜测单词的意思。根据第二段的最后一句,在1963年以前,大出版商只出版 run-spot-run 读物。即出版内容处于一种相对稳恒的状态。紧接着在第三段第一句中用了转折词 however,说在1955年,Rudolf Flesch 引发了(touched off)一场争论,由此可见,此处的 touch off 必然是"引起"的意思。

5. C。本题为判断题。从第二段中综合出 whole-word 阅读方法的特点:强调单词的意思、没有解码(decoding);由此可知选项 B、D 是错的;在文章的最后一句话,作者指出 Phonics does not devalue the importance of thinking about the meaning of words and sentences,所以选项 A 也不正确。

6. D。本题为细节理解题。第一段第一句与第四句说 "Green-space facilities are contributing to an important extent to the quality of the urban environment... The recognition of the importance of green-spaces in the urban environment is a first step on the right way..."可见,人们已充分认识到绿色场地的重要性。因此,选项 D 应为正确答案。

7. B。本题为细节理解题。第二段第一句中写道"The theoretical separation of living, working, traffic and recreation which for many years has been used in town-and-country planning, has in my opinion resulted in disproportionate attention for forms of recreation far from home, whereas there was relatively little attention for improvement of recreative possibilities in the direct neighborhood of the home."(多年来在城乡规划中人们一直把居住、工作、交通和娱乐从理论上进行分割,依我看,这就使人们过多地注意把各种娱乐设施建在远离家园的地方……)"据此可知选项 B 符合句意,因此,应为正确答案。

8. C。本题为细节理解题。第二段最后两句写道"So it is obvious that recreation in the open air has to begin at the street door of the house. The urban environment has to offer as many recreation activities as possible..."鉴于该句意不难看出,作者建议应在住房附近提供绿色场地的娱乐可能性。

9. A。本题为细节理解题。第二段结论句说"... and the design of these has to be such that more obligatory activities can also have a recreative aspect."可见选项 A 符合此题意,因此,应为正确答案。

10. A。本题为全文主旨题。第一段第一句是本文的主题句,概括了本文的主要内容:城市环境中绿色场地设施很重要,它有助于提高城市环境的质量。最后一段从另一个侧面阐述了该主题,起到了前呼后应的作用。因此,选项 A 应为正确答案。

Section B   Banked Cloze

1. F。上一句话说 Artists and scientists both make valuable contributions to our society,是短文的主题,接下一句必然会就主题的 controlling idea "more"一词进行推展说明。因此,在此空格中应填入 more 最符合逻辑。

2. B。respect 是由前一句话:The fact is that scientists are more 中的 valued 推出。

3. J。该句实际上也是这一段的主题句。根据其后的推展句进行逆向推导可知能够反映时代和文化的应该是 arts。因为后文所提及的 painters 或 writers 都属于这个范畴。

4. C。performers 意为"表演者",与 actors 相并列。

5. D。entertain 意为"使娱乐"。因为这是 singers 和 dancers 的天职。

6. E。这里主要谈的是艺术家的作用:提醒我们想象力有多么美好,多么令人激动。

7. G。根据逻辑,各种艺术都是人类的精神所需,符合逻辑。

8. H。meals 与前面的动词 cook 相对应,cook meals 即"烧饭"的意思。

9. K。这一段又回到谈论科学家作用的主题上。根据前文中所讲:计算机在生活上对我的帮助可以说这些功劳应该归功于科学家。选填该词符合逻辑。

10. L。该句的意思是"电影是科学的结晶",符合上下文逻辑。

Section C　Reading Comprehension（Skimming and Scanning）

1. Y。全文推导。

2. Y。参见第七段第一、四句。

3. NG。参见全文。

4. Y。参见第三段第二句。

5. NG。参见全文。

6. N。参见第三段倒数第二句。

7. Y。参见第四段第一句。

8. old technology
   参见第三段倒数第一、二句。

9. conditions in any one country
   参见第四段第二句。

10. make the installations commercially viable
    参见第七段第四、五句。

II　Comprehensive Test

Section A　Cloze

1. A。起始句中谈到人们将20世纪电视的发展和15、16世纪印刷术的传播作了比较。接着说,然而在此期间发生了很多事情。可见,between 指的是这两个时期的中间一段时间。符合上下文的逻辑联系。

2. D。It was not until...that... 是惯用句型,意为"直到……才……"。

3. C。medium 意为"媒体",根据上文出现的 newspaper 可以断定这里指的应该是一种媒体,因此,应该选择 C。means 意为"手段,方法",如:a means of communication（交际工具）;measure 意为"措施,步骤,判断标准,程度"。

4. B。in the company of 为惯用搭配,意为"伴随着,同……一起",符合题意。in company 的意思则为"当着别人的面,一起"。如:She feels shy in company.（当着外人,她感到害羞。）in the process 意为"在……进行

中",如：I started moving the china ornaments but dropped a vase in the process.（我动手搬那些瓷器饰品，但在移动中摔了一只花瓶。）in the light of 意为"鉴于，考虑到"；in the form of，意为"以……形式"。

5. B。speed up 的意思是"（使）加快速度"；gather up 意为"收拢，鼓起勇气"。例如：He gathered up his strength for the hard job.（他振作精神全力以赴来做这项艰难的工作。）；work up 意为"引起，激起；逐渐上升，向上爬"；pick up 意为"加速等"，指从不动到动或慢速行驶后增加速度。

6. A。介词 on 置于某些不及物动词后表示行为的"延续"。根据上下文，该句意指"继续下去"，其他介词都不可与 lead 连用。因此，应该选择 A。

7. D。lead...into the 20th century world of the motor car and the airplane.（继续往前……进入20世纪的汽车和飞机世界。）其他3个选项均不能构成结构上符合上下文的逻辑。

8. D。该题为惯用搭配题。in perspective 意为"正确地，合理地"；concept 意为"概念、观念"。in effect 意为"实际上"；dimension 意为"方面，程度，重要性，范围"，常用复数。

9. C。从上下文的逻辑意思来看，此句表示语气转折。因此，选项 C 应为正确答案。本句的意思是，20世纪初开始使用计算机，随后在60年代发明了集成电路，这就大大地改变了第一段最后一句中所谈及的过程，尽管这个过程对媒体的影响并非立竿见影。

10. B。followed by 意为"（被）紧接，跟随"。符合上下文的逻辑。

11. D。此句上文提到彻底改变，而下文中又讲此影响没有显现出来。由此可知这两部分之间的关系式是让步关系。

12. A。apparent 意为"明显的"；desirable"可取的"；negative"负面的，消极的"。该句中上文提到的变化很彻底，但影响却不明显。由此可以推断，此处只有 apparent 才切题。

13. A。institutional 的意是"习以为常的，体制化的"；universal 意为"全体的，普遍的，完整的"；fundamental"基本的"；instrumental"起作用的，有帮助的，器械的，器乐的"。根据逻辑推理。与 personal 相对的应是 institutional。因此，选项 A 为最佳选项。

14. C。storage capacity 意为"存储容量"。capacity 的基本含义是"容量，生产量，能力"。如：breathing/vital capacity（肺活量），annual capacity（年产量）；ability 意为"能力，本领，天资"。如：to the best of one's ability（尽自己最大努力）；capability 意为"技能，力量"。如：capability to do sth（做事能力）；faculty 意为"技能，天赋"。如：the digestive faculty（消化功

能）。

15. B。in terms of 意思是"就……而言,从……角度;用……（表示)",为固定词组。

16. D。此题为逻辑型词义题。此句中能修饰 distance 的形容词只有 smaller。

17. A。context 意为"语境,背景,环境"。如:within the general context of the present political situation（鉴于目前总的政治形势)/ The only child behaves nicely in his context.（在这种环境中这个独生儿童表现良好。);range 意为"范围,领域,类别"。如:in the higher ranges of society（在社会高层);scope 意为"范围,见识,余地";territory 意为"范围,领域"。

18. C。influence 意为"影响,支配";effect 用作动词时,意为"使生效,实现";impress 意为"使留下印象,使感动";regard 意为"看待,认为",常与 as 一起连用。

19. B。controversial 的意思是"有争议的";competitive 意为"有竞争力的";distracting 意为"令人分心的,困惑的";irrational 意为"不合理的,没有理性的"。如:an irrational belief（荒谬的信念)。根据四个选项的词义及语句环境,只有 controversial 符合题意。

20. C。weigh A against B 意为"权衡,斟酌 A 与 B 之间的关系";weigh with"对……有重大影响;被重视";weigh against"对……关系重大,阻碍"。由此可见选项 C 应为正确答案。

Section B　Error Correction

1. of which 改为 in which。

   which 这里指代的是先行词 fable。in which 相当于 in the fable。

2. at the most 改为 at most。

   该词组为固定用法,意思是"最多,至多"。

3. rest 改为 the rest。

   该词在这里指的是 the world 中的其他部分。因此,the 不能省略。

4. keys of 改为 keys to。

   key to 为固定用法,其中 to 为介词,其后应跟名词或动名词等。

5. soon or later 改为 sooner or later。

   该词组为成语,意为"迟早。"

6. compete for 改为 compete with。

   compete for 的意思是"为……而竞争";compete with 为动词固定用法,意为"与……竞争"。

7. 无错。

8. so 改为 as。

   "as + adj/adv + as + 从句"为固定用法,其中第一个 as 为副词,可以用 so 替代,第二个 as 为关联词,引导一个从句。

9. of 改为 to。

   这里 to 是动词 sacrificed 所要求的,意为"牺牲"。

10. 无错。

Section C   Short Answer Questions

1. is not likely to appear in the fossil record

   参见第一段第二句。

2. It is likely that they will be buried rapidly

   参见第一段第四句。

3. Because erosion there contributes to the destruction of skeletal remains

   参见第一段第四句。

4. The swamp environment reduced the amount of bacterial decay.

   参见第一段倒数第二句。

5. Because they are decayed and changed into something else.

   参见第三段第四句。

Test Eight

I   Reading Comprehension

Section A   Passage Reading

1. A。该题为细节题。相关的信息在文章第一段第四句和第二段最后一句中: According to one NBC executive, no difference exists in the peak sound level of ads and programming. In regular programming the intensity of sound varies over a large range. However, sound levels in commercials tend to stay at or near peak levels. 由此句可以得知商业广告的音量并未超过其他节目的音量。因此,本题的正确答案应是选择项 A,即其最大音量没有超过其他节目的音量。

2. B。本题为原因题。根据文章第三段内容,技术人员运用不同技术使得音量一直保持在峰值状态,从而让人们觉得商业广告节目的音量很大。因此,本题的正确答案应是选择项 B。

3. C。本题为具体细节题。文章第三段倒数第二句"Because people become

adapted to the type of sounds coming from programming, a dramatic change in sound quality draws viewer attention." 指出,因为人们已经习惯了节目中的某种声音,突然听到一种变化了的声音会吸引观众的注意力。因此,本题的正确答案应是选择项 C。

4. D。本题为具体细节题。根据文章第三段,技术人员运用各种方法使得商业节目的声音与普通节目不同,从而吸引观众的注意力。因此,本题的正确答案应为选择项 D,因为这些商业广告中具有某些使得观众觉得有什么非同一般的事情发生的声音特性。

5. D。本题为目的类试题。作者在文章中着重介绍了人们如何运用各种方法使得商业电视节目具有不同于普通节目的音响效果,并最终吸引观众的注意力。据此可以推知本题的正确答案应是选择项 D,在电视广告中如何利用声音吸引人的注意力的特性。

6. C。本题为具体细节题。根据第一段所说的内容,如果妇女年复一年地受到无情的剥削的话,那只能怨她们自己。因为女士们一想到自己在众目睽睽之下穿着一身过了时的服装就不寒而栗,这也正是她们总被时装设计师和大商场利用的原因。由此可以推知,时装设计师和大商场总是靠不断变换妇女的时装来赚钱的。所以本题的正确答案应是 C。

7. B。本题为具体细节题。文章的第二段指出,许多女士不惜每年耗费大量的钱财更新那些几乎从未穿过的衣服;有的女士花不起那么多钱买新的,就宁可浪费许多时间,改造现有的服装。而且第二段第一句话就指出,不断变化的时装本身就是浪费。因此,本题的正确答案应是选项 B,作者认为把过了时的服装拿出来改来改去是浪费时间。

8. C。本题为推导题。根据文章第三段的内容:时装设计师和大商家正是利用了女士们的这些弱点,在设计时很少考虑服装的保暖、舒适和耐用等特性,他们只考虑服装的外观,作者断言,不断变化的时装简直是在有意制造浪费,对社会没有做出一点点有益的贡献。因此,本题的正确答案应是 C,即 comfort(舒适)。

9. A。本题为是非判断题。针对四个选项所提供的信息,结合原文内容,可以推断出,本题的正确答案应是 A 新潮时装的产生是对妇女的商业剥削行为。其他选项都不符合原文内容。

10. D。本题为结论题。文章在最后一段提出的两个问题:一是女士们不断更换时装是不是反映了她们反复无常、见异思迁的本质,二是男士不爱服装式样是不是反映了他们始终如一、稳重可靠的品质。作者虽然没有正面回答,但是问题的答案尽在不言之中,即男士在个性方面较为稳重可靠。因此,本题的正确答案应是 D。

Section B Banked Cloze

1. D。上文中提到了两种情况,该句所提到的则是后一种情况,意思是两者中的"后者"。

2. E。spend 意为"花费(时间)"。

3. F。作为学生学习理所当然是学生的首要目的。因此选用 goal 符合题意。

4. G。根据本文的观点,(对学生来讲)只有学习的生活是不平衡的生活。

5. H。broaden his range of experience 的意思是"扩大经历面"的意思,符合上下文逻辑。

6. C。根据上下文可以推知,作者是赞成学生走向社会的。因此,把交结来自社会各个领域的人视作一个好机会是很自然的事。

7. J。结构上 problem 是动词 solve 的宾语。

8. K。pocket money 的意思是"零花钱"。

9. I。sense of responsibility 意为"责任感"。

10. L。benefit 意为"获益,受益"。

Section C   Reading Comprehension (Skimming and Scanning)

1. N。参见第二段。

2. NG。参见全文。

3. Y。参见第九段。

4. N。参见第十段。

5. N。参见第十七段。

6. Y。参见第十三段第二句。

7. N。参见第二十二段。

8. with less legitimate excuses
   参见第六、七段。

9. his notes from the school appear on the site
   参见第十三段段。

10. take his operation nationwide
    参见第十九段。

II   Comprehensive Test

Section A   Cloze

1. B。本句要求回答段落主旨句对未来住房提出的问题,transaction(交易,买卖),definition (定义)与 assumption(假定,设想)都不合句意。A good

deal 为固定词组,意为"大量,很多",符合题意。

2. C。本题主要考词组搭配。in terms of 意为"根据,在……方面";think in terms of science fiction and the space age 即"从科幻小说和太空时代的角度考虑",符合文意。其余选项常用搭配为:in reference to 的意思是"谈到";with respect to"关于";in consequence of"由于"。

3. C。本题主要考句型。possible 一词做表语时常用 it 做形式主语,而把做逻辑主语的动词不定式放在后面;it is at least possible to assume...即"至少可以设想……",是正确选择。用人称代词表达"能够",可以"做某事"要用 can do,be able to do 等句型。

4. A。科幻作家在作品中表达看法,即向广大读者"传达,传播"自己的观点,因此应选用 conveyed。其余选项都不适用:conceded 意为"构思,怀有";deduced 意为"推理,推断";formulated 意为"用公式表示,系统阐述"。

5. C。conceivable 的意思是"能够想到的",符合句意:未来的人们将过着极为舒适的生活,拥有一切可以想到的设备装置使生活安定、健康和方便。conceptual 意为"概念的";considerate 意为"周到的,关心他人的";complimentary 意为"称赞的,恭维的"。

6. A。if not 常用来表示让步的意思,作者在这里讲科幻作家眼中的未来人们的生活即使不能算很幸福的话,起码也是很舒适的。其他选项均不合逻辑。

7. D。本段讲下一代人面临的人口问题"除非立即采取行动限制世界人口的增长或开发新的食品资源,或双管齐下,否则数以百万计的人将会死于饥饿。"unless 意为"除非",即 if not 的意思,符合句意。

8. D。吃不饱或营养不良(under-feeding)总比饿死(dying of starvation)强;故 for the better(好转),in the least(毫不)与 at the most(至多)都不适用,只有 at the best(至多,充其量不过)符合逻辑。

9. C。before this century is out 意为"在本世纪结束前",符合文意。

10. A。从本句定语从句"房子可用轻便材料建造"及并列句中"或生活水平低的落后地区"等可推知 hottest 符合文意。

11. D。customarily 意为"通常地,惯例地";habitually 意为"惯常地,习惯做地";conventionally 意为"常规地,惯例地"。生活水平"一贯很低"要说 traditionally low。

12. B。kind 意为"种,类",为可数名词。every kind 不合逻辑;this kind 指代不明;a certain kind 意为"某种",在文中缺少冠词;some kind 符合语法要求与文意:但即使最低限度的住房(庇护所)也需要某种材料。

13. A。waste of 是常用搭配,意为"对……的浪费"。

14. C。从语法角度分析,这里需要的是不及物动词,因此排除及物动词 raise (使升起)与 arouse(唤醒,引起)。rise 意为"升起,上涨",也不在此列。

15. C。millions of 是不确切的数字,所以用 precisely(精确地)来修饰不合逻辑,numerically(数字地,数字方面)用在这里为赘语;previously 意为"以前地",与文意不符。literally 意为"确实地,不夸张地",符合文意。

16. A。swell 意为"使变大,增大,隆起",符合文意。inflate 虽也有"增大,使膨胀"之意,但主要用于指价格的上涨或给……充气使之膨胀;diverge 意为"使岔开,使转向";delete 意为"删除,擦掉",不符合题意。

17. C。该句的意思是"除需采取措施避免肮脏和疾病等问题外,还要防止犯罪行为的增加"。spread 的意思是"散布,传播,蔓延",符合用词搭配的要求,应为正确答案。extension 意为"延长,扩展",expansion 有"伸展,扩张,膨胀,发展"等意思,这两个词都不能用于修饰 crime。disposal 的意思是"布置,处理,控制"。

18. C。从下文原因状语从句的解释可知,世界将面临的大问题,不只是住房问题,故应选 merely(仅仅)。其他选项均不合逻辑。

19. A。accompanying 是 accompany 的现在分词,意为"随之而来的",符合文意。associate 的意思是"使有联系,与交往";escort 意为"护卫,护送,陪同";"attach"意为"附上,使隶属,使相关"。

20. D。draw upon 是固定词组,与 draw on 同义,有"利用,依赖,凭借"的意思。stretch out 意为"伸展,探出";stick to 意为"坚持,紧跟";take in 意为"收留,吸收,容纳",不符合题意。

Section B Error Correction

1. for voting 改为 to vote。

   permit sb. to do sth "允许某人做某事"permit 要求接不定式做宾语。

2. practiced 改为 practice。

   could own land and (could) practice most professions,为两个并列谓语和宾语,动词用在情态动词之后应使用原型。

3. high 改为 higher。

   高等教育是 higher education,而不是 high education。

4. and 改为 or。

   为两个否定句并列用连词 or,肯定句应使用 and。

5. a little 改为 little。

   根据上下文,此处应为否定含义。

6. worked 改为 have worked。

　　因为句子的时间状语是 throughout the history of our country。

7. establishing 改为 established。

　　因为与被修饰词 school 之间的关系是被动的关系。即 school（which was）originally established only for men，所以应用过去分词。

8. about 改为 with。

　　因为"对……不满意"，要求接介词 with，即 are dissatisfied with。

9. fewer 改成 less。

　　付工资多或少用 pay much 或 pay less 来表示，为不可数概念。

10. overwhelming 改成 overwhelmingly。

　　因为在此句中 overwhelmingly 修饰的是分词 held。因此，应使用副词。

Section C Short Answer Questions

1. It was not so large as that of industrial workers.

　　参见第一段第四句。

2. The proportion has decreased.

　　参见上注。

3. Physical work.

　　参见第一段第三句。

4. less important than awareness of being a good employee

　　参见第二段。

5. to be more successful in his career

　　参见第二段。

Test Nine

I Reading Comprehension

Section A Passage Reading

1. C。短文在第一段开首句就切入了主题"Long before they can actually speak, babies pay special attention to the speech they hear around them."，随后又谈到了婴儿在出生早期对不同声音所做出的不同反应。在此后的几段中，作者分别提到小婴儿甚至能够区分细微的声音差别，识辨铃声与人的说话声，以及从声音中所获得的乐趣，尽管他们并不明白语言所表达的真实意思。由此可知选项 C 为正确答案。

2. C。根据第一段第二句"Within the first month of their lives, babies'

responses to the sound of the human voice will be different from their responses to other sorts of auditory stimuli. "可知作者之所以在此处提到铃声的目的是对此句的进一步推展说明,解释小婴儿是如何区别不同的声音的。

3. D。noted 的本意是"注意到",与 observed 同义。

4. B。根据第二段第二句"One researcher observed babies and their mothers in six diverse cultures and found that, in all six languages, the mothers used simplified syntax, short utterances and nonsense sounds, and transformed certain sounds into baby talk. "可知经观察发现,来自六种不同文化的母亲与婴儿交谈时所采用的方式都是相同的。因此,选项 B 符合题意,应为正确答案。

5. C。根据第一段第一句"Long before they can actually speak, babies pay special attention to the speech they hear around them. "可见婴儿对语言的兴趣不是通过别人传授的,而是与生俱来的。因此,正确答案应为 C。

6. B。本题为细节理解题。在第一段中作者讲到人们意识到要改变饮食习惯,即更多地吃天然食品"... have become aware of the need to change their eating habits, because much of the food they eat, particularly processed food, is not good for the health. "(因为他们所吃的大部分食品,特别是加工食品,对健康不利)。也就是说人们想吃对自己更有益的食品。因此正确答案应是选项 B。

7. C。本题为细节理解题。作者在第二段第二句中说:"... that the soil has been nourished by unused vegetable matter, which provides it with essential vitamins and minerals. "(这些土壤受到没有用过的蔬菜质的滋养),与选项 C 的意思相吻合,因此,应为正确答案。

8. D。本题为段落归纳题。在第三段第一句中作者写道:"Natural foods also include animals which have been allowed to feed and move freely in healthy pastures. "(天然食品还包括在卫生的牧场上喂养并自由走动的动物。)言外之意,在笼式养鸡场的鸡挤在鸡舍内不能自由走动觅食就不能叫做天然食品。

9. B。本题为推理判断题。在第四段中作者提到"This is actually a nonessential food!""we can in fact do without it. ""the quantity we use has grown steadily over the last two centuries and in Britain today each person consumes an average of 200 pounds a year! Yet all it does is to provide us with energy, in the form of calories. There are no vitamins in it. no

minerals and no fiber."即"糖实际上并不是一种必需食品"（"糖所起的作用无非就是以卡路里形式提供能量"，可是"我们使用糖的数量在过去200年内持续增长"。）由此可以推导出，糖的使用是饮食习惯形成的。因此，选项 B 符合题意，应为正确答案。

10. A。本题为细节推理题。最后一段第一句说："It is significant that nowadays fiber is considered to be an important part of a healthy diet.（值得注意的是如今纤维素被认为是健康食品的重要组成部分。）"接着作者又阐明了理由。由此可见，作者认为，吃富含纤维素的食品更有益于健康。选项 A 符合题意，应为正确答案。

Section B　Banked Cloze

1. K。本文主题谈的是办公室秘书与电话接听的事，说人们所获得的第一印象是通过电话的接触。因此，此处应该选填 telephone。

2. I。按常理说，如果一个人打电话时总是没人接听，会感觉很不好的。因此，此处选填 feeling 符合逻辑。

3. A。根据前半句 If a call is answered rudely，主句的主语显然就是 caller。

4. D。该句与前一句是结构并列的一个句子。因此，也需用 if 引导一个条件状语从句。

5. E。she 这里用作泛指。

6. N。secretary 为泛指。

7. G。好秘书处理电话业务必然是迅速而有效的。因此，在此处选填 efficiently 符合逻辑。

8. F。这里的条件句是另一种假设。根据后文 or become angry 这个假设应该是与之相应的一个假设，即 impatient。

9. C。通常打电话的目的要么是为了咨询，要么是了解信息。因此，这里选填 information 符合逻辑。

10. J。calls 用于指电话呼叫。

Section C　Reading Comprehension（Skimming and Scanning）

1. Y。参见第一段第二句。

2. Y。参见第二段第一、二句。

3. NG。参见全文。

4. N。参见第三段第四句。

5. N。参见第二段最后一句。

6. N。参见第四段第五句。

7. Y。参见第四段第六、七、八句。

8. providing them with specific benefits

参见第二段第三句。

9. (to create) undesired effect.

参见第五段第一句。

10. where appropriate with their own facilities

参见倒数第二段最后一句。

II Comprehensive Test

Section A   Cloze

1. A。give thought to 为惯用搭配,意为"思考,考虑";give sb. an idea of 意为使某人了解……的情况;give an opinion of/on 意为"发表对……的意见";give sb advice on 意为"给某人一些劝告"。本句中只有 give thought,to 为固定用语。因此,选项 A 应为正确答案。

2. B。strengthen 意为"加强,巩固";stimulate 意为"刺激,使兴奋,鼓励,鼓舞";enhance 意为"提高,增强";accommodate 意为"留宿,收容,供应,供给",此处作"适应"解,符合句意。

3. C。本句译文:成长着的身体需要运动和锻炼,但不仅仅在强调竞争的方面。care 意为"小心,谨慎,照料";nutrition 意为"营养";exercise"练习,训练,锻炼";leisure 意为"空闲,闲暇"。exercise 与 movement 在逻辑与含义上属于同类概念,符合上下文逻辑。

4. D。从逻辑的角度看,该句主句表达的意思是"年轻人正在努力适应各种挑战"。而从句的意思则是"这些年轻人变得爱面子并且需要信心",两者之间是因果关系。因此,只有 Because 符合上下文的逻辑要求。

5. C。assistance 意为"帮助,援助";guidance 意为"引导,指导";confidence 意为"信心";tolerance 意为"容忍,耐性"。从逻辑的角度看,取得成功和知道他们的成就会被羡慕会给这些年轻人带来信心,所以只有 confidence 符合句意。

6. B。claim 意为"要求,声称,主张,索赔";admire 意为"钦佩,赞赏,羡慕";ignore 意为"不理,不顾";surpass 意为"超过,胜过"。根据上下文可知信心会由此而产生。因此,只有 admired 符合题意。

7. D。由于竞争现象的存在,设计活动时注意重优胜轻劣汰自然应该是明智之举。根据此逻辑可以断定 wise 应为正确答案。improper 意为"不适当的,不合适的,不正确的";risky 意为"冒险的,风险的";fair"公平的,相当的,尚好的"。

8. C。本句意:"出版学生写的书刊评论简报、展出学生的艺术作品和主办书刊讨论俱乐部"都是对前面提到的"安排活动"的举例说明。因此,只有 for example 才符合上下文的逻辑。

9. A。display 意为"陈列,展览,显示";describe"描述,形容";create"创造,创作";exchange"交换,调换,兑换"。根据句意,选项 A 符合题意,应为正确答案。这里出版许多学生写的书刊评论简报、展出学生的艺术作品和主办书刊讨论俱乐部是对上半句的进一步推展。

10. D。durable 意为"持久的,耐久的";excessive"过多的,过分的";surplus"过剩的,剩余的";multiple"多样的,多重的"。从上下文来看,既然是多种小型俱乐部,当然就能提供多种机遇。因此,multiple 应为正确答案。

11. A。group 意为"群体";individual 意为"个人,个体";personnel 为集合名词意为"全体人员,人事";corporation"公司"。因此,四个选项中,只有 group 才可以与 dynamics 搭配,意为"群体动力",引申意思是"团队精神"。

12. D。consent 意为"同意,赞成";insurance 意为"保险,保险费";admission 意为"允许进入,接纳";security"安全,保障"。根据词义和上下文逻辑,security 为最佳选择,因为 shy students 需要安全感是出于人的本能。

13. B。barely 意为"仅仅,勉强,几乎不",相当于 hardly,强调"几乎不,简直没有"的意思。如:She has barely enough to eat;particularly"特殊地,特别地";definitely"明确地,肯定地";rarely"很少,难得",强调"不经常发生(的事)"。如:They were rarely seen together and certainly didn't travel together。本句意:那个在幕后支持他们的老师是几乎看不见的,因此,选项 B 符合题意,应为正确答案。

14. D。根据常识,年轻人往往不能长久地把注意力集中在一件事情上,再从下一句来看,各种活动应该组织得让参加者保持活跃。所以无论从常识还是从上下文逻辑,只有 short 才最适合句意。

15. C。这里 so that 引导了一个目的状语从句。

16. D。everything 和 nothing 在此句中不能使句子逻辑意义完整。anything 一般用于否定句和疑问句之中。

17. D。let sb. off 意为"宽恕,从宽处理";let sb down 意为"使失望"。如:The company now has a large number of workers who feel badly let down。let sb out 意为"放掉,放出";let sb alone"不干涉"。本句意为"让其他参与者感到失望"。因此,选项 D 符合题意,应为正确答案。

18. A。on the contrary 意为"正相反"与上文形成对照;on the average"平均,一

般说来";on the whole"总的说来";on the other hand"另一方面"。

19. C。making for 意为"有助于,有利于";standing for"代替";planning for"计划,安排";taking sth for"把……看作,把……当作"。本句中应为"安排"。因此,选项 C 符合题意,应为正确答案。

20. A。capabilities 意为"能力",根据逻辑推理,所安排的活动应该限制在学生的"能力"范围之内。因此,选项 A 符合题意,应为正确答案。responsibilities"责任";proficiency"熟练,精通";efficiency"效率,功效"。

Section B   Error Correction

1. needing 改为 needed。

   need 的逻辑主语是 sum,在此句中应使用过去分词形式,表示被动的意思。

2. in 改为 on。

   on a permanent basis 为固定搭配,意思是"在……基础上,根据"。

3. invited 改为 inviting。

   句中 invite 的作用是进一步说明情况,其逻辑主语是 companies,表示主动的意思。因此,应使用现在分词的表到形式。

4. 无错。

5. in home 改为 at home。

   at home 常用的意思是"在家里",在此句中的意思是"在国内"。该词组有两种表达形式:at home 或 in the home,但不能说 in home。

6. some saver 改为 some other saver。

   此句中必须加上一个 other 表示所 sell 的对象不包括 he 本人,即所谓"排他"的意思。

7. is 改为 are。

   该句的主语是 Many of the services,因此,系动词应使用复数形式 are。

8. could 改为 could not。

   根据上下文可知,作者是想用双否定的表达形式来说明 hospitals, roads, electricity, telephones, railways 的重要性。该句如省略了 not 一词,将会于情、于理都说不通。

9. lonely 改为 alone。

   alone 的意思是"独自(一人),单独";lonely 的意思是"孤独的",不符合题意。

10. 无错。

Section C   Short Answer Questions

1. Difference aspects which have been stressed in defining human intelligence. / Human intelligence has different definitions because of different emphasis.

   参见第一段第二句。

2. effective adaptation/the importance of adaptation to the environment/ effective environment adaptation

   参见第一段第四句。

3. lies chiefly in changing oneself to cope with the environment/involve coping more effectively changing or finding a new environment/changing to cope environment, change or find a new environment

   参见第一段第最后一句。

4. perception, learning, memory, reasoning, and problem solving

   参见第二段第一句。

5. Intelligence is an effective drawing together of many abilities. /Intelligence is the combination of nature and abilities.

   参见第二段。

Test Ten

I Reading Comprehension

Section A Passage Reading

1. C。词汇释义题。第一段倒数第二句写道："Even judges are softer on attractive defendants.（甚至法官对有魅力的被告也会显得更温和。）"紧接着作者用 But 一词使语气产生了转折,也就是说,前面讲美貌的长处,后面则要讲美貌可能成为一个人的"短处"。因此 liability 的意思应为 disadvantage。

2. A。本题为细节理解题。乍看起来,似乎4个选项都有道理。这时需要严格按照文章提供的确切信息来进行取舍。第六段第三句中作者写道:Thus, an attractive woman bas an advantage in traditionally female jobs, but an attractive woman in a traditionally masculine position appears to lack the "masculine" qualities required.（一位富有魅力的女子在传统的女性职业中占有优势,但是在传统的男性工作中她就显得"男子汉"素质不足。）可见,选项 A 符合题意,应为正确答案。

3. D。本题为细节理解题。文章在最后一句中做了总结:"结果表明,英俊的男性候选人全部击败了非英俊的男子,但是被列为最漂亮的女子的得票率却总是最低的。"可见,如选项 D 中所述"魅力对女子与其说是长处还不如说是障碍"符合题意。when it comes to 的意思是"当谈到……时";be more of a...than a... 的意思是"与其说是(后者)还不如说是(前者)"。

4. B。本题为推理判断题。纵览全文可知,当人们把美貌与幸福,工作、职业,能力,成就等联系在一起时,常常会产生偏见。因此选项 B"有偏见的"应为正确答案。

5. A。本题为篇章主旨题。从文章的字里行间可以看到,本文着重分析美貌对女子所带来的不利影响。因此应选择 A。选项 C"为妇女要求平等权利"意思太抽象笼统,且与本文的议论主题"美貌"无甚关系。

6. D。本题为细节理解题。作者在第一段第六句中说到了"Today the majority of jobs in America, Europe and Japan (two thirds or more in many of these countries) are in the service industry, and the number is on the rise.(如今,美国、欧洲和日本的大部分工作(这些国家中三分之二或三分之二以上的工作)是在第三产业。这个数目与日俱增。)"由此可以判断正确答案应为选项 D。

7. B。本题为细节理解题。作者在第一段最后一句中写道:Long-held notions about jobs and careers, the skills needed to succeed, even the relation between individuals and employers—all these are being challenged.(老的工作和职业观念、取得成功所需要的技能,甚至个人和雇主之间的关系——所有这一切都正在重新认识。),句中谈到就是老的工作和职业观念需要重新认识,即 are being challenged,意思是说老观念行不通了,这点与选择项 B 的意思相符。因此,应为正确答案。

8. B。本题为细节理解题。在第二段中作者回顾过去,展望未来技术发展的前景。接着又在第二段第三句中写道:Tomorrow's achievements in biotechnology, artificial intelligence or even some still unimagined technology could produce a similar wave of dramatic changes.(明天在生物工程、人工智能或甚至无法想像到的某项技术中所取得的成就会产生类似的巨大变革冲击波),与选项 B 的意思恰好相吻合。因此,选项 B 应为正确答案。

9. A。本题为细节理解题。作者在第二段第四句中写道:But one thing is certain: information and knowledge will become even more vital, and the people who possess it, whether they work in manufacturing or services, will have the advantage and produce the wealth. Computer knowledge

will become as basic a requirement as the ability to read and write.（拥有信息和知识的人,不管他们在制造业工作还是在第三产业工作,将独占鳌头,创造财富),与选项 A 意思相符,应为正确答案。

10. C。全文主旨题。作者在本文的第一段第一句中写道:"一个新时代即将到来。"这一句实际上也是全文的主旨,紧接着又具体阐述这个新时代的特点和内涵,依次对文章的主旨进行推展说明可见选项 C 符合题意,应为正确答案。

Section B　Banked Cloze

1. L。该句子是承接上一句 with commercials thrown in every three or four minutes 而来的,谈的都是同一个主题。

2. B。第一句话把乘坐公汽车比作看电视节目。当人们睡觉闭上眼睛时,显然就什么都看不见了,就好比关上了电视一样。因此,此处应填入 television。

3. C。此处 somewhat exciting 的意思是"有点令人激动",显然是作者对这一感觉的认可。此外,somewhat exciting 与 comfortable 由 and 连接。根据表达习惯 and 所连接的成分应该在意义上一致,结构相等。因此,此处应填入该词。

4. D。根据该词所修饰的名词的结构(并列结构)可以推知此处应填入该词。

5. G。开公共汽车的人,自然应该是 driver。

6. A。这里 lane 的意思是"车道"。通常汽车司机需要加速或减速时需要更换车道。

7. H。pass 的意思是"度过时光"。

8. J。food 是根据前一句话推导而出的。因为前一句中谈论的是 food。

9. K。这里 beginning 是相对 The end of the ride 而来言的。

10. F。hands 指把手放在脑袋后面做悠闲状。

Section C　Reading Comprehension

1. NG。参见全文。

2. Y。参见第四、七段。

3. NG。参见全文。

4. Y。参见最后一段。

5. N。参见全文。

6. N。参见最后一段倒数第二句。

7. NG。参见全文。

8. nuclear power and renewable energy

参见第十段第一句。

9. generate electricity
参见第十段倒数第二句。

10. intervene in the market
参见倒数第三段。

II Comprehensive Test

Section A　Cloze

1. C。本题测试惯用搭配。make towards 相当于 make for,go towards,move in the direction of"朝……走去"。

2. B。though 用于引导让步状语从句。因为从句主语与主句主语相同,从句谓语又包含系动词 be,所以从句中的主语和助动词均省略了。

3. C。根据上下文,本句中从句与主句之间是因果关系。因此,选项 C 应为正确答案。其他词均不切题。

4. D。该题测试词义搭配。fallen 和 flown 均为不及物动词,不能用于被动语态。blow 意为"吹到",适合题意。该句子的意思是:这里我们没有发现什么雪,因为大部分积雪似乎已从山上刮走了。

5. A。该题主要测试词义搭配。此 view 意为"看见的东西,景色"。例如:Your house has a fine view of the hill。(从你的房子能看到这些小山的美丽景色。)本句意思是:看不到远处的山,因为云层正在我们四周形成。

6. A。come up 意为"发生,形成"如:A snowstorm is coming up. (一场暴风雪正在酝酿中。)因该句中使用了 suddenly。所以选用 came up 比选用 came on 更符合句意。

7. B。该题主要测试词义搭配。notify 相当于 inform sb of sth;report sth to sb,意为"通知,报告"。glance (at)相当于 take a quick look at,意为"看一眼(强调行为的动作)"。notice 相当于 become aware of;observe,意为"注意到,留心,看到(强调行为的结果)";view 相当于 look at or watch carefully,意为"仔细察看,注视(强调行为的过程)"。可见,此句使用 noticed 最合题意。

8. B。该题主要测试逻辑搭配。其译文:我们本来应该注意到风暴的来临,但那时我们的注意全部集中在开车上。我们还来不及采取任何措施,就已被白雪照得眼花缭乱。

9. A。前半句提到"不能上下走动",所以"不得不一动不动地等待"。根据这个逻辑,选项 motionlessly 应为正确答案。

10. A。in spite of 意为"尽管",主要用于引导让步状语短语,用在此处符合题意。in relation to 意为"关于,至于";in case of"万一";in the event of"万一,发生"。

11. C。do something ＋ to do 常译为"采取措施以便能做……"。在否定句中常用 not...anything 或 nothing。例如:I can do nothing to get rid of the embarrassing situation.(我实在无能为力摆脱困境。)本句意思是:这种情况持续两个小时以后,我才意识到为免冻死在这里我们必须想点办法。根据句意,选项 C 应为正确答案。

12. B。made out 相当于 see and identify with effort or difficulty,意为"辨认出"。

13. D。out of the question 相当于 impossible,意为"不可能",用在此处符合题意。without question 相当于 beyond question,意为"毋庸置疑";in question"所谈到的(作后置定语),正谈到的"。

14. D。pinch,意为"搭,捏"。该句的意思是"……我们在脚下挖出一个平台,在上面搭建帐篷。"pinch 用在此句中符合句意。wrench,意为"拧,扭,歪曲(实事)";wedge"楔入,插入",wedge oneself into a crowd,意为"挤在人群中";pad sth. with cotton 意思是"为……填棉花"。

15. B。cut away 意为"砍掉",此句的意思是:我们爬上那里,开始吹掉冰块。cut off 意为"打断,中断";cut out"删掉"。

16. B。situation 意为"形势,情况";position 意为"工作,职位";occupation 意为"职业,工作"。

17. D。died down 相当于 disappear or subside gradually,意为"逐渐地消失,止息";die out"消失,死绝";die off"相继死去"。

18. D。at last 意为"最后,终于",指经过一番努力后,最终做成某件事,用在此情景下符合逻辑。

19. C。as best one can/could 意为"尽量好地"。如:Do it as best you can.(你尽量做好那件事。)

20. D。crawled 相当于 move slowly, pulling the body along the ground;climb 相当于 go up or over sth., esp. using one's hands and feet。

Section B　Error Correction

1. entertained 改为 entertaining。
   此句中作者的意思是"这类采访具有很强的娱乐性",因此,entertain 在这里所起的作用是表语。应此应采用-ing 形式,即现在分词,而非过去分词。

2. necessary 改为 necessarily。
   根据句子结构可知,这里所需要的不是表语,而是修饰系动词的副词。因此,应该使用 necessary 的副词表达形式。

3. 无错。

4. whose 改为 which。

whose 是 who 的所有格,而此处根据上下文推导指的应是"哪一个地区",即 which area the news-people select。

5. ingoing 改为 outgoing。

outgoing 的意思是"外向的",ingoing 的意思是"内向的"。根据下文 who are willing to appear on the air 可知这类人不应是内向的人,而是外向的人。因此,应用 outgoing。

6. 无错。

7. samples 改为 sampling。

这里 sampling 的意思是"取样"。

8. exercises 改为 exercise。

情态动词后边的动词应使用原型。

9. is 改为 are。

该句的主语是 problems,是名词复数,因此应使用 there be 的复数表达形式。

10. 无错。

Section C   Short Answer Questions

1. people from place to place as airliners are doing now.

参见第一段。

2. a rotating device topside

参见第二段第一句。

3. To be widely used by average individuals.

参见第三段第二句。

4. They have been widely used for various purposes.

参见最后一段。

5. For urgent mission to places inaccessible to other kinds of craft.

参见最后一段倒数第二句。